T0354928

Where's My TOMORROW

Where's My TOMORROW

by W.M. Fisher

Order this book online at www.trafford.com
or email orders@trafford.com

Most Trafford titles are also available at major online book retailers.

Print information available on the last page.

ISBN: 978-1-4269-7418-2 (sc)
ISBN: 978-1-4269-7419-9 (e)

Trafford rev. 09/07/2016

North America & international
toll-free: 1 888 232 4444 (USA & Canada)
fax: 812 355 4082

Looking out over the blue and white of the sky almost makes me forget for a moment that the past ever happened. But there's not enough sky to ever erase the years of black that will always be burned into my memory. It's sad to think what a person has to go through just to have a glimpse of freedom. Freedom... sometimes that word just means to me, the absence of pain. Pain which is doubled when it's that of a child being robbed of their freedom by an adult; an adult who is supposed to love and care for them.

How empty those words seem to me now. I can't recall exactly when it all started; those black days that is, it just seemed to me...that it always was.

I remember as a baby the cold rejection thrown at me because I wasn't born blonde and blue eyed, compounded by the fact that, God forbid, I was born female. That, to my immigrant mother, was considered to be an even bigger curse than being childless; for you see, females only spread disease and produce unwanted children. The only light at the end of the tunnel for a woman was that she may, if blessed, give birth to males. That was the premise that I was raised under. That you live to serve men!

Chapter 1

I tried to be happy, but sometimes at three years of age most of your happiness is contingent on the whims of adults. It's especially difficult when you feel that one of your parents hates you and the other one doesn't even know that you exist. It's the latter that is almost more disheartening to me now.

My father was a big, silent, hardworking man who had the hardest job in the world, being married to my mother.

Mother, that word still seems foreign to me, and also more than a bit frightening. You see, as a child, the things that "should have" frightened me didn't, and where I was supposed to feel safe and secure is where the real horror lived. That was a place called home!

When I think back to my childhood, I felt the safest when I was alone. I'd walk through the prairies that surrounded my home for hours, and felt great solace by running in the high weeds and throwing rocks. That's when I would experience something wonderful, a feeling known as freedom!

I would feel as though nothing on earth could stop me. That would be until I would hear the unbridled and piercing broken accent of my mother. The harshness of her voice was like an executioner's bell ringing in my head. Her voice yelling my name, "Madia, Madia", which is Yugoslavian for Mary. It was her name as well, but that's where the comparison ended. Hearing her yell my name would make me feel as though all the blood had been drained from my body. But I knew, blood or no blood, I'd have to run like the wind to her or be ready for the untold suffering for being a disobedient child.

What was the big event that I had to run home for? Well, that day I was to sit on the lap of an old man who wanted to rent a room from us. "Madia," my mother said sweetly, "sit on the lap of this nice man. He wants to give you a pony ride on his leg, and then he'll give you a shiny new nickel. So you be 'very' nice to him Madia."

How my flesh crawled as he started stroking my face and hair. He was dressed in a suit, like a businessman. He was short, fat, and bald and stunk of cheap cologne and cigars. He had a pencil thin mustache, and I kept staring at it to see if it was real or drawn on to keep my mind off of where he was putting his hands. He had a pocket watch in his vest's pocket that hooked to one of the vests buttons. He wanted to know if I wanted to play a game and I nodded yes. He would drop the watch then he would ask me to retrieve it and hand it back to him. It always fell between his legs.

I still thank God to this day, that through my childhood naiveté, I didn't fully understand what this man was doing.

His and many other men's hot and exploring hands were to defile me throughout my childhood years, and just like him many didn't stop at just my face and hair.

People would later ask, "Why didn't you tell your mother?" I could only laugh at them silently and think, what for, I was being a good little girl. After all, wasn't it my mother who gladly handed me over to these wanton men?

I couldn't understand at the time, but later, as I got older, I realized that maybe it was to give her time, time to explore. Yes, my mother always found a way to make money when my father's back was turned. I wonder if that's why he was always so silent?

I know by now you must be thinking, was there any glimmer of happiness in this child's life? The answer is yes. It came by the way of my godmother, I'm sure she had a real name, but I simply called her "Kuma"; it was Yugoslavian for godmother.

She was the kindest, sweetest and most understanding woman alive. She led me to believe that maybe I wasn't the most ugly, stupid and evil child ever born. Because of her soft touch and kind words, I found an invisible sanctuary of love that was truly real. I love her memory today as much as I loved her then. She is the only reason that I never wanted to kill myself. Bless you, Kuma!

To give you a small example of how she made everything okay, I'll have to jump to age thirteen which is difficult for some and impossible for others...I belonged to the latter category.

It was a blazing, white hot day back in the summer of 1939. I still laugh when people say it was simpler then, or they just refer to them as the good old days. Good for what? Good for pretending that you came from the perfect family; that life was "G-rated" and everyone had complete respect for one another? I just think that fear and shame were the great motivators of that era; and it's a shame that so many people were afraid to speak the truth.

There I was looking off into space while leaning on the fence, virtually unaware of my brother and his friends playing ball in the prairie across the dirt road from our house. Even though it was hot, I was chilled to the bone. At the time I assumed it was the shock of our father's death which happened a month earlier. I was wearing my new white cotton skirt that my Kuma had given to me for my birthday a few days before. I didn't have a party that year because we were still in mourning. It always struck me funny how my mother forced us to mourn only on her level. By that I mean, I wasn't allowed to cry for him because *she* felt that I didn't love him enough, and that was part of God's decision that he should take him from us. It was also why we couldn't show any sign of a good time...because that *too* would be a sin.

My wandering mind was swiftly brought back to reality by the crashing sound of "Madia!"

My heart skipped a beat as a knot started to form in my stomach, "Where the hell are you Madia?" I trembled with the anticipation of yet another horror filled day.

Just then she appeared, with her short stocky frame and her enormous bust. She had a light olive complexion and light brown hair that she liked to refer to as blonde. She did that because I was darker skinned and with almost black hair. She would always say that women should be light and men should be dark. She had on a flowered dress with a full white apron over it.

She would only take it off if she was bartending. She said that men wanted something to look at while they were drinking. She needed to wear her glasses all the time, but just like the apron, it depended on the bar clientele. She always wore heels because she was barely five-foot-tall; again, she thought that men expected it. All of this was enhanced by her vulgar mouth.. Oh, never in front of our guests, just her family.

She grabbed my arm, shook me as she yelled the word "Whore" into my face. Before I could even ask what I did wrong, she clutched my skirt in her hand and said, "Only a WHORE would wear this!"

Standing there baffled, I couldn't understand why she would object to my skirt. I thought maybe because Kuma gave it to me and she was jealous, or that it was white and we're still supposed to be in mourning. Then like a bolt of lightening it hit me. The skirt had a trim of the tiniest red rosebuds – which my mother hated and thought were evil. I never gave them a second thought because they were nearly nonexistent.

Slap went her weather-worn hand across my face, and then again the word "WHORE" was hurled at me. I started to cry, and then she started, "God took your father because he knew that you'd be a whore and didn't want him to have to see it! It's because you're so evil that I lost my man to an early grave!"

I couldn't believe that she was saying this to me; it wasn't so much the words because by now I was used to them, but that she was doing this outside where people could hear. At that moment I didn't know if I was going to be killed, all I knew was I wanted to just run away. Then, slam, once again her hand made contact with my face.

Through my tears, I could see that we had caught the attention of my brother and his friends. Embarrassed, I begged for her to calm down, with that she slapped me again for talking back. I turned my back to her and tried to slowly walk away hoping that maybe the boys would just go back to playing ball, but as I looked up and toward them I noticed horror in their eyes. At first, I assumed that it was just the shock of seeing her hit me; until then they had only seen the effects of my beatings and not the beatings themselves. Just then I could hear my mother laughing hysterically. This couldn't be some sick joke, could it? Then all of a sudden it felt like my panties were all wet and something running down my leg. Oh God, I thought to myself, did I pee from fear? With that I looked down…BLOOD!

Was I bleeding from being hit? Quickly I looked up, darting my eyes from my laughing mother to my disgusted brother and then to his shocked friends.

I pleaded, "Mama, help me, please help me. What's happening?"

She got very serious as she pointed her twisted arthritic finger at me and said, "Go and get out of here! That's 'The Curse' you evil little bitch! That's the sign that you are truly evil and you're sentenced to hell! He's coming for you now, so get ready!"

"NO" I screamed.

"Oh yes Madia, you're going to hell for killing your father, because it's a sin not to love your father and to let him die! You evil, sinful little whore. That's what you get for wearing the 'Flowers of Hell' on you."

Hysterical, I just ran and ran to get away not only from her, my brother and his friends, along with the gates of hell, but also from the horrible shame and guilt that I felt. In a way, I did feel guilty about my father - not for killing him, but for not loving him enough. I felt that it was all my fault that I had never bonded with him until I saw him lying there dying. Why didn't I tell him how much I loved him when I had the chance?

I ran frantically through the prairie, praying for someone to help me, even though I knew no one could. I ran and ran and then it hit me - Kuma!

I was nearly out of breath when I got to her house, and by that time my skirt was covered in blood. I pounded on her front door and yelled her name over and over, but there was nothing but silence. With no reply, I just simply screamed, "PLEASE...SOMEBODY...HELP ME!" Then I slid down the wall and sat in my own blood, crying and feeling so alone.

I cried for what seemed like an eternity, and then I heard a familiar voice, "Oh child, what in God's name has happened?"

"Kuma," I cried, "please help me before it's too late!"

"Too late for what, child?"

"I'm going to Hell. I killed my father because I didn't love him enough! I'm evil, Mama said so, and now this blood is a sign that I'm going to Hell! Please, Kuma, please help me!"

With a disgusted look on her face, Kuma said, "Who said this, your mother? My God, she must be insane!"

"Mama said that what makes it worse is that this skirt has roses on it and that those are the flowers from Hell! So please, Kuma, help me, I don't want to go to Hell!"

She took out her handkerchief and started to dry my eyes as she said, "Come on, child, let's go in the house and get you all cleaned up while I explain what this is really all about. No one is going to Hell, except for maybe your mother." She told me that this was natural and all perfectly normal. I was so relieved. She gave me a skirt and panties of hers to wear home. I told her that I felt bad because I'd ruined the skirt. She said, "Oh, child, this is just the beginning of things that you'll ruin by having a period. You'll be cursing left and right every month."

"Kuma, is that why some people call it 'the curse'?"

"Well, I never thought about it, but it's as good of an excuse as anything I guess."

If Kuma thought this experience was horrible, she would never have been able to handle all of the aspects of my life. I learned early on that there were some things that can never be talked about, and in a strange way I think that's where I found my strength.

I felt that if I could somehow stay in control of myself and just keep quiet during many of the uncontrollable situations that I was thrown into situations that were so gruesome and unbelievable - I wouldn't have to tell anyone... besides, who could I tell?

I knew the answer was – no one.

Chapter 2

One of the situations that not only made me stronger but also made me know that I had to begin to become self reliant happened over the Christmas of my fifth year.

Everything started out so perfectly, and I hoped that in this magical season all of the pain from previous years would vanish, like how a snowflake would melt when it touched your cheek. But I was wrong and it would be the last Christmas that we would celebrate together as a family.

Christmas morning started out so happy that I really thought maybe the holidays could make my family whole. I was the oldest girl in our sibling lineup, but the first-born was my brother Sonny, he was my favorite...my parent's favorite too. He was seven and tall for his age with black hair and the most piercing blue eyes. As I got older, every time I would see a picture of the actor Tyrone Power, I would think of Sonny; he was so wonderful.

Then there was me; I was five and a half, very skinny with olive skin, dark brown hair and eyes...quite the disappointment.

Then came my brother Martin, named after our father. He was four, good-looking like Sonny but dark like me.

Finally, the biggest thorn in my mother's side, twin girls. The only thing that saved them, according to my mother, was the fact that they were blue-eyed and blonde. It's sad; I don't even remember their names anymore. I went to their graves one time as an adult, but they didn't have a headstone, just markers with numbers on them. I thought, "What an end?", but who knows, maybe they were the lucky ones.

Everyone was sitting around opening their presents, and I was so happy to get a doll that year; she was beautiful. I went over to hug my parents to show them my doll and how happy I was, but as I approached my mother, the doll bumped her coffee cup and it spilled. I started to say that I was sorry, but it was too late. In a flash my mother grabbed the doll by its feet and hit me across the face with it while screaming at me and calling me names. My father just got up from his chair and silently walked into the other room shaking his head. My mother watched him walk out and then she turned toward me with a disgusted look on her face. I felt like I wanted to die. Then just as I thought that she was going to hit me again, she stood up and started tapping the doll against her other hand and was looking around, she stopped and started to smile. She finally spoke, "Madia, it's for your own good that I'm going to put this doll high atop the cabinet. This way you won't hurt yourself or anyone else. Santa should've known that you weren't big enough to play with a doll like this. If you're good, I'll let you play with it later."

Once again I felt as though I was a big disappointment, not only to my parents but also to my siblings, because by now the tone for the day had changed. Also, I guess I had disappointed someone whom I didn't even know, someone by the name of Santa Claus.

As the day wore on my heart would sink every time I would walk past my doll, she looked as alone as I felt. Everyone else was playing with their toys, and with nothing for me to play with I thought that I'd play with the twins and their toys, but Mama told me to leave them alone.

They were only about two years old, and I would try to mother them as much as Mama would allow. She never wanted me to spend too much time around them; she told me once that I was to stay far away from them – she didn't want any of my ugliness to rub off on them.

So I walked over to the window just feeling that this can't be how Christmas was supposed to be. Then I saw Sonny and some of the boys playing in the street with his new football, so I quickly grabbed my coat and went down that long flight of stairs to be near some happy people.

When I got to the door, I opened it up and yelled out to Sonny, "Can I play too?"

He came over to me and with a big smile he said, "Sure thing, Mary," he was the first person to ever call me Mary and not Madia, our mother hated it, but would never correct her Sonny.

He said, "I'll let you play, but you've got to be quiet because I left my coat upstairs, and Ma will kill me if I get another cold."

You see, he was always a very sickly child and Mama told him that the next time he didn't wear his coat while he was out playing and got sick, she wasn't going to take him to the doctor. I was worried because he had been coughing for a few days already, but I told him, "Don't worry, Sonny, I won't tell Mama, I promise!"

He winked at me, smiled and said, "Thanks Mary, I know I can always count on you!" Just then his buddies said that they wanted to go play on the other side of the prairie, and I wasn't allowed to go there, so off he went. But he looked back at me and kind of motioned that he was sorry, so I just waved at him and he blew me a kiss and mouthed the word - thanks.

Alone once again, but I didn't feel bad. Even though I had to go back upstairs and be alone, I felt good inside because I knew in my heart that with all these people always fawning over

Sonny, it was Sonny who was always trying to fawn over me.

He knew that for some reason Mama blamed me for everything, but he would always tell me when we were alone that I was the bravest little girl in the world - braver than Shirley Temple - and that he was so proud to say that I was his sister.

Finally suppertime came around and I overheard my parents say that my Kuma was dropping by to see us and she had a present for me! Plus I heard Mama say that this would mean that she'd have to give me back my doll so that Kuma wouldn't make an issue out of it. You see, Kuma couldn't have children of her own and she would always say how she wished that she could have me. But of course Mama reassured her that her life would end if anything ever happened to me. Too bad she never said those words to me when we were alone.

I heard the bell and then I heard a familiar voice from downstairs yell out, "Yoo Hoo."

"Kuma, Kuma," I yelled as I ran to open our apartment door. I opened it and looked down to see Kuma coming up the stairs. I started jumping up and down.

As she made it to the landing, she knelt down, hugged me and said, "Oh, child, how I've missed you!" Then she hugged me again. It was always such a wonderful feeling when we'd hug, it was as though our hearts would touch!

"I love you, Kuma, Merry Christmas," I said, and then I looked into her twinkling blue eyes and asked, "Kuma, what did Santa bring you?"

She smiled and said, "Not a thing, and do you know why?"

"Were you bad?" I asked.

With a slight giggle in her voice, she answered, "No, it's just that he knew that I'd be coming to see you, and that's the best gift in the whole world to me!"

I was so happy that my eyes started to tear up, and I hugged her again.

"Now don't cry, honey, otherwise how are you going to see what he left for you!"

"Me?" she nodded yes as she pulled out two beautifully wrapped gifts from a big bag.

She pointed to the smaller of the two and said, "That's the real good one, so save that for last, Santa told me so."

Once I tore the paper off, I could see that it was a shoe box, so I removed the lid and was looking at the most beautiful black patent leather shoes that I'd ever seen. I looked up at her and said, "They're just like Shirley Temple's! I love them!" You see, I always had to wear these ugly brown corrective shoes because of a birth defect of my right foot.

Now it was time for gift number two. I couldn't imagine what could be in such a small box that Santa could think was better than the shoes. But as I opened it up and moved the tissue paper away, I laid my eyes on the prettiest and smallest porcelain baby doll that I'd ever seen. The doll was only about four inches long, and she was dressed in a white lace christening outfit; she was lying in a glass cradle that rocked.

"She's beautiful. She looks just like a little princess!"

"Oh child," Kuma said as she hugged and kissed me, "That's not just any little princess.

It's mine. That means that this doll reminded me of you when you were a baby. Don't you see her brown hair and those beautiful warm brown eyes?"

I felt as though my heart would burst. I thought maybe this day could be saved and this man Santa must be just as wonderful as my Kuma.

After dinner as Kuma was leaving, I heard her mention that she didn't like the sound of Sonny's cough, which by now one of the twins had a cough as well. Mama said, "Well, Kuma, everything is under control so please don't worry."

"Madia, I'm just saying that with all of these children and with running a business, you might overlook some signs that could become serious."

"Well, Kuma, if you had children of your own, you'd realize that colds are just part of growing up."

I could tell that this bothered Kuma, and she looked down and then away from Mama. She looked like she was going to cry, and then she spotted me and said, “Well, Madia, I don’t need to have children of my own when I have Little Madia and the rest of your children. Isn’t that right, Little Madia?” With that she put her hands out to me and I ran into her arms.

“Oh yes, Kuma, we all love you.”

Then there was a loud bang, and Kuma and I looked over toward Mama and somehow a big pot had fallen to the floor. Just then my father walked in asking, “Hey, what’s going on up here?” He looked mad and then he saw Kuma and he started to smile and said, “Oh hello Kuma, Merry Christmas. Are you going to stay for a while?”

Mama blurted out a simple, “No!”

We all were a little shocked, and then Mama nervously smiled and said, “I mean, ugh well, she has a husband of her own to look after and so I’m sure that she has to rush off and make sure that her husband has a Merry Christmas of his own. Right, Kuma?”

“Why yes, Madia, you’re right.”

I grabbed her hand and said, “Please stay for a while, Kuma...please?”

"Oh, child, I wish I could but there are so many stops that I have to make." Then she caressed my cheek with the back of her hand. It was like silk.

I asked, "Kuma, why are your hands so soft?"

Papa answered for her, saying, "Well, Madia, your Kuma was a concert pianist back in Yugoslavia. She didn't have to work in the fields like us." Then he looked over to her and I could see that they just kept staring at each other as he finished speaking, saying, "That's when I first met her. Me and your Uncle Pete used to do work for her father."

Then Mama said, "Martin, don't you have to go back downstairs for our customers?"

He never even looked at Mama, but he said, "Yes, Kuma, I'd better go back. Merry Christmas." Then he stepped toward her.

Immediately Mama said, "Kuma, it's best that you leave right now. Your husband must be very concerned about where his wife is."

Kuma smiled and then she offered some polite good-byes, gave kisses to the girls and then a kiss for me. By then Papa was back downstairs, so I told Kuma that I'd walk her to the door. Mama just mumbled to herself as she turned her back to me and Kuma.

So I walked Kuma to the door where she kissed me one more time and she told me that she loved me and I told her the same and then she was gone. I closed the door and stood in the middle of the dining room alone and silent. It felt like the day never even really happened, that is until I looked back at my gifts, and thought, I'd be willing to give them all back to Santa if he would just let me go home with Kuma.

By bedtime I heard some noise downstairs and went wandering. I was freezing because someone left the door open. Then I realized that someone was holding it open; it was Sonny. He turned as I called to him, "Sonny, aren't you freezing?'

"Stay back, Mary, or you'll catch cold."

"What about you, Sonny? Aren't you freezing?" I asked.

"No, Mary, it feels great – I think I have a little fever, and if I tell Ma, she won't let me play football tomorrow, so please don't tell."

"OK, Sonny, I promise!"

"Thanks Mary. Now get back to bed before we both get in trouble." So I ran back up the stairs and tried to be as quiet as I could as I slipped into bed.

I heard Sonny come back in and go directly to the twins' room. Mama told him earlier to stay with them because their room was drafty and she wanted him to help keep them warm, plus if they needed anything she wouldn't have to get up.

Until I feel asleep, I could hear him cough. It sounded like he tried to muffle it with a pillow, but I could still hear him.

By morning Sonny was really sick and looked bad, and the twins didn't look or sound much better. I asked Mama if she was going to take them to the doctor like Kuma suggested. Sometimes at five and a half years old I'd forget the fear and open my mouth without thinking of the consequences.

Mama just glared at me and said, "You and your Kuma could both go to Hell!"

Well, I don't know how or why, but I looked at her bravely and said, "I would go anywhere, even to Hell, if it meant that I could be with my Kuma!"

Incensed, she slapped me across the face so hard that I fell to the floor and my little baby doll from Kuma fell out of the pocket of my robe. Mama looked at it and then back at me, then while staring into my eyes, she put her foot on the tiny doll's head. I thought no - she's not going to hurt my new doll. She's just mad cause I talked back.

But then she said, "Remember one very important thing, Madia, *I* am your mother, not your precious Kuma!", and with that I heard a crunch…I wanted to die.

"Mama, Mama – You killed my baby!" I cried.

She started to chuckle as she turned and walked away, saying, "Don't worry, Madia, there'll be another Christmas next year. Maybe your Goddamned Kuma can get Santa to give you another doll." Then she started to laugh.

I crawled over to see if there was anything left that I could save, but the doll was almost dust, so I just took the doll's outfit and put it in my pocket.

I could only think to myself, how could Mama do this to me? And that this was the worst Christmas ever. Little did I realize that this was just the beginning of the Holiday Horror that was about to unfold and would stay with me for the rest of my life.

All that night I was awake, between my crying and the terrible coughing of Sonny and the twins, I didn't get any sleep. When dawn finally came around, breaking the silence of the morning I heard the voices of my parents coming from downstairs.

I peeked out of my door and saw my brother Martin. I told him to be quiet and together we snuck down the long staircase that led to our tavern on the first floor. On our way down we could hear them even better. I heard Papa say that he thought Sonny and the twins might die because they were all so sick. Mama told him that he was crazy and to shut up! We just made it into the tavern and hid under the bar so they couldn't see us. We watched as Papa got so mad that he hit her in the face, as he said, "I must be crazy to have married a pig like you!"

She turned back around holding her face and stared right at him and said, "A pig is all you deserve for a wife. Hell, even a pig is too good for a bastard like you!"

Again Papa slapped her across her face and this time her mouth started bleeding. Mama wiped her hand across her mouth and looked down at the blood. She looked back at him and with a piercing look of steel in her eyes she said, "Thank you very much Martin. I was wondering when you'd give me my Christmas present."

Disgusted, Papa just stormed off and went back upstairs, not even acknowledging us.

I couldn't believe what we'd just witnessed; we both just stood there. Then all of a sudden Mama turned and walked toward us mumbling something about how she didn't have time for this bullshit and that she had to clean the bar.

Trying to show that I was concerned as well, I spoke up saying that Martin had already told me that Sonny and the twins were worse and she just nodded.

But then again I went too far when I said, "Mama, remember what Kuma said ...," but before I could go any further, I could see that the second I said the word 'Kuma', her eyes turned to fire and I knew I was doomed.

Instantly she came around the bar after me. She grabbed a nearby broom on the way, and with one fell swoop she hit me broadside so hard that I flew into the wall, bounced off and hit the floor. My brother tried to run over to help me, but like a giant brick wall Mama stood there between us saying, "Don't touch her Martin. She'll get you sick because she was near Sonny - she might have the disease too!"

"I don't care!" he yelled, and with that she slapped him.

Immediately she turned back to me yelling, "See how evil you are, you little bitch? You made me hit your little brother!"

She repeatedly hit me again and again. "Run Martin, run!" I screamed, "I'll be OK!"

I could see that he had tears in his eyes as he started to run back upstairs. I didn't know if they were for me, him or the both of us. They should have been for the entire family, because by nightfall our world was to be turned upside down.

"Madia", my father's bold voice rang out. "Call the doctor. I can't wake up Sonny!"

My mother had a sudden look of panic and then she turned to me and said, "I'll take care of you later, you little bitch!"

Thank God, I thought. A reprieve for a little while anyway.

Then I thought about that look of panic on my mother's face. I mean it frightened me because of Sonny, but it also brought me a little joy, because nothing ever made my mother afraid, except for our father when she would finally push him to his limit. Plus, I was just so happy that when Papa yelled, "Madia!" from upstairs, that it wasn't for me.

Chapter 3

The doctor arrived before noon, and by 2:00 p.m. one of my favorite people in the whole world was in a coma and dying. The doctor started his examination with the girls because they were so young. It seemed as though it took forever. I tried to peek in through the crack in the door and I could see him taking a lot of things out of his bag. Then out of nowhere came my father's hand. He pulled the door shut and said, "Madia, get away from there and don't get in the doctor's way. Go sit on the couch or go downstairs."

So I sat on the couch and watched my mother walk back and forth.

She kept saying to herself, "Why is he spending so much time on them? He needs to check on Sonny. Can't he hear him coughing?"

I could hear Sonny coughing the entire time too and I was wondering the same thing as well. Finally he emerged and said that he was done with the twins and he wanted to examine Sonny. He was in there less time and when the door to Sonny's room opened, the doctor didn't look very happy.

Mama said, "Well is he OK?"

The doctor looked at her and said, "Well, Mrs. Zovko, the girls..."

"Who the hell cares about them, what about my Sonny?"

The doctor looked at her with a puzzled expression and said, "I'll take the girls with me, but Sonny is far too sick to leave. The shock of going out in the cold could ruin any chance that he might have. I gave him something for his cough, but he'll have to stay here, and I'll check on him again tomorrow morning."

With that prognosis he opened up a virtual Pandora's Box.

"What kind of Goddamned doctor are you?" screamed my hysterical mother. "You want to save these little bitches just so you can let my Sonny die! Without him, what use do I have for any of these little bastards?"

My father grabbed her by her shoulders and said, "Quit talking crazy. The doctor knows what's best!"

"Best?" she screamed as she pulled away, "Best, well he is the best!" now pointing to Sonny's bedroom door, "And if he dies, then I don't give a shit if all the others go to Hell… and you fine doctor", as she now spoke directly to him in a venomous way, "you can go right to Hell with them!"

With that my father slapped her across the face saying that the doctor was doing his best to help all of the children.

She stepped back yelling that if Sonny died, she'd kill the doctor! Slam went father's hand again across my mother's face. He yelled, "Shut up! The doctor knows what he's doing."

"He doesn't know shit!"

And my father went to slap Mama again but the doctor stepped between them and said, "Everyone needs to calm down. The most important thing is to think about the children. *All* of the children."

My parents stepped back, and my father glared at my mother and said, "I've got a business to run, Doctor, do whatever you want." Then he walked away and went downstairs leaving me and Mama with the doctor. Mama walked away in a huff. The doctor tried to ask them both for help bundling up the twins. No response. Then as Mama was almost out of sight, she yelled back, "That little bitch will help you. Madia, help the doctor."

He looked so disgusted. He was getting ready to yell back to her but he looked at me standing there, and he just kept shaking his head. He let out a big sigh, and his face was so red. He finally said, "Well, Little Mary, this is what big sisters do for their little sisters. Will you help me?"

"Yes, Doctor, what do you need?" "Some warm clothes and blankets so that they can keep warm in the car."

"Sure thing." I said as I ran over to the dresser in their room and pulled out all of the warmest things that I could find. Then I went to my room and got some blankets from the chest at the foot of my bed.

"Here, Doctor, will this work?"

"Yes, Little Mary, these are perfect."

As he was putting away the last of his things into his big black bag, I noticed that his mood was harsh, not toward me, just in general. He was putting his things away in a deliberate manner. Even as a child I could tell that he was obviously appalled by the display he had witnessed. That's why I really hated to bother him, but I had a question that was burning in my heart. I was so compelled by what I felt that I had to approach him. I had to know if Sonny had gotten sick from the cold weather.

"Doctor, can I ask you a question?" he looked up, and as he stared at me his mood started to soften.

"Of course, Little Mary...What's on your mind?"

"Doctor, is Sonny sick because he was outside without a coat?" I asked.

"Little Mary, Sonny has a virus that he caught from somebody else who was sick."

My guilt was starting to fade, then he went on, "But of course, if he was exposed to the cold for too long, then, yes, it could have lowered his resistance and made him worse, why?"

Feeling as though I now wanted to die, I just looked down and started to walk away. He touched my cheek and turned my face toward him and in a kind manner he said, "Oh, Little Mary, if you're worried about catching this, don't worry, just keep yourself and Martin away from Sonny until he gets better, and you'll both be fine. I'm going to get the twins settled in at the hospital, then I'll come back to check in on Sonny and make sure that everything around here goes back to normal."

All I could think was that was an impossible task…even for a doctor.

But his words kept ringing in my ears about the fact that the cold could have made Sonny worse. Why did I keep my promise to him? If only I'd told Mama, maybe Sonny wouldn't have gotten so sick. Maybe I should tell her now?

As I looked over toward the kitchen I could see that she was sitting all alone and I truly felt sorry for her. I knew that she loved Sonny more than anyone else on earth. I could see that she was still crying, and then all of a sudden she just got up and walked like she was in a trance toward Sonny's door.

"Mama", I said, "I have something important to tell you."

Slowly she turned toward me and said, "What could *you* possibly have to tell me that is more important than my Sonny dying?"

A chill ran through me, and hesitantly I said, "Nothing Mama, nothing at all, I'm sorry."

"Now go away…and leave me and my son alone."

Silently, and with enormous guilt, I slowly walked out of the apartment door and down that long staircase that led to our tavern, trying not to think about everything. As I got nearer to the tavern door, I started to lose my concentration, due to all the loudness coming from inside. The noise was loud and happy in there that night. Everyone was filled with the holiday spirit. Who would have known of the grieving that was going on upstairs?

I walked in the tavern unnoticed and observed everything the way I thought it would be. The only thing that seemed out of place in my mind was my father, who was by now behind the bar laughing and carrying on as if it were any other night. I was really confused. Here was my father, our father, the father of dying children, a man who tonight during this grieving could only console his wife by beating her in front of not only us, but also the doctor, and now he's laughing and having a good time...didn't he love us at all? I guess Mama was right. He *was* no good, and maybe all men *were* pigs!

Through the noise and smoke I spotted a small, dark figure...Martin. I was so caught up in my own guilt that I'd completely forgotten about him. As I walked over to him sitting all alone in the corner, I could only notice how scared he looked. I was twice as scared, because not only was I worried about my siblings, but also for myself. For in my heart, the guilt of not telling my mother the truth about Sonny, was beginning to rumble inside of me like a volcano.

"Martin," I said softly, "everything will be okay."

"I'm not so sure Mary. What if Sonny and the twins die? Then it's just us against them."

I thought to myself, oh my God, I never thought about that, for sure we wouldn't have a chance, but I couldn't say that to him. I'd have to be strong for his sake! Bravely I said as I hugged him, "Martin, there's no us or them. We're a family."

We sat there in each other's arms for the longest time. I didn't want to let him go, because at that moment, I felt as though he was all I had.

I don't know how long we sat there, but before we knew it, the doctor had returned from the hospital.

He walked in looking rather blank as he approached our father and whispered something into his ear. Papa looked a little upset, yet he stayed very cool as he waved over a friend to bartend for him. Then he and the doctor headed upstairs.

I said to Martin, "Something's wrong, let's go upstairs."

We pushed our way through the crowd and I could feel the fear mounting. I knew I'd have to be strong for Martin's sake.

As we started to ascend the stairs, I felt a new emergence of guilt blending with fear. Suddenly a scream, it was my mother's voice.

Then I heard her yelling, "No, no – it must not be true!"

As we got to the top of the stairs, I could hear the doctor explaining that God works in mysterious ways. Then like a madwoman, Mama started yelling, "Fuck You and Fuck God!"

Finally we made it to the threshold; we were frozen stiff with fear. I was never so scared in my life. From what I could comprehend, the doctor was there to tell them that the twins had such a high fever that it wasn't looking too good for them. Then he went directly into Sonny's room to check on him…Sonny was dead.

Papa just kept yelling at Mama for saying the "F" word, saying that it was bad enough when a man said it, but he had no use for *any* woman that would say it. Then he grabbed her by her arms and said, "Madia, I know you're upset, but that still doesn't give you the right to act this way!"

With that, she broke away from him. She looked him square in the eyes and slowly said, "And Fuck You!"

Slam went my father's iron hand against my mother's face.

The doctor stepped in yelling, "Are you both crazy? This is when you need each other the most! You still have other children to raise."

Coldly and blankly, my mother stared at him saying, "I have no other children."

"Mama," I said, "yes, you still have us!"

Slowly she turned her head and stared directly at my brother and said, "That's right…I still have my Martin."

With that she began to smile and reached her arms out to him. He slowly let go of my hand, and like a magnet, he was drawn into her waiting arms.

I couldn't even speak, because I felt as though, not only was I unwanted and unloved, but now…I wasn't even here.

The doctor, amazed by the whole scenario, tried to bring a sense of normalcy to the scene by saying that we're all in shock. He also told us not to worry about anything, and that he would be taking care of all of the arrangements for us.

I wished at that moment that I was one of the arrangements that he was going to take care of, because already, in those few moments, I felt a renewed sense of aloneness.

I tried to keep saying to myself that Mama didn't mean it, and that she was just in shock. But I knew that those were her true feelings of contempt for me. Plus, it was the first time she'd ever verbalized them, and it cut me to the bone.

You see, not only did I have to deal with her rejection, but I also had to cope with my own deep seated guilt. Yes, I did feel like I had killed my brother through my silence. Being engulfed in those feelings, I could only walk silently away back to my room, leaving behind my family as they mourned one son's death, one son's rebirth, and the nonexistence of me.

It seemed as though I was alone in my room crying for days instead of hours. Then all of a sudden there was more erratic talking. It was my mother on the phone with the doctor, who was by now, back at the hospital.

Coldly, she said. "Don't worry doctor, there's nothing there that matters to me. What's most important is that I still have my Martin. OK, call me if there's any change in the other one... if you want."

With that, she hung up the phone and just sat there alone holding a family photo, petting the black and white image of her dead son.

Bravely, I approached her and said, "Mama, please, I have to talk to you about something."

Without even looking up, she said, "Ok if you want, but first your little sister is dead - now go on, what's bothering you?"

A strange silence took over the room, and then I asked, "Which one Mama, which twin is dead?"

Hauntingly, she replied that she didn't know, nor did she care, just as long as she had her Martin.

Feeling that I might unleash all kinds of horror, I didn't care…I had to tell the truth! Hysterically I said, "Mama, I killed Sonny, and I guess I killed the baby too, it's all my fault! Everything!"

She turned her head, and coldly she said, "What the HELL are you talking about?"

"Mama," I screamed, "Sonny made me promise…but I didn't know he was going to die!"

Slowly she rose to her feet. With the hate from a million lifetimes, she stared at me, and slowly started to walk toward me. I felt as though I would pass out from fear.

Then she finally spoke, "Madia…what promise?"

Tearfully, I explained about Sonny playing football without his coat, and that I saw him sitting by the open door.

"I wanted to tell you Mama, but I didn't want Sonny to be mad at me. I love him!" With rage in her eyes, she responded, "Loved him you mean!" She screamed into my face, "Your brother is DEAD because of you! You murdering, little, BITCH!" Slam went her fist against my head. She'd hit me so hard that I fell down, then she screamed for me to get up. When I didn't get up fast enough, she kicked me in the back, and then lifted me up to my feet by my hair.

"Please Mama, please don't kill me. I'm sorry, I'm so very sorry!"

She screamed at me, "Sorry, I'm the one that's sorry! Sorry that I didn't kill you at birth!" She reached down, picked me up, and put me under her arm like a sack of dirty laundry and started walking. I prayed that someone would come upstairs to save me.

Then as we approached the door to Sonny's room, she said, "Let me show you what your silence did to *my* Sonny!"

She flung open the door and there was Sonny's lifeless body. She threw me down on the bed and on top of my dead brother. I tried to run through the door to get away, but she grabbed me by my hair and dragged me back to the room. She shoved me back through the door, and yelled, "Tell him you're *sorry*!" and she slammed the door behind me.

I kept screaming, "Please come back for me Mama. I can't stay in here. I can't. I'm scared. *Please* don't leave me alone!"

She was outside the door, and she said, "Madia, you're not alone. You're with your brother. See how well he can take care of you, when you keep a promise for him!"

Standing there, frozen in disbelief, I didn't know what to do. Is this really happening, or is this a bad dream?

I felt so lost, and so alone.

Then, after a while, I slowly walked over to his bed. With my tear filled eyes, I looked at my dead brother's face. There was soft glow to his face from the moonlight coming through the lace curtains. I said to him, "I'm so sorry, Sonny. I wish I could have been strong and told Mama that you were out playing in the cold. Because I'd rather have you mad at me, than dead." I already missed him and didn't want him to leave me. So I decided that I wanted to lie next to him one last time. I trembled as I crawled into bed next to him. Then lovingly, I leaned over and gave him a kiss on the lips, and whispered "Good-bye."

I cried all night. And instead of being afraid, I could only feel a strange sort of security. Because even though Mama thought this was to be my punishment, I felt safer being in bed with my dead brother, than being out there with my very much alive mother. As I closed my eyes, again I could only express my sorrow over and over to my brother, and tell him that I loved him, and that I would love him forever.

CHAPTER 4

I woke up hoping it was all a bad dream. Maybe Sonny was alive, and for a brief moment everything was really okay. Then I turned my head; and the harsh reality of his death was staring me in the face.

Sonny was now an unbelievable color. So very cautiously I reached up and I touched his face. It was so cold that I pulled my hand back. The real horror of his death set in. I no longer felt secure with my brother's body. I could only feel panic and fear.

I jumped out of bed and started beating on the door for someone to let me out. "Help! Help! Mama, Papa, Martin! Somebody *please* let me out of here!"

I heard the click of the lock. The door opened, and there was my father. Standing tall, he filled the doorway with his presence. With a shocked look on his face, he asked, "Madia, why did you lock yourself in the room with Sonny?"

"Papa", I said, "Mama put me in here, because she was mad that I killed Sonny."

"What?" my father said, "Your mother wouldn't do that. Don't lie! And just how do you think *you* killed your brother?"

"It's because I didn't tell Mama that I saw Sonny outside without his coat," I replied.

"So what!" Papa yelled, "That's nothing - and that still doesn't give you the right to say bad things about your mother!"

Then in a calm tone, he said, "Now get washed up. People will be coming over soon."

How strange I thought, first Mama went crazy, now Papa doesn't even care.

Maybe the way he acted was the right way, just accepting life as it was, or maybe he just didn't care about anything; his wife, his children, their lives or their deaths….just money and business.

Looking back now I realized that many men back then weren't included into many inner-family things until something like death entered into it. That could be why he always seemed so mechanical about everything.

It was now time for us to grieve with family and friends, as they waked Sonny's body in our home on the couch. That's what they did back then. Someone even took a photo of him lying there and later gave it to us as a gift. Many people came by, and after a while they all seemed alike. That was until my Kuma walked through the door.

She expressed true sorrow over Sonny and the twin's deaths. Oh yes, right before the mourners had arrived, we were notified that the other twin had died too. There would be no wake for them, only Sonny. No one bothered to come over to tell me. I just overheard it from the adults.

"Oh child," I heard a soft and familiar voice say as to console me, "I'm so very sad for all of you."

"Oh Kuma", I said as I threw my arms around her. Then after she kissed me, she led me to my room.

She said, "Sit on the bed child. I'm here to ask you how you're feeling and if you need me for anything."

How wonderful I thought, finally somebody realized that I was grieving too. I should have known that the first kind words would be from my Kuma.

"Kuma" I said, "I have to tell you something that is going to make you hate me forever. I told Mama and she hates me now."

Softly she said, "I could never, ever hate you."

As she held my face in her hand, I said, "Kuma, I killed Sonny!"

"What?"

"And the twins." Then I started to cry.

"Oh my God, child, that's impossible. They died from pneumonia!" She then quickly clutched me to her chest while she rocked me back and forth as we both wept together. Tearfully I said, "It's true, it's true! I knew Sonny was outside without his coat, and I didn't tell Mama. Then he was sitting and letting the cold wind blow in on him, and I *still* didn't say anything."

"Child, a virus like theirs isn't caught over night. They had to be sick with it for a long time. It just didn't show up for a while. That's all. Just be glad that you and Martin were lucky enough not to have caught it."

"Oh, Kuma, why didn't I catch it instead of them? Sonny was so good, and he was a boy. They're better than girls you know and the twins were blonde and blue-eyed, and *so* pretty. Not like me."

"Now child, you're so precious to me, like a perfect diamond, only better. And if you died, well, I don't know what I would have done. And who says that boys are better? And what's wrong with brown hair and brown eyes? I think you're beautiful and I wouldn't trade you for a *million* boys. Madia, you look me in the face and you tell me, 'Kuma, you never lied to me, and if you say I'm wonderful, than I am. There is only one of me in the *whole* world and I'm special. I know that not only will many people love me throughout my life, but most of all, my Kuma loves me!"

I repeated those magical words back to her and I did feel better. Because I knew that no matter what other people said, including my mother, my Kuma was kind, good, and so full of love, that if this is the kind of person who loves me, then I couldn't be as bad, ugly and evil as Mama told me I was. From that point on, I knew that I would have to try to *not* be like my mother, but more like my Kuma.

Chapter 5

Many weeks of silence came my way from my mother, especially when we were alone. I didn't mind because Kuma's words would go through my head like a song. The strangest part of our new family dynamic was that I noticed the strange behavior involving my younger brother, Martin.

He was getting all of the attention from not only Mama, but also now Papa joined in on the family band wagon.

We were playing outside one day, and he fell down. He immediately wanted to go in. I asked him what for, it was only a scratch?

He replied, "Mama told me that I'm *all* that she had left. So if I got hurt or anything, I should hurry and find her."

All she had left, I thought, "What about me?"

So I said, "Martin, there are still the two of us – not just you."

"Girls don't matter, Mary, you know that."

How could my little brother say this to me? He's the one who said, "It was going to be us against them."

Well from that point on, I knew it was me against all of them, and all I could think about was, Thank God that summer was almost over and I was going to be starting school. It was the fact of knowing that I was going to be away from all of them - all day!

Mama informed me we were going shopping for school clothes. She always dressed us beautifully. She told us since we had a business, people expected it.

We would always go to a shopping area that people referred to as 'Commercial Avenue'. It was the shopping district in South Chicago; an area in Chicago near our home. It was just far enough that you had to take the streetcar.

"Now when we get there Madia," my mother would say, "you know what I told you, don't you?"

"Yes, Mama, I'm to walk far in front of you."

"That's right!" she said sternly.

"Why do I have to do that Mama?"

"Never mind, just do as I say!"

"But why Mama, why?"

"Shut up, I'm your mother and if I say you're to walk on your hands, you'll do it! Now don't argue with me, you little bitch!"

"But what if I get lost?"

"Don't worry about that Madia, I couldn't get that lucky!"

I hoped she was only joking, but I somehow knew she really meant it. It was those types of words that always brought back all of the old negative feelings.

Again, I asked why?

"God damn it, why, why, why, is that all you can say? Well…if you must know, I'm going to *pretend* that you're not my daughter, because you're so dark, and I'm so fair. I don't want anyone to think I have a child that looks like a Mexican. That's it, you look like a dirty, filthy, little Mexican bitch! There, you wanted an answer - well that's mine. Now let's go!"

"But you like Martin," I said, "and he's dark."

"Like? I *love* my Martin! I love my Martin because he's a boy...and boys are supposed to be dark. Girls are supposed to be fair, like me."

Fair? I thought, there is nothing fair about her. Not only in her actions, but she wasn't blonde or blue eyed. She had brown eyes and light brown hair that she put something on to make it a little golden. Her skin was lighter than mine, but not fair, not like Jean Harlow, or anything?

Even to this day, I still don't understand her 'fair' obsession.

So off we went. It was always so exciting – all the big buildings, and the hustle and bustle. Of course I had to sit in a different seat from her, which would scare most children, but by now I'm sure that you can tell that it was a pleasure.

She gave me 'The Look' when we approached our stop, so that I could get up and she wouldn't have to speak to me in public. She would only speak to me in public if we were around people that already knew that we were related.

As I walked along the street I would keep glancing back so that I could keep track of her. I would always get a little panicked because I would have to try to keep track of where she was all the time, since she would pop into stores and not let me know. I couldn't cry when I was afraid because she would hit me and tell people that I was trying to run away. This was compounded by the fact that, 'God forbid', she'd have to actually admit that I was her child.

Chapter 6

As time went by, I finally understand that everything she did with, to, and for me, was a battle of power, combined with the fact that what she *really* wanted for me was to be strong.

It took many years of therapy in my adult life before I was able to see this, and to also understand her distorted perception on *how* to make someone strong.

For example, the summer of my sixth birthday, I experienced one of the most horrid weeks of my life. I can only thank God that I've never had to repeat anything like that again. Even to this day, to remember it makes me feel paralyzed, humiliated, and afraid. For instead of the happiness of soon being a six-year-old little girl, who only wanted to feel the joyful anticipation of being 'the birthday girl', I had to endure my mother's unbelievable perception of strength and courage...perceptions that were beyond distorted.

I'm sure that in her own way she thought that she was doing her best to make her weak female child strong. It's just too bad that she went about it in such an abusive and cold-hearted manner. It was that summer when the evidence of her twisted child rearing hit its peak.

It was unbearably hot, and everyone was trying to get ready for the big 'Fourth of July Celebration', that we always had at our tavern. I was trying to be happy because not only was it a holiday, but it was also ten days until my sixth birthday. I was in the bar's kitchen, thinking that I was staying out of everyone's way, when my mother yelled for me to go outside.

I said, "Mama, everyone says it's over 100 degrees."

"Quit thinking only about yourself and get outside."

"I feel hot!"

"You know how I feel about people who always start *all* their sentences with 'I', so quit making yourself seem *so* important and get out of here!"

I thought to myself, 'I' better get out of here before 'I' get hit! So I moved swiftly out the door and onto the back porch. The back porch led to our big backyard where we would have a lot of our outdoor parties. I went out there and I found a cool spot in the shade of one of our tall Cottonwood trees. There was a breeze and I thought, gee, Mama did me a favor – this is heavenly. As I lay on the grass, I was just so happy to be enjoying the quiet of the day when I heard a car pulling up onto the gravel driveway next to our building. I sat up and saw a familiar car, "Kuma!" I yelled as I got up and ran to see my favorite person in the whole wide world.

With her arms wide open, she yelled, "Child, how are you on this big holiday?"

"Great now that you're here!" I said as I got swallowed up by her embrace.

"Kuma, I was feeling hot before, but I'm better now."

"Hot?" she asked, "when was that?"

"Oh, back when I was in the kitchen, with Mama. You know, while she was getting some of the food ready for the party."

With that I got silent, and Kuma said, "Child, what's bothering you? Are you sure you're not sick?", and as her soft pink hand caressed my forehead, she said, "Oh my! You are hot!"

Trying not to wreck the moment, I said, "It's just that I'm a little warm from being in the kitchen with Mama, and from running to see you, that's all."

"Well if you're sure?" Then her tone changed back to being happy. "You know what we almost forgot, don't you? You never told me what you wanted for your birthday. It's almost here you know. What will it be child? Tell your Kuma!"

"Well, Kuma, I'm going to tell you a secret wish, but you have to promise me that you'll never tell anyone, not even Mama. Especially, not Mama, O.K.?"

"O.K.", she replied, and as she smiled, "I promise. What is it?"

"Well, Kuma, the best gift, if I could really have it, would be to wake up and find that you were my mother and not Mama. I know some people would say that it's bad to wish for something like that, but I don't…" then I looked up to her twinkling blue eyes to find them welled up with tears.

She looked at me and with a smile on her face she said, "Madia, my sweet, precious child – I love you sooo much, that I couldn't love you any more, even if God had granted me you as my very own child."

Those words made me feel as though I were ten feet tall, yet also a little sad at the same time, because I'd never heard those words from my mother's lips.

"Oh Kuma, I love you so much. I don't want anything from you, because *you* are my present, my birthday present from God."

Unable to hold back her tears, she just clutched me to her and held me as she tried to compose herself. She asked softly, "Please Madia, there must be something that you'd like?

How about a new doll, and this time I'll make sure that it's not porcelain like the one you got for Christmas from Santa."

"Santa's still not mad at me, is he?"

"No, and he never was! He knows that accidents happen. I don't know what happened, Santa's normally so smart. I don't know how he could've forgotten that you live on the second floor. With all those stairs, he should have known how easy it would be to drop a tiny doll like that! Well it's probably because he's such a busy man. But don't worry, I'll find you one that can take a drop or two. That reminds me that next Christmas, I'll have to let Santa know that too. You know child, all this talk of Christmas has helped me cool down, how about you?"

"Oh yes, Kuma, I feel much better now." But I was too busy thinking about things like, if Santa knows everything, he'll know that I lied to Kuma about the doll. But if he *really* knows everything, then maybe he knows how much Mama hates Kuma, and that I had to lie so that they wouldn't fight? I couldn't think straight because I just lied again, and I was burning up.

I didn't say anything to Kuma because I didn't want her to worry.

"I don't know child – you look a little flushed. Let me feel your forehead." She barely touched it and said, "Child, you're burning up. Come on; let's go tell your mother."

"Please Kuma don't, don't tell her, otherwise I'll miss the party!"

She stooped down and looked me in the eyes and said, "Now child - wouldn't it be better to miss the party tonight so that you can be well for your big day next week?"

"Well…I guess so Kuma, Mama's in the kitchen."

We headed toward the building and as we walked through the back door, I heard Mama say to Papa, "I see your girlfriend's here."

"Shut up Madia, that's a disgusting thing to say. She's a married woman. Don't be ridiculous."

"Really? I don't know whose worse when she's around, you, or Little Madia. The whole world stops when she walks in. Why is that Martin?"

Papa stopped dead in his tracks, turned, and coldly stared at Mama, and said, "Because she's a lady, a lady filled with goodness."

Just then Kuma's hand tightened. She put her finger up to her lips to motion to me to be quiet and to go back outside with her.

Once outside, she nervously said, "Child, I think that I forgot to get some things for the party, so give me a big hug and a kiss and I'll see you later. Don't forget to tell your mother that you might have a fever…bye-bye!"

As she got into her car, I waved goodbye and yelled, "See you later Kuma!"

She waved back, blew me a kiss, and she was gone.

I stayed outside for a while hoping that I would cool off, but I was feeling worse. Then the smell of the roasting chickens and lamb started to make me feel even sicker, so I decide to go inside. I peeked into the bar and could see that there were already a lot of people gathering, so I decided to go back to the kitchen with Mama – who by now was quite alone – and tell her that I wasn't feeling well.

"Mama, I think I have a fever – but I don't want to miss the party."

She slammed the meat clever down into the butcher block where she'd been preparing the food, turned around and glared at me with a cold steely stare, and said, "You'll do anything to fuck this day up for me – won't you?"

"I'm sorry Mama, but I'm sick." I said sheepishly as I looked at the floor.

"Ouch!" I screamed as Mama grabbed a hold of my hair.

She then got face to face with me and said, "Well, Madia, let's get you into bed right now before you spread this disease too. We don't want to infect your brother, Martin – because you know if anything happens to him, I'll kill you – and this time you know I mean business!"

She dragged me by my hair all the way upstairs, and when we got about mid-way, we stopped on the landing and she yelled to my brother, "Martin, Madia is sick and I don't want you to catch her cold, so go to your room and grab what you'll need for a few days away!"

"Yes Mama." he replied.

"She might kill you like she did your brother and the twins!"

Ironically, whenever she referred to Sonny, and my sisters, she would make the sign of the cross. Funny, this coming from a woman who couldn't even remember the twins' names.

"And you're not allowed back up here until she either gets well or dies! Do you understand?"

He poked his head out of the doorway and said, "Yes Mama – Bye Mary!" and he was gone.

I tried to yell back, good-bye, but just then there was another horrible yank on my hair from Mama's death-grip, and I was dragged up the rest of the stairs.

"Mama, you're hurting me!"

"Shut up you little bitch. Do you think that I have nothing better to do today than babysit your ass? I'm very busy, and I don't want to have to deal with you until tomorrow! So you'll stay in your room until then...do you understand?"

I nodded yes. But as we got closer to my room, I said, "But if I stay in my room, I'll miss Kuma when she comes back for the party."

She stopped dead in her tracks, and in a slow and evil tone, she said, "Oh yes...What will you do without seeing your precious Kuma? Maybe you'll have to listen to ME for a change! Come on; let's get you into your room. With that bad fever, we wouldn't want you to catch cold or anything - you might die! Oh that's right, I don't have to tell *you* about that, now do I?"

Mama always reminded me, every chance she got, of last Christmas. I always wondered if she'd ever forget or forgive me for that...she never did.

"Get in there and strip!" She ordered, as she pushed me through the doorway of my room. "We're going to bake that fever right out of you!" With that she went around the room and started closing all the windows of an already hot room. My room always stayed very hot because it was on the west side of the building, and the sun would just pour through the extremely tall, wide windows.

Then up went the shades. Next she started pushing my bed into the direct line of the window with the most sunlight, and she said, "Madia, come on, get into bed. I'm going to make *sure* that you're going to stay here until we break that fever. We'll do it by burning it right out of you. Now get into bed."

Standing there naked, I said "Please let me wear some pajamas, Mama. What if somebody comes up here? Like the boarders, or Papa, or Martin?"

"Don't worry; I'm going to tell everyone that you're sick, and that you have to be left alone so you can break the fever. They won't come. They will be too afraid they'll catch it and die." She said that with contempt for me, not only in her voice, but also with her eyes. "Besides, you don't think anybody wants to see you naked? Ha!" she laughed. "Who would want to see a skinny, ugly, little girl like you?"

Just then, there was a "snap," sound. It was from one of the rat traps that we used in the attic.

We lived only a few blocks from the river and many times the large river rats would make their way into buildings.

Terrified, I sat up, and said, "Mama, please don't leave me alone, I'm not feeling good and I'm scared of the rats in the attic!"

"Shut up and lay down!"

"But Mama!"

"Shut up, you evil little bitch!" Then with the speed of light, 'Slap' went her hand across my face.

Then she waved her finger in my face and said, "What the fuck did I tell you? Don't you understand fucking English for Christ's sake? You stay in that goddamned bed - or else!" Then there was a long pause. Suddenly, she got up, and started riffling through my chest of drawers. She pulled out long stockings and shirts.

Held them in her hand, and said, "So, you want to give your mother a hard time by not staying in bed, do you?" And before I knew it, my mother started tying my hands and feet to the bed frame.

Then she said, "Now I won't have to keep checking on you to make sure that you're obeying me!"

She stood there for a moment surveying her handy work and wiping her hands together. She looked rather pleased with herself, she said, "Now - that's perfect!"

"No Mama, it's too hot in the sun like this…I feel like I can't breathe!"

"Shut up! Just shut the fuck up! God damn it!"

Then 'snap', another trap.

"Oh Mama," I screamed, "If the rats come down from the attic, what will I do? I can't move my hands or feet!"

She slowly slithered up to my ear, and softly said, "Oh Madia, don't you know? That's how I'll know if you're lying to me about being sick." She started to stroke my hair, almost like a real mother, and then said, "Yes, Madia, the rats know that you are in here alone, and helpless. But that's OK, because if you are *truly* sick with a fever, when the rats come, they won't touch you. But," she said, now while sadistically smiling and still stroking my hair, "if you are lying to me, they will know, and they will come and crawl up inside you from in-between your legs, and they will eat your guts. Then finally, they will eat those soft brown eyes right out of your little head."

"No!" I screamed.

"Then, if they're still hungry, they'll eat that ugly little face of yours."

"No Mama! No!" I screamed, thrashing back and forth.

"Oh yes Madia, and they *will* come."

"No! No! No! Mama, No!" I cried, "Please don't leave me alone...please!"

I screamed hysterically, and then another snap. Another trap went off, and it seemed louder than ever.

As she leaned over me, she gave me the coldest, meanest look that I'd ever seen.

My mother was almost nose to nose with my tear and sweat soaked face, "Now just lay there and be quiet - or else."

I whispered the word, "Mama."

And before I could say anymore, she screamed at me, saying, "I told you not to say another fucking word! God damn it!" she yelled, "I've never seen a more disobedient child!"

Swiftly, she dug into her enormous cleavage, and pulled out a used sweat soaked handkerchief, and rammed it down my throat.

"This ought to keep you quiet till your fever breaks, my little darling. Ha, Ha, Ha," she laughed as she got up and out of my bed. "Remember, keep your eyes shut!" She taunted, as she just kept laughing while she walked out of my room, which by now was like a furnace.

As her laughter and footsteps faded, I couldn't believe my mother just ignored my muffled moans and my tears. Then 'snap' went yet another trap.

All through the night, it seemed that I kept hallucinating about the amount of traps that kept going off. Also, I imagined giant rats coming for my eyes and guts. As I silently pleaded to God for help, I still couldn't understand my mother. How could she do this to me? How could she tell me all of this? I prayed to God, and asked him, that if I survived this torture, maybe he could perform some kind of miracle. So when I woke up, that this, and my entire life of almost six years, would all have been a very bad dream. And that Kuma was really my mother, and that my life was in fact, wonderful.

Well I survived, and I guess dreams don't come true. It was morning when I finally heard the lock being opened. It made me realize, that first, I wasn't dead. Secondly, I didn't have a fever anymore, and most of all…the rats never came.

"Madia?" my mother's now soft voice said, "How are you feeling, better I hope?"

She was smiling as she walked toward me and removed the rag from my mouth.

Bravely I said, "Yes Mama, the fever's gone, and look, I still have eyes."

With no reaction on her face, she only said, "That's nice."

As she began to untie me, she asked me if I was hungry.

"Yes, Mama." I replied. "But first, may I have some water? I'm really thirsty."

"You should be, Madia, look…the sheets are soaked with your sweat!"

"I know Mama." Then sheepishly, I said, "But some of the wetness is also my pee."

Angrily, she turned on me, and yelled, "You little bitch! I don't believe a big girl like you, pissed in your own bed! Well maybe you're not as grown up as everyone thinks. Wait until I tell your friends, you pissed in your bed."

I begged her, "Mama, please don't tell anyone."

Slap went her hand across my face.

Being weak, I fell to the floor, and I started to cry. As I laid there naked on the floor, my tear filled eyes watched her as she stripped the bed.

Staring at the floor, I said, "It's only because you left me here for so long. People will understand if I tell them that."

Feeling pain to my head, I realized I was being pickup up by my hair.

"Ouch, Mama!" I screamed, "It hurts!'

"Not half as much," she said sternly, "as a child who would talk against her own Mother!" Then another slap!

I covered my face and begged for her to stop hitting me in the face.

"You're right Madia, your little ass will do just fine!"

Crack against my butt went her hand. And she asked, "Now, what are you going to tell people?"

Crack again, "Nothing Mama, nothing," I said.

"Oh yes you will, Madia. You will tell them that you have a wonderful mother, who takes good care of you and who loves you. Then you will tell them that you love your mother more than anyone else in the entire world. Because it's your mother, and no one else, who takes care of you when you are sick. After all, Madia, I broke your fever for you, didn't I? Now get dressed, and be happy, or I'll hit you again! Are you happy?"

"Yes Mama."

"Now, who loves you more than anyone in the whole world?"

"You, Mama, you." I said, as I now sat in the fetal position. Feeling so alone, and beginning to cry I said, "Only you."

Chapter 7

Days passed, and July fourth just seemed like a bad dream. I was sitting alone on the back stairs when the mailman came by.

He said, "Little Mary, I have something for you, a letter."

"How do you know it's for me and not for Mama? We have the same name."

"I know this is for you, because it's addressed to 'Little Mary the Birthday Girl'."

He asked, "Now, don't you suppose that, that means you?"

Happily, I said, "Yes sir, Mr. Postman. You know my birthday is in a few days."

"How old are you going to be Mary?"

Proudly, I answered, "Six years old!"

"My," he said, "what a big girl you are. Say, would you like me to read the card to you?"

"Yes, please! That would be wonderful." I answered. "You know, I can read a little, but I don't want to miss a word. And I bet I know who it's from."

He smiled, and said, "Oh really? Who do you think it's from?"

With a warm feeling in my heart, I said, "My Kuma."

Opening it, he said, "Well you're right and it's so pretty."

"Let me see it."

"Sure," he said, "here, feel the velvety part."

He held the card below his belt, flat against his pants. Now Little Mary, rub the velvety part hard and fast. It'll feel good."

So I did. He was right, it was soft and fuzzy. Then I noticed that his breathing quickened, and I asked him if he was sick.

Slowly, he said, "No."

I heard my mother yell for me, and before I knew it, the postman ran off. I yelled to him to come back, because he was supposed to read me what the card said. He just yelled back that he was busy and had to get back to work.

"Who were you talking to Madia?" asked my mother sternly.

"The postman Mama. He said that he was going to read my card from Kuma to me, but he was too busy."

"Oh is that all?" She took the card from my hands, and harshly, she said, "Madia, do you think that anybody really cares what your Kuma has to say to you?"

"I do." I said softly.

"Well then, I'll tell you. It says, Madia, I didn't know anyone could get so stupid and so ugly in only six years!" With that she laughed, threw the card on the ground and walked back inside.

With tears in my eyes, I slowly bent over and picked up my card with the 'now dirty' fuzzy pink kitty on it. It was wearing a birthday hat that had a big blue number six on it. I knew that my Kuma would have never said something like that to me. So I sat back down, and with tears in my eyes, I tried to make out the words.

I saw the words, "Madia, Love, and Kuma." So once again, I knew that Kuma loved me and my mother was just being mean.

As I sat there, one of our boarders named Tony, came outside.

Softly he said, "Little Madia, what you got?"

"A birthday card Tony."

"Oh yeah. Then why you, no happy?"

"I can't read it." I said, "Will you read it to me?"

"Oh Madia, I can't read either, unless it's in Yugoslavian. Sorry, my English is no good."

He thought for a second, and said, "Wait a minute, I be right back!"

He came right back with another boarder, named Kimo. They were the only two that ever made me laugh, and they were the only two men that never touched me, you know…in that funny way.

"Kimo," Tony said, "you tell Little Madia, what the card say, she know what it means."

"Sorry Little Madia, I can't see the words, I got drunk and lost my glasses."

Tony said, "Now look at us Madia, see what happens when you drink too much and when you don't go to school?"

We all laughed as we sat there together.

I said, "You two are like having two older sisters to me."

They sort of giggled.

"I mean, you'll play dolls with me and you're never mean, or touchy, or anything." So I gave them a kiss on their cheeks, and told them how much I loved them both.

Then, I said, "Kimo, I know my alphabet. How about if I tell you the letters and you can tell me the words?"

He nodded yes, and we deciphered that it said, 'Have a Perrrrfect Birthday!' And that Kuma loved me, and couldn't wait to see me on my birthday.

I was so happy that I kissed Kimo and Tony again. Then I thought how happy they must be for me, because they kissed each other too. How nice these two men got along, I thought.

It's funny, how as you get older, you can see how the innocence of a child can really put things into their proper prospective, without the destructive prejudice that you're bombarded with as an adult.

CHAPTER 8

It came at last, my sixth birthday! I couldn't have been any happier, even if I was given my very own Daddy Warbucks, just like Orphan Annie.

I got up early and I went into Martin's room. He was still sleeping, but I shook him and said, "Wake up, it's my birthday!"

"Oh Mary, Happy Birthday!" he said, as he hugged and kissed me.

I thought, it's a wonderful day already.

"Martin," I said, "I'm going to see if Mama and Papa are going to wish me a Happy Birthday."

"Be careful, Mary, OK?"

"Don't worry. It's my birthday. Nothing bad can happen to me today."

As I approached the kitchen, I smelled something wonderful. Then I saw Mama and I said, "Good morning, Mama, something sure smells good."

"Well, if it isn't my Madia, my little birthday girl. Come give me a kiss. You should always give me a kiss on your birthday, because without me,…you wouldn't be here."

I thought, Mama's being so nice. Why couldn't she always be like this? So I kissed her on the cheek. Then I asked her if she meant that I was here, because she loved Papa so much, like the church said.

You see, I was told that only people who are *truly* in love with each other, were granted children by God.

Mama laughed, "What, me, love your father? Oh God - I hate him. He's a pig - just like all men. Don't talk stupid. I'm trying to be nice to you on your birthday."

I looked down, and said, "I'm sorry, Mama".

As she got up from her chair, she said, "I thought you wanted to know what smelled so good? Well it's your birthday cake."

"For me!" I said, as I stood there in disbelief. My only thought was, this must be a dream.

A dream that I never wanted to wake up from and to my surprise, the entire day went along beautifully.

That is until later, when Kuma showed up, and instantly my mother's mood changed.

"Kuma!" I yelled, "I'm so glad to see you!"

"Oh child, an earthquake couldn't keep me from you today!"

I smiled as she hugged and kissed me.

"Here child, I hope you like this." she said as she handed me a big pink box, "And child, did you get my card?"

"Yes Kuma, thank you. It was so pretty. Me, Tony, and Kimo read it, and then we all kissed."

"That sounds…so sweet. Now, go ahead and open the box." she said.

I lifted off the lid to the box, and I pulled out my very own"

'Shirley Temple Doll'.

"Oh Kuma," I said with a sigh, and tears welling up in my eyes, "She's so beautiful. Thank you a million times!"

With that, Mama came by and said, "Yes, Kuma, it is a very beautiful doll. It's a shame that you never could have any children, because then you'd understand how a gift like this, only spoils children. You see, I got Little Madia something she could use for school, some books."

Kuma looked my mother straight in the eye, and said, "Madia, I bought this doll for Little Madia, because it's a Godmother's responsibility to make sure that any happiness that is not given to her by her mother, was taken care of by someone who loves her enough to take her mother's place. If something bad should happen to her, like jail or death."

"Well Kuma," my mother said smiling, and without a blink of an eye, "not only haven't I heard a siren lately, but I've also never felt better."

Softly, Kuma said, "That certainly is a blessing, now isn't it?"

Stooping down near me, Kuma said, "Well Madia, I just remembered that I have to help a very sick friend. I'll see you later today, OK?"

"Sure Kuma, I understand. And every time I look at my Shirley Temple doll, I'll think of you."

Kuma smiled sweetly, and looked into my eyes, and said, "You do that child."

Out of nowhere, came my father's voice, "Kuma! You're not leaving so soon are you?"

And before she could answer, Mama stepped in between them, and said, "Martin, you know we can't be so selfish. Kuma has to go and spread herself around. You know, to do good deeds somewhere?"

Kuma stared at Mama, and said, "Yes Madia, we all spread ourselves around, one way or another."

From the kitchen, I heard a snicker of laughter coming from either Tony or Kimo, who were sitting together. My father must have brought them up the back stairs with him.

Papa always found them odd jobs to help them pay their rent.

I knew even at that young age, that even though they weren't yelling, Mama and Kuma were still fighting.

Throughout the rest of the day, we had all types of guests, young and old…I had a wonderful birthday.

That night as I knelt to say my prayers, I knew that Mama was looking on, but I didn't care - I was still *so* happy.

Softly, I said, "God, thank you for the happiest day of my life and maybe sixth birthdays were magical, because everything went so nice."

I asked him to bless *everybody,* including my new Shirley Temple doll from Kuma.

Again, I said, "Thank you God, for giving me a beautiful day."

Out of the dark, from the next room, I heard Mama saying to me, "He gave you such a beautiful day today…but where's your tomorrow?"

I should have never ever thought about it. I try not to even today.

CHAPTER 9

A new day started and already I woke up to a different kind of morning. My parents were screaming at the top of their lungs at each other. So I snuck out of bed so I could listen. I heard Mama say, "But *why* do you have to go over there! What the hell are you supposed to do, bring him back to life, or something?"

"Shut up, Madia!" said my father's commanding voice.

"Don't tell me what to do!" she yelled back. Apparently out of control, she followed him down the back stairs, and then she screamed over the fence to him, "And why don't you take your daughter with you? That way you can both just stay there, forever!"

With that, Mama tore down an entire clothesline of freshly hung clothes. I stood in the back doorway, just staring at my mother's rage.

Just then she looked up, and said to me coldly, "I suppose you'll be next to go and want to console your precious Kuma!

I gave her a questioning look, and she said, "Her husband died last night!"

"Oh no!" I said, as I covered my mouth with my hands. I felt bad, even though I really didn't know him. I only saw him a few times, you see he was always very sick, and couldn't leave the house.

"You know if your Kuma worried about her husband just *half* as much as she worried about *you*, he'd be alive *today*!"

In a flash I thought, is this Mama's way of trying to say, that indirectly, I've now killed Kuma's husband, too?

"Oh Mama, no please, tell me it's not my fault!" I said as I started to feel tears welling up in my eyes.

Surprised, Mama looked at me sternly, and said, "See Madia, you robbed Kuma's husband of her love, so he died, so what! Now go upstairs and play with that God Damn doll she bought you, rather than taking care of her poor sick husband – go on!"

Shocked, I slowly walked up the back stairs and as I walked, I could only think, first Sonny, then the twins, and now Kuma's husband. God, I'm only six, and I've killed four people already. Mama must be right. I must be the most evil child ever born.

Then, while at the midway landing, something caught my eye. It was the tiniest mouse I'd ever seen, and he was so cute. I sat on the stairs and looked into the little mouse hole. There he was, he looked so adorable, just like a little toy. I thought, this is the only toy I should have, after all, how could I ever look that 'Shirley Temple Doll' in the face, knowing how I was a killer.

Searching through my pockets, I found a small piece of a cookie, so I put it by the mouse hole and he came out, nibbled, and ran back in. Oh how I started to laugh, and now feeling better, I wiped the tears from my face with my sleeve.

Mama could hear me laughing all the way outside, and as she was picking up the laundry, she yelled, "Madia! What the hell are you doing? Get upstairs!"

"I found the cutest little mouse in this mouse hole Mama..."

"Rats!" Mama yelled, "Rats!" Then she threw down the laundry and headed through the door and up the stairs toward me.

When she finally reached me, she said, "Is that the kind of toys you like? Why you ungrateful little bitch! You know your Kuma searched high and low for that God Damned doll, instead of taking care of her poor sick husband, and now he's dead! So you could at least have the decency to play with the God Damned thing!"

Feeling guilt ridden, and empty inside, I simply replied with, "Mama I was only pretending the mouse was my toy, pretending, that's all."

"Pretending hah! Well, there's no time to pretend in the real world! So now you think you're some God Damned movie star or something? Pretending? Well, it's about time you do something real. So you don't want your new toy? You'd rather play with rats, hah! Well, let's get rid of all of those toys that you don't want, OK?"

With that, she grabbed me by the hair, and dragged me up the stairs, and to my room.

Through my tears, I pleaded with her to let me keep my toys!

Coldly, Mama said, "Oh no Madia. You've got those live rats for toys!"

"Please Mama, don't throw away my toys – I love them!"

By now we were at my bedroom door, she pushed me threw the doorway and said, "What would you do with these; they don't do anything but sit there – right?"

She let go of me long enough to scoop up all my toys in my arms. I tried to head for the closet with them, but she got me by my hair, and we barreled back through the apartment, and down the stairs like lightening.

Once outside, Mama yelled over the fence and across the dirt road, to the neighborhood children playing in the prairie, "Kids, come over here if you want free toys!"

"No, Mama, no!" I screamed, "Please don't give away my toys, I'll play with then, honestly I will!"

Softly, so only I could hear, she spoke to me in a sarcastic way, "Oh no my dear Little Madia, you had your chance…and now you'll see on the faces of these children, what being truly grateful is."

"Here children, take these dolls and toys with you. Madia says that since she has so much, she would like to share these with all of you; and if you can't use them, give them to your brothers or sisters. Now enjoy them. Bye!" She said sweetly. Then yanking my hair, she said, "Say goodbye to the children."

The children kept thanking me, but I couldn't answer them because I was so distraught.

Again, she whispered in my ear, "Say goodbye to them, or I'll kill you, you little bitch."

Faintly, I gulped out the word, "goodbye", but I wasn't saying that to the children, I was saying goodbye to my toys. How guilty I felt since the Shirley Temple Doll cost Kuma's husband his life, and now a stranger, somewhere, had it.

Mama made me stand there till all the children were gone, then she let go of my hair.

"Mama," I said, "what will I tell Kuma when she asks me what happened to my Shirley Temple Doll?"

"Tell your Kuma, I'm sorry Kuma, but I'm so stupid, and ugly, and evil - that a little girl like me doesn't deserve a nice doll like that. And it's a shame that your husband had to die over it, especially since some other little girl will be playing with it, and not me."

With that, my mother broke into hysterical laughter.

Tearfully, I looked up at her, and said, "How come you hate me so much?"

Puzzled, she squatted down to me, and looked me in the eyes, and said, "I don't know Madia, maybe it's because you're just so ugly."

I burst into tears, and could only think, run, run, run, until you can't run anymore!

Of course, I only made it to the alley, when her iron fist grabbed my hair. With one giant yank, she pulled me backwards, and said, "Where do you think you're going?"

"Leave me alone," I cried, "I hate you, I hate you!"

"Hate me, do you? Don't make me laugh. Do you think for a minute that I give a fuck if you hate me or not? Why you stupid little bitch, *you* hate *me*! Well, that's only a speck compared to how much I *hate* you!" Then a slap went her hand across my face. She hit me so hard, that I fell in the dirt. "Now get up!" She commanded, "Get up!"

I just sat there, hoping that either someone would come by and save me, or that I would simply die.

Slam again went that hand against my face as she yelled, "Get up, and tell your mother how sorry you are for talking back to her. Come on, tell your mother you're sorry or else!"

I just sat there in the dirt…silently, and then her voice sounded like she was really was going to kill me!

"Stand up you little fucking bitch! Or so help me, I'll fucking kill you!"

Still nothing from me.

Finally, she just grabbed me by the hair and pulled me straight up onto my feet, and said, "You god damn little stubborn bitch, won't you ever learn not to disobey me!" Slam went her hand against my face, and again I was sprawled out into the dirt.

"You'll talk to me, or I swear I'll tear your fucking God Damned tongue out of your ugly little head!"

Just then, she got quiet, and I noticed, that she was staring at something nearby. I wanted to get up and run, but I was too weak, and too afraid.

Then all of a sudden Mama grabbed me and stood me up, and said softly, "Madia, I'm so sorry about your toys, but don't worry, I've already found you a new doll, its right over there." I looked, thinking why is she now being so nice? And what to my shock and horror did I see, but a large, dead, river rat. I looked up at my mother, and said, "No, Mama, NO!"

"Pick it up!" She said. "Pick it up or I'll beat you!"

"Why Mama? Why?"

"Because Madia, you like rats for toys. You told me so. So what's the difference if the rats are small or big? Now, pick up your new doll."

I just shook my head no because I was unable to speak.

Slam went my mother's hand across my face, and again I was down in the dirt! "And while you're down there", Mama said, "Pick it up!"

I cried, "Mama, I can't!

"Pick it up, or I swear to God I'll kill you!"

A simple, "no" came from my lips.

And with that, I felt her shoe come in contact with my stomach, as she now had resorted to kicking me. Slowly and sinisterly, she blankly said to me, "Now get up. I mean it Madia. Get up and on your feet."

With what little strength I had left, I managed to get up and onto my feet, even though my entire body was racked with pain. I looked on as my mother picked up the rat, and forced it into my arms. But my limp arms dropped it. And with that, she stood on my crippled foot, and pressed down on it, saying, "I'll crush it worse, and then they'll probably have to cut it off, so pick up the goddamn rat."

Goddamn rat, I thought, I'm the only thing that's damned in this alley. So slowly I bent over, and picked up the rat. It was stiff, and there were flies swarming all around its face.

And as I stared down at it in my arms, my mother slowly said, "Now Madia, aren't you going to sing, rock-a-bye baby to your new baby doll? Come on, after all, she's so pretty, she looks just like you when you were a baby. See those wonderful, warm brown eyes? They're just like yours when you were a baby. Now sing God Damn it, and go through the alley to your friend Bonnie's house and show her your new baby doll!"

I cried, as I walked through the alley, gulping the words rock-a-bye baby, to the dead rat in my arms. I rocked it back and forth, and while I slowly sang, I could hear my mother's laughter coming from behind me. Even though I walked for about fifty yards to my friend Bonnie's house, I could still hear her revolting laughter. I prayed, right then and there, that God would be merciful toward me, and simply strike me dead.

As I approached Bonnie's house, she was outside playing hopscotch by herself. Bonnie was sort of a loner, but we always got along because our mother's were very good friends, and quite similar in their actions.

"Mary", Bonnie yelled, "What's that in your arms? OH GOD! I'm going to be sick!"

Then out of shear frustration, I just threw the rat away from me. Unfortunately it landed near her feet, and she let out a bloodcurdling scream.

Then she yelled, "Mother, mother! Mary's throwing rats at me!"

"Shush Bonnie, I didn't mean it, I just had to get it away from me, please don't call your mother! Please!"

But it was too late. Apologetically, I looked up at Bonnie's mother's pinched looking face, as I uttered, "I'm so sorry, I didn't mean to throw the rat at Bonnie."

Slam went her hand against my already bruised face.

"Madia, what kind of behavior is that from Mrs. Madia's daughter? You should be ashamed of yourself! Bonnie is like your sister; so how could you scare her like that? Say you're sorry to her, right now!"

Feeling nothing but pain, disgust and fear, I looked at Bonnie's tearful eyes through her little black rimmed glasses, and said, "I'm sorry Bonnie; I just wanted to get it away from me. I'd never throw a rat at you, please forgive me?"

She silently nodded yes, and then she finally muttered a faint, "I forgive you Mary."

I started to smile, thinking maybe now Bonnie and I would be left alone to play, just so that I could try to forget about this day.

Then suddenly, a firm hold was on my hair, "Come on Madia, now we'll tell Mrs. Madia what an evil thing you did by scaring my poor

Bonnie. Not to mention walking around as filthy as a pig! Bonnie, you stay here, I'll be right back."

And as I was behind dragged away, I could see that Bonnie now realized what her yelling to her mother had cost me. Even with tears in my eyes, I could still see that there were new tears in Bonnie's eyes, as she mouthed the words, "I'm sorry Mary."

I could only think to myself. I'm sorry too Bonnie.

It seemed like only a matter of seconds flew by, and we were back at my house. Loudly Bonnie's mother yelled out, "Mrs. Madia, where are you? Madia?"

In a flash my mother appeared at the back door, and looking concerned.

She said, "Mrs., what has my Madia done wrong?"

Well here came the story, *her* story, and the only story that my mother would believe.

"Mrs. Madia, Little Madia picked up a dead rat, and threw it at my little Bonnie!"

Before even asking me, she slapped me across the face.

By this time, I thought that my face was going to fall off and hit the ground, it was so sore.

"Did you beat her yet, Mrs.?" Mama asked.

"Yes, I slapped her once."

With a look of pure delight, my mother said, "Go ahead; slap her again. I want to see it. Besides, she's got to know, mother's are like sisters, we can punish each other's children when they're bad, and we're not around to discipline them."

Slap went her hand, and before I knew it my head was spun in the other direction by my mother's hand.

I looked up at her, as if to say, why? But before I could even speak, Mama just simply explained that the slap was to keep me in line.

Cordially, she thanked her friend for coming directly to her with the problem. And again before I even knew it, I was being dragged up the back stairs and to my room. I know my mother was swearing at me, but I can't remember anything specifically, it all just seemed the same after a while.

That is, until we got up to my room. Once in there, I noticed on top of my chest of drawers that the little glass cradle to my smashed baby doll from last Christmas; the one that Kuma gave me from Santa, was there. I walked over to it, and thought, this must have gotten lost in the toy giveaway spree from earlier that day.

Softly, a strange tone of genuine politeness emitted from my mother's mouth, "Madia, my little darling, I know you've had a bad day. So why don't you lie down for a while, and just so you're not lonely, I thought that you might like a new tiny baby doll for your cradle.

Now get into bed like a nice girl, and I'll put a surprise in your cradle for you."

Was this a bad dream or a trick? I couldn't tell, nor did I care. I just thought, for a moment, maybe, Mama does have a heart.

She looked back at me, and said, "That's right honey, hop into bed like a good girl." With that she pulled something out of her apron pocket and placed it in the cradle.

Then she said, "Now pleasant dreams, and you can play more when you get up."

I heard the lock click behind her, so I slowly crept out of bed and made my way over to the cradle. I thought it must be another baby doll because it's wrapped in tissue paper, just like the porcelain one at Christmas.

I should have known it was the little mouse I had played with earlier. She must have trapped and killed it. I grabbed it and the cradle, and threw them both out the window as I kept crying and screaming, "No! No! No Mama, how could you do this to me?"

With that I heard laughter coming from the other side of the door. I then realized that my mother never really left and she was just waiting for me to open the gift she gave me.

I heard her then say, "What Madia? I thought you'd love a new baby doll for your cradle.I just don't know about you?"

Hopelessly, I threw myself on the bed and cried myself to sleep. Even through my crying and my pain, I could hear my mother's laughter and foot steps fade into the distance, and I could only think, please dear God, just make Mama keep walking so that I never have to see her again.

I woke up to the sound of knocking at my door. I was afraid to say anything, because I thought it might be Mama checking up on me. Finally, I heard a familiar voice saying, "Madia, are you awake? Little Madia, it's only me, Tony."

Quickly I ran to the door, but there was no key. So I said, "Tony, I'm locked in, just turn the key." And with a click, I was set free. "Tony," I said, "you'd better leave, or else you'll get into trouble, because if Mama catches you, she'll be real mad."

"It's OK," he said with his thick accent, "she told me to come see you because I find something and she say, it belongs to you." He opened his hands, and there was the glass cradle that I threw out. "Mrs. Madia, say you lost it. So here, Madia."

I'm sure mother thought that it would bother me to have this back, but I was going to fool her. It was from Kuma, and Santa, two people who loved me, and now sweet old Tony, who cared enough to climb the high stairs, just to bring it back to me. I took it from his hands, and said, "Oh thank you, Tony, I was looking for this. Thank you." Then I reached over and kissed his cheek. He never mentioned how dirty or swollen my face was. I'm sure that he knew, or saw something, but he was afraid of Mama too.

Then Tony smiled, and he asked why I was locked in my room.

"Well Tony, Mama is mad at me again."

"Oh Little Madia," he said, "how could anybody ever be mad at you, you so pretty and so nice girl. You should be outside, it's a beautiful day. Come, let's go. But you better wash your face first."

"OK Tony!" I said as I set the cradle down. Then, even though I was in so much pain that I could barely walk, I went to the bathroom to clean up. I looked at my reflection in the mirror and I was a mess. That's when I was sure that Tony knew something, but was too afraid to ask or say anything. So I threw some cold water on my very painful, and dirty face, and before I knew it, I was taking his big hard hand in mine, and we went downstairs...I was going to show Mama that she can't hurt me.

As we turned on the midway landing, I saw my father and my Kuma, hugging each other by the backdoor. I said, "Kuma, I missed you, and I'm very sorry about your husband."

All of a sudden, everyone seemed nervous.

My father said, "What are you doing here, Madia?" Then he turned to Tony and sternly said, "Tony, you didn't see a goddamned thing, you understand?"

"Yes Mr. Martin," Tony said nervously, "I know nothing."

"Papa," I said softly, "can I hug Kuma too, like you? Because I feel sad for her."

And before Papa could speak, Kuma said, "Oh yes child, I need a hug from everyone today." She looked at my face and said, "Child, what happened to you?"

"Oh Kuma, I was playing and I fell down – that's all. I'm OK."

And after our embrace, I turned to Tony, and said, "Come on Tony, Kuma said, everyone."

So Tony came over and hugged Kuma briefly, and said, "Sorry Mrs. to hear such bad news."

"Thank you Tony, and thank you Madia, for making sure everyone hugged me."

Well we all stood there for a moment, not knowing what to do, when finally I said, "Kuma, can you and I go outside? I have to talk to you, unless you want me to get Mama so she can hug you too?"

Kuma quickly said, "Oh child, that's OK, I'll see her later, lets go outside if you want. Good bye Tony and Martin. Thank you for the hugs, I'll see you later!"

They both said, goodbye as we went outside to sit at a picnic table in the yard.

"Kuma, I have to tell you that I know something bad."

Nervously, Kuma said, "What child, what do you think you know? And remember, things aren't always what they seem."

"No Kuma, I know this, Mama told me."

And with that Kuma started to twist her gloves nervously, and pulled out a handkerchief to help clean me up a little more, as she said, "Your mother says things that sometimes aren't quite right, you know, she doesn't ...."

"No Kuma, she told me that it's all my fault that your husband died. You know, because I take up too much of your time."

With a look of relief on her face, she smiled, and with teary eyes, she hugged me and said, "Oh my dear wonderful Little Madia, you are the most wonderful thing in my life! And you've got to understand that my husband was always a very sick man. He was born with a very weak heart. I didn't know that when he sent for me from Yugoslavia to be his wife. That's just how life is, and I could have sat with him, night and day, and he still would have died."

"But Mama said..."

"Shoosh, don't even worry about what your mother said, I'm telling you, that's just how some things go in life."

With that, Kuma took both of my hands, and kissed them. With a smile on her face, and tears in her eyes, she looked into my eyes, and said, "Remember Madia, you told me a secret once, about how you'd like to wake up one day and find that I was your mother? Well, I just want you to know that I wish the very same thing."

Out of nowhere, came a loud voice saying, "So you do, do you?"

"Mama." I muttered.

Kuma turned around and said, "Madia, Little Madia and I were just talking."

Coldly, Mama said, "Oh yes Kuma. I know. I heard every God Damned word. Quit poisoning my daughter's mind with your bullshit! I don't believe it! Your husband's body isn't even cold yet, and you're trying to pick up a new family! Well I guess it's true what they say about widows; they're just whores in black dresses."

"Madia," my father's voice rang out from the back doorway, "shut up, you don't know what you're talking about!"

"Oh don't I? I came outside, and she's already planning to be Madia's new mother! And unless *I'm* the one who's stupid, that would make her, your wife! And you know I wouldn't let that happen, unless it was over...my... dead ... body! And unfortunately for you, I'm feeling pretty goddamned good. Oh wait, maybe Kuma will start taking good care of me....just like she did for her husband! In that case I'll be dead in a week!"

With that, Kuma let go of my hands, and she started to cry uncontrollably, as she ran off to her car and drove away.

My father said, "Shut up Madia, or I swear to God, I'll kill you!"

"Go ahead! What? Does the truth hurt?" With that, Mama spit at the ground near Papa's feet.

He raised his hand, and I yelled, "No Papa, please don't hit Mama!" I still can't believe that on occasions like that, I would still defend her. But I did.

Just then, my brother arrived from playing, and asking what all the yelling was about.

Mama stooped down, and said, "Don't worry about a thing, my darling Martin, I'll be *your* mother, forever, and I'll never leave you."

Disgusted, father turned around and went back inside.

"Come on Martin, you must be hungry. Come on in and I'll feed you, my beautiful son."

As they walked away, I stood there alone, thinking I just saved Mama, and now she's turned her back on me, like I wasn't even here.

"What about me Mama?" I said.

Softly, she said to Martin, "Go upstairs," as she kissed him on the cheek. And once he passed the door, she looked at me with pure hate, and said, "So you dream that she's your mother, huh? Well I should beat you this time till your head falls off. But I'll wait for a better time to get even with you, and besides I don't want to touch that ugly little face of yours. I might get my hands dirty. Ha, ha, ha." She laughed as she turned and walked back inside.

I stood there thinking, oh my God…she's going to wait for a better time?

Just then, Tony ran outside, "Madia, come quick, a telegram! Hurry!"

I thought, oh God, someone must have died, because we never received telegrams. As I made my way through the bar, and approached my father and mother, I noticed Mama was crying.

"Mama, is everything OK?"

"Oh Madia, your Grandmother is coming to America to stay with us for three weeks, she'll be here next week." Then Mama went upstairs mumbling, "Oh I must tell Martin his Grandmother can't wait to see him. She can't wait to see my beautiful boy."

Feeling alone, even though the bar was filled with people, I just started walking back outside as tears started to form in my eyes. All of a sudden I felt someone's hand on my shoulder. I looked up.

"Tony," I said, "my grandma's coming, do you think she'll want to see me too?"

He picked me up, and said, "Oh Madia, when she see you, she gonna think, oh, I so lucky to have my Madia."

Chapter 10

Well the day finally arrived; and as I was getting ready, my brother Martin came by my room, and said, "Mary, are you excited about Grandma coming?"

"I sure am, and I bet she's really excited to come here and see us, too."

"But what if she doesn't like us, then what?"

"Oh Martin…why wouldn't she like us? You're being silly…and besides, I don't know what you're worried about. You're her only grandson, you know she'll love you." Then quickly I thought to myself, and I'm only a girl, so I'll have to do everything that I can to make her like me, but will she? After all, Kuma's a woman, and she likes me, and she's not even family. So my own grandmother's got to love me.

Just then, our father's bold voice rang out, "Kids, your grandmother's here!"

"Oh Martin, let's go and meet her."

So I grabbed my younger brother's hand and off we went. As we went down the stairs, Martin said, "Do you think Grandma knows my birthday is coming soon? Maybe she brought me a present?"

"Oh Martin, you and your presents, don't you ever think about anything else?"

She was like a vision, and as we walked through the doorway into the bar, I could only think, how wonderful - my very own grandmother. She was in all black, which was striking against her golden skin and snow white hair that was piled high on top of her head in a bun. I stood there frozen. We smiled at her, and with that, she put her arms out and said, "This must be my little angel."

"Oh Gramma, Gramma," I heard my brother's voice say as he ran from my side to her waiting arms. I started to walk toward them, even though I wasn't invited or welcomed like my brother was.

My father had walked in just then with Grandma's last piece of luggage, saying, "So, I see you've met your two grandchildren."

Puzzled, she stood up from hugging Martin, and said, "Two, oh yes, I forgot, you did say in your letters that there was one female left. Pointing at me, she looked, and said, "Is that it?"

I was crushed. She referred to me as *it*...?

I thought, I am not a chair, I'm a person. Well, if I was expecting any good feelings about myself to come from her, I knew in that instant, I'd have a long wait.

But she did do her grandmotherly duties; she halfheartedly kissed me on the cheek, and patted the top of my head.

After all of the introductions were out of the way, we had a big dinner to celebrate her arrival. It was the start of dusk, which was one of my favorite times of day, when I finally saw a truly friendly face - Kuma.

I ran over to her, and said, "Kuma, I've been waiting for you to come by all day."

Kuma replied, "Well Madia, I wanted to, but I didn't know if I should, and then I thought of my Madia, and I said I'm going."

With that she hugged me, and I noticed that she looked like she was going to cry. So I asked her why she was so sad.

She smiled and said, "Why Madia, I'm not sad, I'm happy, happy because I'm with you."

"Madia," I heard my mother's voice yell, "Where are you?"

Kuma looked up at me, and said, "It's best that I go."

"No Kuma." I said strongly, "If everybody else can have guests here to meet Grandmother, then so can I."

"Oh Madia, but I know your grandmother, and we don't really get along too well."

Happily, I said, "That's OK, because I don't think that Grandmother and I are going to get along too well, either."

With that we started to giggle. Just then, Mama appeared in the doorway. Coldly she looked at Kuma, and said, "Oh you again, don't you ever stay at home? Or maybe someone invited you, Martin perhaps?"

"No Mama" I said, "I did, it's not a party unless Kuma's here, plus I wanted her to meet my grandmother."

Slowly she descended the short steps that lead to the yard. Putting her hands on her hips, Mama said, "Don't worry Madia, my mother knows your precious Kuma from back in Yugoslavia. She warned me about you before I ever came to this country. She told me that you'd try to come between Martin and me one day, but you never will. Do you think that I'll let you be happy with him after all of the miserable years I put in? Well, you'd have to kill me first! And you couldn't."

"Madia, not in front of the child," said Kuma nervously. "You're going to give her the wrong idea."

"Wrong?" Mama yelled, "I only speak the truth; and maybe that's just what you don't want her to hear!"

With that, I noticed Kuma was starting to cry, and my mother looked like she was made of stone, just standing there with the plains of her face and body high-lighted in the contrasting tones of nightfall.

"Besides," she continued, "I think it's about time she knows all, especially since my mother's here to back me up on some facts. First, you always thought you were *so* special because you went to school, and read a lot of books, while my hands were covered with shit! Shit, from not only the farm animals, but also my own."

My mother had a glazed over look to her face as she went on. "Do you know how us peasants had to wipe our asses? Well, all I can say is that you were lucky if the rock you found was smooth and flat."

Hysterically, Kuma finally yelled back at my mother, "Madia, it isn't my fault that my family had money. Don't you think I've suffered too? Remember I just buried my husband."

"Don't make me laugh." said Mama, "You knew he was going to die, otherwise, you'd of never married him."

"How can you say that to me?"

"Because it's true - that's why."

Sobbing, Kuma said, "I know you don't believe this, but in my own way, I *did* love him. And it's true, that before coming to America, I knew he was older and a little sickly, but he wanted me, so I *had* to go. That's the way it is, it's horrible, but it was a fact of life never the less. You know Madia, back then we had no choice - and that goes for rich people as well as the poor! You go with the man that wants you, or at least had the most money."

"Oh…is that it? You mean if Martin would have had more money, *you'd* be his wife instead of *me*?"

"No that's not what I'm saying at all. I'm saying that we didn't have a choice, but little Madia will. America's different, the times are different."

Cynically my mother said, "Yes Kuma, but some things will never change, like the fact that you want my husband."

Kuma looked at me to see my reaction. I think what pulled her through this whole scenario was the fact that instead of me being shocked, I must have had a look of approval because I know that I was thinking how wonderful that would have been.

Mother was also shocked a little when she saw that this little late night girl talk didn't shock me.

After all, her plan back fired, for instead of me now hating my Kuma for trying to break a not so happy home, I could only think, she could have been my mother...it would've been a dream come true.

In a disgusted tone Mama yelled for me to go to bed. So I grabbed Kuma's hand, and sort of pulled her down to me. As I gave her a kiss on the cheek, I whispered, "Thank you Kuma – I love you." She hugged and kissed me and whispered, "I love you too."

Pulling apart, she said, "Pleasant dreams, Sweetheart."

I walked over to give Mama a kiss, and she just pushed me away, and said, "You should have come to *me* first."

Then she looked straight at Kuma, as she said to me, "After all *I* am your Mother - now get to bed."

Her words and actions didn't matter to me... because all that night, as I lay in bed, I tried to understand all of the things being tossed back and forth in my mind. Between Kuma and Mama – and the only thing that I could think about was – wow, Kuma really could have been my mother.

In the morning, I got up early, and as I was on my way to the kitchen, I looked out of the window and I noticed that Papa was outside. He looked so alone. I could also hear that Mama was on her way downstairs to clean the bar, but just as I turned the corner into the kitchen, there she was…'The Grandmother', which was how I would refer to her silently.

"Good morning Grandmother, did you sleep well?" I asked, as if I really cared.

She looked up at me, and for a moment you could see how beautiful she must have been when she was young.

"Madia," she asked, "why are you so skinny? Doesn't your mother feed you?"

Innocently I answered, "Oh yes Grandmother, she feeds me all the time."

Coldly she glared at me, and asked, "Who is she?"

I thought maybe because she's so old, she forgot what we were talking about. "SHE is Mama," I said.

Slap went her hand across my face. "You never say 'She' or 'her' that's 'your mother'! So you are always to say 'my mother' this, or 'my mother' that. Otherwise people are going to think you are stupid, or, God forbid, disrespectful, or both! Now you sit here, and I'll fix you a *real* breakfast." She pulled out the chair, and pointed to it.

Teary-eyed, I looked up at her, and asked, "Then am I to call you 'the Grandmother'?" Thinking to myself how it would make a great name for a monster movie.

"No, just Grandmother, will be fine."

I thought to myself, oh God, I'll never last with the two of them hitting me all the time.

But since we were alone, I thought after last night that I'd ask all about Kuma. "Grandmother, Mother said that you knew my Kuma back in Yugoslavia. Can you tell me about her?"

Even with her back to me, I could tell that I hit a nerve.

"Oh her," she said. "Well, she's from a good family, and your father's people worked for them. What else do you need to know?"

Sheepishly I asked, "Was she good friends with my mother back then. Is that how she got to be my godmother?"

"No, Little Madia, she was friends with your father. But her father made wedding arrangements for her in America, so she had to come here and marry a very wealthy man that paid a handsome dowry for her."

"Grandmother, what's a dowry?"

"Well Madia, that's usually money, or in my day land or livestock, that is paid to a girl's father for the girl's hand in marriage. If for some reason, the girl decides not to marry the gentleman who's paid for her; it is a big disgrace for the family. As a matter of fact, your father and she came here on the same boat. And from all I know, she got married about a week later. Your father was upset by it, so much so, that he had written to his best friend Peter, my son and your uncle, to find him a wife. So Pete wrote back saying he had a sixteen-year-old sister, your mother Madia."

"You mean I have an Uncle Pete somewhere?"

"Why sure Madia, he's still back home in Yugoslavia. You have lots of family back there. Now you be quiet and eat, and I'll tell you stories from back in Yugoslavia." So she set out more food, and as she was cutting some bread, she cut her finger and some of the blood got on the bread. Then she looked at her finger again, and sucked the blood from it.

I looked at her, and at the bread, and thought that I was going to get sick. I guess I must of made a face, because she asked, "Madia, what's wrong? Didn't you ever see blood before? My God, you're just like your mother when she was a little girl."

With that, she picked up the blood stained piece of bread and held it up to my mouth. "Here, eat it." I shook my head no, and I quickly grabbed a clean piece of bread and pushed it in to my mouth, so that there wouldn't be any room for the bloody one. Grandmother just laughed, and as she stared at me, she took a big bite out of the bread, and actually ate the bloodied part right up.

She began to tell me a story. "Madia, back in Yugoslavia, most of us were very poor. We had a little farm, and it was next door to Kuma's family's farm So sometimes Uncle Pete and your Papa, would work there together to help him out since he didn't have any boys of his own. Kuma was an only child, and her father treated her like a princess. He wouldn't let her get her hands dirty, and that's why they were always helping out; plus they needed the money.

"But she was a wonderful pianist; she played like an angel. They were going to send her to Paris or something, when that nice gentleman sent her father the dowry. So, off to America she went. There was a rumor that her father noticed that local boys were getting interested in her, one of them being your father, and he wanted to get her married off as soon as he could."

"Did Mama and Kuma play together; were they friends?"

"No, I kept your Mama very busy with chores, and Kuma's father treated anyone who wasn't rich like they were peasants. It was a small village and most people didn't like Kuma's parents. They would see you out shopping and they'd pretend that they never met you before. Your father is a little like that too."

"Papa?"

"Yes – *your* Papa. I've heard him say that he never met your mother until she came off the boat and landed here in America. But he forgets that not *all* of us forget things. Well I can even remember when he first met your mother, back when she was a child about your age. I overheard your father talking to her one day when she was helping me do laundry outside. He came by with your Uncle Pete after working at Kuma's. He said that while they were doing some work over there, he saw another little girl, and wanted to know if she knew her. So no matter what your father says, he *did* know your mother back in the old country. He would always go on and on about how she was the most beautiful little girl that he'd ever seen, and that he couldn't wait until she grew up so that he could marry her. Over the years as she got older, he kept right on saying it. Well, we'd all laugh, because we knew that her father would never allow it. Imagine, an upper class girl married to a farmhand - ridiculous. Oh, but here is the part of the story that I meant to tell you. One time, at Kuma's farm, he went on about how one of the other farm hands had gotten cut, and there was some blood. Well when the little girl saw it, she passed out. He actually told that story to your mother when she was a little girl right in front of me. He and your Uncle Pete were mending our fences, and while they were washing up, your mother was bothering them, so he turned to your mother and told her that story hoping that she'd run away and leave him alone. But when she didn't, he asked her, 'Little Madia - are you strong or weak?'

"She replied, 'I'm very strong."

'Oh I can tell, but do you pass out when *you* see blood?'

'No,' she said. 'I'm strong.'

Well your father just smiled and went on his way...but it made me think, 'I want to see just how strong she *really* is. So I took your mother out to the chicken coop, because on a farm everyone has a lot of work to do, and you have to know how to do many jobs.'

Like I said, she was about your age, and she had a pet chicken that followed her around just about everywhere, and I would always remind her that there are 'No Pets' on a farm!

So I said to your mother, "Little Madia, today I'm going to teach you how to kill a chicken."

"What?" replied your mother, "But, I love chickens, and I even have a pet one. There, she is my pet chicken, Coco."

So I pointed to one, and said, "This one?"

Well, your mother nodded yes, and with that I grabbed the chicken and grabbed your mother and said - Remember Little Madia - there are no pets on a farm. Then I pointed to all of the chickens, and I said, all of these are just here so that we can live."

"I told her to grab the chicken around the neck, and she said, "But what if it hurts her Mama?"

"Don't worry - its fast. Now squeeze very hard."

"No Mama, I can't hurt Coco!"

I told her, "I'll help you."

So I put my hand over hers, and with a tight grip, we lifted the chicken off of the ground. Then with a sharp snap of the wrist, we spun the chicken in the air by its neck until you could feel the neck bone snap. Your mother screamed and screamed.

Then the chicken's claws scratched her hand, and a couple drops of blood were drawn.

She screamed, "Look Mama, I'm bleeding!"

"So, you're *not* strong. Well, we'll fix that!" I took my thumbnail, found the spot where the neck was broken and then I bit into it to tear its skin and I tore Coco's head off.

Your mother screamed even more as the blood came shooting out. So to show her that there was nothing to be afraid of I held that chicken up to her so it squirted blood onto your mother's face. While that child stood there screaming, I smeared the blood over her face and dress saying, "Now, don't ever be afraid of blood, it can't hurt you. So, do you feel stronger or do we have to kill another chicken?"

"No Mama, no - I'm very strong now! See I didn't pass out."

"Are you sure?" I asked, "Remember a woman has to be strong, because we have nothing else. You can never really rely on a man – they're useless. Then I asked her one last time, 'Madia, are you *sure* you're gonna be strong enough to be a woman?"

"Yes Mama," pleaded the child, "I'm strong, very strong."

"Then I made your mother eat that chicken for dinner that night. She never tried to make a farm animal a pet again. So now you can see, that's why your mother is so strong today – *I* made her strong. That's a mother's job.

Well Madia, did you like that story, or would you like me to tell you another one?"

Horrified, I just sat there speechless and kept thinking - what kind of breakfast story do you call that? It certainly didn't perk up my appetite.

"No, Grandmother," I finally blurted out. Then I told her that was just fine and asked if I could be excused to dress.

She nodded yes, and told me that I did well eating breakfast, but tomorrow morning I'd better eat more. I thought, I will, as long as there are no more stories from Yugoslavia.

Then, as I was making my way from the kitchen to my room, behind me, in the distance I heard her say, "Madia, if you're nice, I'll make you chicken for lunch." Then she began to laugh. I immediately ran into the bathroom, getting rid of breakfast.

Well when lunchtime rolled around, we had grilled cheese sandwiches, because according to Grandmother - that's what Martin wanted. All I could think was, thank God…no chicken.

As we were finishing up lunch, I asked Martin where he was for breakfast. I told him that he missed a wonderful story that Grandmother told about the farm in Yugoslavia, and that maybe, if he were very lucky, he might hear it too.

He said that he'd like to hear it someday, but he couldn't right now, because he was going out to play. Then he told me that he had not been at breakfast because Grandmother served him in bed because he got up so late.

I thought to myself; even though Grandmother had been here for only twenty-four hours, it already seemed like a month…How would I ever last the rest of her visit?

Chapter 11

The days all blended together during 'the grandmother's' infamous visit, but one day that really stood out was the day that I was playing in the yard and some neighbors came by. Their family was in business too - they owned the local Ice House, back then that's how you kept things cold – you would have ice delivered to the Ice Box in your kitchen - God Bless the person who invented refrigeration. Since we had a bar, we dealt with them a lot.

Anyway, they were Irish and Swedish; they had a son and three daughters. The three girls were all so pretty, blond and blue eyed – and their brother Billy was equally as handsome.

The girls and their mother were all dressed up, and as they approached I thought, you know Mama was right, those girls really are the picture of health – they just sparkled. Their brother was already busy playing with Martin in the prairie, and their mother was coming by to ask if he could spend the afternoon with us, because she and the girls were all going shopping.

Mama said, "Yes, of course, Billy and the girls are always welcome here." Yep, Mama was always true to form, because even though she always would go on and on about how pretty they all were, especially next to me, she could only remember the boy's name, and never the girls, even though the girls would come over a lot to play with me.

As they were leaving, 'the grandmother' came downstairs, and as she passed through the doorway, she stopped and looked at the girls. She had a smile from ear to ear, and after pausing just long enough to take it all in, she went right over to them and their mother, and she just beamed as she remarked how beautiful the girls were.

She said, "My goodness, what beautiful children."

Then after all of the introductions, their mother thanked her for the compliments.

Then 'the grandmother' went on even further, and said, "Well, since they're all so well behaved, and because they're all so pretty, I want to give them each a shiny new quarter, so that they could buy themselves some candy while they're out shopping."

Now back then, giving a six-year-old a quarter, was like giving a child five dollars today, or so it seemed. So in front of everyone, she made a big deal about those girls getting their quarters, so I thought, well maybe if I stand at the end of the line, just to save face, 'the grandmother' might give me one too?

Well, when she got to me, she said in a playful tone to me, "Oh Madia, I'm only giving out money to pretty, healthy girls; not to skinny, ugly ones." Then she laughed. Everybody else laughed too, because they thought that she was joking. But she wasn't. The girl's mother seemed to notice that I didn't think it was funny, but she was in a hurry to leave. But she did make the effort to make me feel better by saying, "Well goodbye everyone, and thank you again."

Then she looked directly at me and added, "My girls are so lucky to have a friend like, Little Mary." And it did make me feel a little bit better just knowing that someone acknowledged me, and they did it in a positive way.

CHAPTER 12

That's pretty much how the rest of 'the grandmother's' visit went. But bit by bit, it gave me more of an insight into the 'whys' of my mother's behavior as the early stories of her childhood were unfolded before me. I'm not discounting her actions, I'm just stating that I was beginning to realize that it wasn't that she just hated me, she hated *all* women, especially herself.

I really could only see this clearly for the first time as an adult, which was way too long after the fact of so many years of negative feelings. Now it's nice to know that they weren't directed only at me. In a way, many of the things my mother did were simply her retaliation to the fact that she wasn't a man. Which meant to her that if you were a woman, you can never be free.

This brings to mind probably the only good conversation my mother and I ever shared. It was right after "Grammy" left; I didn't have to say "the grandmother" anymore since she's gone.

It was one night very late, I just woke up, and for some reason I was drawn to the kitchen. There was my mother sipping her coffee and staring out the window.

"Mama," I said softly, "Is everything alright?"

She slowly turned toward me, and in a sweet and genuine tone, she said, "My poor Little Madia, you're always so worried about everybody…even people who are sometimes mean to you. How is it that I could have raised such a sweet daughter as you?"

"Mama, are you *sure* everything is ok? I know you miss your mother, but it's ok, she'll be back again someday."

Mama looked down into her coffee cup and said, "I hope I never see that woman again."

I was a little shocked by her admission, but I knew how Mama felt.

She told me to sit down, and asked if I wanted some milk. I nodded yes, and while she was getting up to get it, she just started talking, it was more at me, than to me. She told me how her mother always told her that it was the biggest curse in the world to be born a woman; and the feelings of worthlessness that those words would instill in her. It was for that reason and that reason alone, that she had always hated herself.

"Madia," she said as she looked into my eyes for the first time during this talk. "I hope that I've shown you, how you *must* be strong to survive when you're a woman. Women have no power against men, unless they push themselves ten times harder than any man, to survive. Men are born lucky, they have it all. We only live to serve them and to be their slaves. The only good thing they can ever do for us is to make a lot of money, and then die."

Even though I was only a child, I knew that these were the words of a very sad and frustrated woman. I could only think, it's a shame that she couldn't learn to love herself... then maybe she could've learned to love me.

We sat there together, for the first time, just like normal people - and I think that she just needed to get things off her mind, and I just happened to be there. Being free of her mother seemed to trigger something in her.

She went on to tell the most incredible story of her arrival to America, and how hard it was to be on a ship full of people, for days and days, that you couldn't even speak to.

"You see, Madia, there were people from all over the world on that ship, and all only speaking in their own language. There we were, all ready to go start our new lives in a new land, and we couldn't even talk to each other about it."

She went on about how the boat trip was only half of the journey. She told me about the excitement that she felt when she finally saw the Statue of Liberty, and what a strong woman she looked like, and how America will give her the chance to be a strong woman too. She also decided right then and there, that she had to free herself of the "old ways" of her country. America was her "new country", and she was going to be an American and live the American Dream, no matter what it took.

She then went on how her dreams were smashed once she arrived to Ellis Island in New York, and how everyone was herded like livestock, and again the women were treated even worse. She was afraid that because she didn't speak English, that maybe she wouldn't be let in, so she paid close attention to the answers that other people gave and just mimicked them.

Luckily, she was able to fool them, but by not really knowing what was being said to her, or what she was saying back to them, she ended up on a road trip that took weeks by train, and ended her up half way across the country, and back.

She told me that she learned big lessons on that trip; first, that she was going to learn English as fast as she could; second, that a woman alone who has run out of money, doesn't need to be able to speak English to get by in America, and finally, that she needs to become Americanized, so that men won't be able to ever take advantage of her again.

Not knowing what she was really trying to tell me at the time, I said, "If you couldn't speak English, then how did you get here?"

"Oh Madia, I was luckier than most, your father sent me my ticket and a little money." Then her mood changed, and in a resentful tone, she said, "He also sent a note and a safety pin, so I could put it on my chest. The note had my name, and then his, and then in big bold letters, it said, 'I belonged to HIM!' Slam went her fist onto the table, "It read, 'I Belong To Martin J. Zovko, Chicago, Illinois, USA'. Oh Madia, how I hated the fact that I had to wear a note that said that I belonged to anyone; especially a man."

She turned, and looked straight into my eyes, and said, "You see Madia - that's *why* it's a sin to be a woman, because we only *belong* to men, we're not really people - just things."

Those words, and that night, haunted me for the rest of my life. Because even today, so many years later, I see women that stay with men that beat and abuse them, all because – "They love them."

So here was a woman, a woman who suffered through the poverty of being a peasant, and still made it to America alone. Who now works hard running a business, and doing things that a lot of people wouldn't dream of doing in back rooms, just to keep it running, all the while dealing with all the challenges that go with that, not to mention having and losing children. Plus, being married to a man that she really didn't love, or even know. Now she's telling me that, that's *not* being strong. Well, if that's not, then I don't know what is.

She then turned to me, and said, "Well, who knows, maybe when you get older things might be different for you; I hope so. Now get back to bed, tomorrow will be here soon." She leaned over and gave me a kiss on the cheek. I remember it so well, because it didn't happen often.

It seemed as though from that point on Mama was a little nicer to me. Maybe it was all of the painful memories brought back to life from her mother's visit. Oh, don't get me wrong, there was still abuse, just not quite as physical, and unfortunately we all know, that mental abuse can scar a person much deeper than any type of physical abuse.

CHAPTER 13

It was in early June of 1939, and I was soon going to be thirteen. Oh how I couldn't wait to be a teenager. I didn't know what was to happen exactly when you became one, but all I knew, was that everybody just couldn't wait until they were one too.

Kuma told me that it was going to be a new chapter in my life; and I know I needed one. It was Sunday, and we were all going to a big picnic that was sponsored by some Croatian organization that Papa belonged to.

It was one of those rough mornings. Mama was trying to prepare some food and Papa was going to donate gallons of homemade red wine. Mama bought me a new blouse to wear. It was beautiful! It was white cotton, and it had the most striking and colorful embroidered pattern on the sleeves and neck. It kind of reminded me of a fancier version of the blouse Shirley Temple had worn in Heidi, except this one had beautiful satin bows that tied its short puffed sleeves. I wore it with a real full yellow cotton skirt, and to be different, I belted it tightly with a black patent leather cinch waist belt to show off my tiny waist. The blouse's embroidery had black outlining, so I knew that I would look spectacular.

I went downstairs and walked toward the kitchen in the bar, to see if Mama needed any help, and as I got to the top of the stairwell I could hear that she and my father were having a terrible verbal battle. So I thought, pretend you don't hear a thing, and just go in there as happy as can be.

With each step, I just gathered all the strength I could, and as I bounded through the door, I said, "Good Morning Mother and Father, isn't it a beautiful day." I felt stupid, trying to sound so cheerful, but I thought, maybe it would help.

I was wrong.

My mother took one look at me in that outfit, and said, "Take that shit off! You look like a goddamned whore, and pull that blouse out. What are you trying to show off, your tits? You don't even have any yet. You'll see, all the old men are going to try and look at them!"

With that, she ripped the blouse out of the waistband, to make the blouse fuller.

"Madia, leave the girl alone!" yelled Papa.

Quickly, Mama turned to him, and said, "Do you really want everybody to stare at your daughter's tits?"

Even though my father's reply was supposed to be directed to me, it really was meant for Mama; he spoke in a very cutting way while he glared at Mama saying, "Don't worry little Madia, the men won't be staring at you; they'll be too busy looking at your mother's tit's."

"You pig!" yelled my mother, and with that, she picked up a giant ceramic bowl filled with coleslaw and hurled it at him. It missed him, thank God, but it went all over the wall and floor. Unfazed by it all, he just looked at the wall and went out the door laughing. But I was the one left stuck with an outraged mother.

"See the trouble you started already this morning? Everything was fine until *you* came in dressed like a whore!"

"But Mama," I said.

"Don't but Mama me!" Slap went that hand across my face.

I just cried and ran back upstairs to my room.

While I was in there trying to pull myself together, my brother poked his head in, and said, "Don't be upset Mary, Mama's just having a bad morning and she's taking it out on you. Besides, I think you look swell."

"Thanks Babe, that makes me feel better."

By now everybody called Martin, "Babe". Mama started it because he was not only the baby of the family, but also her special, and precious, baby. The kids in the neighborhood also called him that because he was a great baseball player, just like Babe Ruth. Although, I think the girls called him that, because he was growing up to be an exceptionally fine and handsome young man.

Well, later at the picnic, we were all having a good time, when this one friend of the family, a very prominent businessman, who was also a drunk, came over to our table and said that if I needed a ride home, he'd be glad to give me one. After all, he'd done it before, and it wouldn't be a problem. My parents turned to me and asked if I wanted to leave?

I replied, "No thank you, I'm having a wonderful time."

Which was really a lie, and would have loved to of had a ride home; but not by him. How I loathed that man. If my parents only knew what kind of slime he really was, they would have never asked me to leave with him.

You see, ten years before, the same scenario had happened, and my father let him give me a ride home. My father was so impressed by his money and political connections; he thought that it was an *honor* that he even spoke to us, let alone to offer to give a helping hand with his child.

He had a big convertible Cadillac and I felt like a movie star riding in it. We stopped for ice cream along the way and he even let me eat it in the car. Upon our arrival home, he pulled into our garage and I thanked him for the ride and the ice cream cone.

He said, "Oh it's not a problem at all. I'll take you out for a drive any time you want. You're a special little girl, Little Mary. Do you want to play a game before you go inside, and it will be our little secret, ok?"

I wanted to be polite, so I nodded yes, and just kept licking my ice cream cone. Then he got out of the car, opened the trunk and pulled out a blanket. He then spread it out on the garage floor and stripped naked. He laid down on the blanket, and then he told me to come over by him. I was a little afraid because it reminded me of other men who…well, treated me inappropriately before, but eventually I did sit down next to him. Then he took my ice cream cone and asked if he could have a lick. I nodded yes.

Then he took my hand, and said, "Oh look Mary, you have some ice cream on your fingers, but that's ok, I'll lick it off for you." And then he had some on his finger, and said, "Mary, would you lick the ice cream off my finger like

I did for you?" I nodded and obliged him. By now his penis was fully erect. He took the ice cream cone and let it drip onto the head of his penis, and once the ice cream was all over it, he handed the cone back to me and said, "Now little Mary", he nodded his head as he held out his penis, "lick the ice cream off of this, ok?"

I just sat there licking my ice cream cone and shaking my head no. I knew I'd never heard of anything like this before, so I thought this has to be wrong. And after all, aren't people always trying to cover themselves up, and not be naked. But before he could even ask me again, I heard my mother yelling for me from the back door of the bar. So he jumped up, and told me that I was never to tell anyone about this, otherwise my parents would be mad at me, and punish me...and then he was gone.

At the time I was too young to understand fully what had just taken place, but as I got older, that memory would repulse me time and time again. Even later I couldn't say anything about it to my parents, because they thought that he was so wonderful, and he was such a good customer, etc.

One of the businesses that he owned was a pharmacy near the beach. I remember as I got older, fighting with my mother to not have to go in there; but she'd make me go in time and time again. Each time he'd see me he'd say how much he'd like to take me for ice cream again sometime…my skin would crawl…and my mother would comment on what a nice man he was. Sometimes he'd be bold enough to come around the counter, and wait for my mother to be busy. Then he'd start patting me on the head, and eventually he'd force my head into his crotch. One time I made a noise, and my mother yelled over from another isle, "Madia, you be nice, and you do whatever he says. You don't want to be a bother."

He yelled back, "Oh she's not a bother, she's perfect." Then he looked down at me and smiled.

And now he's here at this picnic, being bold enough to ask my parents for permission to drive me home…that bastard.

Well time rolled on and I actually was starting to have some fun. It was now about five o'clock in the evening, and the picnic was in full swing. I noticed that Papa was with some man talking in a corner and they were starting to argue. Mama was over there too, and I could see that she was trying to push Papa back, and pleading for the man to just go away. But Papa pushed her out of the way and she fell onto the grass. As he tried to help her back up, this man snuck in a sucker-punch to Papa's mid-section, and Papa doubled over. Then, with Papa doubled over in pain, this man went and gave him an uppercut to his head, and blood immediately began to pour out of his face. It looked like it was coming out of everywhere, and then Papa fell to his knees, and then to the ground. I started to scream; and then I couldn't believe what I was seeing. The man actually went right over to Mama and kissed her very hard on the mouth. He laughed, then turned and he walked away leaving my father lying on the grass bleeding. Someone suggested that we call a doctor, but Mama said that he had no more than a broken nose, and that she'd take him home, and he'd be fine in the morning.

When we got him home, Mama didn't want him upstairs, because of the blood, it would make a mess. So she turned to old Tony and Kimo and said, "Tony, put Martin into your room and you can sleep in Kimo's room with him."

Tony looked a little surprised, and Mama said, "Don't give me that look. I'm not stupid, you sleep in Kimo's room all of the time anyway." Tony and Kimo looked at each other, and then at Mama with surprise. Mama said, "Listen, I don't care what anyone does as long as I get my rent. And Tony, I'll even knock off a couple bucks if you help me get him into bed."

They got him into bed and stripped him down to his underwear, which had blood on them as well. Then Mama turned to Tony, and sarcastically said, "Ok, show's over. I can handle it from here."

Papa started to vomit, so Mama turned to me, and yelled, "Get a bucket so he can throw up in it!" I ran and got one; but when I returned, I realized that I was too late because there was blood or wine all over him, Mama and the floor. Just then, he vomited so violently and with such force, that it actually was caused him to sit up. A stream of red careened through the air and splatters from it hit the ceiling and the walls. I'd never seen anything like it before or since. It looked as though a massacre had taken place.

Throughout the night, Papa slipped in and out of consciousness. Mama stayed with him all through the night. I went down early that morning, and Mama said, "You stay with him and I'm going to clean up, and make sure that your brother Babe doesn't come down to see his father this way."

As I sat there and looked at this blood-drenched man, the piles of bloodied towels on the floor and small pools of blood all around him, I thought how could anyone bleed this much and for this long and not die? Maybe Mama *was* right, some of this just had to be wine.

Papa slowly opened up his eyes and looked at me, then slowly said, "My dear Madia, I'm going to be leaving you soon and it makes me sad to think that I'll never see what a wonderful woman you'll be someday. God bless you my darling daughter. Please take good care of your brother and remember to always do whatever your mother says. But most of all, remember, that even though your father's not going to be here to take care of you, I want you to know that I love you very, very much."

My eyes were filled with tears. How could I have ever thought him to be a mean ogre of a man? When in his dying hour, he only had words of love for me.

He reached out his hand to me and I grabbed it. It was so cold. Then he asked if I could bring him some lemonade because he was so thirsty.

As I reached over to give him a hug and a kiss on the cheek, I said, "Of course Papa." Again, his cold flesh touching my lips, all of a sudden it reminded me of the time I'd spent in bed with my dead brother Sonny and I thought, oh my God, Papa's really going to die.

Then Mama came through the door, and I said, "Mama, Papa wants me to get him some lemonade, so I'll be right back, ok?"

"Sure, you go," she said, "but you better put some ice on those bloodstains on your skirt!"

"OK Mama," I said, "anything you say!" I was oblivious to the blood, because I was so caught up in the realization that Papa loved me. I begged God to please let him live. He can't leave me now that I've really found him.

As I opened the icebox, I saw that there wasn't anymore lemonade left. So I went back to the room and asked Mama if I could run to the store to get lemons for Papa."

As if she was in a trance or something, she said, "Sure, if it makes you happy, go."

So I ran three blocks to the Hi-Lo Food Store, and at first I was unaware of people staring at me, but then there were a few "Oh my Gods!" and I realized that the people were staring because I was covered in blood, but I didn't care, I had to get home as fast as I could for my Papa! I bought a big bag full of lemons, and I ran like the wind all the way home.

As I approached the house, I was shocked to find that the man who had beaten my father was talking on the back porch to my mother. They muttered something back and forth to each other and then she kissed him and said that soon everything will be OK.

"Mama, I have the lemons." I yelled. So she nodded and tried to hurry the man off, but bravely I walked right over to him and said, "What do you, of all people, want here?"

"Oh, I just came to check on your father, to make sure everything was ok."

"Well it will be as soon as *you* leave!"

"Madia," my mother yelled. "You don't ever talk to an adult that way no matter what!"

Holding back my anger, I remembered what I'd promised Papa, and said, "Ok Mama, I'm very sorry, may I be excused?"

She nodded yes and I was off to the kitchen, but first I had to check in on Papa. Softly I said, "Papa I'll have your lemonade in a flash. I had to pick-up some lemons."

He just lay there, and then I saw the most amazing thing, as he was breathing out, you could see a vapor emitting from his mouth, like in cold weather. So I went over to him and I leaned over him and said, "Papa, are you alright?"

"I'm so thirsty Madia, so thirsty."

As he was saying those words, I put my hand up to see if I could feel the vapor. I could, it was cold, so I touched his face and it was even colder than before.

I guessed that with the room being so warm and him being so cold, that's what happens. All I know is that it scared me so badly, that I could only walk backwards slowly out of the room, like a zombie.

By the time I got to the kitchen, the reality of my father dying seemed so close at hand, that I begged God again, "Please God, please don't let that happen. I'm almost thirteen years old, and it's the first time that I've ever felt so close to him. Please God, don't take him away from me now." I thought that over and over again, as I was busy slicing the lemons and wiping my tears away with my arm.

Then I heard some men talking. They were going back and forth from Papa's bedside to the backyard, but I didn't want to stop what I was doing to see what they were doing – Papa mattered most.

Finally the lemonade was ready, and as I brought it in to him I was shocked...he was gone. Not dead, but physically gone from his bed.

I ran back out with the tray, and I started yelling, "Mama, Papa's gone! Mama?"

By the time I made it out to the back porch I saw my father's face in the back window of a family friend's car. There were many people in the car with him and I noticed that Mama in the front seat alongside the man who had beaten my father.

"Madia!" My mother yelled. "We're taking your father to the hospital, so you have to open the bar!" And as the car drove away, I looked and I could see Papa in the backseat. He was so pale that he looked like a ghost and he was just staring out of the window. I wasn't sure if he could see me, but I smiled and softly muttered, "Papa – I love you."

Then I walked back into the empty bar and thought, how can I run the bar? I'm not even thirteen yet. And most importantly, I didn't get a chance to give Papa his lemonade or really tell him that I loved him.

I stood there alone, frozen for a while, before the reality of life started to set back in. My brother came in and said that when Mama was leaving, she told him that he was to see if I needed any help stocking the bar or cleaning it.

"Mary" he said to me, "do you think Papa's going to die?"

I sat down the tray and hugging him I said, "I'm sure everything will be ok." But silently I could only wonder how we were going to survive.

CHAPTER 14

Mama had been gone for hours, and I was bartending like a pro, or so I was told. Just then, one of the customers grabbed my breast and I slapped his hand away.

"Hey!" He said in a rough tone of disappointment. "Your mother never minds a little grab now and then."

"Well I'm not my mother!"

"Yeah, I know - her tits are bigger!"

With that, I threw a shot of whiskey that I had poured for another customer, right in his face. The other men laughed and my brother Babe just happened to see what had just transpired.

He immediately ran over to my side and looked at this man and said, "If you ever touch my sister again, I'll kill you!"

The man leaned forward and said, "Oh yeah?"

"Yeah!" Babe replied, as he pulled the gun my father kept hidden out from under the bar.

I was a little shocked but I had to be tough just like Babe, so I yelled, "Now get out of here! We don't need your money!"

No sooner did he leave when a lot of yelling and whistling broke out from all of the other men in the bar. Then they even started applauding us.

One man stated that our father ought to let us bartend more often. With that, I saw a familiar car pull up and my mother came rushing from it and through the door screaming, "Everybody out! My Martin is dead!"

Everyone looked shocked and confused and as the people filed out, they tried to console her, but she would have no part of it.

"Out! Out! Leave me alone! I'm a widow." Then she went to the back of the bar and sat in the downstairs kitchen and wept.

Once everyone left, I locked the door and headed back to be with Mama. Babe was already there and she told him to get some things because he would be staying at a friend's house for a few days. He kissed her, and then he went upstairs.

I went over to her, and said, "What about me, Mama? Where am I going?"

She slowly lifted up her head and saw the left over tray of lemonade and said, "He never got to drink your lemonade, did he?"

I looked down and said, "No Mama, I guess I didn't make it in time."

Slam went her hand against my face. "It's because you were so worried about your goddamned lemonade that you didn't get a chance to say goodbye to your father! You're always worried about only yourself! You wanted to impress your father with some goddamned lemonade, while he lay dying! You see, that's *why* God took your father away from us. Because you're selfish and only care about yourself! You're so evil! I don't know how you could be my daughter!"

I started to cry.

She slapped me again, as she said, "I don't want to see you shed a single tear or I swear to God I'll kill you! You evil little bitch! You killer!"

Then she quickly got up and walked over to the room where Papa had been. She looked around, and said, "Now Madia, you need to clean up your father's blood. Remember, I have to make money off this room…I'm a widow now!"

And she could see Tony and Kimo outside and she mumbled, "I guess those two queers can stay in Kimo's room from now on. I need to rent this one as soon as possible. Then she turned back to me and said, "What are you waiting for?...Get going!"

As she walked away I said, "Mama, I can't. I mean, this is Papa's blood. I can't."

She slowly turned around and said, "Are you disobeying your mother again? Why you Little Fucking Bitch! It should have been you at that morgue and not your father! I know you won't be happy until you've killed all of us!"

"Mama," I said as my eyes welled with tears, "I never killed anyone."

She quickly raised her hand and said, "Do I see tears in those eyes...the tears of an evil little bitch?"

Quickly wiping my eyes, I said, "No Mama! No! I'm just saying..."

"Shut up! I *know* what you're saying. Well you *are* a killer. First you killed your brother and sisters with your silence, and now, because you didn't love your father, and because of your evil selfishness - you've sent your father to his grave. If only you'd loved him, he might still be alive! Now clean, or else!"

With that, she stormed off and up the stairs to check on Babe. I slowly walked to the pantry and got some cleaning supplies. A bucket, soap and a scrub brush. Once I was in the room alone, I just burst into tears. I kept looking over my shoulder praying that Mama wouldn't catch me. Crying, I knelt down on the floor, and started to wipe up my father's blood. I couldn't believe how alone I felt. I also thought; what *if* I would have gotten back in time to give him his lemonade? Maybe if I had gotten him something to drink, maybe that could have helped him pull through? After all, the church always tells us that with love and prayer, we can make miracles happen.

But would God ever listen to an evil child who let someone die without telling them that she loved them? And as I scrubbed, and cried, I wondered what my life was going to be like now?

CHAPTER 15

It was the day of my father's wake and I was just about at the end of my rope, from having to stare at my father's dead body and being bombarded by people, that I either didn't know or hated, and then came Kuma. She had been crying. When she finally reached me through the crowd she said, "Oh my dearest Madia, what can I say to you except how very, very sad I am for you."

"Please Kuma," I said, "can we go outside, I can't take it in here anymore?"

"Yes of course. But first, I must extend my condolences to your mother."

I thought, now this will be something to see.

As she approached my mother, I could see the seething contempt that she had for Kuma starting to surface.

Nervously Kuma started, "Madia, I can only say, that I am very sorry to you for your loss. I know exactly how you feel."

Mother looked coldly at her and said, "What?...Why, because you loved my husband too?"

Everything went silent and everyone's eyes were upon them.

Bravely Kuma said, "What I meant was that I also lost a husband and I know how you feel."

Mother put her arms on her waist and said, "You couldn't *possibly* know how *I* feel. After all, you *never* loved your husband...although you did love mine...probably enough for both of us!"

Quietly Kuma said, "Madia, I understand that you're upset and grieving, so I'll talk to you later." And she turned to walk away.

Then coldly and loudly, mother was very matter of fact when she said, "Well Kuma, now that my Martin is dead, I really don't see any reason for you to ever have to come around here ever again."

Kuma was shocked. She just looked down as she walked away through the crowd of mourners.

Then as she passed me I reached out and grabbed her hand and said, "Kuma, I'll walk with you."

She slowly looked up at me with tear-filled eyes and smiled as she said, "Thank you Madia."

We both walked proudly past those glaring eyes until we got outside.

"Kuma," I said, "I don't care what my mother just said, all I know, is that it was *you* who truly loved my father, and it's just a shame that you never told him so. I know how you feel Kuma, because I wish the very same thing for me too."

We just stood there and hugged each other tightly.

Then she whispered in my ear softly, "He knows."

CHAPTER 16

Finally it was the morning of the funeral, and as I was getting dressed, I heard Mama yelling on the phone and then hanging up.

"Who was that Mama?" I said, as I walked toward her.

She just glared at me and said, "It was just that bitch Kuma wanting to know if it would *upset* me if she attended Martin's funeral."

I asked what she had told her and she said, "I told her to stay the fuck out of our lives – forever!"

I just walked away in an understanding way, but the minute that I was out of her sight, I ran downstairs to our bar, took a nickel out of the cash register, and used the pay phone to call Kuma back.

"Kuma," I said nervously, "I know what Mama said to you - and I don't care. I want you there and I know that Papa would want you there too. So please come and join us. I'll stand by you, just like at the wake."

Tearfully, she said, "Madia, where do you get your strength?"

"From you Kuma...only from you."

As we hung up I thought, please God, make it be OK. I know that this is probably the stupidest thing that I've ever done, but please help me to be strong, for me and for my Kuma.

When we arrived at the church there was no sign of Kuma outside, so I thought that maybe she was already inside. As we ascended the stairs leading into the church, I could only nod at people as I scanned the crowd...then it hit me, the sight of Papa lying in state. It was real...and I became transfixed on the image of him in the casket in the church. Even though I saw him at the house, seeing him in the church made it seem, I don't know, more official...and final.

As was our custom, everyone that passed by his casket, had to lean in and take a turn kissing his dead body and I thought – there is no way that I can do this.

Just then, from the back of the church, came this figure of a woman dressed in black... Kuma. Suddenly, I felt as brave as anyone; so I leaned in and I kissed Papa on the lips, and when I looked up, I saw Kuma, and smiled as I extended my hand to her.

Out of nowhere came my mother, looking first at me, as if she wanted to kill me, and then at Kuma, with an even more disgusted look, she said, "You have some nerve coming into a house of God."

Without missing a beat, Kuma looked at me, and then at my mother, and said blankly, "If you can walk into one my dear Madia, then I suppose anyone can. Excuse me won't you? I have to say goodbye to a dear and life-long friend."

Mama looked as though she was going to explode.

But Kuma was strong and unfazed, as she proudly walked over to the casket. She looked down at my father's face, and sweetly said, "Goodbye my dear friend, you'll never know how *much* I'll miss you." And with that, she gave him a kiss on his lips too.

Then she walked over to me, and she said, "Well Madia, you know what this means don't you? It means that now that you only have one parent - it's time for me to be a bigger part of your life. You see, when one loses a parent, that's when it is the duty of their godparents to become a very important part of their lives." Then she kissed me and gave me a big hug, and then she whispered in my ear, "Oh Madia, this is just the beginning of rocky times for you, your mother and me. So be careful and be strong."

I could only think, 'heck', every day of my life has been rocky, so I'm pretty used to it.

Then as she was walking toward the exit, she passed my mother and Mama spit on the ground in front of her.

Coolly, she paused, and then kept right on going, showing Mama that she was *going* to be in our lives and would really be someone to contend with from this day forward...I guess she was getting stronger too.

Mama didn't speak or even interact with me for the rest of the ceremony. But then after the funeral, as Mama, Babe and I were all walking back into our bar, she sent Babe upstairs, and the minute that he was gone, she turned toward me with an evil glare and said, "So you and your Kuma *think* you really put on a show! Well here's the finale!"

Slam went her fist into my stomach, and then slap across my face went her hand. She then pulled my head back by my hair and she put her face a fraction away from mine and said, "You tell your fucking Kuma what I did, and she'll get the same. *And* - if I *ever* see her near me or you again, I'm gonna have to kill the both of you – do you understand me? Now get the fuck away from me you fucking little traitor!"

She shoved me with such force that I ended up sprawled out on the floor. I covered my head in the anticipation of a punch, kick, slap or something, but there was nothing…just her footsteps as she walked away from me with a very deliberate gate. I still didn't dare get up until I made sure that she was really gone. So while I was there on the floor and in pain, I could only think about the fact that from this moment on Kuma was never going to be allowed in the bar or our home. But that wasn't going to stop me – and it didn't. Every chance I got, I'd sneak away and go over there… sometimes Mama would find out and beat me. But I didn't mind, the beatings didn't last long and I knew that I'd have those memories forever.

Chapter 17

Well, time went on and I found high school to be a Godsend. There were a lot of new kids, so many things to do, and I joined everything.

I was always good at sports, and now there were teams and clubs to belong to. I thought; this is going to be just great! Especially with all the practices and the games, it meant that I wouldn't have to be at home as much.

There was also something new…'Boys!' I never thought much about them because Mama always told me they were pigs, and often enough, some men proved her right.

She also told me that they only wanted one thing. It's just she never told me what that one thing was. I mean, if she never explained menstruation to me, you know that reproduction was never a spoken subject.

She always threw the word Whore around; but I just thought that it meant that you were the type of girl that liked to go around kissing a lot of men.

So it was a shock one summer night at a friend's house, when they decided to play, Spin the Bottle. Well no one had ever kissed me, and I couldn't get over why it always took so long in the movies; because the only kisses I'd ever had up to this point, were just pecks on the lips from family and friends. So when it was my turn to spin, I spun it and it landed on my best friend's cousin. I didn't know what he meant when he asked me, "Do you French?" I thought it must have meant something like, do I like it? In the movies they show how passionate the French people kiss, so I said "yes", meaning that I've seen movies about France.

Well I was shocked and mortified when he slipped his tongue into my mouth. I got up and said that he was disgusting. And he, being the poor sap that he was, took it as meaning that I thought he was a lousy kisser. He turned red and went home saying how crushed he was, and that he hadn't realized that I'd 'been around'.

These innocent misunderstandings led to an unusual chain of events; like when after I'd left the party, someone's mother overheard the girls talking about how they wondered *who* I'd been kissing that made me such an expert.

Well that mother told another mother, who in turn told another mother, etc. So you can just imagine how blown out of proportion this story was by the time it reached Mama.

My mother was so incensed by the story, that the minute I walked through the door, she said, "Madia, I *hear* that you've become a whore! Well you little bitch – I am so pissed off right now, that if I hit you, I'll probably kill you!"

So she held back as much as she could, then ordered me to my room all the while the word 'whore' was hurled at me in English and then in Yugoslavian.

Once upstairs, I ran into Babe and asked him what Mama was talking about? He explained that Mama heard through the grapevine of crazy mothers that I'd been kissing a lot of boys, and was showing everyone at a party how to kiss.

In the meantime, I was the hit at school when this story got around, and I was immediately pledged to a club. I told them that I would love to be a member of a sorority and then I asked, "What do I have to do?"

As it turned out, there were five of us juniors that were to be pledged all at the same time. Our initiation was to scrub down the sidewalk in front of the local movie house, called the Commercial Theatre, in South Chicago.

We all had to dress in costumes that were a cross between scrubwomen and clowns.

The morning of the pledge event I met everyone in front of the theater. They brought the costumes, and it was so much fun. Even though that street brought back a lot of painful memories, due to the many tears that I had shed on that sidewalk back in the days of when Mama and I would walk separately down the street because she thought that I looked Mexican and so I couldn't be seen walking with her.

It was ironic that even though it took years, I was finally finding happiness on that street.

While I was scrubbing and laughing with the other pledges, I was looking down at the sidewalk when I noticed a familiar pair of shoes standing next to me...Mama. I looked up, only to find that she was looking down at me. She was silent for a moment, and then she coldly said, "What the fuck do you think you're doing? Is this what I raised you to be - a goddamned scrub woman?"

I stood up and said, "Mama, this is only a joke. It's a test to get into a club at school. We all have to clean the street. Please don't embarrass me."

"Oh, Madia, I would never embarrass you." She said in her snide way, "I've come to help you. So you want to clean the scum and filth of the other people? Well then clean this!" With that, she spat on the ground near my feet.

Then she demanded, "Now you get back down on you knees and clean that."

With tears welling up in my eyes, I just slowly shook my head as I asked, "Why Mama?"

Then slap went her hand against my face, and she just repeated, "Now clean that up!"

So I slowly sunk to my knees, and cried as I scrubbed my mothers spit from the sidewalk. Then, without another word, she just started walking away. I was too afraid to turn toward the other girls. Then all of a sudden, I felt a hand touch my shoulder, and a friendly voice that said, "Mary, it'll be OK "kiddo" - don't worry. Hey, we all understand, you're not the only one with a crazy mother, now come on... look at me."

I turned to find the smiling face of a classmate of mine named, "Vicky". She put her arms out, and said, "Let it on out honey, you'll be OK."

I just threw my arms around her and burst into tears, and before I knew it, all the girls had joined in to form a big group hug...I could only thank God for sending me such a wonderful group of friends.

Well, as it turned out, the rest of the day went fine and they told me that I was made a member. I thanked them but I had some doubts that were bothering me, so I turned to them and asked if I was made a member because of what had taken place earlier with my mother.

And quickly, a girl by the name of "Toots" said, "Mary, is it *so* hard for you to accept that people can *actually* like you? We wanted you even before the initiation."

"Really?"

"Come on! You're fun, you're pretty and you're popular, of course we want you in the club. Honey, it's getting late, but we'll talk to you later. We have to run."

Then they all hugged me, and said, "See you later - Sorority Girl!"

I answered with, "Good-bye, and thanks… and I love you all very much!"

As I waved bye to them it hit me. They said that I was fun, pretty and popular. I stopped to think - well I did always like to have fun… but I'm neither pretty nor popular. But all the way home, I would keep catching glimpses of my reflection in the windows of the stores, and I kept thinking – Gee girl, you do seem to be looking pretty good. But what do I really look like? I couldn't wait to get home so that I could get a real good look at my face. The girls had put the make-up on me, so I had assumed that it would be like clown make-up. I could only think, well maybe some of it washed off, and maybe now it didn't look too bad.

As I got off the bus in front of our tavern, I noticed this handsome man, and he was smiling at me. He said, "Little Mary, my, how you've grown up, and beautifully too."

I could only think, boy, this has been the most incredible day.

"Well thank you, Sir." I replied nervously, but for the first time, with a bit of confidence.

"Sir?" he said. "Come on Mary. Don't make me feel too old. Don't you remember me? It's Bill - Bill Fisher, your old pal? The war's over, and you certainly aren't that skinny kid that used to cheat at checkers."

Well I had completely forgotten about him. He was always so nice to me, and he *would* let me cheat, and he'd never get mad. But I couldn't get over the fact that he was at least ten years older than I was, and now he's paying attention to me.

Bill had been a friend of my parents for years; he started doing odd jobs for them as a child, and I remembered that he would just wander in and out of our lives. He had to do odd jobs because he was one of thirteen children, and they needed all the money they could get. Mama told me that as a child, they would even hire him to run beer for them in his wagon during prohibition.

Later I asked him about that story and he told me that when he was just a boy, he was pulling his wagon that had a keg of beer in it, (my parents thought that no one would suspect a child as part of a boot-legging operation), when all of a sudden, a big black car turned the corner, and some men rolled down their windows, and they shot holes through the wooden keg. It scared him, but he stayed right where he was, and didn't run.

Then one of the men yelled to him and said, "Kid – Now go tell your boss that this was just a warning to let them know that this shit is gonna stop NOW!" Then he threw some money at him and they sped off. He turned to look at the wagon and he could see that the beer had leaked all over the ground. He told me that even though it was scary, it wasn't half as scary as having to go back and tell my parents that he didn't make his delivery. So his affiliation with our family went way back to before I was born.

But none of that mattered to me at that moment, because as I stared at him, I could only see a cross between Burt Lancaster and Kirk Douglas, and he was talking to me!

As he smiled at me, my whole body sort of shivered with a feeling that I'd never experienced before, and I nervously said, "Well it's great seeing you too Bill, but I'm late and Mama will yell, so I've gotta run…bye. I'll see you around."

He smiled again, and tipped his hat as he said, "Sure thing Mar, you can count on it."

I walked into the bar and headed straight into the woman's bathroom, so that I could wash my face before Mama could see me - because I thought Mama would just kill me if she saw me in make-up. But to my surprise when I got in there and saw myself in a real mirror, I looked beautiful, well beautiful compared to my usual unmade face. Not like a model or a movie star or anything – but just kind of pleasing to the eye. So I left it on, and I was willing to take a chance.

I walked into the bar's kitchen, and cheerfully said, "Hello Mother, I'm back. Do you need any help with anything?"

She looked up and stood frozen for a moment and even started to halfway smile, but then in an instant, her look turned to anger.

She finally spoke and said, "So you think by putting makeup on an ugly face, that you're going to turn in to a 'God Damned Movie Star' now? Well you look like a whore. But leave it on if you want, because I'd rather look at a whore, than an ugly girl. Now get out of here "Movie Star", I've got work to do...GO!"

Hurriedly, I ran out the back door because I didn't want her to have the satisfaction of seeing that I was getting ready to cry. Then I thought, Oh no, not this time...then I got the brainstorm to go by Kuma's house. Let's see what *she* thinks!

So I went back in the bar to use the pay phone, and this time the light was streaming through the front windows on me, and the men at the bar got to see me made up for the first time. They started whistling, and saying, "Hubba-Hubba", and things like that. But as much as it made me feel good, it also made me feel a little dirty, because a few of the men in there were the same ones, that in my youth, had groped me against my will.

I finally reached the pay phone and rang up Kuma. She first asked if Mama had beaten me or something, and I reassured her that I was fine, and then I said, "Well, I'm coming over. I have something to show you."

CHAPTER 18

As I approached her house, I could see that she was rocking on her big porch swing. All of a sudden the swing stopped and she leaned forward, she put on her glasses just to make sure…and then she jumped up and started down the stairs toward me yelling, "Oh my God child, I didn't know if it was you or Hedy Lamar! Why you're pretty enough to be a model!"

Being embarrassed I said, "Kuma, you don't *really* think so, do you?"

"Child, now would I still be wearing my glasses in public if I didn't think so?" With tears forming in her eyes, she held me by my hands and said, "God has turned you into a beautiful woman."

I said quickly, "Yeah, with a little help from Max Factor."

We both laughed as we hugged.

Then she looked around to see if anyone was watching as she quickly took off those glasses that she hated so much.

"Kuma, why don't you wear them all the time? You look nice in your glasses."

"Well Madia, I guess it's just the vanity of an old woman."

"You're not old Kuma."

"Well I'm not young either. Come on, let's go in the house. Now *I've* got something to show *you*!"

She led me over to her sofa, and she sort of pushed me down into it. Then she just stood there for a minute tapping her chin with her finger. You could tell that the wheels in her head were spinning in high gear. Then all of a sudden, she pulled out a copy of a movie magazine that she had tucked away in her bookcase. She held it up in front of her face…it had a big picture of Hedy Lamar on the cover, and she explained how now that I had make-up on, she could *really* see the resemblance.

For as long as I can remember, Kuma loved *anything* to do with Hollywood. I'm sure that it was her only escape from being trapped in a loveless marriage and regretting the fact that she didn't marry my father, and seeing how unhappy he was. Even as a widow, she still couldn't be free to be with the man that she wanted, because he was dead and she felt that she was now destined to be alone. Plus she knew the torment in my life, and how different my life would have been if *she* would have been my mother. That's why she had to live in her fantasy world, a world that she gave to me too, and how it helped me escape my life as well.

"Kuma, you're crazy," I said, "she's beautiful, and I look like Olive Oyl, not Hedy Lamar!"

I started to get up and she yanked me back down to the sofa. She sat down next to me and said, "Now child, you're not calling your Kuma a liar are you?" With that she popped back up and said, "Now Miss Lamar, you just sit right there, and we're going to work some Hollywood magic for you."

I just laughed and went along with her, because it did make me feel good, not to mention the enormous ego boost, which I could always use.

During the trauma of an eyebrow arch, she gave me a glass of wine …and soon it didn't feel as bad. Then she brought out some of her makeup and didn't say a word as she worked her Hollywood magic on me. Then all of a sudden she stopped, and did a little nod of approval to the masterpiece that she had just created.

Still without speaking, she took me by the hand and directed me to her bedroom and made me stand in front of her full-length mirror. I looked for a minute and couldn't believe that it was really me that I was looking at. I thought, even though I was hardly Hedy, I *was* looking simply wonderful, and I was beginning to believe her.

Then she said, "Wait here, I want to get something!"

Off she went into one of her spare bedrooms, and soon she came out with the most beautiful long black beaded gown.

"Here, let's try this on. I know it's outdated, but just in case you ever go shopping for something like this, you'll have an idea. Now you go and change into it, and I'll wait in the kitchen. You call me when you're finished!" And she ran off.

I slipped off my jeans and plaid flannel shirt and then slipped into a gown, fit for a movie star.

"Oh Kuma!" I yelled, "You can come in now!" So I struck a pose, holding my empty glass of wine high in the air. I heard her getting close so I said, "So what do you think of your movie star now Kuma?"

She just walked toward me like she was in a trance and then finally she broke her silence with, "Oh my God Madia, you're even *more* beautiful than Hedy Lamar."

Jokingly, I responded with, "I think it's because of the shoes myself," and with that I picked up the gown's hem to show off my bobby socks and saddle shoes.

We both laughed and she called me a silly goose as we fell back on her bed with laughter.

"Now Madia," she said after a minute or two, "I'm serious, it's the truth. You could easily be a model!"

Then I could see that she had another brainstorm brewing.

She grabbed me by the hand and dragged me back to her living room and said, "Now you just wait right here and don't change. Then you go in the dining room and when you hear me yell to you, just strike that same exact pose!" she paused again for a second, "Oh, but first, wait," she mumbled as she went into the spare room again. This time she returned with the most beautiful pair of black satin pumps that had a rhinestone cluster on top of the instep.

"Here child, try and squeeze into them, they're a little stretched out, so try…just for a minute."

Even with my bad right foot, I had managed to get them on, and I made my way to her dining room. Then I finally heard her yell from the kitchen, "Get ready!"

I assumed that she went to get her camera, so in my best movie star pose. I stood there pretending that I was an Erté Statue. She walked in but she wasn't alone. She had brought with her, two of her neighbor ladies, and they had with them, the most beautiful blond man that I'd ever seen. He was a bronze Adonis and he had the most chiseled looking profile. He looked a lot like the actor Buster Crabb, back when he played Flash Gordon - I couldn't believe that he was even real.

"Now Madia," Kuma said, "these are to be three independent judges to say in a secret ballot, if you should pursue a modeling career. Now let me get some pencils and paper."

But before she could take two steps, the women both grabbed her by the arm and said that they didn't need a secret ballot. Their votes were definitely 'YES!'

With that the shorter of the two women approached me and said, "My goodness Madia, you have grown up to be quite a beautiful young lady. Oh by the way, I would like you to meet my nephew. He's here for a few weeks. He's from Boston. Madia, meet Kenneth Bennett III, no less."

As he took my hand, I went to shake it, but as he stared me in the eye, he said, "No, this hand is much too beautiful to be shook, it's only purpose in life should be to be kissed and donned with beautiful and expensive jewelry. I'd like to cast my vote as well. It's a definite yes."

I thought that I had died and gone to heaven. Then I thought to myself – and when and if I get there, I hoped that all of the angels would have crystal blue eyes, wavy blond hair, and a golden tan, just like Kenneth Bennett III.

I joked that if they thought that I looked good now, they should have seen me in my saddle shoes.

The ladies laughed and Kuma said, "Madia, we're being serious. Oh she's always kidding around." Then I could see her wheels turning as she put her hands on the shoulders of the two ladies and said, "Let's go in the kitchen and get some coffee." She glanced back at me, looked Kenneth up and down and gave me a wink.

With them on their way to the kitchen, Kenneth picked up my saddle shoes. As he handed them to me he said, "It's rare to meet not only such a beautiful girl, but one who also has a sense of humor."

"Well Kenneth, my old chap, when you look like me, you have to have a good sense of humor to survive. This is all make-up and make believe. I'm sorry that Kuma dragged you over. You must think we're all nuts or something, I'm sorry…really."

And ever so politely, he replied, "Don't be, I'm not…not at all. The problem is that you're not seeing what everyone else is seeing. You belong on a magazine cover, and if I'm not being too forward, would it be alright with you if I walked you home?"

"Kenneth, you don't even know where I live."

Assuredly, he said, "It doesn't matter. I'd walk anywhere with you…and why don't you call me Ken? What can I call you? I've never heard the name Madia before, so I don't know what it's short for?"

"Oh Ken," I said nervously, "it's Mary, just call me Mary." I was getting lost in his eyes and I thought, "Kiddo, just be you! He's probably just being nice for his aunt's sake." So now with a little more confidence I said, "By the way Ken, you sure are smooth. Do you always talk like you're in a movie?"

He explained, "Only when I'm in the company of a beautiful woman."

"Oh really, well then I'll go wash my face… that should bring you back to reality quick enough."

He laughed, and said, "Oh Mar, you're a riot."

"Oops Ken, you slipped. You almost sounded like a real person there for a second. Keep up the good work pal." I said as I patted him on the shoulder, while I was passing him to go change. I stopped at the doorway and turned to look back at him and said, "I'll meet you on the porch after I've changed, OK?"

"Sure Mar," he said, as he smiled.

Then while I was changing, Kuma came in and she said, "Well Madia, I think we have to talk seriously about your career."

I grabbed her hands and said, "Wait Kuma, I want to thank you for being so wonderful to me today, because the morning had its rough spots, but you can't be serious?"

Firmly Kuma grabbed my shoulders and said, "Now Madia, I am being *very* serious. It's *you* that needs to realize that you have blossomed into a beautiful young lady. Now come with me over to the mirror and for just a moment, pretend that you aren't you and look into the mirror. Look at yourself from all angles. What do you see?"

As I looked from head to toe, I thought the light from outside must be coming through the window at just the right angle, because whoever that is in the mirror, certainly does look pretty... I hated to think it, let alone say it, because according to the church, vanity was a sin, but here goes nothing, "Ok Kuma, in this light, and just for this moment, I look…ok. Now can I change?"

She just gave me a look like, "We'll see."

Soon I was back in civilian clothes, but before I could even say good-bye, Kuma said, "Wait, here's a picture of Bette Davis in jeans and a shirt, very similar to what you have on. You just need to perk yourself up a bit, that's all."

So I let Kuma play with turning up the collar, and rolling up the sleeves. But I wanted to die when she tied the bottom of my shirt in a knot at my waist.

"Kuma, I think you're going a bit too far, don't you?"

"Not at all child," she said, "Oh and wait here." Again she ran off to the spare room, and emerged with a pair of sandals that she bought for me and that I had always been too afraid to wear. It was because of my bad right foot. I always tried to hide it.

I said, "Kuma, I can't, my foot, and Ken wants to walk me home."

"That's precisely why *now* is the perfect time!" She explained that between the hair and the make-up, not to mention my new 'sporty look', that she'd given to my old clothes, the walk would be wonderful. She said that she was going to prove to me, once and for all, that no one cared about that damned foot except me.

So before I could retaliate, she grabbed my shoes and socks and threw then into the spare room.

"Oh Kuma, now what are you doing? I'll never find them in there. Then I took a deep breath and said, "What am I going to do with you?"

Then she smiled at me and I thought, "Well, maybe she's right."

I smiled back at her and I said to myself, "Well, we'll see."

She winked and said, "You'd better hurry or I'll grab *Kenneth* for myself. Now run along and I'll try to find your shoes. You can pick them up tomorrow, now run along...and I *dare* you to prove me wrong."

She hugged and kissed me, and even with being scared, I thought, heck – even if she is wrong – he lives in Boston.

But then I saw him standing there, looking like a Bronze God, and all of those insecurities came flooding back into my brain. I didn't know what to do. I stopped dead in my tracks and looked down and said, "I'm sorry for being so forward Ken, believe me, I don't know what's gotten into me today."

He then took my hands and he nudged my chin up so that I'd have to look at him face to face. As I looked up into his beautiful blue eyes, it looked as though they were welled up with tears.

He said, "Mar, I think you're swell, I've only known you a few minutes, and gosh, it seems I've known you my whole life." Then he embraced me and kissed me on the cheek. He quickly apologized for being so forward. He said, "Mar, I normally don't act like this either, but I've never met someone as wonderful as you."

Well by this time, I really felt like I *was* caught in an M.G.M. musical extravaganza, and that there should be a hundred dancers coming out of nowhere at any minute, but there were none. Just me feeling like a new person and an attractive one at that. Being admired, even if it was only briefly, by probably what I considered to be the most handsome young man on earth. It was the most wonderful experience in the world.

Our silent gaze was broken by Kuma's voice yelling from the porch, "Remember to call me tomorrow, Hedy!"

We both broke up. Laughingly I yelled back, "OK, Cecil B.!"

She waved good-bye and as we walked away, she waited until Ken turned his back and that's when I noticed that she was putting on her glasses for a better look.

As we walked I thought, well now is a good time to face reality. So I said, "Ken, you haven't said anything about my deformity."

He looked at me as though I had lost my mind and said, "What deformity?"

With that I stuck out my foot saying, "Didn't you notice my foot? Isn't it horrible?"

"What do you mean? Your big toe? What happened, did something fall on it?"

"No, I was born disfigured like this."

He then took my chin again in his hand, and said, "Don't you think you're over reacting? It just looks a little swollen or something. I wouldn't of even noticed it if you didn't bring it up."

With those words, I felt as though the weight of the world had been lifted off my shoulders. And to hear them coming from someone so perfect looking. I couldn't believe it. I turned toward him. I stopped and grabbed him by the shoulders and said, "Do you really mean it or are you just pretending to be in a movie again?"

Taken aback he said, "Mar, I'm serious. You know I've never thought that I'd meet a person as insecure as I am, especially one who was so beautiful."

With that I hugged him and gave him a little kiss on his cheek. Then I said, "Insecure? You? Why you're the real movie star here – look at you – you're gorgeous!"

He said, "Mar, this is as new to me, as it is to you. I was always the runt and sickly, so I had to try and make myself stronger, and well, now I look like this, but inside, I'm still the runt. That's why it hurt me to see the doubt that you had in yourself earlier…I know how you feel. My father was killed in a car accident when I was three years old and my mother a nervous breakdown, so that's why my Aunt had to help raise me. My Aunt is my Dad's sister, and when my mother got better – which didn't take long – she immediately married the first guy that she met, which caused some bad-blood in the family. My Aunt really never forgave her, not to mention that she's had two more husbands since him. We moved around a lot and each guy had more money that the next. Plus, some of the guys weren't too happy about having a sickly stepson. Their solution was that I would be shipped off to boarding schools…and kids can be cruel to the new kid, especially to the sickly, runt of a new kid. So I decided to get strong, that way I could defend myself. I also thought that then maybe my mother wouldn't mind having me around. Well that's my life story – What's yours?"

I paused for a moment, trying to absorb all that he'd just told me. Finally, I said, "Well it's pretty boring. There's not that much to tell; except that Mr. Runt turned Movie Star, you have given me the most perfect day of my life!"

"I hope not," he said, "because even more perfect days are ahead for you if I have anything to do with it. Besides, you never want to be perfect, and you wanna know why?"

"Why?" I said.

"Well, because if you're perfect, they'll all want to hang you on a cross at Easter!"

I laughed and said, "Ken that's blasphemy, you're not supposed to say things like that!"

"Oh loosen up Mar, after all, I learned it in the Seminary."

A loud crash came into my mind. I thought, Ken was going to be a priest?

"Did you say you learned that in the seminary? Like the priesthood kind of seminary?"

"Yeah Mar," he said, "Hey, don't let it make you nervous. Irish Catholics always send their sons there, but c'mon - me a priest? Hardly!" He winked and then he looked me in the eye, and said, "Hey, why do you care?"

I replied with, "Hey, none of your business - ok!", then I could feel butterflies in my stomach and nervously said, "Oh, there's my house! Thanks a bunch and I hope to see you again soon."

Laughing he said, "Wait now. Isn't that supposed to be *my* line? Come on, we've seen the same movies."

"Oh, you're such a nut!" I said, as I reached up and ruffled up the top of his golden locks. "Oh your hair is so springy. I like that."

Then he touched my hair and said, "God Mar, your hair feels like silk. I could do this all day."

We just stood there for an awkward moment and then he kissed me…Wow! I didn't know what to say or do, so I just did what I always did when I was nervous, and made a joke.

My retort to him was, "Pardon me Father, before we *both* sin?"

He laughed and it broke the tension. He smiled at me and I thought that I'd melt, so I just blew him a kiss as I broke away from him, and started running toward my yard.

Then he yelled to me, "That settles it. We're going out tomorrow. I'll get your number from your Kuma on the way back to my aunt's. Sweet dreams and I'll call you tomorrow."

As I got to my gate I turned around to get one more glimpse of him, and what do you know? He was doing the same.

God it made me feel so good.

But as I approached the back doorway, reality was waiting – Mother.

She snidely said, "So Miss Movie Star, I suppose you're to become Blondie's whore?"

"Mama, he's just visiting from Boston. Don't worry."

"It's my job to worry. That's what mother's do, worry about their children until the day they die."

As she said those words, I could only think - My God, she's finally considered me her child. There was nothing that she could say that was going to bring me back to earth. So I just went past her smiling as big as I could, and I went upstairs to take my bath and to daydream about this glorious day.

As I was doing that, I could only wonder what Ken was doing, and if he meant all the wonderful things he said. I especially hoped that he was serious about seeing me tomorrow. But I quickly said to myself, that even if he didn't call, it would be ok too, because even though I didn't have my tomorrow yet, no one could take away my today.

As I was enjoying my long soak in the tub, I kept replaying the events of the day and kept thinking nothing but wonderful thoughts. It seemed as though I had soaked for hours when a siren in the distance broke the silence of the night. I thought how sad it was that someone out there has to be experiencing sadness, when there was so much joy to be had.

Chapter 19

For some reason I got up a little later than usual, and I happened to walk in to the living room to catch my mother swearing at someone on the phone. As she was hanging up I said, "What's the matter Mama?"

In a frustrated tone she said, "God damned kids. Always making prank phone calls! I must have had ten hang up calls since 5:30 this morning."

"Well what do they say Mama?"

"Nothing! Not a goddamned thing! I'm so pissed off, that I'm gonna rip this goddamned thing right out of the wall the next time it rings!" Then she said, "Here - you stay up here with this bastard phone. I've got work to do. I'm not like my movie star daughter, who can stay in bed until nine o'clock!"

Just then the phone rang again and Mama just kept shaking her head and swearing as she went downstairs.

I picked up the receiver and said, "Hello?" expecting to be hung up on; but instead I could only hear the sobbing voice.

"Oh Madia, thank God I've finally reached you."

"Kuma, what's wrong? Was that you calling all morning?"

"Yes Madia, but I heard your mother's voice and hung up; I knew eventually I'd get you. Madia, you must come over quickly."

"Kuma, please tell me what's wrong?" I begged.

"No Madia, not on the phone, please come to my house."

"Ok Kuma, but you must calm down. I'll be right over." As I hung up I thought what kind of excuse could I give Mama? Suddenly, I heard Mama yell up to me, "Madia! Get dressed! You have to run to the store for me. I need some lemons for the bar. So get moving!"

I yelled back, "OK Mama, I'll get dressed right now!" Thank you God for giving me an alibi. But as I began to walk toward my room, I froze for a moment, thinking back on the last time that I had to run out for lemons...Papa. Tears started to form in my eyes, and I said to myself, "Now Mary, you're just crazy - what - every time you're sent out to the store for lemons someone dies? Oh, pull yourself together girl."

As I approached Kuma's, I noticed that she was coming through her front door carrying some food. As soon as she saw me, she set the food down on her swing.

"Madia, my darling child" she yelled, "thank God you've come."

I ran to her, and said, "What's wrong Kuma?"

She hugged me so tightly, and then she started to cry, but quickly wiped her eyes, and told me to sit down on the porch steps with her. She took my hands and said, "Child, do you remember yesterday? That fine young boy Kenneth?"

I nodded yes and said, "Of course, we're supposed to go out sometime today, but he hasn't called yet."

I noticed that Kuma's eyes were now tearing uncontrollably.

"Kuma, has something happened to him? Is he ok?"

Kuma said, "Well, while he was taking his bath late last night, he had some kind of a sun lamp thing on him, I guess that he did it all the time, anyway, they think that he went to make sure that the radio wouldn't fall in or change the station and somehow he pulled the cord and the lamp fell in. He was electrocuted and died."

"No Kuma!" I screamed, No! It's not true ... It can't be!"

Kuma nodded, and softly said, "Madia – it is true."

Then I burst into tears and looked up to sky saying, "Why God, why do you kill everyone I love or that tries to love me?"

Kuma embraced me tightly and said, "Oh child, that's not true - I'm still here and nobody loves you more than me. Come now, you've got to pull yourself together." she added, "We have to bring some food to his aunt's house.

"Kuma I can't…I just can't." I couldn't even move let alone think of *trying* to be social. Then I just looked at her and said, "Why him…it's not fair."

She hugged me tightly and whispered in my ear softly, "Come on child, you must be strong now, if not for yourself, then you must for his aunt's sake. She has lost so much too…we mustn't be selfish…think of her."

I looked at the table covered with all of the food that she had packed up, and I said, "You're right Kuma, she must be devastated. Ken told me that she was like a second mother to him… let's go." I knew that Kuma was right and I *was* being selfish. I was in shock and I only knew him for a day. She knew him his entire life. I thought, Ken - I'm doing this for you. "Come on Kuma, I'll be OK – let me help you carry this to her."

I felt stronger with every step. Because I knew in my heart, that somewhere out there, this would make Ken happy, and it was a way of paying him back for the happiness that he had given to me.

As we walked, I just kept replaying all of the wonderful things that Ken had said to me the day before. As we approached her front door, I just kept saying to myself, "Be strong Mar…be strong."

I took a deep breath before we walked into her house and thought, "You can do this." But as soon as we entered and I saw that sweet little woman, who had said such nice things to me the day before, I could feel her pain. She looked so alone and I knew how she felt, but I didn't want to be the one to add any more sorrow to her day. After setting down the tray of food, I approached her and said, "I'm so very sorry to hear about your nephew, I…I..." then I burst into tears.

She got up and hugged me and said, "Oh my dear sweet Little Madia, you don't have to say a word. Kenneth told me that he thought you were the most wonderful girl that he had ever met. As a matter of fact, I'm sure he'd want you to have this. He'd shown it to me right before… before he went in to take his...well last night."

And as she fought back the tears, she handed me an eight by ten black and white glossy picture of him, signed "To Mar - My Favorite Movie Star! From Your Biggest Fan! With All My Love - Always, Ken"

Then she said, "He asked me if it looked like it was the kind of picture that movie stars gave out?" She added, "I said yes, even though I didn't know what he was talking about; but it sure made him very happy. Madia," she said softly as she took my hands, "Let me just say thank you for giving my nephew Kenneth, one of the best days of his short, short, life. He told me that you had made him feel as though he never wanted to go back to Boston." She then kissed me on the cheek.

I gave her a big hug and then I asked, "Where will he be waked? I really want to see him."

"Why Madia he's gone. They've already shipped his body home to Boston."

My heart sank.

She could see the disappointment in my face. Then she gave me a warm smile and said, "Just keep your memory of him as he was yesterday.

He'd like that." Then she grabbed my hands in sort of a consoling way to me, and said, "You know Madia, I told him not to bring that damn thing into the bathroom, but he just wouldn't listen. He said that he had a big day the next day and that he had to look perfect." She just shook her head, gave me another hug, and sat back down on the couch.

A cold chill went through my body at that moment, because I could only think - he's dead because of me! Yes, that's it. He wanted to look good for our day together and now he's dead. Again, it's my fault...I just wanted to die!

Kuma could tell that something was wrong, so she pulled me to the side and she asked me if I was ok.

"Kuma," I said in a whisper, "Don't you see? He's dead because of me...of me!"

Shocked, she just looked at me for a second, then looked around to see if anyone had heard me, and she said, "Oh child, let's go outside."

Once on the porch I completely broke down. She tried to console me, but I could only feel an intense guilt mounting.

"Kuma, I exclaimed, don't you see? He was doing that for me!" She had tears in her eyes and a puzzled look on her face. I began to cry even harder. I threw my arms around her and clung to her, as I cried on her shoulder. Then she moved us further away from the doorway and we sat down and cried together on that poor grieving woman's steps.

Kuma rocked me back and forth, telling me softly over and over to shush, and that it would all be ok.

Then she said, "Oh my dear, dear, Madia. How could that woman raise you to think that everything is *always* your fault? Someday you'll see that none of us can control life *or* death. And you can't look at death as a punishment to you. After all, aren't you lucky to have known Ken, even if only for a day, than not at all? And maybe the brief happiness that you felt with him was just a sample from God, of how you will, and *should* be treated in the future by men…like a lesson. Remember, everything happens for a reason."

I looked into her eyes and said, "Well, I know the reason God sent me you Kuma. You helped me to survive - and I know that without you, I could have *never* made it this far. Thank you Kuma for giving me a life."

Then I looked up to the sky and I said, "And thank you God, for giving me my Kuma." I looked back down and we just stared into each other's eyes and tearfully smiled and hugged.

Then she said, "Oh child, you'd better be on your way before your mother gets suspicious."

"You're right. Say Kuma, do you have any lemons at your house? I'm supposed to be at the store getting some for Mama."

"As a matter of fact child I just bought some. I was going to bake and well now, I won't have any time. I have to help out here. They're in the icebox, so take all them if you want."

I kissed her on the cheek and jumped to my feet and said, "Kuma, you're a lifesaver." We both smiled and I made my way toward her house.

"Oh child, there's a bag on the counter that has your shoes and socks in it, so don't forget to take them too!"

Once again, she had saved the day.

I ran to her house, picked up the lemons and the bag with my shoes, and I ran back out. I looked back to the neighbor's house and there was Kuma standing there waving good-bye and yelling, "Madia, I love you!"

I yelled back, "I love you too Kuma! Bye!"

I could only think on my way back, "Kuma, I love you more than you'll *ever* know."

When I got back home, I left the shoes on the porch and brought the lemons into the bar. As I handed them over, Mama asked me if I went to California or Florida for them because I'd taken so long.

I politely said, "I'm sorry Mama, but I ran into some friends from school and I guess I lost track of the time."

Jokingly, she turned to one of the bar patrons and said, "Oh yes, you know my Madia thinks that she's some kind of movie star around here. So I'm sure that everyone wanted her autograph!" Then she and some patron's started to laugh.

Oh God, I thought, that reminded me - I forgot Ken's picture at his aunt's house. I've got to call Kuma.

"Madia," rang my mother, "you bartend for a few minutes, I have to go up to the Avenue to pick something up. I'll be right back."

"Sure Mama," I said. I thought this is perfect. This will give me a chance to call Kuma. So as soon as Mama left, I went to the pay phone and rang up Kuma, but there was no answer. I thought, well she's probably still helping out at Ken's aunt's house, so I'll give her a few minutes and then I'll try again.

But it only seemed like a few moments before Mama appeared back at the door.

I said, "Gee Mama; that was quick."

"Well you know Madia; some people are quicker than others." While she was saying that, I had noticed what looked like an envelope in her hand. Then in a superior tone, she said, "Madia, the funniest thing happened while I was out, I ran into one of your friends, and she wanted me to give you something. Come in the back." She nodded her head toward the bar's kitchen and then she turned toward Tony, who was sitting at the end of the bar, and said, "Tony, watch the bar. I won't be long."

He quickly jumped up and got behind the bar. I'm sure that he sensed the very unusual vibe that was now in the room.

With every step I felt impending doom, I couldn't imagine what was going on, but I just knew that she was up to something. The very second that we were out of everyone's sight, she turned to me and started.

"So you little fucking bitch - you went to see that slut Kuma of yours. Well don't try to deny it, because I just so happened to run into a woman who was on her way here to give you something."

"Your only clue will be is that she has a dead nephew...Does that ring a bell? You lying little bitch!"

Then slap went her hand across my face. "She told me how you had forgotten this when you were at her house this morning with your Kuma!" Slap again went her hand. "She also said how you had told your Kuma that you felt *so* guilty about her nephew's death. Then she just assured me that it was just the shock of the news, and that you shouldn't blame yourself! Well, I should have told her that murdering people was your hobby - next to being a god damned movie star that is!"

With that she opened up the envelope and pulled out Ken's picture and waved it toward me.

"Oh, don't let me forget the Grand Finale - a picture of Blondie that's signed, 'To Mar - My Favorite Movie Star!' What does he think you are a horse, you're not *Mar*, you're Marion or Madia or Mary, but only a disrespectful, fresh pig would call you *Mar*!"

"Stop it Mama!" I yelled.

She stopped dead in her tracks for a moment and then she looked me coldly in the eye and said, "If you *ever* raise your voice to *me*, your mother, again, I swear to God I'll kill you!"

"Now let me finish," she said," 'From Your Biggest Fan! With All My Love - Always, Ken"

I thought to myself, oh how cheap and dirty she made it all sound, especially something that was meant to be so beautiful.

I extended my hand to her saying, "I'm sorry for yelling Mama. I've just been a little upset. May I please have my picture?"

She became very animated, and it all didn't seem real for a moment.

"Oh Madia," she said, "don't you know that when you defy your mother, there must be some type of punishment given? Now let me see?" she said, in a slow and deliberate way, "What should it be?" First she looked around the room, and then acted sort of surprised as she noticed that she was holding the picture. Then she stared at the picture and then she looked back at me.

I said, "No Mama, not the picture please, I beg you no."

And with that she turned on the burner to the downstairs stove, and slowly moved the corner of the picture over the flame. She never broke eye contact with me. Then finally, after what seemed like an eternity, the picture caught on fire. I stood there watching as she destroyed the only proof that a gorgeous young man once admired me. I was so sick to my stomach that I thought that I'd throw up right then and there;

but I refused to let Mama get any satisfaction from this, so I only said, "Well, if that's all you wanted, may I please be excused?" then I turned my back to her and walked away.

Frustrated by my indifference to her disgusting little show, she could only say, "You'll thank me and God, someday, for saving you from being his little whore! God took care of him, and now I'm taking care of you!"

As I slowly ascended the back stairway to our apartment, I could only think - No Mama, that's where you're wrong - nothing can ever wipe him and that glorious day from my memory…nothing.

Chapter 20

Well thank God the rest of my junior year wasn't as traumatic, although every time I saw a young man with blonde hair it would bring back Ken's image. Not that I minded, it's just as happy of a memory today as it was the very first time I laid eyes on him.

Throughout the rest of high school, I didn't ever get the chance to date one on one, my mother wouldn't allow it.

But finally, as a senior, I did get to do a lot of *group* things. I met a lot of wonderful kids through all of the different clubs, teams and such.

The days just flew by and before I knew it, it seemed as though summer was almost upon me. It also meant that I was continually being hounded by Kuma to consider a modeling career.

I just laughed, but she kept on reassuring me that nothing was impossible. I remember one day in particular where she said, "Why are you so against trying it? After all, look at how well that Higgins's girl is doing with her modeling career! Why she just won Miss South Chicago, didn't she?"

"Kuma, she's a beautiful girl. I know her, she goes to my school, and she has the most incredible blue eyes that you've ever seen."

"So, you could be the model with the most incredible *brown* eyes!...I know," she went on, "We'll get some pictures of you in one of those new two piece bathing suits. You know, just like in the magazines."

"Oh Mama would *kill* me!" But she wasn't paying any attention to me. She started scheming. You could tell by the far off look in her eyes.

She said, "Somehow we're going to have to go downtown and do some shopping or something. Child, start thinking of a way to get your mother to let you go downtown and then we can go to some modeling schools to see what they think."

"Ok, Kuma." I said, just to appease her, "but now I've got to get home. I'll talk to you soon. Bye-bye." And I starting hurrying away to get home.

"Bye, child, oh excuse me, I mean Miss Chicago Model!"

I yelled to her, "Kuma, I think that you're starting to lose your mind!"

"Child, I'm entirely *too* young to be senile!"

I just kept walking and shaking my head... but secretly, it did make me feel good that at least someone thinks that I'm not ugly – even if it was just Kuma.

I was enjoying the walk and just kept laughing to myself about how I can always count on Kuma to make my day, when I heard a soft voice say, "Mar?"

I looked over, and standing in the shade of a big tree was the sister of a friend of mine from school. Her name was Babs.

She said, "Hi Mar, I know that you really don't know me well, but I'm Shirley's sister."

"Hi Babs. Of course I know who you are. How's Shirley?"

"Oh she's just fine. She's the one who told me that I should come over and talk to you. I wanted her to do it, but she said that you were really nice and that if you could help, you would, and that I didn't need to drag her into this."

"Well Babs, I like a good mystery as much as the next guy – so what do you need from me?"

Nervously she said, "Well, I've met this guy who wants to take me to Florida - and I'm going - even though my parents told me not to. They told me that if I go, that I'm to never come back home! So I said, "That's fine with me!" My family is nuts and now they've forbidden my sister to talk to me, so that's the other reason that she didn't come with. But she said that you were a real trooper and that you would help anyone out if you could."

This whole thing was sounding a little crazy, and I couldn't wait to find out what she could possibly need my help with. Plus I wanted to tell her – Sister, if you think that your family is nuts – boy do I have you beat!

Then I thought, wait, you're going to Florida...with a boy, and you've told this to your parents, and you're still alive? They can't be that bad. Then I said to myself, I don't think that they're the ones that are nuts.

"Sure Babs, if I can. What do you need?"

"Well, I know that you've got a few bucks, and believe me, I'm not asking for money or anything, I just want to know if I could borrow some summer clothes. I mean, you always dress so nice, you know, classy and all. It would only be for a week or two...what'd ya think?"

I thought to myself again, "Thank you God!"

"Babs, by any chance you wouldn't need a bathing suit, would ya?"

"Yeah, I sure do!" She said.

"Well, follow me and take your pick!" With that we both ran upstairs to my room. I found three cute outfits and three bathing suits. I explained that they were from last year, but they're still very much in style.

She said, "Oh Mar, you really are swell. Shirl was right."

Then I put everything in a bag and I told her to come back at dinner time and to pretend she was returning them to me, in front of my Mother.

She asked why, but I just told her that if my plan worked, she could keep them!

"Oh boy, sure thing!" She said happily, "See you around six?"

"Better make it six fifteen…and Babs, be there on time ok?"

"You got it kiddo!" She said as she ran off.

I hoped that this plan worked – I knew Mama like the back of my hand – but Babs was a little flakey.

Well it was dinner time and there we all were; my brother Babe, Mama, and me having our dinner. Our friend and boarder, Tony was bartending for us, so we could eat as a family. I kept looking at the kitchen clock, then finally at 6:15pm sharp Babe said, "Hey, you know who's walking this way, it's that girl Babs. You know

Mary, your friend Shirley's sister. They say she's quite the number. You know, on the fast side."

I thought that this couldn't have been better timing if I'd have planned it and told Babe precisely what to say. Plus, since Mama always listened to everything that Babe said, I could tell that she was processing what he had just said, and I could also tell that she knew exactly what he meant when he said that she was 'fast', so this was perfect!

Innocently I said, "Oh Babe, I barely know her but she's always seemed so nice. I just think that boys like to talk. Mama, she doesn't look like a tramp to you, does she?"

Mama looked out the window toward her, and asked, "Does she live on Avenue 'O'?"

"Yes Mama," I said.

"Then she's that 'party girl' I heard a couple of guy's mention. You don't hang around with her, do you?"

"No Mama, her sister Shirley and I are sort of friends from school. Shirley said that her sister Babs was always out for a good time, but she was really a very sweet...Oh look, she's coming here."

I got up to answer the back door, and as soon as we made eye contact I winked to her, and said, "Hi Babs, what's up?"

"Oh hi Mar, I just wanted to return these clothes."

"Oh," I said loudly, "You must mean the summer outfits and bathing suits that I let you borrow last year." Again I winked.

"Oh yeah," she muttered, "I thought, gee, it's almost summer again, and you might want'em back. Boy, those bathing suits sure did fit great; all the guys *really* liked them!"

I could hear my Mother's chair move from behind me. Then Mama started, "First, what's going on here? And Miss Babs, don't call my daughter a horse! Her name is Mary, not Mar!"

Then she turned to me, with a look like, 'Have YOU lost YOUR Mind!' then she said, "And Madia, why did you give away these new clothes?"

Nervously, I said, "Well Mama, it was almost the end of summer, and Babs happened to see me at the beach and wanted to know if she could borrow some stuff. Isn't it nice of her to bring them back so that now I'll have something to wear this summer?"

I then looked down into the bag and said, "Oh, so you didn't have time to wash them, well that's OK. I'm sure that they'll wash up just like new."

Babs now caught on and crudely said, "Yeah Mar-Oh I mean Mary-I sure hope they don't stink or anything, because you know, I did almost live in them all summer."

Well that was just enough for Mama, and she finally spoke.

"Oh Babs, Honey, you know what I think? Since you like them so much, I think that you should just keep them. Madia won't mind, will you?"

Mama glared at me, and I said, "Of course not Mother, whatever you say."

"Good, then it's settled. Now Babs you run along home and enjoy the clothes. We have to finish dinner."

Babs said, "Thank you!" As she started to walk away, she stopped, turned back and checked out Babe from top to bottom, and said, "Gee Marty, I sure know why they call you Babe. I hope to see a lot more of you at the beach this summer. Bye!"

I wanted to burst out laughing because that was the topping on the cake, and the best part about it, was that she was serious.

As soon as Babs was out of sight Mama looked at me and said, "Madia, are you crazy? That girl's a whore! You let her wear your clothes? And then you were going to put on a bathing suit once worn by *her*? Oh my God! How did I raise you? You know you can get all kinds of dirty woman diseases from sharing bathing suits and underwear! Why do you think they're so funny about that stuff in the store?"

Babe started giggling, and Mama asked him, "What's so funny?"

Babe said, "Gee, I'm sure glad that I'm a guy."

"Hey!" Mama responded quickly, 'The same goes for men! Don't you ever let someone wear your underwear! Oh these crazy kids!" Mama said, as she shook her head while she finished her dinner.

Babe and I kept tapping each other's foot trying not to laugh. Slowly in a very wide-eyed innocent sort of way I asked, "But Mama, that means that I won't have anything to wear this summer."

"Well Madia, we'll go shopping one-day next week."

"Mama," I said, "would it be possible to go shopping downtown? And if we do, do you think that we could see a movie?"

She slammed down her fork and knife and said, "Well, I suppose now we're both to be a couple of movie stars, huh? Well if you want to bullshit around downtown all day, you'll have to take one of your friends! I'm a hard working woman and I don't have time to play around like you!"

I thought, my plan is working perfectly, thank you God!

Then I asked, "But what if I can't find anyone to go with me?"

"Well," Mama said, "Then you just will have to go bare-assed to the beach this year!"

Babe laughed and Mama said, "What are you laughing at? Can't I talk without everyone laughing! Oh, you crazy kids!" She just shook her head, then she stopped and said, "But just remember what I've told you before, that when you *do* go to the show - if you see a Chinese man, don't sit next to him. Because I heard that they're injecting people with opium and killing them – or worse! So Madia, you go, and you have a nice time."

After Mama left the room, we both just started laughing, and Babe said, "What was *that* all about? Chinese guys...Opium...Murder?"

"Who knows Babe? Hey, maybe it's just Mama's way of saying that she cares?" then we just laughed.

Later, as I was doing the dishes, Mama came over and said, "Buy something nice. I don't want to be embarrassed by you when you're at the beach. Remember, people expect us to look nice." With that she handed me two one hundred dollar bills. She then added that this was to be an early birthday present.

I went to hug her and she quickly stepped back saying, "Don't touch me, are you crazy?

You've got soap on your hands!" Then she went back to the bar.

I'm sure that other kids would have just enjoyed the money, but I thought, I'd gladly give it back for one true hug from my Mother.

So once my chores were completed, I went into the bar where I saw Mama engaged in a conversation with a fairly attractive man. I tried to get her attention, but she was lost in conversation. Finally, the man kind of nodded his head toward me and Mama looked over. I started to ask her if it would be ok if I went up to Ewing Avenue for some ice cream. She went back to looking at the man, and without even saying a word to me, she just waved me off. So I took that as a – I'm busy so go do whatever you want, and I was on my way. On my way to Kuma's that is, to make shopping plans.

As I arrived I noticed Kuma in her garden. I yelled to her and she waved me over. She told me that she'd been snipping some flowers for her dining room table. She took a pink rose and put it in behind my ear and said, "Oh, how beautiful you look my precious Madia."

We hugged and kissed then I took the flower out and stared at it. I asked if she had a daisy instead of a rose.

"Now child, she scolded, you're not listening to your Mother again, are you?

Laughingly, I said, "No, I just prefer daisies, that's all."

"Then that's ok. As long as it is *your* choice, and not some crazy made up thing by your Mother."

"Kuma, are you turning into a psychologist or something?"

"No", she said, "but I bet I'd of made a good one though."

Then she got a far-off look to her as she said, "You know Madia, you're so lucky to have been born and raised here. Because in America, things are so very different than where I grew up. Why you can do almost anything that you want here and I know that someday - the way things are going - men and women *will* be equal. And I sure do hope that I'm around to see it!"

"What do you mean, Kuma? What makes you think that they're not?"

"Oh child, we really are. That's my point!" She turned to look at me and smiled, then quickly asked, "Oh, and what about that modeling career?"

"Now Kuma, slow down," I said, "but I do have some great news. What are you doing tomorrow? Mama gave me $200 to buy summer things. So do you want to go downtown?"

She got so excited. She took my hands and started hopping up and down. I asked her if she had lost her mind.

She responded with, "Yes! And I hope I never find it!"

Chapter 21

The next day we got an early start. We met at the South Chicago train station so that no one would spot us together and tell Mama. Yes - I was *that* paranoid and I didn't want anything to wreck my big shopping day with Kuma.

I saw her waiting for me on the platform. She was holding two cups of coffee and as she handed one to me she said, "Child, here you go. Drink this. We'll need all the energy that we can muster up if we're going to do some power shopping at Marshall Field's. She knew that Marshall Field's was my favorite store downtown. Not to say that we wouldn't hit them all, but that *was* my favorite. It was an enormous store. There was floor after floor of some of the most beautiful and elegant things that you could imagine.

While we were shopping, I found the most beautiful bathing suit. It was a black satin two-piece. So I quickly showed it to Kuma on the mannequin, and before I could even ask her for her opinion she yelled, "It's perfect. I just love it...Oh child, you'll not only be the talk of the beach, but it will be great for pictures. Oh, you'll look just like a movie star!"

I shook my head and took her by the arm saying, "Kuma, Kuma, Kuma! Whatever am I going to do with you?"

While I was in the dressing room, Kuma went off and came back with a pair of black satin platform heels.

"Here," she said, "put these on - and don't argue - just do it."

She then told me that since no one was around, that I was to go over to where they had a raised platform area in front of a three-way mirror, that I assumed that they used for long evening gowns, and that I was to stand very tall and strike a pose.

I knew that there would be no living with her until I did it, so I went along with her wishes. And I had to admit, I looked good, not great, but good.

"Oh Madia," she said with glee, "You look superb! You *must* get it, and I'll get you the shoes.

I looked at the tag, and it said $45. "Kuma," I said, "Look, its $45."

"So are the shoes," she said, "and that's a nice round number, $90, yes, I like it!"

"Kuma, I'll buy the shoes, I'm not having you spend your money."

"She snapped back, "I won't hear of it, after all, it'll make me happy. Oh, you know what would be divine with this?" she said, "A large man's cotton shirt. You can use it like a cover-up. Why all you'd have to do is put up the collar and push up the sleeves. I saw it in a movie magazine – everyone's doing it. Now you have to promise me that the first time you wear this to the beach, you'll wear it just that way!"

"Fine." I said, "Whatever you say, you're the boss."

"That's right!" she added, "And I'm going to make you a star! Oh by the way child, stay here for a moment, ok?"

And before I could answer 'sure', she was gone. She came back, of course with a sales lady, and said, "Now, Mary,"...Mary, I thought, she's *never* called me that before. "Mary, strike that pose will you?"

"Certainly, Mr. Ziegfeld." I said, as I smiled at her.

She asked the sales lady, "There...What do you think?"

The woman said, "Why yes, you're quite right, she'd be wonderful."

"My dear," she said, as she now directed her questions to me, "Do you have a portfolio yet?"

Bewildered, I asked, "What kind?"

"Why a modeling portfolio my dear. Because if you really want to be a model, you'll have to start out on the right foot, and the first thing that you'll need will be a portfolio of photographs of yourself."

I thanked her and said that I would take her advice. She then told me that I would have no problem getting work, especially runway modeling because of my height. As she left, I waved my fist at Kuma.

She just laughed, and said, "Oh...go on and change. We have a lot more shopping to do!"

Just then the sales lady came back with a business card of a photographer for me, and Kuma snatched it right up. We said our thank-you's to her and made our way out of that department. Kuma was so excited, that you would have thought that she'd just won a million dollars.

The rest of the day she would say little things like; it's in the cards – I can feel it, you're going to be a star. Mentally, she already had me living in Hollywood. I didn't have the heart to burst her bubble by reminding her that I didn't have any talent, because I could see that she was on cloud nine, and so happy for me...and her.

Well after hours of being in store after store, I was depleted of cash, and I just wanted to get back on the train and head for home. But Kuma was still raring to go! I knew that it was because she was still riding high on the fact that she had a phone number to an *actual* photographer in her purse.

The ride home was relaxing and extremely enjoyable, because I got to see Kuma beaming the entire time. I hadn't seen her this happy since my father was alive, and I knew that where ever he was, he was as happy for her as I was.

Once I returned, I was just about to go in, when my friend Millie, from down the street, came over to me and said that she had to talk to me. That it was a matter of life and death!

I could only think, not today, my feet are killing me, but since she looked so troubled, I said, "Well come on up to the apartment so that I can get these shoes off." And then I had an idea. I said, "Mill, has anyone seen you out today?"

"Why no, I was at our cottage by the lake all day. I just got back now when I saw you."

"Great, want to help me out?"

"Sure Mar," she replied, "What do I have to do?"

So I told her to say that she was with me shopping downtown all day and that I'd tell her why later, Ok?

"Sure thing!" she said, "But I have a crisis that I *have* to talk to you about in private!"

"OK, OK, calm down – let's go inside." We went up the front entrance so that we wouldn't have to go through the bar.

Once we got upstairs, she said, "Let's go in your room and close the door."

As we sat on my bed, she started to tell me about some guy that she met while she was out dancing a few weeks back. But as I opened my purse, I found a note that totally eclipsed whatever it was that Millie was trying to tell me. The note was from Kuma. It read, "My dearest Madia, seeing you today made me realize exactly how much I love you. I always knew it was a lot, but my darling, if I ever would be asked to lay down my life for you, I would. You are the sweetest, dearest, and most wonderful girl that God has ever created, and I am so blessed to have you in my life. I want you to have your money back, plus another $100. That way I don't have to go shopping for your birthday. God bless you and remember, no one will ever love you as much as your Kuma. Well maybe a couple more will come very close later on. Bless you my child, and P.S. No arguments about the money, Ok?

"Mar, aren't you listening?" yelled Millie, "What am I supposed to do?"

"I'm sorry, Mill, I wasn't listening, my Kuma did something so absolutely wonderful."

Hurriedly Millie said, "That's great, but what am I going to do?"

"About what?" I asked.

"About the baby!"

"What baby?" I said.

"My baby!" she exclaimed. "I'm pregnant, and now I don't know what to do!"

I nearly fell off the bed. My friends and I never talked about sex, or anything like that. I was always either playing sports, in some club activity, or being kept busy with the bar. Plus, as far as I knew, you were never to fall deeply in love with a man and be alone with him, otherwise God will bless you with a child; and that is supposed to only happen once you're married.

I thought, well, she *must* really love him; otherwise God would *never* let this happen? (Talk about naïve.)

I asked her, "What *are* you going to do?... Because I don't know nothin' about birthin' no babies."

"Cut it out Mar!" She exclaimed, "This is serious!"

Just then the door opened, it was my mother.

"Hi Mama," I said nervously, "Millie and I were just looking at the things I, ah we, bought."

Coldly she said, "Madia, leave the room, you're not to hear this, now go."

It was so surreal. Mama was stone-faced and Millie looked panicked. I couldn't imagine what was going on. So I just got up and took my purse because if Mama saw the money or the note, I'd be killed. I headed for the door. Once I was out, I wanted to listen at the door, but I had another mission at hand. I quickly went downstairs to the basement and put the money in my underwear. I lit the note on fire and put it in the furnace. Only after that task was done, did I think about what was going on upstairs. I couldn't imagine what Mama and Millie were talking about. So I decided to go back upstairs to see if they were through chatting. I had gone up the back stairs and through the apartment, and just as I got up there Millie was walking out.

I said, "Bye Mill" and she waved back.

She turned and started to say something, but Mama yelled, "Millie, you do as I say, or else!"

Then Millie just nodded, looked down, and made her way down the stairs silently.

Mama, then almost cheerfully, said, "So, did you have a nice time shopping downtown?"

"Yes, but what about Millie, Mama? She's having some trouble that she wanted to talk to me about, but..."

In a flash Mama's mood changed, "You are to *never* ask me about that. *And* you are to *never* talk to her again. She's spoiled, and you're not to hang around with her kind...do you understand?"

"But Mama, you don't understand. I'm not supposed to say anything, but she's going to need me and all her friends, now more than ever! Mama, she's going to have a baby!"

Then, without even a glimpse of emotion, she said, "No she's not. I'll see to that. If her mother knew what kind of daughter she's raised, she would die. So you must pretend that she was never here, or ever even a part of your life. Do you understand me Madia?"

Sensing that anything but an affirmative answer could turn into an instant nightmare, I simply just said, "Yes, Mama, I do."

"And Madia, don't you ever breathe a word of this to anyone, not even your brother, especially him, because he doesn't need to know how dirty and evil women can be. He'll find that out soon enough on his own!" Then she turned and she was gone.

Puzzled by what had just taken place, I went back to my room. As I laid on my bed, I started thinking, do other people lead such action packed lives? For their sake, I certainly hope not.

The entire event was a mystery that had no answers for me, so I just thought, go to bed.

You can try and sort all of this out tomorrow when everyone has had a chance to cool down.

So the next morning, I got a call from my friend Vicky and she wanted to know if I wanted to go to the beach. She lived nearby and said that a few of the kids were going and she wanted to know if I'd go too. I yelled to Mama in the kitchen, "Mama, is it ok if I go to the beach with some of my friends today?"

She yelled back, "Who's going?"

"Vicky" I said. And Mama replied that it would be fine. Babe had poked his head out of his room to tell me that he and his buddies were going too. Then he said that I could use his new bike, because his friend Pete was going to get to use his father's car. Babe's friends were always a little older than him; but he fit in because he always looked like he was their age, because of his height, so he was my younger/older brother. I asked him if I could borrow one of his shirts as a cover-up at the beach. He said yes, so I told Mama that I was going to borrow one of Babe's shirts as a cover-up. I knew that it'd be a lot easier than explaining why I *really* wanted to borrow one. Plus I told her that I really didn't want to spend any money on something that was just going to lie on the sand, and could get blown away or lost. Mama liked that because she thought that I was being frugal *and* I was making sure that I was covered up on my way to the beach. She was always worried that someone was trying to stare at me and get ideas.

When I got to Vicky's, all of the girls, minus Millie, were there. I took off my jeans and opened the shirt to show them my new bathing suit. They all loved it but they said, "You can't wear that. It's just too scandalous!"

"Oh come on." I said, "It's the latest thing at all of the downtown stores."

Vicky said, "So what did your mother think about it?"

I said, "Well let's just say that to avoid any arguments, I did the smart thing…I didn't show her." We all laughed and we were off to the beach!

When we got there I saw some friends and they all wanted to take pictures of me in the suit *and* for the first time, boys were actually noticing me, and it felt great!

Just then, a car pulled up, and my brother Babe jumped out. He looked crazy as he looked me up and down, and said, "You get your ass home right now! You look like a whore!"

I walked right up to him, and said, "Remember one thing, my darling *little* brother, I'm almost two years older than you, and you have *no right* to tell me what I can or cannot do! You're *not* my Father! You're my brother, my *little* brother at that! So run along little boy!"

The second that I turned my back on him and before I knew what was happening, he had grabbed the shirt and ripped it right off my back. He screamed at the top of his lungs, "Well if you want to look like a whore, than you may as well show the world! There everybody, she wants you to look at her, looking like a whore! Here - have an eyeful!"

I turned to him, and said, "Babe, how could you humiliate me like this in front of all of our friends? My God, I'm your sister!"

He stood there coldly, and said as he looked me in the eye, "I have *no* sister."

With that, he threw the shirt into the car, got in, and then they sped away, leaving me standing there wearing nothing but my new bathing suit and shame.

One of the other guys at the park gave me a shirt, and I told Vicky that I had to go home.

Vicky said, "Do you want to get your stuff at my house?"

I just shook my head no.

"See ya Mar, talk to you tomorrow?"

I didn't respond. I just got on my bike and rode away. As I rode down the street I couldn't stop crying. I was feeling so low that I just wanted to die. Then out of the clear blue sky, I saw a great looking guy in a convertible and he was waving at me. I was going to ignore him until he yelled my name, so I stopped. He got out of his car and started to walk toward me.

He had on a beige satin bathing suit, which almost made him look naked, and then I realized that the guy was my old checkers pal, Bill Fisher.

"Hey Mar, you're not leaving are you? It's early."

As he said those words, I thought, gee, he doesn't seem repulsed by my suit, and then he said, "Great suit, you're gonna have to get yourself a baseball bat to keep the guys away."

I smiled and said, "Yeah, but do I get to use it on my family first?"

"Why?" he asked, in a truly sympathetic tone.

So I explained about Babe and told him that I was sure by now Babe had told Mama, and she'd probably react in the same way, if not worse!

"Whoa!" he said, "You've lost the war without even fighting a battle yet. Come on, your mother loves me. She won't get nuts if you're with me, and besides, I think you look just great! I'll be the proudest guy on Ewing Avenue if you'll accept a ride from me."

I looked into his beautiful blue eyes and said, "Why not? You can only die once!"

Jokingly he said, "Oh, you've seen me drive before, huh?" With that he opened up the trunk and put my bike in and we were off.

As I rode with him, I thought, why couldn't everybody be this nice to me? Here was this guy, whom throughout my life has wandered in and out, and he has *always* made me feel special.

As we pulled up, my brother and his friends were just pulling away and Mama was standing by the back gate looking furious.

Bill yelled, "Hey Mary, I'm delivering to you, the most beautiful girl from the beach. Before you say anything, I think she looks great! I think that anybody that doesn't like the way she looks, is just jealous! Now Mary, don't you think that this daughter of yours looks like *real* class? After all satin bathing suits are the in thing, look at mine!" And with that, he stepped out of the car; obviously Mama noticed that he nearly looked naked. He walked around the car to let me out. "Now look Mary," he added, "Don't we look like we fell out of some big time fashion magazine?"

Still nervously distracted by his incredible physique, Mama muttered, "Why Bill, you look so handsome, and Madia, I wasn't upset at all. It's just since Babe's Papa died, he thinks that he has to protect all of us. Why Madia, you do look very nice. Bill, are you hungry? I've got a roast in the oven and if..."

"No Mary, I've got to get home, but thanks anyway. Bye Mary and Bye Mary, see ya!" Then he gave me a wink like – I told you it'd be ok.

After he left, Mama turned to me, and said, "Your brother's right, you *do* look like a whore! And now you're acting like one *too*!" Slap went her hand across my face, and then said, "Now get upstairs, you little bitch and go to your room. I'll deal with you later."

I went upstairs and changed and when I came back down to eat, I encountered Babe and told him that under no circumstances, was he to ever embarrass me like that again!

He apologized and said, "Mar, I didn't know what to do - all the guys were saying what a looker the girl in the black bathing suit was, and when I saw that it was *you*, I didn't know what to do. Now I realize that I should have been proud, but I don't know...I'm really sorry."

So I hugged him and said, "It's ok, but next time you're getting a knuckle sandwich." We both laughed and went into the downstairs kitchen for dinner. As we walked in we were almost oblivious to the fact that Mama was already sitting in there.

She turned and said, "So Babe, I see we're to have dinner tonight with a whore."

Babe said, "Ma, cut it out. I told Mary I was sorry."

"Shut up!" she yelled. "That's your job as the man of the house. You're not *supposed* to let your sister walk around like some cheap little whore, are you? Well are you?"

"No Mama," Babe yelled. "But it's over, ok?" With that he stood up and yelled, "I'm getting out of here…you're both crazy!"

And as he walked through the door Mama reached over, slapped me and said, "See, by you acting like someone special, like some whore, you've driven your brother from his home, you little bitch! Now get out of my sight before I kill you!" She screamed.

So I quickly got to my feet and ran back upstairs. Once in my room I thought, will this day ever end?

I then looked at my packages and thought, this will all blow over, just relax. Emotionally exhausted, I decided to take a little nap. After a couple of hours, I got up and thought, I'll take a nice long bath and put on my new silk pajamas and robe. While in the tub, I heard that Babe had finally made it home and that Mama was trying to be extra sweet to him, because he was still a little upset.

I often wondered what it must have been like to have a mother that would wait on me hand and foot. I always wanted to ask Babe.

As I was drying off I noticed that I had only brought my white silk robe with me. So I tried to dry off especially well, because I knew how transparent silk was when it got wet. As I emerged, I tried to walk as quickly as I could past the kitchen doorway so that the two of them in the kitchen couldn't really see me, when all of a sudden I felt a hand at the shoulder of my robe. And with a mighty tug, I could hear it shred from the shoulder seam all the way down, exposing my buttocks.

It was Mama, and she started yelling, "So, you want to expose yourself... well *there!* I hope you're happy!"

I cried as I ran back to my room, and I could hear Babe yelling at her, asking if she were crazy.

Mama just laughed and said, "I told her I'd get even! So I'll buy her a new Goddamn robe... who cares?"

I lay on my bed thinking that's right Mama, who cares? I'm sure no one.

I felt that way most of that summer, until I realized that every so often it seemed that one person kept popping up, Bill Fisher. It was getting to where every time I'd be out and away from home, I'd bump into him. I thought that either we had a lot in common, or maybe, he liked me...?

Chapter 22

Having graduation on my mind was the only thing that kept me going. Just knowing that every morning I'd be getting up, out and away from Mother and one day closer to freedom, was all I needed. By now every day was a power struggle with her. I didn't know why. She'd always accuse me of seeing boys, even though I'd have loved to have gone on a date, who had the time? Also, the only unhappy times in school, would be when I would run into my old friend Millie. Every time I would try and approach her, she'd run away. It really bothered me, so one day when it was just she and me in the girl's locker room, I stood in her way and said, "Millie, what's the matter with you? I can't stand it, please, what's the matter? You've got to tell me!"

So with tears in her eyes, she looked up at me and finally said, "Oh Mar, I've missed you too, but I promised your mother," she then turned away.

I spun her back around, "My mother? What does my mother have to do with this?"

She looked at me and said, "You remember last summer when I came over and I said that I, I...had a problem? Well your mother helped me out and part of our deal was that I was to *never* associate with you ever again."

"But why Millie, I don't understand?"

She looked at me with a surprised expression and said, "You mean your mother never told you?"

"Tell me what?"

"Mar, didn't you ever wonder about the baby?"

I just looked at her and said, "Well Mil, I just assumed that you lost it or…I don't know?"

She then stared at the ground as she told me that she had an abortion, and that Mama had not only arranged it, but she also paid for it; with the stipulation that she was never to talk to me again.

"But why, Mil?" I asked.

"Well Mar," she said, "Your mother told me that I was no longer a 'good girl' and that she didn't want her daughter to hang around with trash."

With tears in my eyes I just reached out and hugged her saying, "Oh Mil, is that all? You're my friend, not trash. So you made a mistake, but it's over. I'm just glad that you're not mad at me or anything, and besides, we can still hang around at school. Then when school's over, we can do whatever we want!"

She looked at me and said, "Gee Mar, you're swell. What did I ever do to deserve a friend like you? I mean, here you thought that *you* did something wrong…and I assumed that you thought I was trash."

We hugged one another and then both took a deep breath, pulled ourselves together and went into the gym, and for the rest of our lives, we never discussed that summer again.

CHAPTER 23

As the days rolled by, life did take some fun turns, and thanks to a push from Kuma, I got the nerve to finally bring up the subject of modeling school to Mama, and surprisingly, she went for it.

It really was an exciting change for me, plus there was one photographer who really liked me. He would tell me over and over how great my bone structure was, and fabulous my shoulders were, and my smile was so beautiful, and on and on to where there were days where even though I would never dare to say it out loud, but in his photos, I *was* beautiful. Plus he taught me how to walk, stand and basically be a lady.

Things just got better and better, but when it was time for our final shots, he asked me if I knew that in some of the photos I would be required to be shot in only a slip, and that I just had to trust him. Well since I was raised to never trust a man, even ones who are nice – especially ones who are nice, I didn't say anything.

All the way home on the train I debated on what to do. Because I thought on one hand, it's no big deal, I've worn less at the beach. On the other hand, what did he mean by 'only a slip'? Wouldn't that be see-through?

Since it bothered me so much, I thought ok, let me see what the culprit who started this dilemma had to say, so I was off to Kuma's.

When I explained it to her, she said that I wasn't being silly or childish and that many girls were too naive and trusting, and that I was right in telling her. She said that if it made me feel any better, she would go with me. I thanked her and I told her that I'd let her know.

So as I walked home I thought, Kuma took this news very well, and if she came with, I know that nothing bad would happen. But just to be sure, I thought, since its photos that I know somehow, someway, Mama was sure to see them, so I'd better give her a heads up.

Plus, for some reason, I figured with Mama's past, that she would either be supportive or would say, "Who would want to look at an ugly, skinny girl like me anyway?"

Soon I was home and as I walked through the back door of our bar and into the kitchen, I saw Mama at the sink. I asked her if I could talk to her about something serious.

"Now what do you want to bother me with? Can't you see I'm busy? What is it? Are you in some kind of trouble?"

"No Mama, well, I don't know really?"

"Spit it out. I don't have all day."

"Well Mama, the photographer said..."

"Goddamnit! Don't scare me. I thought that it was something important."

Then mocking me she said, "The photographer, the photographer – what – did your face break his camera and he wants me to replace it? Tell him to get his money from your Goddamned Kuma – she started all of this Bullshit! You know Madia, there are more important things to worry about in this world other that YOU! Is it always about you? Who the Hell do you think you are? You're gone all day, so I have to do everything, and now my Goddamned Movie Star daughter has a problem…a photographer? Who the hell cares?"

I thought, just ignore her ranting and ask the question, after all, how much madder can she get?

"Mama this sort of concerns you too. The photographer wants me to do my final photos in only a slip. What should I do?"

Then, with her back to me, she just stopped moving and there was complete silence. Then she calmly turned and stared at me with an intense look on her face. She answered slowly and deliberately as she said, "Would you ever want your children and their friends to look at a photo of you in a see-through outfit? Think about what could happen years down the road. Do you want those kinds of pictures of you floating around?" Then she just turned back around and said, "I didn't raise you to be a whore."

I just looked down at the floor and thought, I still don't know what to do…Then crash went a small stack of three of four plates that Mama threw to the floor. Still with her back to me Mama said, "Now get the fuck out of my sight."

I quickly ran upstairs to our apartment and into my room. Still afraid of what might happen, I stopped and I thought, Mama's right, I'd never thought about it before. I mean, I know how I felt about things that went on with Mama when I was young, and I would *never* want my children feeling that way about me…no, I can't do it. I'd never want any of my children to feel about me the way that I've felt about Mama.

So when the day came around, I called Kuma and the photographer and told them that I was sick. Kuma kept trying to get me to reschedule, but I never went back. Later, when I finally told Kuma of my concerns and what Mama had said, she told me that she understood. She also told me that it was my decision and that she supported me in it 100 percent. She also added, "I will tell you one thing Madia, when you're my age, you'll wish you *had* those photos." Then she smiled and gave me a big hug.

Chapter 24

Modeling was out, but I still had a lot of activities going on with school and everything. One of the things that stand out most was that Christmas. I'll never forget it.

It was early and Mama was getting things ready for the big Christmas buffet that we always put out for our patrons, when there was a knock at our back door. As I answered it, I couldn't believe it. There was Bill Fisher, the phantom man in my life.

"Hi Mar," he said, "Merry Christmas and here's a little something for you." Surprised, I told him that he didn't have to get me anything.

"Come on Mar, I had to."

"Oh really? Why is that?"

"Well because you're a special person in my life and I just thought that you should know it. So here, take it."

With that he grabbed my hand and placed a wrapped gift box in it.

He said, "I've gotta run and get back home. You know what a big family I've got and it'll be a madhouse over there real soon, so Merry Christmas!" He then simply kissed me on the cheek and was gone.

If I wasn't holding the gift in my hand, I would've sworn that it didn't even happen because it was all so fast.

I looked at the present and thought, "Well ok? Don't question it – just go with it."

As I was opening it up, I thought what in the world would *he* get me? He doesn't even know me – not really – what could it be? As I got the last bit of paper off, I saw that it was a square black velvet box. I opened it up and in it was the most beautiful three strand pearl necklace.

I could only think what an unusual guy... and what a *great* gift! Then I thought, I can't keep this, but just then Mama walked in and asked what I had.

I told her the story and then I explained that I simply had to give them back because it just wasn't appropriate for me to accept such an expensive gift from a stranger.

"He's no stranger to this family. He was working around here before you were born. Just keep it."

"But Mama…?"

"Don't but Mama me. Listen Madia, a woman *never* gives back jewelry. If a man is stupid enough to give it to us, we take it, and the only way they get it back, is off our cold dead body. So Merry Christmas! Now get your ass back upstairs."

Chapter 25

Bill Fisher – the man of mystery. Every time I wore or even looked at the pearl necklace, it made me wonder about the thing that he said about me being special. If I was so special, why did he only seem to wander in and out of my life, and not try to ask me out on a date? Maybe because I was Croatian and he was Serbian? Oh well, it certainly didn't stop him from popping up like that during the months leading up to my senior prom. I would catch glimpses of him here and there. He was always smiling, waving and with a different girl…so much for *me* being special. It made me wonder what kind of deal he had with a jeweler and if he got the 'bulk rate' on pearl necklaces. He was the closest thing we had to a playboy in our neighborhood, but he always went out of his way to say hi…and sad to say, I liked it. The truth be told, I used to daydream that he was my secret admirer. But back to reality; it was time for our High School Senior Prom.

I was asked to go and be the date of this guy named Bob, who in a way reminded me of my dear ill fated friend Ken, so I jumped at the chance and said yes!

When I told Mama she said that she didn't know him, and *she* thought that it would be better if I went with someone that *she* knew.

Crushed, I walked from the bar's kitchen where our discussion had taken place, back up front towards the bar and got myself a Coke. I took a seat at the bar near the front window and just stared out into space. How was I going to tell Bob, that now I couldn't go with him? He would have been the perfect date. He was tall, blonde, and handsome and had the most beautiful blue eyes. Plus he was funny, and liked to dance...like I said – perfect!

I thought, I have to find a way to pull this off. There must be a way to sneak around Mama, so that I can go with Bob...but how? While I was sitting at the bar and lost in my plotting, there was a tap on my arm – it was my pal, Bill Fisher. I was oblivious to the fact that he had walked in. came over to me and was trying to get my attention, because I was too busy in my own little world of Prom Espionage. He asked me what was wrong and if I was ok.

So I explained the situation to him and he told me that he would try to help. He asked where Mama was and I pointed to the back. He smiled at me, winked and was gone. He was back in a flash, and Mama was following right behind him.

Mama said, "Madia, what Bill just said to me in the kitchen made a lot of sense. So you go with that nice boy and have a wonderful time." As I got up to thank her and before I could say anything to her, she just simply walked away. Confused, I turned to Bill and asked him what he could have possibly said to her that would've made her change her mind so quickly.

He just headed out the door, paused for a second and said, "Well Mar, I guess that I'm just a smooth talker. I gotta run – see ya around." And he continued out the door. I followed him out in the hope that he might slow up long enough to tell me something, but all he did was yell back to me as he was crossing the street, "Have a good time at the Prom!"

I yelled, "Thanks Bill!" and he was gone.

Just then the pay phone by the front door started to ring. As I approached the phone I looked out the door and I caught a quick glimpse of Bill driving away in his convertible, and I thought, either I'm getting older or he's getting younger, because I sure could go for somebody like him...oh well.

I said, 'Hello' into the phone and it was Kuma, who by now was using a fake voice on the phone until she was sure that she had actually reached me. We figured out that it would be best if she had to call, plus it gave her a chance to try and impersonate one of her favorite movie stars. One time she's Bette Davis, and another time she could be James Cagney – you never know.

After hearing a voice that sounded like Katherine Hepburn asking for me, I said, "Hi, what's up Kate?" I was always careful not to mention a name other than her character. She wanted to know how it went with Mama and if we were off to buy a prom dress? I told her yes and that we'd be going tomorrow. I told her that I had a very unusual story for our train ride.

She said, "Oh I love intrigue! Is it a good love story? Does it involve romance?"

"I don't know...but I'll call you back - Bye for now!" I hung up and went upstairs and called my friend Vicky. I told her that I needed a cover for tomorrow. Would she either call or drop by and leave a message with Mama, that we would be going dress hunting?

"Sure kiddo!" replied Vicky, and then she said, "Mar, what 'is' the deal between your godmother and your mom?"

"Oh Vick, it goes so far back that I don't even remember a time when they *did* like each other. All I know is that it turns into the 4th of July around here, at the very mention of the name Kuma. Well I've got to go." And jokingly, I said, "See ya tomorrow!"

Giggling as I hung up the phone, I sprang to my feet and there was Mother. Nervously I smiled and said, "Oh hi, Mama - you startled me, I didn't hear you come in."

She stood there for a moment, looking at me coldly, before she finally said, "Madia, who was on the phone?"

"It was Vicky, Mama, why?"

She slapped me and said, "Don't fucking lie to me, you little bitc., Now who was it?" she demanded.

With tears in my eyes, I rubbed my cheek and said again, "It was Vicky. Honestly Mama, I wouldn't lie!" Slap again went her heavy hand.

"Why you little fucking liar. I just heard you on the phone and you were talking to that bitch, Kuma!" she screamed.

Shaking my head, while trying to gain some control I said, "No Mama, Vicky and I were talking about her godmother, and then she asked if I had one. I was just explaining how you and she don't get along anymore, and that you haven't for years - that's all. Please Mama, call her back yourself and ask her if you don't believe me!"

She just stood there and said, "Well Madia, I don't! So you dial her number for me and I'll ask her myself!"

I dialed and there was no answer, so I tried again and there was still no answer. Looking victorious, she stood there and said, "Well *liar* – what do you have to say for yourself *now*?"

I told her how Vicky said that she might stop by, and...

Laughing, Mama said, "And just how fucking *stupid* do you think I am, you lying bitch? I'll fix you up. So you said that she might come by? Well, we'll see!"

With that, she quickly ripped the phone wire out of the wall and said, "See? This way you can't call and arrange anything with her, and then we'll see *if* you're telling me the truth!"

She turned and started winding the phone cord around the now dead phone, as she stormed back through the apartment. While she was walking away I got up and as I was making my way back to my room, I ran my foot accidentally into a chair, and mumbled, "Son of a bitch!" By the time I made it to my door way, I felt a presence behind me. I turned and there was my Mama looking outraged and wielding the phone.

She screamed at me, "How dare you call your Mother a bitch? You ungrateful, lying little whore!" And with that, I saw the black phone heading straight for my face. I turned, but I was too late. The receiver caught me in the nose and eyes and the base of the phone caught my back and shoulder.

"Mama," I screamed, "Please don't. I wasn't calling you that, I was talking to the chair. See how red my last two toes are? I ran into the chair that's all. I'd never say anything like that to you, never!"

By then I was too late. She had lifted up the phone once again and it came crashing down hitting me with full blown force in the face. I heard my nose break from the force of the blow. Then again, this time to my left shoulder. The third blow went straight into my back. I felt an electrical shock go up my spine and whatever nerve she hit, dropped me to the floor and I couldn't move – not even to wipe the blood that was pouring out of my nose. She kicked me and screamed, "Get up you little lying fucking bitch!"

She stopped and didn't say another word. She walked away silently.

Wracked with pain and seeing that I could now move, I tried to get away, even though the pain was getting more and more intense. I crawled into my bedroom and pulled myself up and flopped onto the bed, not knowing what to do first; rub my foot, back or face. All of a sudden a cold wash cloth came flying through the door way and I could hear Mama's muffled voice saying that my nose was bleeding. I grabbed the rag and put it on my face. I could feel that the bridge of my nose seemed too close to one side. I gathered all the strength that I could and I sat up long enough so that I could get a glimpse of my face in the mirror. My left eye was almost completely shut and my nose leaned to the right. I couldn't believe it. I had to get closer to the mirror. It was worse than I thought. My nose looked so funny that I thought I've got to do something quickly so that it doesn't mend like this. I took a deep breath and thought – It's now or never! So I pushed my nose back where it belonged. I heard it click inside. The pain was blinding. I thought that I was going to faint, but had to get it back in place. I'd seen it done a hundred times before downstairs, because there was always a fight over something. I held the washcloth there and applied pressure as I laid back on the bed. I just kept saying to myself, "Soon it'll be graduation and I can get the hell out of here, and away from her forever!"

All of a sudden I heard a familiar voice yell up, "Mary, are you up there? It's me, Vicky!" I thought to myself, thank you God, please have her give the right information to Mama.

Once upstairs, she took one look at me, and all of the blood and said, "Oh My God! What happened to you? Should we call an ambulance? Does your Mother know? Who did this to you?"

I put my hand up to my mouth to shush her and said, "Don't worry about me. Did you talk to Mama? What did you say?"

Looking puzzled Vicky said, "Well yeah, I just got done talking to her. She's the one that sent me up here to see if you needed help, because you tripped and hurt yourself, but I wasn't expecting a murder scene. There's blood everywhere! You've got to go to the hospital. What the heck did you trip over…an elephant?"

I stopped her long enough to say, Vic, I'll be ok. I just need your help getting me into the bathroom so I can get cleaned up."

"Ok Mar, but before we do that, what do you say we get some ice in the kitchen for that face? I'll have more room to help clean you up."

"Sure," I said as we walked toward the kitchen. I asked Vicky again to tell me word for word, everything that was said between her and Mama. As she started, a strange look came across her face. She looked me straight in the eye and said, "Tell me the truth Mar. Your Mother did this, didn't she?"

I looked down, nodded yes and said, "But it doesn't matter. It happens all the time. I'm used to it by now."

She stood up and said, "Mar, are you crazy? No one is *ever* supposed to do something like this to you, *especially* not your Mother, for God's sake! You have to tell somebody about this before she kills you!"

Suddenly the back door from the porch to the kitchen opened, and standing there was Mama. She slowly walked in, nervously smiling and said, "Madia, Vicky explained everything, and here is some money for a new dress and accessories. There's also some extra money so that you can treat Vicky to a wonderful lunch downtown tomorrow."

She then turned and walked away, leaving three $100 bills on the table. Vicky just sat there with her mouth hanging open and said, "I can't believe it. She didn't even say that she was sorry to you! What good is this cash? Is this supposed to erase what she's done to you? Oh kiddo, no one knows what you've had to go through, do they?"

"Oh Vic," I said as I got up and walked over to the window, "It's not so bad, honestly, after all…I'm still alive aren't I?"

She walked over to me and said, "Physically sure, but Mar, it's gotta hurt inside?" With that she put her hand on my shoulder. I winced with pain and she asked me to take off my blouse.

"Here?" I asked.

"Sure Mar, I want to see if there's a bruise."

"Oh no Vic, let's go to my room. If I take my blouse off here, Mama will kill me."

"Well it wouldn't take much more at this rate, but ok, whatever you say Mar."

We slowly made our way back to my room with the ice and some towels. Once safely inside my room, I slowly tried to take off my blouse, but it hurt to lift my left arm, so Vicky helped me. Even though I couldn't see the bruise, the look on Vicky's face told me that it had to be a doosy.

Looking shocked she said, "What did she do, shoot you out of a cannon or something? I've never seen anything like this …not even in the movies."

I turned so that I could get a good look for myself in the mirror. I thought to myself, Oh my God, that's turning into the biggest and blackest bruise that I've ever seen! Trying to make light of it for Vicky's sake I said, "Well I think a strapless is out, don't you?"

We both giggled, then Vicky stopped abruptly and said, "Mar, quit making jokes… this is serious!"

I just looked at Vicky and said, "Please Vic, be my friend, and don't say anything about this to anyone, ok?"

She nodded yes and with tears welling in her eyes and said, "Mar, you must be the bravest and strongest girl I've ever met. I'm awfully glad that you're my friend."

"I'm glad that you're mine too Vic. Hey, why don't you come with me tomorrow? I'll treat you to lunch at 'The Burghoff'. It's a wonderful restaurant and the waiters are pretty cute too."

"Thanks Mar but I can't. I have to help my brother, but call me when you get back so that we can come up with some story to tell your Mother about what a *wonderful* day we had, ok?"

We both laughed, I think to stop from crying. Soon she had me all cleaned up and wanted me to lie down, but I didn't want to go to sleep. I told her that I remembered hearing someone say that it's best to sit up in a chair to help with facial swelling or bruising or something like that, so I sat up in a chair in the living room, and she brought over an ottoman for my feet. She got me a glass of ice water, blew me a kiss and was on her way.

No sooner had she left when old Tony came up to bring me a plate of food. "Hello Madia," he said, "your Mama said you should eat upstairs tonight." Then he looked at me and said, "Oh my God Madia…were you in a car accident or something?"

"No car accident Tony, but it was something like that. I tripped over a chair in the apartment."

He walked away with an 'Oh…I understand', look on his face. Then he paused at the door, looked back at me and then at the ground. He shook his head as he walked away. I sat there thinking to myself, why is everybody making such a big deal about this? Then it hit me. Was I so used to this type of abuse that I've been numbed by it? Maybe this type of treatment really *was* horrible and I had just become unaware of its severity because it was so commonplace for me. I thought for a minute and it made me look at it in a different perspective. I know that if I walked in on Vicky and she looked like this, I would be outraged. I guess after being told all my life that I was no good, and worse yet, that I was made to *feel* as though I 'was' nothing, it had finally caught up with me. The conversation went on in my head, after all, I was a living, breathing, human being and so what if I am 'female'? Some of the most admired people in the world and throughout history are women. Why was I letting all of those negative words from my Mother affect me so much? I needed to change deep down inside how I really felt about me – and soon! I couldn't believe that I finally was having a revelation. I decided that my life would start to become meaningful, if not to anyone else, then to me! It was like the fog that I was living in had lifted. It hit me that the most important thing of all was to be important to yourself: today, tomorrow, and always – and never tolerate this type of behavior – especially from someone that is supposed to love you.

And all through that night, I would re-cap some of the most gruesome moments of my life and think, 'My God, I survived them all and I'm still here!' I was finally feeling good about me and thought, once I'm out of high school,

I'm going to get a life, far, far away from my mother. If she wants to be miserable, over the fact that she was a woman, well then that's fine for her, but it's not for me. All of the things that Kuma had said to me throughout my life came flooding into my brain and I finally knew that she was right. It was going to be a new day for me from now on.

KINDERGARTEN GALLISTEL SCHOOL

Chapter 26

In the morning while I was getting dressed, I had already made up my mind that I'd have to lie to Kuma. It would kill me to, but I wanted us to have an enjoyable day. As I entered the bar to say that I was off shopping, the bar was already half filled with patrons. Somebody asked if I'd gotten the number of the truck that hit me.

I said, "I think that I'd fallen down the stairs or was it that I walked into a door…I'm not really sure anymore? I think you'll have to ask my mother what it was that happened."

Mama just stood there motionless. It felt so empowering to be a bit snide when it came to Mama and her lies…especially with people around so that Mama couldn't retaliate.

I yelled 'bye' to everyone, then Mama yelled for me to be careful.

I quickly turned and feeling like I was Joan Crawford, I stared at my mother and said "I intend to be. That's why I'm not going with you. Good day Mother." I smiled and quickly turned around and went out the door.

Feeling victorious, but still shaky, I never realized it before, but having an audience made it so easy to stand up to Mama. I also knew that eventually I'd have to go home and have to be with her alone. It wasn't going to stop me because I was going to have a glorious day with Kuma. The one woman I knew who *really* relished in being a woman and who always told me that it was always a blessing to be born a woman. Once she told me, that you can be born female, but it's an acquired art to become 'a woman'! Once you've become one, you would never need anything or anyone to make you feel good about yourself.

She was always so wonderfully melodramatic.

I saw her waiting at the entrance to the train platform. She noticed me and started waving, but as I got closer to her, she stopped and pulled out her glasses to try and figure out what had happened to me.

I yelled, "Hello Kuma...what do you think of your movie star now?" Looking concerned, she asked what had happened. I made up some story about how the stairs to the basement were wet and that I had slipped.

I said, "Now don't worry. The doctor said that everything's just fine, ok?"

She gave me a look like, "I don't really believe you, but we're here to have fun so it'll have to do...for now."

I grabbed her by the arm and told her that I had a surprise. I explained to her that Mama had given me money to buy a prom dress and that she had to guess how much.

First she said, "A hundred dollars?"

I shook my head no.

"Two hundred?"

I still shook no and held up three fingers.

"You mean to tell me that your mother gave you three hundred dollars to buy a dress?"

"Yep. Mama gave me three hundred to get a dress, complete with shoes and accessories."

She looked straight ahead and mumbled loud enough for me to hear, "Maybe if she'd have broken your arm, you'd have gotten a thousand."

I tugged her arm and just laughed.

You could never fool Kuma and I was sure at some point during the day I'd hear a speech. But for now, we just settled for girl talk. I brought up how I was going to the prom with a handsome young man, named Bob, and that he reminded me so much of her neighbor's late nephew, Ken.

"Kuma," I said, "You know if Ken hadn't died, I know we'd have gotten married. Sure there were other boys, but he was different - not to mention how just being near him made me tingle all over. Is that true love Kuma?"

Then I asked, "Is that how you felt about your husband?"

The train was crowded and so we had to sit across from each other. I noticed that as she started to talk, how peaceful, yet teary eyed she looked.

She started, "Oh child, that's definitely love. It's meant to be beyond wonderful. I do know how you feel, but there are times that even though you love someone with your whole heart and soul, you can never have them." Then she just gazed out of the window.

I said, "But Kuma you were married to him, for a while at least, so you really know what it's like."

She went on, now with tears rolling down her face and being trapped in her handkerchief.

"No Madia, the man that I *truly* loved was married to someone else. He was....never mine."

"Kuma tell me the truth. Was that man my father?"

She turned and smiled at me and said, "You're such a clever girl. You've known all the time haven't you?"

I nodded yes and said, "Even as a child, I could see that your eyes and his, would light up, at the mere mention of each other's name."

"Do you hate me child? After all, he was your father."

I grabbed her hands and said, "If two people love each other, how could it be bad, especially when they *should* have been together all along."

She looked at me and said, "Have I told you how much I love you?"

I nodded yes and said to her, "Kuma, if it's possible, I love you twice as much, and to me, you'll always be my *real* Mother. I know that not only do you love me, but you dearly loved my father and I know that he loved *you* very, very much. I saw how much his heart would break every time you'd leave us after a visit."

All of a sudden, a little chubby lady in a big flowered hat started to cry, and in her Irish brogue she said, "That's so beautiful, but please stop. I can't take anymore. This is such a sad, yet beautiful conversation. I'm so sorry for eavesdropping, but I couldn't help myself."

Kuma and I looked at each other and then back at her, and knew that this was a major moment in both of our lives. I could tell that she wanted to tell me more, but there'd be a better time and place. Plus, we had to keep trying to console the flowered hat lady. The lady told us her name was Bessie. She started telling us about her life, and how she should've married a Frenchman, who was the love of her life. She monopolized most of the conversation during the train ride, and I would periodically catch Kuma smiling at me as we both listened to Bessie's tale. I could tell that she was happy to have had my approval and acceptance of her feelings toward my late father. Finally Bessie's story was winding down, so I jumped in and started to bring up my story about Bill Fisher, and how something he told Mama in private, made it ok for me to attend the Prom with Bob. I told her about how lately everywhere I go - he's there.

She said, "Oh child, you're probably just imagining these things…or maybe he likes you."

"Kuma, I was wondering the same thing. He's really gotten to be quite handsome with age, but he's got to be *at least* ten years older than me."

She smiled and before I could ask her what was really going on in her mind, I noticed that we were getting ready to reach the first Loop Area stop.

Kuma said, "Let's get off at the last stop, over on Randolph Street, so we can go right to Marshall Field's first. We may as well start at the best!"

Chapter 27

Once in the store, I got a little nervous as we approached the more expensive dresses. We were greeted by a saleslady and she remarked how we looked so familiar and that there were just a few seats left for the Fashion Show, so we'd better hurry.

She said, "I'm so glad that the two of you could make it to the private showing of our new arrivals from Paris. Weren't the invitations simply lovely?

"Oh yes," said Kuma.

I looked at her and she gave my arm a squeeze, so I kept my mouth shut. "My niece is just recovering from a terrible skiing accident and I thought that this might be the perfect thing to cheer her up."

The lady said, "Where do you find snow in May?"

Kuma, not missing a beat said, "Switzerland of course. It's the *only* place to ski this time of year you know."

The lady agreed and led us into the private showing area. There were only about two dozen women or so and their clothes alone, looked like a fashion show.

I nudged Kuma and said, "What's with the lie about Switzerland? You were never there."

"Yes I was," she said, "I rode through on a train as a child."

"Well, *I* was never there, Kuma."

"Who knows child?" she went on, "You're young, and maybe one day you will. Now let's sit down."

I shook my head and sat down. Before I knew it, I was in awe as I got to view the most beautiful clothes I'd ever seen. Outfit after outfit, one was prettier than the next. After I thought that I had seen all that I could see, in came the evening apparel. The gowns were breathtaking and then, there it was. The most beautiful gown that I'd ever seen. It was strapless and made of silver satin with a combination of light blue, silver and white organza and chiffon. On the front was a starburst of sequins, beads and rhinestones that seemed to trickle off into infinity throughout the gown. It came with a sort of throw/boa sort of wrap made of organza. It too was dusted with the same sparkles. It also had something that I'd never seen before, custom shoes made to order. They were made of the same fabrics as the dress, plus they had the same matching starbursts covering the top of the toe area. The model wore long, pale bluish, gray gloves that were beaded. To top it off, she was wearing a single large rhinestone cuff bracelet. She looked magnificent!

I thought, my God, she had dark hair and eyes like me. I turned to Kuma and said, "I know I could never afford it, but do you think they'd at least let me try it on?"

I could see the wheels turning in Kuma's head. So after the showing, Kuma told me to stay seated and that she had some wheeling and dealing to do. I tried to stop her, but she was off.

In the meantime, the model who had worn the gown came out and sat down near me. I leaned over and said, "My, you looked just lovely in the last dress. Do they ever let you keep any of the clothes?"

She politely smiled and said, "No."

Then she asked what had happened to my face.

"Oh…a skiing accident." I said. I didn't know why I lied. I think I'd just been around Kuma too long.

"Too bad." she replied coldly, and she said, "So, are you going to be buying the dress?"

"Oh I could never afford it. I'm not rich. I only have $300 to spend, and that has to include shoes, lunch, train fare and I'm sure that it costs a lot more than that."

She laughed and said, "You had me going for a minute kid. Skiing accident? That's pretty good. So what really happened to you?"

I gave her a Reader's Digest version of the story, and then added how I was going to my high school senior prom and was looking for a dress.

I got up enough nerve to ask her what the actual price was for the complete blue dress ensemble.

She looked at me and said, "$1200.00."

"For a dress?" I said "Oh my God, who has that kind of money?"

She said, "Jerks, that's who. Then she paused for a minute and said, "I've got an idea kid. Wait here and don't move!"

Off she went in a hurry, she almost knocked Kuma down, who was just returning.

Kuma seemed a little startled by the girl's fast getaway and said, "She's in a hurry!"

She sat down next to me and took my hand and said, "Child, I love you - but do you know how much that entire ensemble costs?"

I said, "It's $1200.00."

Looking baffled she said, "Good guess child. You're exactly right."

I giggled and had to confess my conversation with the model.

Kuma said, "Well I'm sorry but there's not a dress in the *world* worth $1200.00…unless a trip to Paris comes with it!"

I looked at her and said, "Would you settle for Switzerland?"

She said, "Why, you're never going to let me forget that now, are you?"

"No never." I responded and we both giggled like a couple of school girls. All of a sudden we heard all kinds of yelling coming from the back. The model burst through the draped doorway and as she hurriedly walked by me she said, out of the corner of her mouth, "Have a great time at the prom, kid!" She winked and just kept going.

I looked at Kuma and she looked at me, but before either one of us could speak two men and a woman, all screaming at each other half in French, half in English, came through the same drapes holding the dress.

Kuma just had to know what was going on. She deliberately walked over to them and said, "Excuse me, is there something I can do?"

"No Madam," the man exclaimed, "There's nothing that *anyone* can do."

"It is ruined, because of that stupid model! She tore the underlay of the gown with her big clumsy feet! Who would pay good money for a gown that has now been turned into a rag?"

I stood up and said, "Me! That's *if* the matching shoes fit, then maybe we can talk, ok?"

He looked surprised and then said, "First let me see if she's destroyed them too!"

After he left, Kuma looked at me and said, "That was some quick thinking child. You learn fast."

I grabbed her hand and said, "Well I had a wonderful teacher."

She went on how she could fix that dress, so that no one could ever tell. Then the man appeared and said, "Well, these shoes were made for an adult model and not a young lady such as you, so they're probably going to be too big. But here, let me get someone to help you. I took them right out of his hand and thought, even with a broken toe on one foot and a large bent toe on the other, I'll make them fit! Since they were worn before, maybe they were stretched to where they would fit. I had to give it a try, so I stood up and said, "I don't have to wait for a saleswoman." With that I slipped them right on.

They fit perfectly, so I turned to the gentleman and said, "I'll give $300 cash, if you'll throw in the bracelet, gloves and wrap."

He said, "But those shoes are one-of-a-kind, and they alone are worth a hundred dollars."

I said, "Well of course they are. I know that, and I also know that they are one-of-a-kind to a dress that's now a rag…so do we have a deal?"

He looked at the assistant and the saleslady, and said, "Deal. I'll get the dress boxed."

"No," I said, "I'd like to try it on."

So before he could change his mind, I opened my purse and took out the three one hundred dollar bills. I said, "Here," to the saleslady, "Now where's the dressing room?"

They quickly hustled showing us the way, and treated us like we were the Rockefeller's or something.

Once Kuma and I were in the dressing room alone, I let out a sigh of relief. "Oh Kuma, I was so scared. I can't believe we pulled it off!"

Kuma said, "Not we, *you*. You did it all on your own. Oh child, I think you're beginning to grow up."

I was so excited about putting the dress on but then thought, with all of my big talk, what if the dress doesn't fit? I told Kuma that I was worried and she said, "Don't worry child, we'll make it fit."

As I got undressed I could see the shock on Kuma's face, because she finally got her first glimpse of all of my bruises, especially the large bruise on my back. She went to touch it and then stopped, asking me if it hurt. "Don't worry, I'm fine." I said. "And besides Kuma, you're missing the best part…it fits."

She took my hand while still eyeing the bruise and said, "No dress is worth this." Then she looked into my eyes and said, "Madia, you must promise me that you'll never again, let something like this happen to you. Especially from someone who is *supposed* to love you. It's wrong child."

I could see that she was dead serious and I told her that once school was over, I was going to be free of everything and everybody…except for her.

She smiled but I could see tears forming in her eyes and she turned away.

As I was getting changed I could tell that she didn't even realize that she had mumbled out loud, "I could kill that woman myself."

I tried to change the subject by saying, "You know Kuma, if we went home right now, we might have time to try and repair the dress so that I could bring it home with me,…otherwise Mama might get suspicious."

Kuma, trying to compose herself said lovingly, "Don't worry child, I can get this done in no time." She just smiled at me and said, "It'll be ok. I promise."

All the way back on the train Kuma was rather silent. I asked her what was wrong. She tried to tell me that she was just thinking about mending the dress, but I knew that seeing me hurt, also hurt her.

I responded with, "I don't know Kuma. You're not as good of a liar as you used to be."

She looked at me with a smile and said, "Only to you child, only to you."

Chapter 28

Once at Kuma's, the dress was fixed before I knew it. I remarked how extraordinary I thought she was. Her only reply was that she thought that I was also.

"Now run home Madia, or else we'll have to find crutches that match this dress."

I looked at her and said, "Now Kuma, be nice!"

She told me that she didn't have to be nice, as she headed me toward the door. She gave me a big hug and told me to hurry along.

When I got home, I immediately ran up to my room to try it on again. Once I was by myself alone, standing there looking at my reflection in the mirror, the reality of how beautiful the gown was, against my battered body, hit me. I started to cry as I stood there thinking, I'll never look normal by prom. Just then Mama entered my room.

The moment was surreal, because I didn't know if her look of surprise was for my dress, or for me. In a way it had almost seemed as the beating was a Godsend, because it showed me that my mother was human. I say this because it was the first time I'd ever seen a remorseful look in her eyes. I suppose that the harsh realization of the fact that she could see actual evidence of her mistreatment of her daughter was too much for her to bare.

She only told me how beautiful the dress was and how pretty I would be at the prom, then she quickly exited my room and didn't bother me for the rest of the day.

As I sat there in my room, I could only look at the dress, that now hung from my closet door frame, and think, if these bruises don't go away no one will ever get to see this spectacular gown. Then the phone rang and it was Vicky. I told her about my dilemma. She told me that her mother had some makeup designed for varicose vein coverage and that it would be *perfect* to cover the bruises. She said she'd be right over.

"Oh and Vic," I said, just in case Mama was listening in the other part of our apartment, "Did you ever see such a beautiful silver blue gown?" Picking up on it, she said, "I get ya Mar. Kiddo, you'll be the belle of the ball!"

I thanked her, not for the compliment, but for being a good friend.

By the time she showed up I was sitting in the bar, having a coke, and Mama was bartending.

"Hi Mar," I mean, "Mary" she said. "I've got the stuff."

"What stuff?" Mama asked.

I thought, well, let's go for broke. "Oh Mama, since the dress is strapless, I didn't want the bruises from the accident to show, so Vicky told me that her mother had some special makeup that might cover it. I guess I could try to get a tan too...because I wouldn't want people to think that you beat me."

Mama didn't say a word or react.

I smiled and took Vicky by the hand and we both ran upstairs giggling.

Once we were in my room with the door closed, I looked at Vicky and said, "Vic, did you see Mama? She didn't say a word."

But Vicky had noticed the dress and I lost her. She didn't hear a word that I was saying, because she just kept going on and on about how beautiful the dress was. As I slipped off my blouse, I could see the look on Vicky's face change, as she got another look at my bruises, which had gotten even darker.

Vicky realized that she was staring and quickly turned around and said, "Well, let's get to work and see if this stuff is as good as my Mom says."

As she began applying the makeup, she stopped and asked, "Let me know if this hurts, ok Mar?"

"Vic, don't worry. I'm pretty tough."

Shaking her head, she said, "You'd have to be, in order to go through what you've been through."

I just shrugged it off and thought, I can't think about any of that right now. I just stared at my beautiful dress hanging there, waiting to be put on.

When she was done she said, "Mar, look in the mirror and see what you think."

I took a hand mirror and looked at my reflection and it didn't look too bad.

"Thanks Vic. It's perfect!"

But I couldn't get an answer out of Vicky because she was going on and on about the dress.

I thought – well that's half the battle – but now let's see what my face will look like in a week.

Chapter 29

A week had passed by and it was the morning of my prom. After my bath I stood in my room and after surveying myself, I thought, well the bruises are still there, but the makeup *should* cover them completely. No one will ever be able to tell. This was already looking like it was going to be a great day.

Kuma had made an appointment for me to get my hair done. It wasn't at a local place either, because she wanted it to be special. I was going to a beauty salon in South Shore, a very affluent area where everything was very exclusive…and expensive. I was to have my hair done, make up applied, a manicure and even a pedicure. I had always been leery of anyone seeing my feet, let alone touching them, but I was feeling so unstoppable that I couldn't believe I was going to actually do it. It was all like one big dream.

I had worked it all out with Vicky. She was going to cover for me. But while I was downstairs, the pay phone rang, and before I could get to it, a bar patron answered it and said that it was my friend Vicky and she was just checking to see if I was on time.

I took the phone, conscious of the fact that Mama was eavesdropping, and said, "Sure Vic, everything's swell."

But in actuality, I was conversing with Kuma. She said she'd pick me up three blocks away, as usual.

I said, "Bye Vic, see you soon!"

Mama came around the bar and reached for the phone receiver and said, "Why Madia, you didn't say hello to your friend Vicky for me, but that's ok, I'll do it myself." She ripped the phone out of my hand and said, "Hello Vicky", and then turned toward the front door and said, "That was fast."

My heart sunk as the door behind me clicked and I heard Vicky's voice say. "Ready to roll Mary?"

As Mama hung up the phone she said, "Madia, I have something *very* important that I need to speak to you about – in private. Come with me to the kitchen. Now."

"Oh Mama," I said nervously, "I'll be late for my appointment at the beauty shop."

Almost sarcastically Mama said, "Oh then you run along dear. And while you're gone, I'll press your dress for you."

Oh My God, I thought, she's going to destroy it if I go! So even though I knew that it meant trouble, I knew that I'd better go into the kitchen or else. With every step that I took, I tried not to let myself envision any kind of unpleasantness. This was supposed to be the best day of my life.

Before we actually made it into the kitchen, I said, "Mama, I know that you want me to have a nice day, so can we discuss this tomorrow?" I turned to walk away when I felt her hand grab hold of the back of my hair. It almost knocked me backwards as she dragged me through the doorway to the kitchen.

Mama spoke in a low tone, so that only I could hear her. She whispered in my ear, "So you're still a fucking liar, – aren't you?"

She gave a sharp yank to my hair and said, "If you scream…well then, I won't care if the whole fucking world watches me kill you, - you little bitch!"

With tears in my eyes, I decided that I had to try and explain, even if it did mean my death, because I was sick of being a liar. So I said, "Ok Mama, you want the truth? Here it is. Kuma is going to treat me and Vicky to a day at an expensive beauty salon on South Shore Drive, that's all! I know you hate her so I didn't want to upset you. That's the truth!"

In a surprised tone she said, "That's it?… That's your big secret? I don't give a shit if that stupid bitch wants to spend her dead husband's money on you. Take everything that bitch ever offers you. That's all she's good for is her money."

She stopped for a moment and with a half cocked smile, she looked me up and down and coldly said, "It's only going to take *one* day to try and do something with that ugly face of yours? Well my darling daughter, I don't think one day will be quite enough. You should have been there a week ago!"

Bravely and without even looking at her, I said, "When Mama...When I was all black and blue?"

Slap, went her hand against my face, as she screamed, "Shut up!...Shut up! I don't want you to ever bring that up to me again or else I'll..."

I rubbed my face and said, "Or else what Mama? You're going to kill me, right? Well Mama, you can only die once and as long as I live here, I'm already dead. But don't worry Mama, after graduation you'll never see me again. I'm moving out."

"Where?" she yelled, "Where would a stupid girl like you go?"

I looked coldly at her and said, "Anywhere Mama, as long as I am far away from you."

Then 'Mama's look' changed. It was somewhere between shock and fear. After a second or two of silence, she smiled and nervously said, "No Madia, my Madia, you must promise me that you'll *never* leave me. Please, please promise me that you'll stay with me forever."

It scared me because I've never seen or heard her act like this before. It was as though time had stopped.

"Ok Mama...but I have to go now. It's getting late." I walked slowly away, trying to assimilate all that had just transpired. I'm sure I looked like I'd seen a ghost as I walked back to the bar.

Mama poked her head out of the kitchen and yelled to us, "You girls go and have a good time."

As I approached Vicky, she asked if everything was alright. I just nodded and said, "Let's go. We'll be late."

As I was walking out, I stopped and looked back toward the kitchen. There was my mother still standing there...looking small, sad and alone. I could only think, maybe this was her way of trying to tell me that she loved me.

Vicky broke the awkward silence by asking if we should take the dress to her house for safe keeping. I told her it would be fine right here and I looked at her and said, "And so will I, come on."

Outside I made Vicky promise not to say a word of this to Kuma. She nodded yes and said, "Come on, let's get beautiful!"

Chapter 30

The salon was amazing, like something you'd see in a movie, and I told Kuma that if this was all a dream, I didn't want to wake up.

I hadn't seen Vicky since they whisked her out from the hair dryer to do her makeup and then I spotted her, or what I thought was her.

They turned her around toward me and Vicky looked beautiful. She smiled and said, "Get a load of you!"

"Me? Vicky it's you that looks amazing."

"Oh yeah, just wait." and then they turned me around. I was speechless. I didn't even know myself...but I liked what I saw. For the first time in my life, I could actually see for myself, what Kuma had seen in me. I realized that I wasn't ugly, and it was all due to the handiwork of a rather flamboyant man named Arthur. He did my make up, and of course Kuma went through her Hedy Lamarr routine, which he loved and went along with completely. I heard their chatter but I was so engrossed with the surroundings and the people, that I really didn't pay attention to what Arthur and Kuma had been going on about. When I finally saw their finished product – me – I was in shock.

I looked at Arthur and said, "Arthur, you truly are an artist."

He said, "Why thank you Miss Lamarr, but it's easy when you have the perfect canvas to work with."

I smiled and quickly changed the subject, since I didn't take compliments well, and just joked about how I've never had that much make up on before in my entire life. I told them both that Mama would not be happy about all of this and that I probably was going to get in trouble...again.

Arthur told me that if I got thrown out of the house, I could always move in with him and his friend, Anthony. I just laughed and thought, gee whiz, there were so many amusing and unusual people out there in the world, and someday I'll get to meet them all!

On the way home, after we dropped off Vicky, I asked Kuma if it was wrong to be going with one boy, while thinking of another.

Kuma said, "Do you mean that guy that you told me about, Bill Fisher?"

I yelled, "Bill Fisher, my goodness, no, I was talking about Ken."

"Oh child, you can't keep thinking about the friends and loved ones that have passed on. You must let them rest and stay acquainted with the living. All we have is life…until it's over. So that's why you must always *feel* and *be* alive! Life is so short. Take it from someone who's been around for a while."

Kuma's philosophy always amused me, but she did always speak the truth.

This time I told Kuma, "Well let's give this feeling alive thing a try and drop me off right in front of the bar, ok?"

She laughed and said; "Now child, you know that you'll be playing with your life, don't you?"

"I don't care Kuma, Mama wants honesty, so let's give her some."

So Kuma pulled right in front of the bar, and as I left her car, I asked her to say a prayer for me, and was off. As I walked in everyone went wild with amazement; whistling and clapping. I felt great, but I could only think of what Mama would say.

I sort of looked around and then Tony, who was tending bar, pointed up, so I knew that she was upstairs. Bravely I went up to meet the enemy.

As I entered the apartment and before a word could pop out of her mouth I said, "Mama, thank God you're here. I need you to help me cover what's left of the bruise on my back, ok?" And quickly I dropped the back of my blouse to expose it, as a reminder to her.

She stayed very silent and responded with, "Sure Madia, anything you want. It's your day."

I couldn't believe my ears.

I told her that I would go and get changed into my slip and that I'd call her in when I was ready. She just walked away and muttered, "That's fine."

I couldn't believe that she was really going along with everything. Knowing Mama as I do, I quickly made sure that my dress, shoes, etc, were all ok. Everything was fine, she hadn't touched a thing. I changed into my undergarments and yelled out, "Mama, I'm ready if you are."

In seconds she appeared. She told me how pretty I was, and then I handed her the jar of makeup. She started to rub on the makeup and asked if the pressure of her hand was hurting me.

I thought, boy…that sure must be some kind of prayer that Kuma's saying. Out of nowhere, Mama started to talk to me like she was in a trance. Never looking at my face, just staring at my back.

She told how as a young girl in Yugoslavia, things were so very different. "You know Madia, as a girl, I never went to a dance or anything, because my mother thought that those kinds of things were just made up by men so they could get to see women's bodies wiggling, and then that would lead men to force themselves on to decent girls. Girls who would have normally waited until their wedding nights to give themselves to their husbands. So you see, Madia, your grandmother knew, even way back then, that men only want to use women, and that's why we have to be twice as smart as men. If they want something from you, then make sure you get something in return. So Madia," she said as she turned me around, "You make sure every time a man touches you that you get something back."

To break her strange mood, I asked if the make up had covered the bruise. She smiled, as she looked me straight in the eye and said, "Madia, it looks fine, no one will ever know that you had an accident."

"Accident?" I said, "But Mama, this wasn't an accident."

Quickly she snapped back, "Yes, it was, Goddamn it! Now not another word!" She turned and walked away. On her way to the kitchen, she stopped dead in her tracks the second that she heard me utter the words, "Some accident."

"What did you say?" she asked, as she stood there frozen with her back to me.

"Nothing, Mama," I replied, "I was just talking to myself…sorry."

She slowly spoke after a moment or two. "That's what I thought." and then she was gone.

I let out a sigh of relief. I took my hand mirror and looked at her handiwork in the mirror. I looked great and thought, sure, it covered the bruise and the physical pain was gone, but real pain, the emotional pain, was worse than ever. I hoped by Mama having to see the physical evidence of her handiwork in broad daylight, that perhaps for once, she might show at least a small sign of remorse. I was wrong, because somehow in her sick mind, she has twisted this all into her own reality… her reality of this being only an accident. How could she even have said that to me? Especially when we were alone? Who knows, maybe that's how she's been justifying everything in her life, by making believe that her version of everything was actually the truth. If that truly was the case…then I guess I'm glad to be alive. My eyes started to fill with tears and I thought, oh no… not this time…and not tonight.

Chapter 31

It was a beautiful night. The weather was warm, but not too warm. As I finished touching up my lipstick, I looked at myself in the mirror and thought that this can't really be me. I got up from my vanity and stepped back. I was truly amazed and I could only think, if this is a dream please God, don't let it end. I was almost afraid to say it out loud, but I had to remark at my reflection and say, "Well whoever you are in that mirror, you sure do look like a movie star and tonight is your night to shine."

As I walked out of my room, I heard a whistle. It was Babe.

He stood in the dining room and said, "Hey big sister. You look swell! Just like a movie star or something...I can't believe it's you?"

I laughed and said for him to stop, and then all of a sudden he turned very serious on me and said, "No Mary, I really mean it. You *are* beautiful and now the whole world is gonna know it!" And with that, he embraced me and said, "Hey kiddo, you have a great time tonight. You deserve it." Then he kissed my cheek and ran down the stairs.

I felt good inside and out. Babe will never know what it meant for me to get not only his approval on the way I looked, but also for the brief tender moment that we shared. It made me feel better than any dress or make up ever could.

The second that I walked through the doorway of the bar, everybody cheered and applauded. I felt so foolish, but also internally, I felt a little grand and proud. Not only for the way that I looked, but for the way that I felt inside. I really liked, no loved…me. I said thank you to all of them and just as I started to ask where my date was, he walked through the door. He took one look at me and then looked back at the front door to make sure the address was correct and said, "Excuse me Miss, I'm looking for Mary…Mary Zovko. Have you seen her?"

I replied in a grand manner, "Well she couldn't make it so I guess that I'll have to do. That is if you don't mind?" I batted my eyes and we all laughed.

As we were leaving Mama yelled, "Be good." As I went to reply, I bumped into someone. I went to say I'm sorry and noticed that it was my pal, Bill Fisher, who looked quite dashing himself in a tan suit.

He looked at me with those piercing crystal blue eyes and said, "Hey Mar, you sure are a dish," and with that he kissed my hand and turned to my date and said, "Buddy, I guess you're the luckiest guy in the world, because tonight, you'll have the most beautiful girl in the world on your arm."

I knew it was a line, but I didn't care, because to me it was like I had begun to walk on air, and I loved it.

As we walked to Bob's car, Bob said that he thought the guy was being fresh. I reassured him that it was just my friend Bill, and he was just being nice. Then I turned to Bob and said, "Jealous?"

He glanced at me, smiled and said, "Who wouldn't be?"

Nervously I said, "Come on, let's get going. We'll be late."

"Late?" he said. "Oh Mary, don't worry, we have lots of time."

"Well I didn't want to say it inside, but we have one stop to make first, if that's ok? We have to go to my Kuma's house."

"Sure thing. Say, what kind of name is Kuma?"

I explained that it was a Yugoslavian term for Godparent, or witness for a wedding, or actually anything, even close friend. A kind of a catch-all phrase for someone special, and/or important in your life. I thought to myself, she was both.

"What should I call her when I meet her?" he asked.

"Just call her Kuma, everybody does."

As we pulled up to her house, there she was standing on the porch. I heard her yell, "Oh child, how breathtaking you look. Tonight I think you'd even outshine a movie star."

I rushed over to her, did a twirl and then we hugged. I told her thanks for *everything*, and that if it hadn't been for her, none of this would have been possible.

She looked at me and said that God, and not her, had made it possible and that *He* knew I finally had to have a 'shining night', all of my own.

I introduced her to Bob and she made us take some pictures. She whispered in my ear that he really did look a lot like Ken, and that she knew that he was smiling down on his movie star tonight. I started to get a little teary-eyed, so I knew that I had to change the subject.

Quickly I said to Bob, "Would you take one of me and Kuma?"

"Oh child, I'm not dressed or anything."

So I quickly took off my organza stole and flung it around her and said, "There!...Now we're both movie stars!"

CHAPTER 32

Well the prom was going beautifully, and it only got better when I was approached by the most handsome boy in school and he told me, that not only did I look "lovely", but that he would die if I didn't dance with him. His name was Vince and every girl in school thought he was "dreamy". He was not only tall, dark, and handsome, but he also looked just like a young Clark Gable. Plus, he was the only boy in school who had a moustache. The principal allowed it, supposedly because he has a horrible scar underneath, but we all knew it was because his family was wealthy. As we danced I tried to see if I could find a scar, but all I saw was perfection. My friend Vicky danced by and told us we looked like Rhett Butler and Scarlet O'Hara.

Jokingly I said, "Vivian Leigh, gee, I thought I was more the Hedy Lamarr type?"

I giggled, but noticed how Vince looked so serious when he said, "Not even for a second Mary, because you are much more beautiful." With that the song ended and he kissed my hand. He then asked if we could dance again a little later. I told him sure and before I knew it he was gone.

Vicky came rushing up to me and said that she wanted to scream when he kissed my hand. I could only joke with her, saying that this made it twice tonight that my hand had been kissed and I sure hoped that my fingers weren't getting pruney. We both laughed and then went to sit down for dinner.

As I sat there, I kept looking around, taking in the entire experience. I felt like it was all a dream or a movie. But the feeling that I was in a dream or movie quickly ended as someone bumped the waitress' tray, and a sea of shrimp cocktails were hurled all down the front of my dress. I quickly got up and ran toward the restrooms, leaving a trail of shrimp and sauce behind me. Once in the powder room, I saw the damage in the giant mirror. I looked as though I'd been shot in the chest. Then Vicky appeared out of nowhere to help me. We both cried as we tried to salvage the dress…and the prom.

As we were leaving the powder room, I noticed that Vince was waiting for us in the hallway and he said that he had come back for another dance.

"Gee Vince I don't know; I'd hate for you to get any sauce on your white tuxedo jacket."

"Oh come on Mary, it's rented *and* you look like you need to be swept off your feet."

So I relented, and did feel great when he smiled at me and took me by the hand. He made me feel as though we were the only couple on the dance floor and I *was* cheering up.

That is until Vince stopped dancing, and he started looking a little puzzled, looking at his sleeve. Then it hit me, the make up!

"Mary, is something wrong with your back?"

"Well Vince, it's makeup. I had an accident."

With that he started to laugh and said. "Hedy Lamarr, I think it's more like Calamity Jane."

I wanted to die. I started to cry and ran off.

Vince kept following me and yelling to me that he was sorry and that he was only joking, and for me to come back. I made it into an open elevator and the doors closed just as Vince got to them. I could still hear him outside of the elevator doors begging me to come back. I couldn't go back; I just felt as though no matter how I try, I'm just never going to be good enough for anyone or anything. As soon as the doors opened, I ran through the lobby and out of the hotel. I even ran across the street through traffic, and sat on a park bench in Grant Park.

The fresh air started to make me feel better. I sat there looking at the city's lights and staring at that beautiful building, and thought…is this always going to be my fate?

But before I could dwell on that - it hit me, "What about Bob?" He was still in there thinking, God only knows what? How was I supposed to go back in there and tell him that I just wanted to go home? I didn't want to wreck his night too. Even if I hopped in a cab, how would he know where I was? Then out of nowhere came a voice asking if the seat next to me was taken.

I was just about to use some language comparable to my mother's, when I noticed that it was the familiar voice of Bill Fisher.

"Bill, what are you doing here?"

"Well Mar, I was stood up."

I was confused, then he said that he was kidding and he explained how he knew a lot of the kids at the prom and thought that he would do their families a favor and see if anyone got a little too drunk or tired and needed a ride home. He asked, "What the Hell happened to you?"

"Hit and run with some shrimp cocktails. It hasn't been exactly the best night of my life."

Then it hit me. I could send Bill in there. I asked him if he would go and find Bob and let him know that I was ok.

"Sure Mar, I'll be right back."

Soon he reappeared and said, "Well, Bob really didn't want to leave, but he will since he was your date. I reassured him that you wanted him to stay and have a good time, and that I would take you home."

I really couldn't blame Bob for wanting to stay and I thanked Bill. I told him that I would take a cab home so that he could wait for any other kids that needed a ride.

Bill told me that he'd give me a ride home, because I looked like I needed a ride the most. He added that he didn't mind at all, especially since it was such a beautiful night *and* because my family was always so good to him. It was the least he could do. He topped it off with it was not only his pleasure, but an honor. When we finally made it to his car, he opened the door of his convertible like he was my chauffer. It was all so silly.

Once he got in I said, "Bill, could we ride with the top down since it's such a beautiful night? It'll help my dress dry out."

We both chuckled as I took my wrap and used it like a scarf to keep my hair from blowing around during the drive.

As we drove, I kept noticing that Bill would smile every time he'd look at me, so I finally had to ask him what was up?

He said, "Well I'm just looking at the most beautiful woman that's ever been in this car."

"Oh brother – do girls really fall for that line?"

"Mar, it's not a line, I'm just stating a fact, that's all."

"Really?"

"Yep."

"Well Mr. Fisher – are you making a pass?"

"No Mar, it's just that I've never seen a girl look so good in cocktail sauce before."

I laughed and thought – who knew that Bill could be so witty?

As we drove I thought of something that he had said earlier, so I asked him, "Bill, just how long have you known my family?"

"Before you were born, Mar."

Then he started to tell me some wild, wild tales about prohibition and how he ran bootlegged beer for my parents, when he was only eight years old. He went on how *'my mother'* really got to be good friends with all the well-known gangsters, from Al Capone on down.

I was fascinated, because even though I had heard bits and pieces of these kinds of stories, before my father's death, I wasn't sure if they were really true or not; plus all the stories died with him. My mother would never talk about them,...probably with good reason.

Before I knew it, we were home. I thanked him for a wonderful ride home and some fascinating stories. We both smiled for a moment and it seemed a little awkward, when all of a sudden Bill took my hand and again, he kissed it. Then he said good night and before I knew it, he was gone.

I felt a little tingle in me as I watched his tail lights disappear in the distance. I wondered if Bill felt it too?

Mama was waiting for me at the top of the stairs. She asked about the stain on the dress. I thought that she would have asked me about the prom first, but I really didn't care. I wasn't really paying too much attention to her while I was answering her, because my mind was still on the "tingle".

CHAPTER 33

Graduation day was here and I was so excited, not about the graduation, but the party afterwards. Mama told me that she wasn't really throwing the party for me, it's just that it was expected of her, being in business and all. And she added, how could she be happy for me when I didn't have any kind of future. Well maybe she was right, but I didn't care, because a party was a party.

I really *didn't* know what I wanted to do with my life, but whatever it would be, I knew that it meant work and not college, because according to Mama, college was for boys. Mama always told me, "What good is a diploma to a woman,...unless it's to wipe a baby's ass?" It really bothered me that a few of my friends were going to be going to college and that I wasn't, especially since I was such a good student.

Well the bar was filled with friends. They all had parties earlier of their own, but they all ended just as mine had begun, so the bar and yard were packed. I was having a wonderful time, and then all of a sudden it got even better,

"Kuma!" I yelled, and then I made my way through the crowd toward her. When I finally reached her, we hugged and kissed as she said, "I have a big surprise for you." She then called over to my friend, Bonnie, who had also just graduated, and said, "Go ahead, Bonnie. You tell Madia the news."

"Well Mary, as you already know, I'm going to be going away to college, and before I go, I'm going away for a vacation, because my mother thinks that I need to see the world,…or at least Montana."

I thought that I was hearing things or maybe this was all a bad dream - why would Kuma do this to me? She knew how badly I wanted to go to college. Then I thought, Montana? Boy, Bonnie's mother must really want to get rid of her?

Then I realized that Kuma was shaking my arm, and said, "Didn't you hear me. I'm paying for you to go out west with Bonnie on vacation, for a whole month!"

"What?" I yelled, "Me, for a month? Oh, Mama would never...."

"She can't do a thing about it, just watch me." With that, Kuma got up on a chair, and told everyone to quiet down because she had a special announcement.

Mama came out of the kitchen holding a bowl of beets.

"Everyone," started Kuma, "Now I know you've never seen me up on a chair before, but I want the whole world to know that next to Madia's mother, I'm the proudest person in this room of my little Madia, and to show it, next week when Bonnie leaves on her month-long vacation to Montana, I'm going to send Madia with her and I'll pay all her expenses. I know Mama back there won't mind, because after all, we were younger than this when we came to America. So can she go Mama?"

The whole bar turned and waited for her to answer. Kuma and I both knew that in front of a crowd she would be a lamb.

"Of course," said Mama, "if that's what she wants."

"Oh yes, Mama!" I yelled. "I do!" And with that, I hugged and kissed Kuma. Everyone was clapping, then we heard a crash and I looked back and there were beets all over the back wall.

Mama said, "It slipped!" And then she returned to the kitchen.

I looked at Kuma and at the same time, we both said "It slipped?" Then we just started to laugh.

Later, after everyone left, I was helping Mama clean up the bar, she finally broke her silence and spoke.

"So you and Kuma think you're so smart, well we'll see."

"Mama, just think, I'll be gone for a month and…."

"A month?" she screamed, "And what the Hell am I supposed to do for a month around here without you….Who will help me clean?"

She walked right past me without making eye contact as she headed toward the kitchen.

"You'll find somebody Mama," I said, as I slowly turned and made my way back upstairs. Once up there, I just cried and cried as I laid on my bed thinking - I can't believe that I let myself imagine that even for a second, that she was really going to miss *me*...and not my cleaning expertise.

CHAPTER 34

Well the big day was finally here and I was so excited – not about Montana – but about being away from Mama for a whole month!

Bonnie and her mother, Zorka, were already at the bar with her luggage, which Bonnie's brother Pete dropped off. Bill Fisher was going to drive us to the train station downtown. Pete had loaded all of her luggage into Bill's car, but while I was watching Bill put my luggage in, I began to feel really bad for Bonnie. She was a wreck, and her mother was trying to console her because Bonnie had never slept in any bed but her own her entire life, and now she'd be gone for a month. This was going to be interesting.

Unlike Bonnie, my mother would cart me off to people's houses from time to time when I was a child, when things got too intense between her and my father. One time, I was forced to stay at the home of the businessman who had tried to molest me when I was younger. He actually got to finish what he had started in our garage.

She didn't want to let go of her mother, but in contrast, you could see that her mother couldn't wait to get away from her. They've always had a strained relationship, not as bad as my family dynamic, but still not healthy. The one thing that they did have was a touch of a loving interaction. They did the, "I love you's, and I'll miss you's". I wasn't sure if they were real expressions of love or not, but it didn't matter. It still made me a little sad because I knew that there wouldn't be any of that between me and Mama.

Bill was pointing at his watch, letting us know that we needed to get to the train. As Bonnie and I were finally getting into the car I thought I'd give the 'loving family thing' a shot, so I turned to Mama and said, "I'll miss you." and then I gave her a peck on the cheek.

She could only stare at me coldly, and respond with, "You're supposed to, I'm your Mother."

"Mama" I said, "are you going to miss me?"

"Hurry, you'll miss your train." And then she walked away.

I felt so empty as I got into the car. All I could think to myself was, "When are you going to face the fact that Mama is not, nor will she ever be, like a regular mother? Thank God that I have Kuma."

Which made me wonder, where *was* Kuma? After all, this is one of those times where we didn't have to rendezvous in secret at the train station. We had spent days and days with her helping me pack. Just as Bill began to pull away like the cavalry, I saw Kuma's car pull up. She got out and ran over to us. I got out of the car and she gave me a big bear hug and told me that she'd be *so* lost without me, and that I was to only write if I *wasn't* having fun. Because no news, meant fun! We both laughed and I thanked her again. Little did she realize that my thanks weren't for just the trip, but mostly for her love. I asked her to come with us to the train. At first she shook her head no, but then she saw what a mess Bonnie was and she changed her mind, hopped in, and off we went.

At the train station, I hugged Kuma one last time and then I noticed that she was slipping an envelope into my pocket. I tried to stop her but she said, "No, that's for the train ride and *not* before…Ok?"

I smiled and said, "Ok Kuma, whatever you say."

Then she looked me square in the eyes and said, "You go and experience life child. There's a great big world outside of all of this, and when you get back, I want to hear about every second of it. It's time that you started making some memories, some happy memories that you'll have for the rest of your life." She hugged and kissed me and said, "Now hurry child, or you'll miss your train."

I grabbed Bonnie's hand and we followed the porter, who had put all of our luggage on a cart, and headed to our train. Once we were there I tried to tip the porter, but he said that my boyfriend had already taken care of it when he checked us in. I thought, boyfriend?...Bill?... how funny. Then I thought, how wonderful of him, especially since I was caught up in my moment with Kuma. What a good guy.

My thoughts were interrupted by Bonnie, who was still crying, and she said, "I don't think that I can do this Mary. I really don't, I…"

I stopped her immediately, grabbed her by the arm and said, "Bonnie…you can do this, you can…and besides, your mother and Kuma will lose *all* of their money if we don't go, because it's too late for a refund."

I didn't know if it was true, but I had to think of something quick and I know that money meant a lot to her mother. She finally agreed and I pushed her on the train as fast as I could. Montana, here we come!

Chapter 35

The train ride seemed to take forever, but we met a lot of nice people along the way, probably because Bonnie hadn't stopped crying since we left Union Station. I was reading all about this"

'Dude Ranch' that we would be staying at, when a deep voice said, "Excuse me Ma'am?"

I looked up and saw a man pointing to my brochure as he said, "I see you're heading to a place that I'm pretty familiar with." He stuck out his big leathery hand and said, "The name's Jack. I work there part time."

I shook his hand, and said, "My name's Mary, and this is my friend Bonnie. What do you do the rest of the time?"

"Well," he said, "that's a secret, for now anyway. Say, what's wrong with your friend?"

"Oh she'll be fine, she's just a little homesick, I guess. Say Jack, I've never seen a dude ranch before, never even heard of one, except in the movies. What's it like?"

He went on and on about what to expect and then I noticed that he had a wonderful twinkle in his eyes when he spoke. I thought, considering he looked so rugged, he was still very handsome and he was really very sweet and gentle towards us. He asked if he could dine with us and I said, "Sure, see you in the dining car."

While we were washing up, Bonnie beleaguered me about Jack and asked if I had lost my mind. She said, "What if he's a killer? What will we do?"

I mumbled under my breath, "Hopefully, he'll get you first."

"Mary, I'm being serious!"

"Bonnie, we're on a train filled with people, so relax!" With that she started crying all over again.

We met Jack in the dining car and had a wonderful dinner. It was great to have someone to actually talk to, that wasn't crying all the time. Plus, we got to hear from a *real* cowboy, what the Wild West was actually like.

Jack really made the rest of the trip very enjoyable. I found not only his stories charming, but him as well. I don't know how to say it, other than he was just so comfortable to be around. He was so secure in his own skin and calming, which I needed, thanks to Bonnie's continued hysterics.

After what seemed like an eternity, the train finally stopped and the conductor welcomed us to Bozeman, Montana. It was beautiful. As I stepped off of the train, I was amazed by the beauty and grandeur of its raw, open space and vast sky. As Jack helped us with our luggage, I told him that also. His only reply was that if I wanted to see real beauty, all I had to do was look in the mirror. Then he gave me a wink. I just smiled at him and then I heard Bonnie scream. I rushed over to find out that some cowboy was trying to be helpful, and had lifted her into a truck by her waist. She started hitting him with her purse, and then she called him a wild beast. The cowboy apologized, but she'd have no part of it. She just kept saying, "We should have never left Chicago."

At that moment, I started looking around again at those beautiful mountains, and for me, Chicago didn't even exist anymore.

Oh, and the fresh cowboy turned out to be from the dude ranch. He was just trying to be helpful. His name was Buck and he worked with Jack, who assured us that Buck was really a great guy, and I thought if Jack said so, then that was good enough for me. Bonnie tried to start up again and I leaned over to her and said, "Bonnie - just shut the hell up!" She folded up her arms and wouldn't look or talk to me, all the way to the ranch. I thanked God for her little snit, because it gave me time to really enjoy the view.

When we got to the ranch, I could see that it wasn't fancy, but it was rustic and charming. After looking around for a while, I realized that I didn't see any other women there, except for an older lady with her white hair pulled up into a bun. She worked in the kitchen and you could see how respectful all of the men were to her. Then I looked around some more. It looked like all of the people that I saw there were all workers.

It finally made sense to me *why* Buck wanted to really go out of his way for us. It was because he knew that Bonnie and I were the only guests at the ranch. I asked Jack about it later and he explained that the ranch catered to all types of people, especially families, and that two families had cancelled last minute, which meant that Bonnie and I were their only guests.

I said, "For a Ranch Hand, you know an awful lot about the guests."

"Well Mar, it's a small ranch and word spreads pretty fast. Let me show you to your suite."

"Suite? We have a suite?"

"Don't let the outside fool you. You know what they say, never judge a book…"

"Oh Jack, that's not what I meant. After all, the lobby or parlor or whatever this area is, is beautiful. It's just that I thought, that Bonnie and I would have separate rooms, that's all."

"Can't say as I blame you..."

Then out of nowhere came a loud, "I can hear you!"

I said, "Oh hi Bonnie, I didn't see you."

Sarcastically she said, "Apparently. Where's our luggage?"

Jack said, "I had Buck and one of the hands, put it in your suite right from the train."

Bonnie snapped back, "You mean to tell me that some strange men might be going through my things as we speak? Oh my God!"

In a calming tone Jack tried to reassure her, by saying, "They're just putting the luggage in your suite for you – that's all."

"Well we'll see!" she said, and then she turned away from us.

I just shook my head as I stared at her as she went marching up the hallway. I turned toward Jack and he just smiled.

We finally stopped in front of a set of double doors and as Jack opened them up, it was like in The Wizard of Oz, when Dorothy opens the door and enters Munchkin Land. It was beautiful!

"Jack," I said, "This room is magnificent."

"Rooms you mean, and thanks, we're quite proud of this one. There's a private bathroom, two bedrooms, this parlor and a small study. After all, you'll be here for a month, and we want the two of you to be comfortable."

"Bonnie, isn't this fantastic? This had to cost a fortune?"

Bonnie, still trying to be snotty said, "It'll do."

Then she walked by one of the bedrooms and said, "This one's mine."

Jack offered to help move her luggage to her bedroom, but she'd have none of it. "I'll do it myself! My luggage and I, have been manhandled enough for one day. Thank you!"

Then we watched her struggle, as she tried to carry and drag her luggage to her room. It was so comical that I wanted to burst out laughing, but I didn't dare upset her anymore than she already was.

Jack excused himself, because he looked like he wanted to laugh as well. I quickly opened my purse, and could only find a twenty-dollar bill, which was a lot of money for that time, but I had to give him something. As I handed it to him he said, "No Mary, that's ok."

"Jack you have to take this. After all, you drove us up from the train, and…"

"You know what I'll do Mary, I'll give it to Buck and the guys, if that's ok with you?"

"It's yours Jack, so do whatever you want with it…and thank you again for everything."

He tipped his hat to me, but then he yelled, "See ya later.", real loud towards Bonnie's room as he let himself out.

The second that the door shut, Bonnie popped out of her room and said, "It all makes perfect sense now. Look at this room; they all think that we're rich! *That's* why *your boy* Jack has been *so* attentive."

Calmly, as I started putting my luggage into my room, I said, "Well then I just fueled that fire. Because I just tipped Jack twenty dollars."

"Twenty Dollars?! Are YOU Crazy?!"

"Guess so." I said as I shut my door, leaving Bonnie to be aggravated all…by…herself.

Later, once Bonnie got hungry, she became a little more congenial and even *she* had to admit that the ranch was just wonderful. So we got all dressed up and made our way to the dining room. The minute that we walked in all of the guys stood up, and there was a hint of a whistle by one of the cowboys, who was immediately elbowed by Buck.

Dinner was delicious, and we were treated like gold, which made me wonder if they *were* really going all out because, like Bonnie said, they thought that we were rich. The truth was that I didn't really care what they thought – I was having fun.

Buck eventually made his way over to us and asked us what time we'd like our horses ready.

"Horses?" we said in unison.

"Sure," he said, "this *is* a Dude Ranch and that's why people come here."

So I looked at Bonnie, who wasn't paying attention to what Buck was saying, just to the fact that he was inches away from her.

I jumped in and said, "Right after breakfast – Ok Bonnie?"

"Sure." she said in a far away voice.

Buck said, "Alright ladies, see you in the morning. Have a good night."

A simple, "Bye Buck," came out of Bonnie, and then a slight sigh.

It dawned on me that there was the conspicuous absence of Jack at dinner, but I figured that on a ranch this size, there's a lot to do, and he must have had to work the night shift. Then I thought, Mar, why do you care?

Back in our room, I was brushing my hair and I thought how wonderful it felt to not have to think or worry about anything or anyone, anyone that is, except for Kuma, and how wonderful it was of her to have made all of this possible.

I walked out onto the large porch that was attached to our room and just stared up at the stars. They looked incredible out there on the range and I looked up and said, "Thank you God for giving me Kuma."

Then I heard a voice saying, "Talking to yourself Mary?"

It was Jack.

"Sure – that way I'm always in good company." Then I asked, "What are you doing out here…just getting off work?"

"No Mary, my work never ends around here."

"Well if you have to work all the time, what were you doing in Chicago?"

"Well Mary, I was meeting with some meat packers. We're working on a business deal. This is also a working cattle ranch."

"I didn't know that. Where do you keep them?"

He pointed off into the distance and said, "They're all out there."

"Wow, you have to work day and night *and* do business deals? You need a raise."

"Well Mary, you'll have to tell the boss, when you see him."

"I will, just point him out."

"I will Mary. Now you better get some sleep because you've got a big day tomorrow, Good night."

"Good night Jack."

I thought, gee, it's kind of creepy that he knows everything that we're doing. Then I tried to *not* think about it.

As he disappeared from view, Bonnie came through the doors from her room and onto the porch and asked, "Who were you talking to Mar?"

"Jack. He was walking by after his shift…I think?"

"Oh, is that all." Then she perked up and asked, "Was Buck with him?"

"No Bonnie…it was just Jack."

Looking disappointed, she thought for a minute and then she said, "Mar, you don't think that he's a peeping tom or something…do you?"

"Bonnie, why do you always think the worst of people? Good night."

I went to my room. Secretly, it did cross my mind, because I thought that it *was* a little weird, but I was sure that it was just a coincidence.

Chapter 36

In the morning, I was up early and raring to go. There was a knock at the door and when I opened it, there was a little Chinese man with a tray. He said that it was our complimentary breakfast, and that if we wanted something else, we could go to the dining room. He turned to leave and I said, "Please wait. I'll have to see if my friend has some money so that I can give you a tip."

I knocked on Bonnie's door. She yelled, "What do you want?"

"Bonnie, do you have any money…I need to tip the, the…waiter?"

"Waiter? Wait a minute…what did you order?"

Her door opened. She was still half asleep, and her hair was all pinned up in pin curls, and she was just about to really let into me when she realized that the man was still there and that she was only wearing her nightgown. She slammed the door and yelled for me to wait while she got her purse. It seemed like it was a few seconds when the door opened again, and this time she had on her robe and her head was wrapped in a towel. She opened her purse, and when she went to hand me a quarter, I snatched a dollar bill and handed it to the man before she could say a word.

He kept nodding as he thanked us, and then he went out the door.

Again, she asked me what I'd ordered and I replied that the man said that it was a complimentary breakfast and that if we wanted something else, we'd have to go to the dining room.

She said, "See, I told you that they think we're rich…they're trying to butter us up, "Butter us up for what Bonnie?"

"I don't know…but I don't trust'em."

I took off the food covers and saw enough food for ten people – not two. I put a little on my plate and then I watched as Bonnie started to shovel food onto her plate. I said, "A little hungry this morning?"

"No, but if it's free, we're gonna eat it all. Plus, I want to get my dollar's worth."

Once we finished our breakfast I said, "Well Cowgirl, let's get a move on."

Oh yes, Kuma, Bonnie and I had gone shopping before we left. It was really hard to find Western Wear in Chicago – but we found some – and we were ready to Yee-Haw it up!

I couldn't wait to put on one of the Cowgirl-ish outfits that we brought.

As we were making our way over to the stable, I knew that I was ready for our big day of horseback riding, but Bonnie kept going on and on about how she was certain that she wasn't going to like any of this, and that she was afraid that it would make her sick because she was sure that she was allergic to horses.

I just shook my head and kept walking.

Once we got there the ranch hands pointed out a trail and said that the horses knew the route by heart, so we would be ok on our own.

It made me a little bit nervous for us to be by ourselves, but I wasn't about to let Bonnie know that.

Finally dressed, we made our way to the lobby and saw Buck waiting outside with two horses. Bonnie said, "How do I look?"

"Just like a real Cowgirl."

"Do you think that Buck will like it?"

"I don't know…I think the one that you *should* ask is the horse. That's the one you'll be riding."

"Mary?"

"Good morning Buck." I said as we walked out onto the front porch, "I hope that you weren't waiting too long?"

Bonnie chimed in with, "I was ready a long time ago, but you know how some people are."

Buck looked a little confused and asked, "Who?"

I said, "Never mind Buck, she's had too much coffee, that's all. Where do we go?"

Buck said, "Well we're real busy here today branding some cattle, so we thought that you gal's might just want to stick to a trail so that you can get the lay of the land for yourselves…if that's ok with y'all? The horses know the route, so y'all can just sit back and enjoy the view."

I said, "That'll be fine Buck…thanks."

Then he pointed in the direction, and the horses rode off, just like Buck said.

Bonnie waved and yelled back, "Bye Buck. Thank you."

The minute that we were out of ear-range from Buck, Bonnie lit into me. About, how *dare* I monopolize the conversation with Buck, so that she couldn't get a word in.

I just blew it off and before I knew it, I was taking in some breathtaking views. It was beautiful, even Bonnie seemed to be adapting and was appearing to be enjoying the ride. As we rode along we just talked and talked – it was so relaxing.

After riding for a while, I turned to Bonnie and said, "Ok, we've done the trail thing, now let's really ride."

"No Mary, Buck said to stay on the trail and that's exactly what I'm going to do."

"Suit yourself. Giddy up!" I yelled as I smacked the horse on his butt with my hand… and he took off!

Bonnie was yelling at me, but I didn't pay any attention to her. Then I looked back and saw that Bonnie was trying to catch up but she was still trailing far behind me. She started to scream even louder and I heard her scream for me to duck. I did and as I did, I heard a whoosh over my head. There was a steel cable, used for skiing or something, and I thought, 'Oh my God - I was almost decapitated.'

Just then Bonnie got off her horse and immediately passed out.

I saw some water in a nearby stream, so I went over and I filled my boots with water and poured it over her head.

She yelled at me, and asked if I was trying to drown her. I paused and made a face, like…. well, maybe? Of course she started to cry and said, "Well that's the last time that I'll ever try to save your life!"

By the time we got back to the ranch, my feet were really sore. I saw Jack and told him about the cable, Bonnie, and my feet. He told me how badly leather shrunk once it got wet, so he had me sit in a chair on the front porch and told me that he'd try to help me pull them off.

Well Bonnie went crazy and said, "Jack - no one is allowed to touch her leg like this in public." She looked around and continued with, "What will people think?"

Jack just smiled and said, "Ok. Let's move inside then."

We all went inside as Jack apologized. I told him to just ignore Bonnie. He smiled and said in a low voice so that she couldn't hear, "I try to, but it's tough."

"I heard that!" she barked.

Then he looked at me with an 'Oops' expression and told me that I should grab a hold of the piano leg for leverage, and Bonnie could be the one to hang onto my boot. The problem was that while Bonnie pulled she kept sliding on the wooden floor. Just then Jack saw Buck and called him over to help. Jack slid a chair over and told Bonnie to sit in it. He said, "Here's what we're gonna do Bonnie. You keep hangin' on to Mary's boot as hard as you can, and Buck will pull your chair, and if I need to, I'll pull on Buck – but we're gonna get'em off right now."

Bonnie had told me again, earlier on our ride, that she thought Buck was so cute, so I knew that she would allow this.

Sure enough Jack had to jump in and pull Buck from around his waist. The chain of people trying to get my boots off was the funniest thing that I'd ever seen - but it worked - and at last they were off.

After we all had a good laugh, Jack took the boots and said that he'd fix'em back up to look like brand new. He said that he knew a way to stretch them back out.

The next day we thought we would try riding again, but before we could leave, I remembered that Jack still had my boots. So I asked Bonnie if she would get my boots from him since she was always ready before me. She agreed to pick them up and as she went out the door, she said that with any luck, she might run into Buck. I thanked her and I went back to getting dressed. While I was doing one last hair and make-up check, there was a knock at the door. When I opened it, there was Jack, and he was hiding something behind his back.

"Cinderella," he said, "Let's see if they fit." He presented me with the most beautiful boots that I'd ever seen.

"These boots are beautiful, but they're not mine Jack."

"They are now, I bought them for you Mary. Oh yeah, and this too…." He reached down and from the hall and picked up the biggest bouquet of flowers I'd ever seen!

"Oh Jack, they're gorgeous, but I can't let you do this." And before I knew it, he embraced me and kissed me. It was magic! Then a scream from down the hall...it was Bonnie. She came running down the hall toward us, and as soon as she reached us she started slapping him, and calling him 'fresh' and a monster.

Jack just laughed, then he said, "I'm sorry Mary, but I couldn't help myself. Good bye, see ya later." He paused for a moment, then said, "Oh yeah, it was nice to see you too Bonnie." Then he winked at her again, and she screamed.

Again, I could only laugh as I headed back into our room and started putting on the boots.

She started with, "Mary, how could you just stand there and let him kiss you?"

"Easy Bonnie, I just puckered up."

"Oh my God! Mary, what would the nuns at St. Francis think?"

I stood up in my new boots and I looked at her and calmly said, "Who gives a shit?"

"Oh my God," she yelled again, "You've been out here with these *heathens* too long. I want to go home. I can't stand it another minute!"

Quickly I put the flowers in an empty vase that was on the table and said, "Then go, but I'm staying. By the way, are you ready to ride?" I walked into the bathroom to put water in the vase of flowers.

She just stood there frozen...and I didn't care, because I had made up my mind. If she wants to be miserable; then let her be, because I'm here to have fun, and no one was going to spoil it for me. I set the flowers on our little dining table, grabbed my hat and walked out of our room. She followed behind me, not saying a word.

Chapter 37

She stayed that way for most of the flat terrain of our horseback ride. While up in the mountains, she appeared to be actually having a good time. She started with some small talk about the weather and things like that. And then, out of nowhere, she said, "Let's go faster Mar."

I thought to myself – finally – and I said, "Well all right – let's race!" And after a little 'Yee-Haw' to our horses - we really took off!

It was magnificent. We were riding so fast through the trees that I felt like I was flying and totally free. Plus Bonnie didn't have time to bitch or think about anything except if she was going to be able to stay on the horse or not.

Meanwhile, the trees were getting denser and denser, and I hadn't noticed how the branches were whipping at us as we rode, not to mention that they were starting to tear holes in my new cowgirl shirt. I loved that blouse because it had mother of pearl snaps instead of buttons. I felt just like Annie Oakley. The snaps were no match for the trees. Bonnie started yelling something, but I wasn't paying attention. All of a sudden, before I knew it, I was practically topless except for the bra and a few shreds of my blouse.

I heard a voice yell, "Do you always ride bareback?"

It was Jack, and he was already taking off his shirt so that he could give it to me. At first I was so embarrassed, but his smile made it seem ok, and I was kind of getting lost in the moment.

Bonnie yelled for me to cover myself up, but I could only stare at Jack's golden tanned and muscular body. I didn't realize I was smiling and staring at him, and then I uttered the word 'perfect'.

Never breaking eye contact with me he said, "I beg your pardon Mary?"

Nervously, I quickly blurted out, "Oh, your shirt. It's perfect."

He winked and said, "Yeah…that's what I thought you'd said."

Bonnie was flapping her jaws the entire time but I couldn't tell you a word she said because I kept staring at Jack.

He rode back with us and being a perfect gentleman, he never once mentioned seeing me in my bra. He escorted us back, and took our horses back to the stable for us so that we could get ready for dinner.

Once in our room, as you can imagine, there was absolutely no living with Bonnie. I kept telling her that I couldn't hear a word of what she was saying because I was too busy getting dressed, but she still kept going on and on. All of a sudden she got very quiet and said, in a pleasant tone, that she'd meet me in the lobby, and then she just left. Thank God.

Over dinner, while she had me trapped, she went on about how we just had to leave as soon as we could, and that these cowboys were too wild for us and that it was just too dangerous.

"Mary, they are just too 'different' from us and the way we were raised."

"Really Bonnie? And just *how* were we raised? Our lives were shit growing up...that's *how* we were raised!"

I looked at her and said, "Anyway, I like danger Bonnie, and as for 'different'- well different doesn't mean good or bad - it just means different, that's all. Isn't that *why* we traveled thousands of miles…to see something different?"

She was just getting ready with round two when her mood suddenly changed and she said, "Oh hi Buck, it's such a nice night, isn't it?"

"Why yes Miss Bonnie, it is. Did you ladies enjoy your ride today?"

"Oh it was beautiful. I really understand why you love it out here in the West."

I thought – oh brother, he should have been here a minute ago. Then I thought – wait a minute, he's not acting odd, so I wondered if Jack didn't tell any of the guys about my blouse incident, so I asked, "Buck, didn't Jack tell you what happened today on the mountain?"

"No Miss Mary, what happened?" he said, and he seemed sincere.

"Well, we were riding, when all of a sudden…"

But Bonnie immediately jumped in with, "Oh Mary, that's nothing; don't bother Buck with any of that. Buck we just love the outdoors, but what do you have here *besides* horseback riding?"

"Well Miss Bonnie, we're also known for our fishin'…you like to fish?"

"I adore it." Bonnie said.

I thought, oh brother…Bonnie's never fished a day in her life…so I said, "Buck, that sounds wonderful. When can we all go? It could be the four of us; you, Jack, me and Bonnie. What do you think?"

"Oh Miss Mary, I'd have to ask the boss. We're not supposed to do things like that with the guests."

"Well Buck, tell the *boss* that you have two guests. The only two guests, from what I can see, and they want to learn how to fish. You don't have to let him know that Bonnie is a pro. Let us know what he says tomorrow."

"Sure thing…good night ladies."

"Good night Buck." I said.

Then Bonnie chimed in, "Good night Buck. See you tomorrow." Her eyes followed him until he was out of sight, then she turned toward me where I had a smirk on my face, and she said, "What?"

"You *adore* fishing…really, since when?"

She said, "There's a lot about me that you don't know, now shut up and eat."

I just thought – oh…this will be good.

Chapter 38

The next morning at breakfast, I noticed that Buck was heading our way and I kicked Bonnie under the table. She was getting ready to yell at me when I said, "Good morning Buck."

He tipped his hat and said, "Mornin' ladies"

Bonnie's attention was now solely directed on Buck as she said, "Good morning Buck, isn't it a beautiful day?"

"Why yes Miss Bonnie, it surely is. I just wanted to let you ladies know that Jack and I would love to take you fishin' today, if that's still ok with you all?"

Bonnie never took her eyes off of him and said, "Of course it is. What time are we going?"

"How about… in about an hour…will that be enough time for you ladies?"

I said, "That's perfect Buck. We'll see you in the lobby in an hour.

He went to walk away, but quickly turned back and added, "Oh, just in case we're a little late, don't be worried. We're just waitin' on a calf to be born in the barn. Say, would you ladies like to watch?"

Bonnie said, "Oh yes Buck, the miracle of birth is *such* a beautiful thing. We'll be right there."

He tipped his hat and was gone.

Bonnie was so busy being chatty an animated with Buck that I wondered if she realized what she'd just said yes to. So I said, "Bonnie, have you ever seen anything give birth? It's not pretty. I saw our dog give birth to puppies many times and the first time that I watched it, I almost threw up. Are you sure that you can handle it?"

"Don't be ridiculous Mary. What do you think – that I'm a child? Come on and finish your breakfast. We don't want to keep Buck, I mean the guys, waiting, do we?"

"Bonnie there'll be no waiting for anything or anyone when you're dealing with birth so you go ahead and I'll be there in a minute…ok?"

"Ok – but hurry!"

At last she was gone and I could finally enjoy my coffee in peace. I noticed Jack standing in the doorway by the kitchen and he was smiling. As he approached my table, he was still smiling, so I asked him, "You look awfully happy. What's going on?"

"Well besides the fact that you look lovely this morning – I was enjoying the show."

Then it dawned on me and I asked, "Did you purposely send Buck over to tell us about the calf?"

"Well Mary, sometimes ya gotta charm a Polecat to get it out of a tree."

"Oooh – don't call Bonnie a Polecat. The Polecat's will get angry. So you put him up to that…and here poor Bonnie was starting to think that he likes her."

"Oh but he does, and by the two of you agreeing to go with us fishing. Well I guess this makes us the two luckiest guys in Montana."

"And why is that?"

"Because we get to spend the day with the two prettiest fillies in Bozeman."

"Do you mean us or the horses?"

"He just smiled and asked, "How on earth do you put up with her? She's wound tighter than a clock and you're so calm."

"Really she's normally not *this* nuts…she's just homesick. Buck does seem to be helping. Plus, I'm used to her, I've known her since birth. Hey, speaking of birth, shouldn't we get going? I don't wanna miss this."

"Oh, so when did a city gal get so interested in the birth of livestock?"

"Jack it's not the birth, which I'm sure will be amazing, I want to watch Bonnie *watching* the birth. That'll be the real show." I grabbed his arm and off we went.

As we walked, Jack asked, "How about you Mary? Are you homesick too?"

"God no. I'm so happy to be away, that I haven't thought about home for even a second."

"Not even about the fella that's waitin' for ya?"

"What 'fella'? What has Bonnie told you?"

Being apologetic, Jack said, "No, nothing... after all, she and I don't exactly sit around and chit-chat. I just figured that a girl as pretty as you would have a string of guys all waitin' on your return."

"Well Jack, you may know a lot about ranching, but you've still got a lot to learn about women."

"Yep, I don't get a lot of practice up here."

"Then it's a good thing that Bonnie and I came along, because between us, we offer a broad spectrum of 'womanhood'."

I started to laugh. Jack looked puzzled, so I said, "*Broad* spectrum??? It's a joke." Before he could answer, our attention was drawn to a little action at the entrance of the barn. It was Bonnie. She came running out of the barn and around the corner and there was a ranch hand chasing after her. At first I thought, what's going on, and where's Buck?

We went running toward them, and that's when we could see that Bonnie was ill. I asked the hand, "Well...is it a boy or a girl?"

He tipped his hat, and explained that he didn't know because he was told by Buck to follow her. "Ya see Miss Mary, Miss Bonnie screamed the minute that it…a…well, got a little messy. If ya know what I mean?"

"Yeah, I know what you mean. I'll take care of her. They need your help more inside than out here, but thanks!"

He tipped his hat again and then ran back in and Jack went with him.

Trying to console Bonnie I said, "Bonnie, it'll be ok. It's just a part of nature…and of life. Someday we'll be going through the same thing when we have kids."

Shaking her head, she said, "Never! Not me! I will *never* go through something that horrible. That was disgusting. I just wanna go back to our room and lay down."

I thought, should I let her go back, or should I throw a little guilt trip at her and make her stay? I knew the latter would be infinitely more fun so I said, "Bonnie, you can't let Buck see you like this. After all, this is *his* life, if you go back to the room, he'll think that you don't approve."

She stood there for a second, and then said, "You're right Mary. We can't let him think that we're just some prissy city girls. Let's go back in, but please don't leave my side?"

I assured her that I would stay close. As we walked in, I heard the word breech, and the next thing I saw was Jack reaching inside the animal to turn the calf around. I was amazed, - but then I heard a thud. It was Bonnie, she had passed out. A few of the hands wanted to attend to her, and I told them to just leave her alone and that she would be fine. This gave me the opportunity to get closer and to really see the miracle of birth up close, and to see Jack and Buck at their best. They were cool as could be, and before you knew it - there she was - a beautiful baby calf. One of the hands called out, "Buck, whatcha gonna call her?" Buck mumbled something to Jack and he nodded yes, then he said, "Her name is Bonnie!"

I looked over to 'the real Bonnie', who was still out cold, and then to the newborn Bonnie, and thought, "How perfect."

When Bonnie finally started to come around, Buck grabbed her hand and said, "Bonnie, I have something really important to tell you." She started to perk up until Buck said, "Bonnie, I named the new calf, Bonnie after you." Buck was beaming, and I could see that Bonnie was starting to not look very happy about it, but I didn't want anything to wreck the rest of the day, so I looked eye to eye at Bonnie and said, "Bonnie, isn't that fantastic?" Before she could say a word, I squeezed her hand and nodded. She said, "Oh thank you Buck, what an honor."

The day was saved…so I said, "Come on Bonnie, let's go freshen up. There's still plenty of fish for us to catch! We'll see you boys in a few minutes." I looked over toward Jack, and winked…he winked back. It was as if we were both saying…Good Job!

Once in our room, Bonnie kept going on and on about how 'primitive' everything was and how she wasn't geared for this 'lifestyle'. I reminded her that our parents came from a very similar 'lifestyle' back in the old country.

Then I said, "So Bonnie, does that mean that if Buck asked you to get married, you'd say no?"

Her demeanor changed in a heartbeat, "Married? she asked, "What did Buck say? Did Jack say something? What happened while I was passed out?"

"Nothing – and no one said anything, I'm just saying..."

Before I could finish, she started running around like a nut and kept telling me to hurry, because we can't keep them waiting. She checked herself one time in the mirror and then pulled me toward the door.

I said, "Gee Bonnie, I never knew that fishing got you so excited?"

"Mary, it's just that we're losing valuable daylight that's all...that's all!"

Before I knew it, we were in the lobby, but there was no sign of the boys. Then through the front door came Jack. He tipped his hat, and said, "Ladies, your carriage awaits."

I said, "Well Bonnie, see how popular we are? We've gone from horses to a carriage."

When we got outside, there was a beautiful shiny black car.

"Is this for us?" I asked.

Jack said, "Nothing but the best for our two Bozeman Beauties." He called us that because on one of our first nights, there during dinner, they said that they were going to hold a Beauty Pageant for us, but since we were both so beautiful, and we were the only two girls at the ranch, that it would've been a tie anyway.

I said, "Jack, did the boss let you borrow his car for our trip?"

"Well something like that – get in."

It was beautiful and Jack explained that it didn't get much use, so to keep the engine running, they needed to take it out once in a while. I thought, 'great story', but I really didn't care. At that point, even if he had stolen it from the boss, I could have cared less, I just wanted to have fun!

As we drove along, I could only think of how this vacation just got better and better. We pulled up to an area with a large lake and Jack said, "Ladies, it's fishin' time! You gals go out and stretch your legs and Buck and I will set up camp."

Bonnie's mood changed and she said, "Camp? What do you mean by camp? I'm not spending the night out in this wilderness!"

Jack tried to calm her down by saying that he just meant a holding area for our stuff, and where we'll cook the fish that we catch.

"Oh no," Bonnie said, "I'm not cooking anything out here – I'm on vacation."

Jack said, "No Bonnie, Buck and I are going to cook for you and Mary. Now go along and cool your feet off or something while the menfolk set up."

Bonnie felt a little foolish, but since she's the kinda girl that likes to get the last word in, she said, "Fine, where do we freshen up?"

Jack pointed at the lake and said, "There ya go Bonnie – get as fresh as you'd like."

I could see that she was beginning to boil over, and I thought – Dear God, just relax Bonnie. So I started to move toward her in the hope that I could drag her away from Jack, but she moved away from me and said, "No Jack, that's not what I meant…and since you're forcing me to be blunt, here you go, I need to use a bathroom!"

Again, Jack not missing a beat, just pointed to the lake, and said, "There you go Bonnie – pee away."

She was furious, "Do you *really* expect me to pee in the lake?"

"Why not, fish do it all the time."

I started to laugh and Bonnie turned and glared at me and said, "Mary – How *dare* you laugh at me? Why you're no better than them! I want to go home right now!"

"Bonnie" I said, "let's go for a walk and..."

She moved away from me and said, "Mary, I don't want any of your crap about..."

Jack broke in with, "Crap? Oh that's at another lake, this is just the pee lake."

Now Buck and I both started to laugh. Bonnie looked like she was going to explode as she stormed off towards the lake. I looked at Jack, smiled and just shook my head and then went after her.

I kept calling to her to stop, but she wouldn't, so I finally had to run to catch up with her. Suddenly she stopped abruptly and I almost ran into her, she turned to me and said, "What do *you* want? Can't a girl *pee* in peace?"

I said, "Bonnie, where did you think we'd go to the bathroom? There's nothing around for miles. Please calm down so we can have some fun."

With that, I grabbed some leaves from a low hanging branch and I handed them to her.

She said, "What are those for?"

"You'll have to wipe, won't you?"

Then I started to laugh all over again.

She yelled, "I hate you Mary Zovko, I *hate* you!" She snatched the leaves out of my hand and marched toward some trees.

I thought…sure she'll be a bitch for a while and I'll have to deal with her,… but damn, it was worth it.

I came up with an idea, so I ran back up to the camp. I said to Buck, "Buck, I'm sure that you're aware that Bonnie's not really happy with this whole 'outdoor thing', so can you pay a little extra attention so that we can all have a nice afternoon?" With that, I handed him a ten-dollar bill, and he pushed it away, saying that it would be his pleasure and that he didn't want any money, because being near Bonnie was payment enough. He said, "Miss Mary, why I've never seen a gal like Miss Bonnie before. She's so fiery and excitin'. Why she'd be tougher to tame than a wild filly, so I don't want yer money."

"You're a brave man Mr. Buck. Take the money anyway. You can use it later for a silver bullet." And then I pushed the money into his hand. He looked confused. I didn't know if it was from the werewolf reference, the money or both.

As I turned to walk away, Jack came up to me and said. "Let's walk."

Then in a really sweet tone he said, "Mary, I know I've said this before, but how, better yet... why? Why do you put up with her? She's ornery, she's hateful, she's..."

I stopped him and said, "Jack, you don't know her like I do. She's really great and she's my dear, dear friend. We're practically sisters. I know she's a little high strung, but her parents made her that way; and I would do anything for her, because I know that she would do anything for me. She'll calm down…she always does."

He looked me in the eyes, grabbed my shoulders with his big hands and pulled me toward him. I wanted to kiss him so bad, but out of nowhere came Bonnie. She sounded almost bubbly as she said, "Come on you two. The fish aren't going to catch themselves are they? Yoo-hoo Buck, we need our poles!" As she walked by us, she took Jack's hands off of my shoulders and just kept walking toward the camp.

Jack yelled to Buck, "Buck, ya better hurry along. We don't want to keep Miss Bonnie from her fish." He looked at me and said, "You sure know your friend. I thought for sure that we'd have to turn around and head back. You're an amazing woman." Then he kissed me with so much passion that all I could think is – Thank God we're not alone – because at that moment, I really didn't want to be a 'good girl'." Someone was watching over us – I guess, – plus we could tell that Bonnie and Buck were near.

I pulled away and said, "Jack, I *do* believe that this is one of those moments that the nuns from St. Francis warned me about. Let's fish."

Chapter 39

We actually began having a great time. Bonnie even started a running joke about 'the different types of leaves' that you'll need when it was time to go to the bathroom.

Sure, there was also a lot of screaming by Bonnie, first the bait, then the fish, etc…but we still had a lot of fun. The guys treated us like queens. They cleaned and cooked the fish. They had even brought some potatoes and cooked them too. It reminded me of when I was a child; me and my brother Babe would go out to the prairie across from our house and cook 'Hobo Potatoes' with some of our friends, around a campfire.

"Bonnie, doesn't this remind you of when we'd do 'Hobo Potatoes' in the prairie?"

"Mary how funny, I was just thinking the same thing."

Jack asked, "Hobo Potatoes?"

"Sure, we use to go out with our friends in the prairie near my house and roast potatoes in a bonfire...somebody said that that was how Hobo's did it, so they became Hobo Potatoes."

"Mary I just don't picture city girls like you two doing something like that."

"See Jack? We city girls have a mysterious side."

He just smiled.

As the guys cleaned up, Jack mentioned that we'd better get a move on, because night falls fast in Montana. I turned to Bonnie and said, "Well Bonnie, ya know what that means?"

"What Mar?"

"One last trip to Pee Lake!"

We all laughed and then got ready to leave.

It seemed that in no time at all, it really did get dark out, but Jack wanted to drive us up the mountain a little, so that we could really gaze at the stars. Gaze at the stars? Well I thought.

So much for him being a gentleman. Here is when he's going to make his move. God help us. We're in the middle of nowhere with two guys that haven't seen a woman since God knows when. Well, if he thinks that we're just some helpless city girls, then I'm ready to shoot this little cowboy down.

But all of a sudden, something that looked like a deer, ran across the road and Jack swerved so that we wouldn't hit it. I still don't know what happened after that, because before I knew it, the car had rolled over and off the road. I think that it rolled a second time. I'm still not sure. It stopped and finally rested on the passenger side. Jack yelled to see if we were all okay. He was on top of Buck and Bonnie was on top of me, but we were all fine. Then as I tried to move to get out, the sharp pain in my back got worse, and I could only think – Dear God – please don't let me be paralyzed. I finally freed my legs from some of the blankets and fishing gear, which had been in the back seat with us, so I knew I could walk, but now the pain in my back was searing.

The guys got out first and then they pulled Bonnie out, but as Buck and Jack were lifting me out Buck said, "Oh Miss Mary, looks like a fishin' hook is stuck in your back."

So he took out his knife and cut the fishing line that was still attached. Jack said that he'd take care of it from there and he asked Buck to see if he could get the trunk of the car open, and bring him a lantern. He thought for a second and then told Buck to forget about the lantern, because some kerosene might have leaked out and he didn't need a fire on top of everything else.

Bonnie was hysterical, of course.

Jack helped move me to the front of the car and said that the light from the car's headlights would be better anyway.

I asked, "Better for what?"

"Well Mary, that hook has got to come out, and it's got to come out now to avoid infection."

"Now?" I asked.

"Now." He said.

Then all of a sudden Jack said, "Mary, wait here."

"Where would I go?" I asked.

He said, "No, I know that you're not goin' anywhere, I just meant I've gotta get something out of the car and I don't want you to move, okay?"

"You're the doctor." I said.

Jack flashed me a reassuring smile and then he got up and crawled back into the front seat of the car. He retrieved a flask of whiskey from the glove box and handed it to me and told me to take a drink. I did and it burned going down. I didn't know what it was so I asked, "Is this whiskey or moonshine or…?"

Jack said, "Just take another drink…and this time make it a big one."

I did and I was starting to feel really warm. I saw Jack pull out a knife and he cut open the back of my blouse. I asked how bad it was and Jack told me that it looked like the hook went in right under my shoulder blade. He took the flask from me and poured some whiskey over the blade of the knife. Then he told me that he was going to have to pour some over the wound and that it would really sting. He told me to take one more fast swig from the flask and then the moment that it left my lips, he grabbed it and poured it over the wound. I wanted to scream but before I could, there was another sharp pain and all I could do was gasp.

"There, it's out and we're all done almost – now hang on!"

Then the burn of another splash of whiskey on my back and I was bursting, wanting to scream, when Jack said, "There you go Mary – good as new."

I finally yelled out, "Shiiiiit!!!" Then calmly said, "*Now* I'm good as new."

He smiled as he took his shirt off and I asked him what he was doing. He said, "Don't get any ideas. This is going to be your bandage." He tore it into strips and bandaged me up and then had Buck take off his shirt to cover me.

That of course hypnotized Bonnie…so the crying finally stopped. Jack got up and went to the car one more time and this time he came back with flares and a flare gun.

He said that someone at the ranch would probably be looking out for a signal from us, since we hadn't made it back yet. He was right, even though it seemed like only a few minutes had gone by, which I'm sure was due to the whiskey, a pick-up truck with a few of the ranch hands showed up to help us. First the men pushed on the car and rolled it back onto its wheels; then Jack helped me into the pick-up truck and asked Bonnie if she wanted to ride up front with me or ride in the back with Buck. He knew that she would jump at the chance to huddle in the back with Buck. He had one of the guys drive so that he could hold me and lean me up against him so that my right shoulder wouldn't hit the back of the seat and irritate my wound. I didn't mind.

All the way back, Jack kept apologizing for the accident and he kept telling me how brave I was. All I could think about was how soft and warn his shirtless body felt.

I remember getting back to our room but everything was still a blur from the whiskey. I do recall Bonnie throwing Jack and Buck out of our room after Jack had redressed my shoulder with a proper dressing. I believe that there was a little more whiskey involved as well.

Chapter 40

The next morning, I thought, was that all a dream? Until I moved and felt the pain in my back. I really was fine. After all of the beatings I'd been through in my life, this wasn't so bad. There was a knock at the door and while I was slowly getting my robe on, I could hear Bonnie in the next room talking to someone. I ran my fingers through my hair and opened the door. There was Jack and he was personally delivering room service to us.

I said, "Jack, you didn't have to do this. I can make it to the dining room. I'm fine."

Jack said, "Now Mary, you've been through a lot and you've got to take it easy."

Bonnie was silent, just watching Jack and I interact as she stood against the wall and then said, "I was in that car accident too ya know!"

Jack, being the diplomat said, "That's why there's breakfast for the both of you." Right on cue, Buck appeared in the doorway with a jar of jam, explaining that he had forgotten it and that he had to go back for it because he knew how much Bonnie liked it.

Immediately Bonnie's mood perked up, and she said, "Oh Buck, you didn't have to go though all that trouble for me…I mean us."

"Oh Miss Bonnie, it was no trouble at all."

Jack chimed in with, "Oh Miss Bonnie, Buck was very concerned about you and that's why he wanted to come along this morning. He had to see for himself that you were ok." Jack glanced over toward me and winked. He was finally learning how to deal with Bonnie.

Buck nodded and said, "Well Miss Bonnie, I would feel awful if something bad happened to you."

She went right up to Buck and softly said, "Were you *really* worried about me Buck?"

Before he could answer Jack reached under the tablecloth of the breakfast cart and pulled out a gift box and handed it to me and said, "I think that I owe this to you since I've ruined yours."

I couldn't imagine what he was talking about but as I opened it up, I could see that it was a beautiful blouse.

I said, "Jack, you didn't have to do this."

"Yes I did Mary, after all, I wrecked yours last night."

"But Jack, you had to cut the blouse to do your roadside surgery on me."

"Doesn't matter, you were in my car, so it's my responsibility and I told the fella in the store that he better stock up on some women's blouses with you here. Shucks, this is the second blouse in ten days and you still have twenty more to go!"

I laughed and asked, "Jack, how did you know my size?"

"Well I just took in what was left of the one that I took off of you last night and he figured it out." I thought how funny. I barely remember last night, except for the periodic pain in my shoulder. I thought, oh my God, Jack had me sitting out in the open, in a hotel room with a man I barely know, without my blouse on – no wonder Bonnie was so vigilant...Mama would flip out.

Speaking of flipping out, Bonnie suddenly wasn't all dreamy-eyed and I couldn't figure out why. Then it dawned on me, I think that it was the combination of Jack being so attentive to me and entertaining guests while still in my nightclothes...or maybe she was jealous that Buck didn't bring *her* a gift...or maybe she's just nuts.

Jack broke the silence by asking Bonnie and me if it would be ok for him and Buck to join us for dinner. I said sure, but Bonnie just grunted and walked out of the room with Buck behind her trying to ask simple things like what time, etc. Jack came over to me and looked me in the eye and apologized for upsetting Bonnie again. He said he wasn't quite sure what he had done, but *was* sure that it was his fault, none the less. Before I could answer, he looked at me again, this time with a warm glow, and told me that if anything had happened to me, he would've never forgiven himself.

I said, "What are you talking about? Accidents happen and…"

But before I could finish, he stopped me and playfully said, "You know Mary, it's indirectly your fault."

"My fault?" I exclaimed, "How could it be *my* fault?"

He sat down on the edge of the bed and moved in close to me. As he looked into my eyes he said, "Because I was too busy staring at how beautiful you looked in my rearview mirror, instead of looking at the road."

"And may I ask *why* you were staring at me?"

Slowly he said, "What man wouldn't?" and then he kissed me. All I could think was, life just doesn't get better than this!

Just then, Bonnie walked in, stopped, looked at us, and then marched into her room and slammed her door.

Jack said, "Oops, looks like we're in trouble again. Is she always going to be like that?"

"Yep,…see ya tonight Jack. You better go."

Jack got up from my bedside and winked at me as he said, "See ya at eight." Then he was gone.

Chapter 41

Bonnie was still in a mood so she wasn't around for most of the day, which was fine with me. It gave me time to rest and to dream about Jack. I thought, how could I possibly feel so passionate about a man that I've only known for such a short time? Was I crazy? I wondered what Kuma would think about all of this. With Bonnie being gone, I decided to write Kuma and tell her everything… especially the fact that this trip would've been a lot more fun if I'd have gone with her and not Bonnie. That reminded me that Kuma insisted that I bring along some of her really elegant evening gowns on the trip. I thought that I wouldn't have any use for them in the old West, but once again, Kuma knows best. Tonight was the night to really show these cowboys what city girls can look like.

When Bonnie finally got back I said, "Bonnie, let's give these Bozeman Boys a thrill." I held up a beautiful black and gold beaded gown. At first Bonnie looked excited, and then she got very quiet. I asked her what was wrong. She said, "Sorry Mar, it's just that I don't have someone to buy me beautiful things like that."

"Well no one bought these for me either. Kuma let me borrow this and there are plenty more. That's why I brought so much stuff, so we *both* can get dolled up! Let's face it. We couldn't dress like this at home, they'd think that we were nuts – but out here, well I think that these guys think that this is exactly how big city gals dress. So let's give'em a show!"

Bonnie got all giddy and I told her to come over and pick something out.

She walked over and I opened a large steamer trunk. I started placing things on my bed. As I pulled out a beautiful pink beaded gown, I could see Bonnie's eyes really light up. I knew that she always liked it, so I brought it for her.

"Mar, could I wear this one?" she asked as she held it to her chin and looked at herself in the mirror.

"Of course…that's why I brought it."

"Oh thank you Mar – I'm gonna try it on right now!"

I was so happy to see Bonnie excited and positive for a change. She came waltzing back with it on and looked beautiful. It fit her like a glove.

Bonnie said, "I feel like a princess. It's perfect!"

"Why yes you do Miss Bonnie…The Princess of Bozeman, Montana."

She said, "It's a little long, but with shoes…"

"Oh my God – Bonnie I forgot the shoes. Did you bring any that might go with this?"

Well that moment of being positive was starting to fade so I said, "I have an idea. Let's wear our boots and then at some point, after they're devastated by our beauty, we'll lift up our dresses and show them the boots. After all, out here cowboy boots *do* go with everything."

Bonnie laughed and thought that it was a brilliant idea. She was really starting to act like her old self and I thought that she may really be starting to settle in. This could really turn out to be the best vacation ever.

When we finally walked into the dining room, everyone's heads turned as we went by, even Emma, the cook came out of the kitchen to look as us. Buck and Jack were waiting at the table for us and stood up as we approached. They were speechless. As they came around to pull out our chairs, I looked at Bonnie and nodded my head, as the signal to lift our dresses. The second that the guys saw our boots they burst into laughter and I said, "See, you never know what city girls will do!"

Jack shook his head and said, "You sure are full of surprises."

Buck chimed in with, "Miss Bonnie, you sure do look pretty tonight."

"Thank you Buck." Bonnie said sweetly.

I just smiled and said, "Well, after all gentlemen, we've noticed that cowboy boots *do* go with everything."

Jack said, "Why yes they do ladies, but I think that Buck and I are a little underdressed. Would you like us to go and change?"

Bonnie grabbed Buck by the arm and said, "No Buck. Don't leave. You look just fine. We wanted to get dressed up for a change, that's all."

I said, "Bonnie's right. We wanted to show you that we can be pretty when we want to."

Jack said, "Well Mary, you're not pretty… you're beautiful."

Before I could answer Jack, Bonnie turned to Buck and said, "What about me Buck? Do I look beautiful too?"

Buck answered, "Oh Miss Bonnie, you're more than beautiful…you look like an angel."

Bonnie was all smiles, not just then, but during the entire dinner. It was the most perfect night. Bonnie was getting Buck's full attention and I was getting Jack's. I didn't want it to end. Out of the corner of my eye I saw a ranch hand coming toward us and he was holding a telegram.

He said, "Howdy Miss Mary. Here, this is for you. It's from Chicago."

I got a little nervous, I hoped that everything was ok at home, so I quickly opened it. It was from my brother Babe. It stated that Mama was very sick and we were to return home on the morning train.

I was devastated, torn between my love for Mama and the chance, for the first time, to be free, not to mention, perhaps in love. My heart sank because I knew that I had to go back, after all, Mama was all I had.

So we excused ourselves and went to our room to pack. With each item that I placed in my suitcase, I felt a mix of disappointment for me and fear for Mama, plus the guilt for being so selfish. Damn Catholic upbringing!

There was a knock at the door. It was Jack. "Mary, I'm so sorry for you...and me, because you're leaving. Here, I made this for you. I hope you like it."

He handed me a small gift box. I opened it up and in it was a gold pin that looked like rope. In script, it spelled *Mary*.

"Oh Jack, you didn't have to do that."

He put his hand on my cheek, looked me in the eyes and said, "I sure did Mary, because I love you." Then he pulled me up against him and kissed me.

I couldn't believe it.

I felt all warm and tingly. Bonnie walked out from the bathroom, still brushing her teeth, and screamed. But this time we didn't care. Instead of beating on Jack, she just reached into her pocket, pulled out a rosary and started to pray, with toothpaste flying everywhere. Our lips parted and we looked at each other, then we both looked over at Bonnie. Jack said, "I'd better leave, she's gone rabid. I'll pick you up and bring you to the train in the morning." He gave me another kiss. It was incredible. Then he turned to Bonnie and said, "Well ya better tell God about that one too." She retreated back into the bathroom and slammed the door. I laughed, but could feel my eyes well up with tears. How could I be leaving him, I thought? Once again, I felt as though I was being punished, by God, for having fun and for being too strong willed.

The bathroom door opened up and this time Bonnie just stood there with her mouth open watching us still in an embrace.

Jack tipped his hat at her, winked to me, as we parted, and turned to leave.

I followed him to the door and watched Jack walk away one last time as he went down the hall. I leaned against the doors frame and just reflected for a moment on the kiss and then I slowly closed the door. Then I noticed that Bonnie was still standing there staring at me. She turned her back to me in disgust and walked away toward the bathroom, waving her toothbrush in one hand, and her rosary in the other, while sternly saying, "How could you let him do that to you *again*?"

She spit the toothpaste into the sink and I followed her. Once I reached the bathroom door I said, "It was easy…*and* it was very nice."

She screamed as she slammed the bathroom door in my face.

Chapter 42

I hardly slept at all that night and before I knew it, it was morning. I barely ate breakfast because I was so upset. Bonnie was chowing down like a champ, mumbling every so often how she couldn't wait to get home. I kept myself since I really didn't have the strength to fight with her, and I knew that she really didn't want to hear how miserable I really was.

There was a knock at the door. I was hoping that it was Jack, but it was just two of the ranch hands there to pick up our luggage and put it in the car. At the time I thought, when did they have time to fix the car?

They told us that as soon as we were done they had sandwiches, ready and waiting for us, in the dining room to take on our trip. I thanked them but nothing really held my attention, because I was so miserable.

Bonnie kept trying to hurry me along, but I felt like a zombie so much so, that she had to hand me my purse and gloves. She even put my hat on my head as she dragged me toward the dining room.

Once we were there, it seemed as though everyone came out to send us off. I only cared about seeing one face…Jack's. We sat down and everyone was wishing us a safe journey and even expressed concern for my mother's health.

Then Jack showed up, and he was trying to be chipper, but I noticed that his eyes looked a little watery as our eyes met. Bonnie told them that I didn't eat breakfast, so the sandwiches will come in handy. They forced me to have some toast and coffee before I left and then before I knew it, we were in the car. I sat in the back and kept staring at Jack's beautiful eyes in the rearview mirror. Periodically I would catch his eyes well up with tears…not bad for a rough and tough cowboy. Buck came with us too, so it was just the four of us, and we were all very quiet during the ride, except for Bonnie. She was talking more at us than to us, so none of us really needed to respond.

Finally we arrived at the train station. It was a sad good bye for Jack and me. Even Bonnie's stoic demeanor slightly slipped as Buck tried to hug her, which she did let him do for a second, until she caught herself and turned it into a handshake. She said, "Well, thanks for everything." Then she hurried to the train.

Jack and I hugged for as long as we could, and then heard the conductor say, "All Aboard." I knew I had to leave, but as I was going up the steps to board, I stopped and turned to Jack and asked, "What ever happened to my shrunken boots?"

He said, "Mary, I hoped you'd forgotten all about them. I kept them so that I would have something to remember you by. You don't mind do you?"

"Not at all Jack…Not at all."

This time *I* grabbed him and kissed *him*!

I thought if nothing else came out of this trip, it showed me that I was beginning to feel like a woman. Thank you Jack.

The train whistle blew and I entered the train and found Bonnie and our seats. As the train pulled away, we waved good bye to Jack and Buck from the train window. I thought it may have been brief, but it was truly wonderful.

Even with tears welling up in my eyes, I could see that Jack was wiping his eyes too, and then he blew me a kiss. I thought, sure these cowboys may have a rough life, but their hearts are soft and pure as gold.

A few hours into the train ride I turned to Bonnie and said, "Don't you wonder what else Jack does besides work part time at the ranch? I mean he can't make a lot of money there."

She laughed and said, "Why they don't pay him, he owns it. He owns the whole mountain! His father found gold up there years ago, and Jack just has the ranch for fun...he's rich!

I couldn't believe it. I wanted to kill her.

"You're so stupid Bonnie! How could you keep something like that from me? Why didn't you tell me before?"

She slammed her book shut and finally looked me in the eye and smugly said, "Because I knew that if I told you, you'd ***never*** have left!"

"Of course I would, after all Mama's sick!"

She giggled, looked back down into her book and under her breath said, "Now who's stupid?"

"What?"

She said, "I sent a wire to my mother, and told her what 'animals' those men were up there, except for Buck. She told your mother, and your mother sent the telegram, not your brother. That's why we're going home. She's fine! *Now* see who's 'stupid'!"

I felt like throwing her off the train by her hair, but I tried to remain calm. Even though I was so mad at her betrayal, I could only keep thinking to myself, so she helped Mama win again.

I couldn't believe that Mama was *still* able to manipulate me, even from thousands of miles away, thanks to a little help from my 'dear friend' Bonnie.

I asked her if I could see her glasses for a moment.

She handed them over, and just that quickly, I flung them out the window. Again, she screamed and cried, but this time it made me very, very happy. We didn't speak for the rest of the ride home.

Chapter 43

Once home, it was the same old routine, and eventually I got a letter from Bonnie, who was now away at college.

It stated that she had now, 're-evaluated' the whole trip, and that *maybe* she was a little wrong and that she was sorry. She also stated in the letter that she had begun dating a boy, who was originally studying to be a priest, but when the church found out that he was mentally ill-equipped to handle the priesthood, they dropped him from the seminary. I thought how perfect for her. For a 'good time' they could say the rosary together.

As for me, I really missed Jack, but what made it a little easier, was that I was getting closer to my pal, Bill Fisher. Eventually he went from being my pal to my boyfriend, which had its share of madness too.

Like the fact that his family treated me coldly because I was Croatian and they were Serbian, which was a big deal back then. It didn't matter to them that we were *all* Yugoslavian. I was still considered 'from the wrong side of the tracks'. It's funny. My parents had always told me the same story, except in reverse.

Little by little, his parents warmed up to me, then his brothers and a few of his eight sisters. To this day, some of them still refer to me as, 'that woman who married our brother'.

It's hard to believe they felt this way, even though I stole money, from my mother's bar, to help them buy a house. In the meantime, my mother who once condoned my seeing Bill, suddenly changed her tune.

One day when I was helping her clean the bar, she told me that I should get a boyfriend.

"Mama," I said, "I have a boyfriend...Bill."

"Don't make me laugh, he's not your boyfriend, he's your watch dog. I'll find you a 'good' boyfriend, and believe you me, he won't be a Serbian."

I thought, this is it, the final straw, so I said, "Mama, Bill loves me!"

Quickly she turned to me and said smugly, "No, he doesn't love you, he loves my money!"

Devastated I looked at her with disbelief, "Mama, what are you saying?" Coldly she pointed her finger at me and said, "That's right, you think that you're so smart. Well, the truth is, that besides being stupid, you're also so ugly that I had to *buy* you a boyfriend! And without my money he'd be gone!"

I wasn't accepting what she was saying. "No Mama, no... that's not true!"

Defiantly she said, "Oh yeah? Well why don't you ask him for yourself? There, ask him!" She pointed toward the back of the tavern, near the kitchen.

I looked over, and there he stood frozen, and had a shocked look on his face. I didn't notice that he had come in the back door.

I slowly walked over toward him. "Bill," I asked, "does my mother give you money?"

He stumbled to find the words, then uttered, "Well, you see, she…uh… well…"

I demanded, "Just tell me 'yes or no' Bill, yes or no?"

He looked at me and with tears in his eyes he simply said, "Yes - but…."

I didn't have to hear another word. Humiliated I ran out the front door of the bar and past Mama's laughter. I ran and ran, crying the whole time. I had a ton of things racing through my mind, like how much I hated him, Mama, but mostly; I hated myself. How could I have been so stupid?!!

When I finally stopped, I found myself on Ewing Avenue, our local shopping district. People were staring at me because I was so obviously upset, and then some people started to say hi to me.

Blankly I said, hi back to them, not even being aware of whom I was speaking to. All of a sudden, I heard the brakes of a car screech to a halt in front of me. I looked up and it was Bill.

I screamed, "Get away from me…you're a monster! I believed you liked me, even loved me! Am I *that* repulsive that you have to take money from my mother to even be seen with me?"

By now everyone had stopped dead in their tracks to watch the show. The East Side is like a small town, and this was just the sort of thing they lived for.

He begged, "Mary, please get in the car. We have to talk!"

Wiping away the tears I coldly said, "How much will it cost me?"

He told me that I was acting crazy as he hopped out of the car. He asked me again to get in the car. I refused and as he went to grab my arm, I screamed, "Don't touch me you bastard!"

He begged again and again, so finally, just to stop the scene on the street from getting any bigger, I reluctantly got in. We drove to Calumet Park and parked near the beach. Then he explained that how when he got back from the Army he needed money, so he asked Mama if she needed help or if anyone was hiring. That's when Mama made him an offer to be my bodyguard, or as Mama put it, watchdog. She thought that since I was getting older, she was afraid that without a father to watch over me, I might turn into a whore.

I laughed and said to him, "That's pretty funny. Mama didn't want me to become a whore, so she turned *you* into one." With that I grabbed the door handle and said, "Good bye Bill, I hope that the next girl you get paid to watch, is at least pretty. Sorry I'm such a dog."

He told me that he would find a way to make it up to me. I just coldly said, "Take me home."

Looking defeated he obliged, and no matter what he said to me, I refused to answer him. We were almost home when we stopped at a red light. That's when Bill made his move. He slid over, grabbed me by the shoulders and kissed me. I broke away from him and got out.

He stood up on the seat of the convertible and told me that he loved me. Then in even a louder voice, he asked me to marry him. Everyone within ear shot started clapping and cheering.

I was infuriated by the whole scene. Who was he doing this for, certainly not for me!

I just had to get away and think so I started to run, with the intention of getting back to the bar as fast as I could. I just wanted to go to bed and shut out the world – I felt so empty and worthless.

It was less than a mile and periodically I could hear Bill blowing his horn and yelling to me, but I just ignored him.

He finally gave up, I thought, but as I approached the apartment entrance to the building, Bill's car cut me off and he jumped out.

He grabbed me firmly by the shoulders and exclaimed, "Mary, if you'll go into the bar with me, I'll tell your mother that I love you and that I'll pay her back all the money, because I really *do* want to marry you!"

I was so confused. I didn't know what the truth was or what was going on anymore.

I composed myself, looked him straight in the eye and said, "Do you really mean it? You'd give back all the money to Mama?"

"Yes Mary...yes I will. Is that so hard for you to understand, so hard for you to believe?"

I looked at him and said, "Yes Bill, it is.... more than you know."

Then he kissed me like he never had before. There was so much passion that I knew he meant every word. He held me for what seemed like an eternity. When we walked into the bar, hand in hand...Mama was speechless.

Bill spoke first and said, "Mary, I know you've given me a lot of money to watch over your daughter, but I'll have to find a way to pay you back, because I'm going to watch over her for the rest of her life, for free. I want to make Mary my wife."

Mama's eyes looked as if fire would shoot out of them at any moment. Slowly and directly she said, "I'd kill her before I'd let her marry a filthy, disgusting Serbian pig like you!" With that she spit on the floor near Bill's feet. "Now get the fuck out of here and never come back!" she demanded.

Bill, being a gentleman said, "Thank you." to Mama, and told me that he would call me later. With that, he was gone. I thought, how funny.

Where is he going? I needed his protection *now,* more than ever. Protection from Mama. She glared at me and said in a low tone, "Get the fuck upstairs and out of my sight, before I kill you!"

For days she went on and on about Bill, especially when she would catch me sneaking telephone calls from him. We would plan brief meetings at Kuma's; because she really liked Bill, and she could see how happy he made me. In the meantime, Bill had gotten a job at a steel mill called Valley Mold & Steel, and the best part was that it was less than a half mile from my house. At the time, it was the norm, for the men in our neighborhood to go to work there, or at one of the other five steel mills in the area.

Of course I got out in the real world too. I tried a few jobs, unsuccessfully, but it gave me a chance to go downtown and really experience life.

I finally landed a great job with the gas company. Not only was the pay wonderful, but my favorite benefit was that there were all types of different women to work with. We'd have all kinds of girl talk, from fashion to sex. They couldn't believe how naïve I was when it came to the latter. To my surprise, when they would discuss certain sex acts and sex play in detail, I realized that I'd already done them as a child. The more they talked the more it bothered me, and I suppressed my feelings of rage and hate toward all of those men…and my mother. It's a shame that the times were so different back then, because today I could have gotten help and avoided some of the emotional trauma that I had to deal with on a daily basis. What I was going through ranged from guilt, shame, mistrust and self hate. I never had to think about it before, because those types of discussions, were always taboo back then. Now with this open dialogue, I began a downward spiral of self hate and lack of self-worth, which would plague me for the rest of my life.

Chapter 44

Time was drawing nearer for our wedding. It was going to be a happy joyous time, or so we thought. You see, Bill was Serbian Orthodox and I was Catholic and this difference in our religions posed an even bigger problem than an inter-racial marriage did because both nationalities have hated each other historically and forever. Even though they were both Christian, and from neighboring states in Yugoslavia, they may as well have been from different planets. I know that by today's standards it seems crazy, but in 1947 and on the south side of Chicago, it was the way it was.

We were finally told that we could be married in the Catholic Church *if* Bill converted to Catholicism and *if* we promised to raise our children Catholic. Since I went to church all the time and Bill didn't, we thought, well that's the way to go.

Bill always said, "There's only one God and he lives in our hearts, not in a building."

To my disappointment and humiliation, I was not allowed to wear white, even though I was a virgin.

Since we were considered a mixed marriage, according to the local custom, I was to wear an off-white suit and we were to have a small, private ceremony on a Sunday after the priest was finished with the scheduled services in the back of the church, in the priest's chambers.

I was so furious at the Catholic Church, that when I had children of my own, I made them go to every other type of church that I could find. I told them that when it came to picking a religion, they're really all the same. God wants us to be kind to each other, and that's all. Everything else was made up by men, who were trying to manipulate people through guilt.

By the time the priest pronounced us husband and wife, I didn't know if the tears in my eyes were for joy in marrying Bill, or the sadness of not having a 'real' wedding. Not to mention, that perhaps it would have been a little better if my mother had come.

Oh yes, I told her when and where Bill and I were getting married, but she never believed me. She said that even *I* couldn't be as stupid, as to marry a filthy Serbian.

Since Mama wasn't coming, I didn't tell many of my friends when the wedding actually was, but I had to tell Kuma. For my side of the family, it was Kuma, my brother Babe and his pal Pete (he was my friend Bonnie's brother, she was away at school), my old buddies Tony and Kimo, and my girlfriends Millie and Vicky. Bill said since Mama wasn't coming, he wouldn't tell his family. He was also afraid that they would have wanted a big event and we couldn't afford it, plus how would I explain Mama's absence without offending them. Bill understood and that's all that mattered to me. Thank god my brother Babe disobeyed Mama and came. It meant so much to me, not only because I loved him, but because he put *me* before Mama. Kuma did host a small reception at her house and even though it was an intimate gathering, Kuma made it lovely.

On Monday morning when everyone re-hashed their weekend activities, I just chimed in, "Oh, I didn't do much….just got married, that's all."

At first they didn't' believe me, so I quickly showed them my rings. They asked me why they hadn't seen my engagement ring until now. They all knew of my mother problems, so it came as no surprise to them, when I said that she wouldn't let me wear it. After all, she didn't want the whole world to know how 'stupid' her daughter actually was. Then they all asked about the 'wedding night'! I told them I was sad because I couldn't spend it with Bill. They all had similar shocked looks on their faces. I told them that tonight after work, we were going to be moving in with Bill's family. They still wanted to know what happened.

I went on with a very embarrassing and unbelievable tale, that started the minute we went to show Mama the marriage license. After the reception at Kuma's, Bill and I went upstairs of the bar to the apartment, and there was Mama in the kitchen, preparing some food. I knocked on the door frame as we entered. She would hardly look at us.

I said, "Mama, we have something to show you". I slowly took it out of my purse and handed her a piece of paper. She grabbed it from my hand, saw the words 'marriage license' and tore it up. She threw the pieces on the ground and then spit on them.

I asked her if she'd gone crazy.

With that she slapped me across the face, and as Bill moved forward to defend me, she pulled a small pistol out of her cleavage. I cried out for Bill to leave, and that I'd call him later. I acted as a human shield as I pushed him out of the door. I just kept hoping that she wouldn't kill both of us.

You see, Bill had no idea just *how* crazy Mama was until then. I didn't want him to get hurt, because even *I* hadn't seen Mama act *that* crazy in front of somebody who wasn't a family member.

With Bill out of sight, Mama turned on me and said, "Don't lie to me you fucking bitch. Nobody gets married on Sunday! What? Did you think that I'd fall for a phony piece of paper, just so that bastard Serb can fuck you? I'm not stupid!"

She slapped me again and through my tears I tried to tell her that the priest was doing us a special favor.

"Why?" Mama chimed in, "Are you pregnant?"

"No Mama, I just didn't see why I should wait, besides, I couldn't wear a long white dress because Bill is Orthodox."

"Bill's a pig!" Mama yelled, "You don't know how many whores he's slept with in the war, not to mention what kind of diseases he could have picked up! Did I raise you so that you could be fucked by some dog like him?"

Horrified I ran to my room and threw myself across the bed. I couldn't believe what had just happened. Then I thought, I'd better call Bill to let him know that I'm ok, but before I knew it, the door was being locked behind me. I got up off the bed and tried the handle... locked. "Mama, what are you doing?"

She responded with "I'll take care of everything!"

The phone rang several times and every time she'd pick it up, I could hear Mama yell into the phone that I wasn't there and hang up. I knew it was Bill and I hoped that he knew me well enough to know, that I'd never leave him. I cried myself to sleep that night. In the morning Mama had breakfast ready and she did let me out to go to work, and on my plate were ten one hundred dollar bills. She apologized and said that it was just the shock of the news, and that the thousand dollars was a wedding gift. I couldn't believe it. She seemed like a normal mother for a moment. That kind of money, in 1947, was enough for a down payment on a new house. I hugged and kissed her and then with teary eyes, I thanked her.

The girls on the train were pretty shocked, but none more than me! Their shock of course, was for the entire story, but mine was for the sudden change in Mama, because I knew her and what she was capable of...and it just seemed too good to be true.

As we parted to go to our jobs, they told me to have fun tonight and they wanted *all* the details tomorrow. What details, I thought?

At work I called Bill and told him what had happened. He couldn't believe it. He couldn't get over just how crazy Mama could be. I guess when I'd told him stories about her in the past he didn't believe me, but he did now, especially after her pistol routine.

Well Bill met me at the train after work, and we went again to see Mama. When we got to the bar I asked Tony where she was and he first pointed to the basement, and then he motioned like she was crazy. I just laughed and yelled down to her in the basement. She yelled up that I was to go upstairs to the apartment. When Bill and I got up there, I noticed that the dishes from breakfast were still on the table. That's not like Mama I thought, because even if she were dying, she'd wash the dishes.

When she finally appeared, she looked a bit frazzled, like she'd been working all day.

"Mama, you look tired, I'm just going to get some of my things and I'll be off ok?"

"Sure Madia, go ahead." She asked Bill if he'd go down to the basement and bring up a case of beer. He obliged, but to me this all seemed so strange. I should have known what was coming next. As I made my way to my room, I heard the backdoor close, and Mama locking it. I didn't think too much about it until I came out of my room and saw Mama tearing the telephone wires out of the walls. As she hurriedly proceeded through the apartment, she was winding the cords around her arm, with a vengeance, as she walked through the apartment toward the kitchen.

I screamed, "Mama….what are you doing?"

At first there was no response, then she stopped walking, and she slowly turned around, and had a look on her face that I hadn't seen since I was a child. My blood ran cold!

Finally, in a calm tone, I asked her "Mama, what's wrong?"

"Nothing Madia, but a Mother has to do what she thinks is right, no matter what others think, that's all." With that she just turned and walked back into the kitchen.

I followed her into the kitchen and once in there, I noticed that the back door was not only closed, but now there were bars over the doors only window, and the door had about three new locks. Not to mention that there were now two 2"x 4" planks of wood that fit into brackets on the back of the door.

Just then Bill had started to knock on the door, and as I went over to try and open it, Mama grabbed me from behind and threw me up against the wall.

As I went near the door again, she picked up one of the wrapped up phones and hurled it at me.

I screamed, "Mama, are you insane? What are you doing?"

Then like a wild animal she started laughing, and then suddenly stopped. Coldly she stared into my eyes and slowly said, "He'll make you dirty. You think I'm stupid? Well I'm saving your life! And besides being dirty, there'll be pain too! Once he climbs on top of you, you'll be dirty forever!"

She looked crazy. I was so scared and shocked that I could only stand there with my mouth wide open.

Just then Bill started pounding like a mad man. He was yelling, "What's going on?"

Mama quickly ran to the door and yelled back that I was locked in and I was never coming out....not for him or any other man! And especially not to be some Serbian pig's WHORE!

Then the noise stopped and Bill was gone. I couldn't believe that Bill would just leave me behind, without a fight. But before I knew it, I heard a different noise. This time it was coming from the living room. It was Bill. He had gotten a ladder out from our garage and propped it up against the building. He was climbing up to get me on the second floor.

Mama was pretty sharp too, and she came out of nowhere holding a broom. The more Bill climbed, the more Mama nudged the ladder over, until the ladder finally slipped and Bill fell into the street.

I yelled to make sure that Bill wasn't hurt. He yelled back that he was ok and that I should hit Mama over the head with something to knock her out!

Mama quickly turned to me and said, "See, I told you he was no good. He wants to turn you against your Mother! Remember what the Bible says," she went on, "You are to 'honor' your Mother, not some pig like him!"

I turned to Bill and explained that there was no way that I could hit my Mother. "I'll burn in hell!"

Then a shot rang out and I heard Bill yell. I looked out the window and I heard another shot and saw Bill jump out of the way. I turned to my right and couldn't believe what I saw, Mama had been shooting at Bill from the kitchen window.

I yelled, "Mama, are you crazy? You'll kill him!"

"I hope so." She yelled back.

I looked back toward Bill and I yelled, "Run Bill, get out of here before she *kills* you!"

He just shook his head, hopped in his car and drove away. I walked back to the kitchen and saw how pleased Mama looked with herself, and then she told me that *someday* I'd thank her.

I just walked back to my room and fell across my bed and started to cry. I laid there motionless, trying to understand what had just taken place. In between my thoughts, I could still hear Mama's laughs and footsteps, as they faded on her way to the kitchen. I couldn't believe Bill left me so easily, but what could he do? After all, she had a gun.

About a half hour had passed when I thought I heard some noise outside my window. I got up and looked, and it was Bill. This time he'd brought reinforcements with him, my brother Martin.

"Babe," I yelled, "Please help me! Mama has me trapped up here."

Babe yelled back that he knew the whole story and it would be ok. He also told me that I should grab everything that I needed and that I could carry out of my room right now, because after this, there would be no coming back!

I knew he was right so I grabbed a suitcase from under my bed and started packing like a madwoman.

Then all of a sudden I heard Mama's footsteps and I could hear her yelling, "What is going on?"

"Oh nothing Mama, everything's fine." I yelled. This was also a cue to Bill and Babe that Mama was on the loose again and to expect anything.

Suddenly my door flew open and she appeared. This time she had a screwdriver and hammer in her hand. In a flash, she'd knocked the pins out of the hinges of my bedroom door, stating that this way she would be able to hear any monkey business. She dragged the door along the floor, all the way to the kitchen. I realized that through her own conniving, she'd missed the *real* plan of escape…the window.

As she walked away she said, "Remember... you stay put! I've got the keys and the gun….so I have your life! One more thing, Miss Movie-star, any *decent* daughter would give back that thousand dollars to her poor arthritic and *loving* Mother!"

I thought, you're right Mama, and that's exactly why I'm going to keep it. From behind me, I could hear something outside.

When I went to look, I saw Bill, Babe, and my friend, Bonnie's brother Pete.

They had his father's flatbed truck and it was pulled up to the side of the building. On it were some box springs and mattresses. Bill put his finger up to his lips so I wouldn't talk and then he motioned for me to jump. I thought, I can't do that…I'd die, literally. But I also knew that I couldn't be afraid anymore and that even if I died, it was ultimately better than living with Mama. So I threw my suitcase down, clutched my purse to my chest and jumped!

It was a perfect landing!

Bill was right there at the side of the truck and helped me down and embraced me in such a way, that I knew everything was going to be ok, no matter what!

I turned to Babe and Pete and thanked them both, then asked Babe how he got involved in all of this? He told me that Mama had warned him to stay put at Pete's house until she called. Bonnie had called from school and told Pete about the wedding. Then Bill stopped by Pete's and asked to borrow the truck, so we all got together and planned your escape! Boy, you sure are brave, not only to jump like that, but to also go against Mama."

"Babe, what about you? *You* still have to go back in there. Aren't you afraid?"

"No Mar, not at all, remember Ma loves me and she'd never hurt me!"

I knew he didn't mean it that way, but to me, I could only hear the words, 'Ma loves me… and she could give a shit about you, Mary.' I also knew that whatever he said was because of Mama's conditioning and sick manipulation. The truth of the matter was, when I needed him, he *came* to my aid. Actions *do* speak louder than words.

We all hopped in the truck and after a few blocks, we stopped driving and pulled up in front of a large brownstone. I asked Bill what was up and he explained, the building belonged to some friends of his family, and their tenant left early, so they were going to let us spend a week there, before we moved into his parents' house. Plus since Bill was one of thirteen, and most of his siblings were still at home, it was going to be loud and crazy there and this will give us some time to be alone.

I thought, how romantic, and "thank you God" for sending me such a wonderful man like Bill. Not only was he *so* thoughtful, but he also *truly* loves me!

He carried me over the threshold, and as the door opened wider, I could see that he had fixed it up a little. He started to apologize for it not being perfect, but I wouldn't hear any of it. I just looked him square in the eyes and told him that to me, it was "paradise", and I loved it and him. Then I kissed him and I asked for a tour of the flat. When we got to the kitchen, Bill opened the refrigerator and he had put some food in there…he's the best. We ate a snack and then he suggested that we should get ready for bed since we had such an action packed day. Then he added that it was going to be an even longer night. I didn't know what he meant at the time, but he was right, it *was* the longest night of my life.

CHAPTER 45

We eventually got ready for bed and when I came out of the bathroom, I was shocked to find Bill waiting in the bed for me, minus a pajama top. It made me wonder two things, first, won't he get cold, and second, what was he wearing on the bottom?"

As I got into bed he told me how beautiful I was, and that he had been dreaming of this night for such a long time. He started kissing me and between his words and his lips, for that moment, I did feel beautiful. Then all of a sudden, it was like a movie from my childhood had started to play in my head. I can't explain it in any other way, and I immediately became repulsed beyond belief. The minute he touched my breast I jumped and cringed. He assumed that I was having a good time, when in actuality, I was remembering back to all of the men that had touched me when I was a child, especially an incident that happened when I was thirteen years old.

I was bartending and a drunk grabbed me, and as I pulled away from him, Mama grabbed me by the arm and said that he was a good customer, and that sometimes in business, you have to give a good customer a little feel....it was just good business. Then I remembered these loving words from my mother, "Besides Madia, you should be glad somebody *wants* to touch you."

Before I knew it, Bill was pulling down my underpants and I started to cry. He looked sort of pleased and said, "Gee, this *really* must be your first time." With that, he got on top of me. I wanted to die the second I felt his erection probe me. I screamed and quickly got out of bed. I ran over to the corner of the bedroom, where I immediately curled up into a ball, begging, "Please don't touch me. I don't want to be hurt anymore!"

Bill got up and put his pants on. He slowly came over to me, reassuring me that everything would be okay. He told me that he could see that it'll take some time, but it'll be okay. We sat there for the longest time. He held me and stroked my hair, trying to let me know that he really *did* care.

When I finally did feel a little calmer, I looked up into Bill's eyes and could see that he had been crying too. All I could think of was, what have I gotten myself into? I smiled at him and he said, "Don't worry Mar, I won't let anyone hurt you anymore. I can wait."

Well, talk is worth the paper it's written on, because the very next night we had exactly the same scenario. Except this time he told me that now I was being ridiculous, and I sat alone in the corner, while he slept.

In the morning he told me that tomorrow we would be moving in with his family, so tonight was the night...no matter what! As he walked away from me, he stopped, turned to me and asked, "What's wrong, don't you want to have children?" Outraged I yelled, "And just what does that dirty act have to do with having children? After all, children are a gift of God! If he feels that two people love each other enough, then he'll grant them children!"

He looked at me as though I had either lost my mind or I was speaking a foreign language. He said, "You've got to be kidding! Do you really believe that crap? God…you do! I can't believe a grown woman still goes for all that bullshit!"

In defense I yelled back, "Well, it's the truth!"

"Truth!" he screamed, "the truth *is*…. that you've got to put something in, to get something out! Didn't you know that?"

Looking down at the ground I simply said, "No."

Shocked, he said, "You mean you never heard of making love? For Christ's sake, you had a best friend that got knocked up and had an abortion! What did you think that was all about?"

Trying to pull myself together, I said, "Of course I remember that, but…well, I just thought that she loved someone too much! And that making love was just kissing and hugging!"

As he started to walk out the door, he stopped just long enough to say, "Well if you don't believe me, then why don't you ask your doctor all about it. No, better yet, why don't you go and ask a priest." With that, the door slammed shut and he was gone.

I knew that I had to calm down so I could go to work. I kept telling myself that I had to act just like it was any other day, and that I had all day to figure out what I was going to do about tonight. I also knew that the train ride with the girls, was not going to be easy.

Sure enough, all of their questions bothered me so much, that I just kept saying that I couldn't talk about it, because there were too many people around. That kept them at bay, but it didn't stop them from talking about their lives, and from all of their talk and with what Bill had said, maybe there *was* something to this sex stuff. As soon as I got to work I called and made an appointment with my doctor, and asked my supervisor if I could leave work a little early and she said that was fine. As she walked away I heard her mutter, "Aah…newlyweds."

Once at Dr. Arnold's office, he was not only surprised to find out that I was married, but that I had spent two nights as a virgin. Although, the real shocker, was when I told him my theory on where babies came from. Thank God that he was a *very* patient man. He took time out of his very busy schedule to explain *everything* to me. By the time he was through, about an hour later, I left his office enlightened and even more scared than I was before, because the entire idea of "the act of intercourse", still made me sick. I didn't know if it was the fact that it involved organs that excrete, or that both my mother and the church always told me that every part of my body that was covered by clothing was dirty. That, combined with the memory of all of those men in my youth touching and fondling me, added fuel to the incredible inferno of bitter memories that I kept, and still keep locked deep down inside of me, that made it seem like a disgusting and impossible task.

My next step was to talk to a priest, and if *he* went along with all of this, then I guess I would have to do…it!

Of course the priest found my naivety refreshing, but he did say that I *'had'* to consummate my marriage, otherwise in God's eyes, it would not be a *real* marriage.

I was told by a therapist later in life, that ninety percent of all mental illness, stemmed from either sex or religion. With me being two for two, it's no wonder how my life went.

Finally it was time for Bill to come home, and we were to have 'the wedding night', and I was a wreck. I tried to remember the advice that both the doctor and priest had given me. They said…the only way for me to find any sort of enjoyment in 'the act', was to forget about my past, and that I would have to really force myself to relax, otherwise it would not be enjoyable for either of us. Enjoyable?...I thought, I can't imagine it. I'm supposed to relax?...Who could relax knowing that some man was going to be on top of me, entering my body, with the part of his body that he urinates from, and that he would leave in my body, a mucus-like discharge. I wanted to throw up at the mere thought of it.

After dinner Bill told me how wonderful dinner was and how beautiful I was and then he said, "Mar, when you're done with the dishes, I'll be waiting in the bedroom for you." I thought, 'How romantic.'

I changed for bed and as I approached the bed, I could see that he was naked and only covered with a sheet. I could see that he was already aroused and erect, so I just had to keep repeating the words that the doctor and the priest kept saying,…relax, relax, relax.

I slid in next to him and he started again in his usual way, kissing me and mumbling something about love, and then before I knew it, I felt him tear his way through me.

As the tears streamed down my cheeks, I couldn't stand his repulsive pumping on top of me. The more furious his pounding became, the more I hated him for making me go through it. All the horrible things Mama had told me about sex and Bill, were coming true.

First it *was* painful, not to mention humiliating, the only thing that saved me was the fact that the entire ordeal didn't even take five minutes. Before I knew it, he was off me and asleep. That gave me time to take a hot bath and try to cleanse my now, defiled body. I just laid in the tub for a long time, feeling my tears running down my face and neck, asking myself if I would ever feel clean again.

CHAPTER 46

Once at his parents' house I had a reprieve, because Bill couldn't have sex under the same roof as his parents, he was physically ready, but not mentally. It didn't matter to me. I would have been happy with that arrangement, for the rest of my life. The only problem with living there were his sisters. Collectively, there were ten women all under one roof. Need I say more? With nothing more than sexual deprivation on his mind, Bill went out and bought a house as soon as he could.

It was less than a month, when he surprised me one Saturday afternoon. He wanted my ok on it, even though he had already put down the down payment. If he hadn't needed my signature for the closing, I wouldn't have seen it until we moved in.

At first I didn't know what to think because it was so small. But inside, it really was adorable, and the best part for me was that we still wouldn't be alone…thank God. His sister Ruth was pregnant and unmarried…so the family hoped that if she moved in with us, none of their friends would ever find out.

Even though she and I didn't get along when we lived at her parents' house, we became much closer, as time went on. I remember one day we were sitting around, just she and I, and I asked her, "Ruthie, why would you let a man do that to you? After all, it wasn't like you're married…I mean you didn't *have* to do it?"

Her only response was that she loved him, and one night, before she knew it, they were doing it, and kept having fun doing it.

I said to her, "You mean, you liked doing it?"

"Yeah Mar, don't you?"

"Oh sure," I said nervously, "but I'm married!"

"Oh that doesn't matter," she said as she rubbed her belly, "because I'm going to love this baby enough for two."

It all seemed to make sense in a way....it was as though it was a test from God. The test was that if you *really* wanted children, as much as most people always say that they do, then he would give them a disgusting ordeal to go through and the end result would be a beautiful baby. I know its twisted rationalization, but it's the only way that I got through it since I wanted a baby so bad. It also got me to look at Bill in a less disgusting way. I thought that he must have known about this all the time, and just assumed that I knew too. Why else would he have put me through it....He wanted a baby as much as I did. That afternoon was the only time I ever really felt close to Ruthie. We probably would have gotten closer, except in the meantime, her family finally found her a husband. He was Yugoslavian and Serbian. He was a new arrival to America, and I'm not quite sure what the details of the arrangement were...but I *do* know that he had a wife and family that he left back in Yugoslavia, which is why they couldn't get legally married, but no one except the family knew the truth. Anyway, she finally had a husband to show the world, so she could move out and she did.

CHAPTER 47

Even though I always had babies on the mind, it took four years for me to finally get pregnant. Once I was 'with child', things seemed to get better. Mama had relented a bit and I felt that I needed to be near her. We sold our house and we took an apartment about a block and a half away from her. It wasn't as big as our house, but it was convenient for Bill's work, for shopping and of course Mama. As far as Mama was concerned, it took her a few years, but she was finally softening up, because I was finally carrying her first grandchild, but she still hated Bill.

Chapter 48

When the baby came I was so happy. She was perfect. Mama was disappointed because it wasn't a boy, but Bill and I were the two happiest people in the world. Her name would be Patricia; Bill was adamant about it. I wanted to name her Cassie, but I thought it was pretty and since it made him *so* happy; I said to myself, why not?

Going through the birthing process was very easy for me, since by the time that I got to the hospital, she was already crowning. I mean it was all pretty wild. Bill was the craziest expectant father that you'd ever seen and I was the calm one.

As we entered the hospital, Bill yelled for a wheelchair. They brought it over and there I sat with my coat and hat on, holding my purse like I didn't have a care in the world. A nurse came over and asked me if my water had broken and I told her that yes it had, about an hour or so ago. She asked what took so long to get to the hospital and I explained that I had to take a shower first and of course, put on some make-up.

She said, "But weren't you in pain?"

"Not really" I answered. Then she looked concerned and turned me toward a corner and said, "I'm going to have a fast look, ok?" and before I could answer she lifted up my skirt and yelled, "Oh my God, we have a baby!" With that, I was wheeled directly in to the delivery room; hat, purse and all. They helped me from the wheelchair and onto the table. Then the doctor on duty said, "We're going to ask you to push and just bare down ok?"

Well I thought that when he said ok, that I was supposed to do it right there and then, so I did. Instant baby!"

They were all in shock.

The doctor said, "Your doctor's not even here yet!"

"But you said ok...right?"

Then I heard the baby cry and I felt wonderful. Everyone just looked at each other in disbelief at what had just happened, then the door opened and it was my doctor, Dr. Arnold.

He said, "Mary, you were supposed to wait for me."

"Well Doc, she wanted out!"

He went over to the baby and said, "Mary, she's beautiful."

I was so happy and said, "Ten fingers and toes?"

"Yep, they're all there."

"How about her big toe…Is it normal?"

"She's perfect. Here, see for yourself." With that he had the nurse bring her over to me and like every new Mom, all I could think was that she was the most perfect baby that I'd ever seen.

Once in my room, I could hear the nurses talk about the miracle baby and how lucky I was to have had such an easy time of childbirth. I didn't really think much of it, until I heard screams coming from down the hall, and asked the nurse, "What's going on down the hall?"

She said, "Honey, that's what the rest of us go through during childbirth. You're just one lucky lady."

I thought...Those poor women. How do they tolerate that enduring pain for so many hours? Then I thought...God must have known that I couldn't handle much more, so he gave me a break.

While I was laying there they brought in my baby, so I could nurse her, which was the only part that seemed normal to me within the entire reproductive process.

I had just finished nursing her, when I looked up to see Bill, being brought in by the nurse. He was carrying a huge vase of flowers for me. He looked a lot different, or at least calmer, than the crazy man that brought me to the hospital. Oh he was still quite the picture of the 'first-time Father' - you know, pajama top instead of a shirt, a cigarette behind each ear, but at least his face was no longer half shaved. He was shaving when I'd told him that my water broke.

I said, "Nice shave."

He smiled and explained that the hospital gift shop had a small shaving kit, so he thought he'd freshen up for me. To me he still looked quite dashing and the nurse even commented on what a beautiful family we were. He was amazed at how beautiful Patty was. He gently stroked her hair and face. He looked mesmerized. I finally got back to a question that I had since we arrived at the hospital.

I said, "Bill, why were you so adamant about naming the baby Patricia, if it was a girl?"

Bill looked deeply into my eyes and said, "Well Mar, it's the name of the one true love of my life, Patty Christokakas. She was Greek and her father wouldn't let us get serious because he demanded that she marry a Greek man, otherwise I'd still be with her today."

The nurse was speechless as she came over to take the baby back to the nursery. As she was leaving through the door, I could hear her mumble the word 'pig'.

Confused Bill said, "What's up with her?"

With tears in my eyes I said, "Don't worry about her. You'd better go…I need to sleep."

He said, "I understand. You get some sleep and I'll see you tomorrow…I love you." And he was gone.

I laid there crying and when the nurse came back, she said to me, "Mrs. Fisher, I know that it's none of my business, but I've been doing this for a long time and I've never seen a more unfeeling husband in my life. My God doesn't he realize what you've just been through?"

I could see whatever good thoughts that she had about Bill were gone, so I felt the need to defend him. I said, "Oh it's ok, he didn't mean it the way it sounded…he's just…"

"He's a bastard. Sorry – but he is. My God, this is your time and your baby's time. What the Hell kind of a story is *that* to tell your wife, right after she has your baby. I even called my mother and told her about this, because I was so upset for you, and her advice is to leave him, – and we're Catholic!"

Again I tried to thank her for her and her mother's concern, and I assured her that it really will be ok.

She said, "Well I guess you're just a better woman than me. Now try and get some sleep and try to forget about this. Pleasant dreams." She turned off the lights as she left me alone in that room.

I laid there all night long, crying off and on, and thought, sure you love me – you *only* love me, because Patty wasn't available? I'm such a fool."

CHAPTER 49

Patty was a fussy baby, but she was beautiful and very intelligent. She walked and talked at seven months. My friends used to tell me how lucky I was because she was so advanced for her age. But they didn't have to try and keep up with her.

Then came my next pregnancy. It was a miscarriage and Mama told me that it was because Bill's seed was diseased.

Always a kind word from Mama.

I really didn't have time to grieve because my brother Babe was getting married and it was a very happy time. He was marrying a Polish girl named Loretta.

Mama flipped out at first, because she wasn't Croatian, but she would always remind me, at least *she* was Catholic.

I thought Loretta was wonderful. She had the most amazing blue eyes and a great figure. They made a beautiful couple, because of the contrast of her being so fair and petite, and Babe being so dark and dashing.

Mama went all out on their wedding. It was beautiful and I kept trying to pretend in my mind, that she was doing it because she wanted to do this for Babe, but I knew that Mama did a lot of it as a way to throw my wedding in my face. She also would make comments along the lines of, there must be something wrong with Bill, otherwise why would I have been so *ashamed* to marry him without my family around? I figured it was best not even to respond.

Now came my third pregnancy. I really never felt right since the miscarriage. I knew my hormones were off and the doctor confirmed it. He told me that my body needed a rest and that I shouldn't plan on trying to have a baby, for at least another year or two. Mama said that she had had five pregnancies, and she was just fine. She also told me to quit babying myself.

Chapter 50

Finally Mama was happy. It had been almost two and a half years since I'd had Patty, and now a baby boy. Again, I wanted to name him Trey, but Bill was adamant about having his first male child being named after him. I agreed as long as we gave him the middle name of Martin, after my father and brother. He liked the idea because he didn't want his son to be a junior, so this worked out perfectly. Little Billy was beautiful, but Mama pointed out that he had been born with the same birth defect that I had on my right foot. A double big toe, except on Billy, it was on both of his feet. The doctor joked that there'd be no confusing this baby. He meant it in a nice way, to try and make me feel better, but Mama just looked at him and quickly said, "In Yugoslavia, we would have drowned him in the river, like a bag of cats because he's defective, just like you Madia.....I guess we should have drowned you at birth too!" Then she just started to laugh and walked away. The nurses looked on in shock.

I could only cry and think to myself, - I guess I'll never please her. Here, I finally give her a grandson and she thinks that he should be killed, for being as defective as I am.

That pressure and guilt, yes I felt guilty, because after all, it was *my* defect that I passed on to this beautiful baby. I still really wasn't feeling like myself from the miscarriage and now, a new baby. The last thing I needed was the added pressure from Mama, but I knew that I had to be strong, if not for me, then for my babies, especially Billy.

A few months after Billy, came my fourth pregnancy, and by now, I was really fearful of having another miscarriage, so much so that I was paranoid about doing anything.

By now, my sister-in-law Loretta and I, were good buddies and she could see that it was all really getting to me. She told me that I needed to get out more, so one day she came over and was so excited because she and Babe had gotten a new jeep for their business, and she wanted to take me for a ride in it. I knew I shouldn't, because the doctor had warned me, but I went anyway. My first miscarriage was due to me just raking some leaves, so I was a little leery about bouncing around in a jeep, but I didn't want to disappoint her.

Babe had gotten a great deal on it, through some people he met through his gas station business. The station was built on the land where our old play lot prairie used to be, across the street from the bar. The second I stepped foot in the jeep, I knew it was a mistake.

We only drove about twenty feet when Lor decided to go through the alley as a short cut. By the second bump I felt something wet, I was hemorrhaging. Lor started crying and kept saying that she was sorry. I just screamed for her to get me to the hospital. She kept crying as we drove and I tried to keep her as calm as possible, because I thought that we'd get in an accident if she couldn't compose herself. By the time we got there, I was a bloody mess and they told me that they were going to have to do an emergency D&C. I didn't know exactly what that was, but I knew that it wasn't good.

During the procedure, as they were scraping me, they punctured my uterus and now, there was even more bleeding. This was all explained to me by a doctor that I'd never seen before, as I was waking up from the anesthesia. He added that there was a chance that I might not be able to have any more children, but they'd know more later…I was devastated.

The next morning, I was waking up as they were changing my intravenous bottle, and even though I couldn't focus, I could make out the word 'penicillin', which I'm highly allergic to, on the bottle. I tried to tell the nurse but she told me to stay quiet and relax, because I needed my rest and then she was gone. Almost instantly, I could feel my throat beginning to close. I tried again to call for help, but it was no use.

At that moment Bill walked in and all it took, was one look at me and he immediately ran into the hall and screamed for a nurse to help.

When she got there she told Bill that there wasn't anyone on duty to do a tracheotomy on me, so she immediately grabbed a piece of tubing and forced it down my throat. At last I could breathe, but my body was starting to swell to the point, where I thought my skin would burst. By the time my doctor got there he was shocked by my appearance, and all Bill could do was cry and keep asking what was happening to me.

My body was nearly three times its normal size. I had dark circles under my almost swollen shut eyes, and now little lesions were forming on my skin and they were oozing fluid.

Within a few days, I was doing a little better, physically anyway. But by now my nerves were shot. Then Dr. Arnold told me that he was going away on vacation for about a couple of weeks and he wanted to say goodbye to me, before he left. He said that I should be released in a few days and that he'd visit me at home, since I'd be there by then.

I had a bad feeling about him leaving and I should have gone with those feelings because, from the very moment of meeting my new fine young doctor, I felt uneasy. I kept trying to put it out of my mind and just focus on my two beautiful babies waiting for me at home. I really felt bad for Bill, because he looked devastated. I told him that he didn't need to stay with me and that he should go and get himself some coffee and something to eat. Bill said that he wasn't leaving me alone in the hospital, he was just going to run down and get something in the hospital cafeteria, so that I could rest.

While Bill was in the hospital cafeteria, I had a visitor, Mama. She stood in the doorway of my room and looked at me sternly and said, "See, I told you that Serbian's diseased seed was no good."

Weakly I tried to defend him and tell her about the puncture, but she'd have no part of it. She told me that all I needed was to go home and take care of my half-breed babies. I told her that I couldn't move for a few more days.

She then walked over to my bed, threw back my blanket and said, "Get up! Quit acting like some goddamned movie star. What the fuck is wrong with you?"

"Mama, the doctors said that I've lost a lot of blood and I have to rest."

"Bullshit!" she said, and then grabbed my left ankle and pulled me off the bed, in hopes of getting me up. Instead, I just fell to the floor like a rag doll. She still kept holding my leg as she said, "So, you don't want to walk, huh? Well then I'll drag you home where you belong!" She yanked my leg and started dragging me towards the door.

Engulfed in pain, I just kept begging her to leave me alone. All of a sudden I felt something inside of me rip and I screamed.

"Shut the fuck up! You're not fooling me... get up!" she said as she started to drag me along the floor toward the doorway. I looked back to see my arm stretched out and still attached to the intravenous bottle. The IV stand was caught on the chair, so it couldn't move and its needle was tearing something in my arm, so I yelled, "Mama, – my arm!"

She looked back and saw the problem, so she went over and tore the tubing right out of the bottle. She kicked me again in the ribs as she passed me and demanded that I get up and walk. I cried and cried as she dragged me through the doorway. I was not only in internal pain, because I began to hemorrhage vaginally, but now I was also losing blood out of the IV tubing in my arm and it was covering the floor. I could only cry even harder as my mother dragged me out into the hallway. By now my gown had worked its way up to my waist, exposing me to anyone passing in the hallway.

Finally a petite nurse came by and started screaming at Mama. With that Mama yelled, "Fuck you! Whore!"

The shocked nurse screamed for more nurses to help her, and the next one that tried to stop Mama got a right hook, that knocked her out cold. Swearing and fighting were the two things that she knew well, from owning a bar.

Before I knew it, there were people coming out from everywhere to help me. A couple of young orderlies didn't realize whom they were tangling with. Mama always wore heavy shoes and she was short and strong. She kicked at their crotches doubling them over as she kept yelling, "Fuck You!" to anyone that tried to help me.

Finally, a couple more orderlies came in and were able to subdue her. As they took her away screaming, swearing and kicking, my new doctor showed up and Mama started swearing and spitting at him.

He yelled, "Woman...you are banned from *ever* coming to this hospital! You better never need any medical attention from this hospital, because I'll *personally* see that you rot in the street first!"

To which she screamed back at the top of her lungs, "FUCK YOU!" and then she spit in his face. Outraged, he ordered the staff to throw her out and get security to lock the door.

Bill heard a commotion, as he was exiting the gift shop in the lobby with some flowers for me, only to see his mother-in-law being taken away by two large men, who were now surrounded by even more of the hospital's staff. He walked further into the lobby and watched as Mama kept trying to kick in the hospital's front door and then she spit again on the front door. Mama noticed Bill in the lobby and even managed to swear at him. She stood out in front of the hospital swearing, spitting and kicking at the door, until she heard the sound of a siren.

Bill frantically tried to ask people what was happening, but everyone was still in crisis mode and didn't want to answer him. Then he could only think, "My God…where's Mary?"

Once he made it to my floor, he looked down the hall toward my room and he saw them cleaning up blood in the hallway. He started running toward my room, completely oblivious to their warnings of the wet floor, and as he finally made it to my door, a nurse told him that he couldn't come in.

He answered, "The Hell I can't!" and he pushed his way in and he stared at my body, half naked and bloody. I didn't see him at first because I was crying with my hands over my face. He stood there frozen with shock, and then he tried to make it to my bedside, but the doctors that were over me, told him that they had to get me ready for emergency surgery. I thought that I heard his voice as they whisked me passed him. He yelled out, "Mary, I love you – you'll be ok!"

But I was in so much pain that I wasn't sure what was real any more. All I knew was that my physical pain was nothing, compared to the mental torture I was going through. I knew that Mama was crazy, but how could she be so cold, so cruel, so unfeeling?

CHAPTER 51

The next day or the day after, I still don't remember, as my physical self was getting better, my emotional self was now completely shot. I didn't want to talk to anyone, I just wanted to die. I was ashamed, guilty, mortified, unloved - you name it, I was feeling it. I had a complete feeling of worthlessness, that I'd never felt this deeply before. Even the darkest days of my childhood couldn't compare to this. And the worst part of all of these feelings was that I had lost that little fighter spirit that kept me going as a child, plus I didn't have Kuma around, to let me know that it would all be ok. Bill told me that she was out of the country, for something or other.

I spent night and day crying, and not wanting to talk to anyone. When Bill would come up to visit, I didn't even want to see him.

Finally after a few days of this, he demanded to see me, so to avoid a scene, they allowed it. They came in to tell me that he was here, and I said that I didn't want to see anyone, the door opened and there he was.

Bill slowly walked over to me in bed and looked at me with tearful eyes and said, "Please Mary, you've got to get better. The kids need you. I need you." Then he took my hand and kissed it, and I cried even more, thinking how I'm not worthy of such a good man. He could see that I was even more upset, so he said that he was going to go, but he'd be back again tomorrow to see me. I just rolled over on my side toward the window leaving him to stare at my back as he left.

As he was leaving, he ran into my new doctor. The doctor said that he'd like to speak to him in private. They went to a nearby empty room and explained to Bill about all the good results they've been having with a new medical breakthrough, it was called, 'S.T.S.',...also known as, Shock Treatment Therapy.'

"It was simple," he told Bill, "All we do is zap her with an electrical current and bit by bit, it erases her recent painful memories, so that in just a few short treatments, she won't remember the last month or so. This way we can wipe out all the bad stuff she's gone through."

Bill, being desperate, said yes to the first eight treatments. They were to begin as soon as my uterus was healed.

In less than a week, they started.

They explained everything they were going to do to me, and were correct, except for the slight pinch I'd feel. It was more like being hit by lightening. I'd wake up a day and a half later, disoriented.

All I knew was I didn't want another treatment. It came anyway, only this time it took almost three days until I knew I was on planet earth. They were getting ready to take me for my next treatment, when I realized that I just couldn't take another one.

So, as the petite nurse came towards me to once again prepare me for yet another treatment, I jumped out of my bed and climbed up onto the windowsill. I put my hands under the slightly opened window and threatened to throw myself out. I didn't care that it was four stories down. As she inched her way towards me, I lifted the window even higher and moved onto the window ledge and threatened again, if anyone came near me I'd jump!

She said, "Mrs. Fisher you're just depressed, and you may not realize it, but you are getting better. The treatments are really helping you."

I said, "Oh I agree that I'm depressed, but these treatments are bullshit!"

Who should walk into the room at that moment, but Dr. Arnold, and he demanded to know what was going on. His associate, that was at his side, tried to quickly debrief him, but I chimed in. I requested that Dr. Arnold and I should be left alone, and *I* would explain everything.

Once they left, he came over to help me down and I burst into tears. I gave him the gruesome details about Mama, the shock treatments, everything, and then I told him that all I wanted was to see my babies.

With tears in his eyes he said, "You'll be out of here in an hour."

I hugged him and told him that he saved my life.

I immediately called Bill - and in an hour, I was out in the fresh air, for the first time in weeks, and it felt great. I felt as though I was cured, just by being in the sunlight.

Once we were in the car, Bill told me that he had a surprise for me. He said, "Mar, we're going on a date, just like the old days."

I told him that he was the most wonderful man in the world, but if it was all the same, I just wanted to go home, relax, and see the kids. Patty wasn't quite three and Billy wasn't even one.

"No Mary, I know what's best for you, and you need to enjoy life. You don't need hospitals and doctors…you need to remember how to have fun."

Since he wouldn't take no for an answer, I went along with it. Dinner was great. We had Italian food and right there, I was content enough to go home.

But instead, Bill pulled up to a movie theater.

He said "It's the new Olivia De Havilland picture. Everybody says it's great and I know how much you like her, so let's go in."

By the picture on the marquee, it looked like it might be a little too intense for me and I said, "No, let's not." But he wouldn't hear of it, after all, he knew best.

I can still hear his words.

"Two adults for 'The Snake Pitt' please."

Well weren't even halfway through the film, when I knew that he regretted taking me to see it. The film paralleled our lives too closely, and by the time they started giving her shock treatments in the movie, I was ready for another one myself. I got so crazy and jumpy, that the people around us were glad to see us leave.

I wasn't much better once we got home. I bathed the kids and put Patty to bed. I had taken a shower and slipped on my new silk nightgown. While Bill and I watched TV together, I rocked Billy and gave him his bottle.

Bill put on the TV show 'Gunsmoke', which was a very popular western at the time. He told me that it looked like something that I'd like, because the lady in it was rocking her little baby boy too. I though to myself, 'well at least he's trying', so I sat back and tried to relax and enjoy the show.

Then all of a sudden, the lady on TV decides that she can't care for the baby and thinks it might be in the baby's best interest, if she puts him in the potbelly stove and kills him, because she can't care for him without his father being around.

I asked Bill to please turn it off but he said that I have to live in the real world, and that this was just a TV show. He went on about how I made such a scene at the theater earlier, and that I just had to start pulling myself together.

By now, on the show, she was holding the baby near the opening of the stove. I didn't want to watch, so I turned to my right to look away, and there was our gas space heater, right in front of me, I thought, oh God please don't make *me* want to put my baby in the space heater. Frantic, I got up and called Dr. Arnold and told him that maybe I *was* crazy. I told him how nice Bill was trying to be by taking me to a movie.

"But Doc, I just couldn't sit through Snake Pit."

"Snake Pit?" he yelled, "What the hell is wrong with him? That's not the kind of movie you need to see. You need comedies or musicals!"

"Well Doc, now he's making me watch a TV show where a lady wants to put her baby into a potbelly stove and I'm afraid. What if *I* want to do that to Billy?"

"Now Mary just stay calm," he said as he tried to reassure me. "Believe me Mary, everything will be just fine. Now let me talk to your husband."

"Bill," I said, "the phone's for you, it's Dr. Arnold."

"For me? What for?"

"I don't know, he said he wants to talk to you."

I handed Bill the phone. From what I gathered from his side of the conversation, the doctor was trying to let Bill know that I was in a fragile state, according to what Bill shared with me, once he got off of the phone. But while he was being enlightened by the doctor,

Bill looked at me as if to say, 'I should have left you in the hospital.'

He looked at me again and said that he was sorry, as he handed the phone back me. I could hear Dr. Arnold calling my name through the receiver.

"Mary" the doctor said, "I've never said this to *anyone* before, but I'm saying this to you. First, move as far away from your mother as possible, because she's crazy, and secondly, get a divorce. I can't imagine any man being *that* unfeeling. Mary please feel free to call me day or night if you need anything, and please take care of yourself and get some rest."

I felt unsettled by what he had said, but I told him, "Thanks for your help and the advice. I'll talk to you soon."

I could see that Bill was mad.

I tried to talk to him but he said that it was probably best if he went to bed. With that, he got up, turned off the TV and headed into the bathroom, before going to bed.

This gave me a little quiet-time for myself and my baby. After I put Billy to bed and checked in on Patty, I decided that I would go to bed and see if Bill had calmed down.

I got in bed and gently called his name but there was no response. I laid there thinking, when will everything go back to normal? After all, I couldn't talk to Mama about things, because she was still mad at me, plus she was now blaming me for the incident at the hospital, and now, even Bill was mad at me. I couldn't talk to Kuma because I finally found out that she had to go to Yugoslavia, because her father had passed away, and that she wouldn't be home for another month. I really felt alone.

Things were strained between Bill and me for a while. It seemed as though we just coasted through our marriage. As the days went by, I started to find solace in food, and before I had realized it, I had gained a lot of weight. One night as we lay in bed, Bill told me that he didn't want to have sex with me anymore, because I was too fat. Even though I was a little relieved to not have to think about doing it, it gave me an even deeper sense of worthlessness. It was one thing to not want to do it. It was another for the man you love, to say, in essence, that he was repulsed by your body. That only made me eat even more.

Chapter 52

For six long years I threw myself into being the perfect mother, housekeeper and cook. I would do whatever Bill wanted, whatever my mother wanted, hell, even whatever strangers wanted. Kuma was the only one that could see through my façade and she would try to get me in touch with the *real* me. I just kept saying that everything was perfect the way it was.

One day she finally said, "Madia, I know you better than anyone, and you are *not* happy and everything is *not* perfect. You can't keep doing everything for everyone else and not thinking about what's best for you."

"Kuma, just being a good mother and a good homemaker is all that I need to be happy."

She said, "Madia, what are you so afraid of?"

"Oh Kuma, I'm not afraid of anything."

"Really Madia, then why are you hiding the *real* you from the rest of the world?"

"Kuma, I'm not hiding."

She looked me up and down and said, "Aren't you?"

I smiled and gave her a kiss and told her that I had to run. I didn't want to have a conversation about my weight. Sure, I knew that I was heavier than I was before we got married, but everyone gains weight once they're married. That was my mental justification.

As time went on, I really didn't feel any better and it got worse when one day, I was doing some shopping and I ran into a guy from the neighborhood, who hadn't seen me in a long time.

He came up to me and said, "Wow, Mary is that you? You've really gotten big. Hell, from the back it looks like two bulls in a gunny sack, lockin' horns and tryin' to get out!"

When I didn't laugh he started to stumble over his words, explaining that he was joking and that I really looked great.

I politely smiled and said, "Have a nice day." And just kept walking.

I was mortified and on the verge of tears, and then I saw my reflection in a plate-glass store window and thought…My God, he's right! I actually started to laugh, thinking, that poor guy is probably so embarrassed, but it's the truth.

I know that this was what Kuma had been trying to hint at, but didn't have the heart to say. So thanks to a stranger, I honestly had to take a good look at *me* for the first time; and came to the realization that it wasn't a 'few' pounds, it was at least one hundred pounds. I thought, Dear God – what have you done to yourself? I felt so hopeless and ugly. I looked up and said, "God, I need to get back to being *me* and not some robot wife, who is so worried about being a 'people-pleaser' that she's let herself turn to shit!" Just then the church bells rang, and I took it as a sign of, 'Welcome Back

Mar! You've been gone a long time – now get back to work!'

Suddenly I felt reborn, and something inside me said, "Mary, you are going to have to be your own person, and no one can do it for you – except YOU!"

So I did.

CHAPTER 53

Secretly I went on a diet, cut my hair short and decided to go to art school. Bill didn't quite know what to make of the new me. Hell, I didn't know what to make of me, but I didn't care. Before I knew it, I had lost 128lbs. I started to look more like a Beatnik than a 1960's housewife. I also got a job with the Chicago Park District and got involved in politics. Plus, because I worked for the parks, I got a big discount on my art classes…so Bill couldn't complain about the cost of the classes.

It was fabulous because I was attending classes at The Art Institute of Chicago, which backed up to The Goodman Theater, and they shared a cafeteria. I would bring Patty and Billy along, and they would see the actors in costume, wandering around, not to mention all my new friends. They were a bunch of kooky artists...and I loved'em! They were like people that you only see in movies or on TV, and nothing like the people in our neighborhood. I also figured that it would make my children more well-rounded and accepting of people and their differences...It did!

One of my new favorite people was my new art teacher. He was one of the most handsome men I'd ever seen and so compassionate. He would give me free tickets to symphonies and of course he was always there, but so were Patty and Billy. They even got to meet Leonard Bernstein, even though it meant nothing to them at the time, it was a great name dropping moment for them as adults...especially for Billy.

So little by little, he got the drift that 'student and teacher', is all that we'd ever be. Ironically, later Patty had him as an art teacher in college, and he asked if I was her mother, because we looked so much alike. He reminded her that he knew her as a child.

There was a rumor later, that she knew him a little more intimately than I ever had. She was quite the free sprit.

There was one other very interesting man, an Asian artist whose name was Ping Pong… no really…it was. When he told me that, all I could do was laugh, because I thought for sure, he was putting me on. But he was serious, and in time he told me that if I got a divorce, he would marry me and show my children, and me, the world. I have to admit that I did give his offer a lot of thought, not only because he did appeal to me physically, but also artistically and intellectually. He was so kind and gentle and we could talk endlessly, about any subject. He was never boring and he relished the fact that I was like a sponge, trying to absorb art, the city, his culture and his life. At home Bill talked about sports and cutting the grass. That was his world, that, and going to work and going out with the guys.

I finally told Ping that even though it didn't appear to be…I really was happy with my life and I thanked him for his friendship.

Of course one day during a disagreement with Bill, I brought this up, and he *demanded* that I quit art school. I think that it was really, this, along with a culmination of the many different stories that I would come home with, and perhaps the figure drawings that I would do of nude men. Bill let me know that housewives from The East Side, just didn't do those kinds of things. Well maybe they didn't, but I did!

He didn't say that I had to quit *all* schooling, so again without consulting him, I signed up and attended a junior college. This school, just like art school, was such a positive experience that I thought I'd finally found my niche. Unfortunately, this too really upset Bill, but on a different level, because he had only gotten as far as the eighth grade. He had to quit school to go to work and help his parents financially. He thought this new education was making me too independent. What it did do, was to make me more self aware of the things that I really wanted out of life, and that maybe being a housewife and mother weren't enough for me.

As I got more involved in politics and my new life, it forced Bill to take a more active part in parenting, which he needed because he also had a new love, and that was drinking. It was something that he and my brother Babe had in common and enjoyed entirely too much. I should have left him, but all the old guilt, from my mother, who kept saying that maybe if I did more, he would drink less. As a matter of fact, getting a divorce from our husbands was a common topic between my sister-in-law, Loretta, and me. The more I experienced the outside world, beyond the realm of the East Side; I could see that I wanted and needed more. It didn't really matter to me what Bill did, it just frustrated me.

Sure it helped working in the park and I had a lot of fun teaching children, but it wasn't enough.

The other big plus was that in a roundabout way, I felt as though I was giving back to the universe some of the goodness, given to me, by Kuma.

In the early 60's women were starting to divorce more readily and they had to take jobs, even if they were just part-time, and had no one to baby-sit on a regular basis, so I started pre-schools at the parks and they were a hit!

I always reminded my co-workers something that Kuma had taught me, that it was the obligation of every adult to be nice to every child that we come in contact with, because they may be the only person that's *ever* been kind to them. Thank you Kuma.

Kuma was thrilled by what I was doing, but to me, it seemed as though I could do a lot more and I told her that.

She said, "Oh Madia, I'm sure that you'll do a lot more. This is just the beginning of your journey; and child, I have a journey of myself ahead of me."

"Journey Kuma? What are you talking about?...Are you ok?"

She giggled, "Oh yes child, I'm fine. Fine, except for the fact that I'm going to miss you horribly."

"Miss me? Where are you going?"

"Well child, I've introduced you to Mr. Miller, you know the banker?"

I said, "Yes, he's a very nice man, but what's he got to do with this?"

"Well, he was offered a position as a bank president in Texas and he's taking the job, and he wants me to go with him and his children."

"What? Texas?...when did all of this happen?"

"Well child you've been very busy with work and school so I didn't want to bother you. I met him through a friend from church and I'm going to marry him."

I screamed, "Oh my God Kuma – I'm so happy for you!" I hugged her and gave her a big kiss and we both had tears in our eyes.

She asked, "So you approve?"

"Of course I do! I mean, I don't know him that well, but no one is a better judge of people than you, so I'm sure he's magnificent!"

"Magnificent...well that is a tall order."

"Kuma, you said that he has kid's?...How many?"

"Six boys, so I'll be busy. And with no girls, you'll still be my little girl."

I was so happy for her. She finally had a family of her own.

I said, "Kuma, how old is he?"

"It doesn't matter, but he's the same age as me...36."

"Kuma, you're not 36, you're almost 46."

"Child, I'm sure that I *don't* know what you're talking about, and if I did, I would still be 36."

Before I could say another word she put her finger over my lips and said, "Just be happy for me child."

"Oh Kuma I am. And I'm not saying that you don't look 36, because you do, but shouldn't you be honest with him?"

"In marriage you have to have some mystery my dear. It's just a good thing that I've always used a lot of face cream and kept my figure. Speaking of figures, Child, you are going to disappear if you lose any more weight. How much weight have you lost?"

"Almost 130lbs."

"Oh my God…that's an entire person."

I said, "Kuma, yes it was, and she was a very unhappy person, but she's gone for good. Enough about me, when's the wedding?"

"Two weeks, and child, will you do me the honor of being my Matron of Honor?"

"Of course!"

Chapter 54

It was a beautiful wedding and Kuma looked amazing - *and* she did look 36. Immediately after the wedding, she and her new family moved to Texas, because he had to start his new job in a week. I was happy for her, but I really did miss her, but like she always said, "I'm only as far as a phone."

She would come to Chicago and visit a few times a year, and that's when I'd give her an update on my life. The newest update was my new neighbor and friend, Gia. She was Italian and when I would get with her, we'd laugh like schoolgirls. She appeared to have the perfect life and I envied her for it. Her husband was an executive and a chemist at one of the Steel Mills and they had a beautiful little girl. They lived right behind us so we could go back and forth through each others backyards.

I would tell her all the time how lucky she was, and then one day she said to me, “Mary, I’d trade my life for yours in a heartbeat.”

“What Gia? Your husband is an executive, he always looks so perfect, your daughter is beautiful and healthy, and your home is lovely.”

“Well Mar, he’s a bastard and I want a divorce.”

“Divorce? If anyone should get one it’s me, not you.”

“No Mar, I’ve seen how Bill looks at you and how he talks to you, he’s a prince. My Michael is cruel and very abusive. I hate him, and now he wants to have another baby. I told him that there was no way I would have another baby with him.”

So on one of Kuma’s visits I started to tell her all about Gia and her situation. She told me that you never really know someone until you live with them. She reminded me how my mother had fooled everyone that she knew by pretending to be ‘the loving wife’.

She also said, "Madia, Gia is so lucky to have you as a friend. She sounds like there's gonna be some rough times ahead for her, and her daughter."

She added that my road to helping people hadn't even begun. About a year later, I knew what she meant.

Chapter 55

It was early on a Sunday morning when the phone rang and it was Gia.

"Please Mar, can you come over right now?...and please don't tell Bill."

"Sure Gia, I'll be right over."

I didn't bother to ask her what was wrong because I could tell that she was very upset. Instantly, I ran out the door and through our yards. When I made it to her back door, I could see through the screen door that she was curled up on the couch in her family room. She motioned for me to come in and immediately I could tell that she had been, and still was, crying.

I sat down next to her and said, "Gia? My God, what's wrong?"

Tearfully she looked at me and said, "That son of a bitch raped me."

"Who Gia?...Who raped you?"

"Michael."

"Michael? But he's your husband…he can't rape you?"

"Mar, I told that fucker that I wanted a divorce a few days ago and he went into a rage. He picked up a chair and threw it at me. He said that we're Catholic and there is no such thing as a divorce. He stormed off and when he came home, he refused to speak to me, except when our daughter Kimmy was around. I hate him."

"But what about the rape?"

"Well, he went out last night and came home drunk and that's when he tried to get me to have sex with him. But when I said no, he hit me and kept hitting me, as I made my way to the kitchen. That's when he knocked me to the floor and tore my clothes off. I wanted to scream, but I didn't want Kimmy to hear and God forbid, I didn't want her to walk in on us. He kept covering my mouth and I tried to bite him. That's when he hit me and tried to strangle me to shut me up, and that's when he did it. I hate him!"

I couldn't believe what I was hearing, but I could see the marks on her neck and the bruises on her arms.

"Gia, where is he now?"

"Where do you think? The good Catholic is at church. I hope he burns in Hell!"

"Gia, what do you want me to do?" I asked.

"Mar, just promise that you won't tell anyone, especially Bill. I think if Michael finds out that I said anything to anyone, he'd kill me."

"Sure Gia, but are you sure that you don't want to go to the police or the hospital or something?"

"No Mar, I'll be fine...unless I end up pregnant. Then we're going to the hospital. Because there is no way that I'm going to have another child with that fucker."

I tried to calm her down by saying, "Gia, don't even think about any of that right now. You'll be fine."

"Thanks Mar, I just had to tell someone. Now I'd better pull myself together before he and Kimmy get back from church. I don't want her to see me like this."

I gave her a hug and I told her that if she needed anything, I'm just a phone call away. It made me feel good to be able to use a Kuma-ism.

As fate would have it, a few months later, it turned out that Gia *was* pregnant. She was going through all sorts of anxiety about it. She had considered an abortion and even suicide, because when she was at the doctor's office, he told her that she was too far along to get an abortion. She was devastated. She came directly to my house from her doctor, to tell me her news. She just kept crying and saying that she wanted to die. I told her that she still had a young daughter that needed her *very* much, and then I added, maybe once she saw the baby, she might forget all about its brutal conception and just want to shower it with love. After all, it's not the baby's fault.

"Thanks Mar, maybe you're right, but I'm not sure. I'm so confused."

"Of course you are Gia, it's perfectly normal. Just take it one day at a time Honey…ok?"

"Ok Mar, but I still think that the best option for me is going to be adoption."

"Adoption? Well if *anybody* is going to adopt this baby it's gonna be me!"

"You?'

"Of course, I love babies. So when the baby comes, I'll keep it. I've always wanted more kids."

Gia got very quiet and you could tell that she was running this through her head. She looked up at me and I could tell that she was getting ready to cry, and thanked me for being a true friend.

She said, "But Mar, I couldn't stand to see my child raised by someone else, even if it *is* you. I hope you understand?"

I reached over and grabbed her hand and said, "Of course I do."

Even though I really was serious, I had to say that to her, to try and get her back to reality, and get her to start thinking more positively about her baby.

She said, "Mar, if I had to look over the fence and see my child calling someone else mother, well, I'd lose my mind."

"No problem, I'd move. We have land in Arizona!"

She said, "Mar, you're crazy - and that's why I love you. Thanks again. I'd better get home now before that bastard wonders where I'm at."

As time rolled on, she wouldn't discuss it anymore, and she even sort of pretended that she wasn't pregnant. When people wanted to ask her about it, she'd change the subject or she just wouldn't answer them.

It was difficult for me to see her go through this, but she was a trooper. I never saw her breakdown once during the rest of her pregnancy. The part that was even more unbearable for me, was when I'd run into her husband, the sight of him made me sick. I would get mad at Bill because he would still socialize with him. I asked Bill, "How can you stand to be around that son of a bitch?"

But you know Bill, all he could say was that he was a nice guy and then told me that I was 'too touchy' about stuff.

"Too touchy?!" I said, "That bastard raped his own wife!"

Bill grabbed his coffee and headed for the door saying that he was going to water the grass, then he mumbled something about 'how could a man rape his own wife,…ridiculous.'

I wanted to go after him to make my point, but I thought, why bother? He lives in his own little world and he'll never change.

The person that I did find solace in talking about this, was Kuma. We spent hours on the phone. She told me that it was wonderful that I had so much concern for my friend, but she reminded me that I had a family of my own to worry about.

"Madia," she said, "Gia has many things to think about, and as her friend, you'll have to stand by her decision, no matter what it is…ok?"

I told her that I understood, but deep down inside, I thought that if she gave the baby away to someone other than me, I'd be crushed. It occurred to me that what would be even worse, was what if she *did* keep the baby, but ended up treating it badly? I knew that she really wouldn't mean it, but I was afraid that she wouldn't be able to control herself. I tried not to think about it, but it was rough. Because I knew that she was really a loving and wonderful person, and under different circumstances, she would feel blessed by having another child.

I could only think of this poor beautiful baby coming into the world and having a mother that didn't love it. I knew those feelings all too well, so I made up my mind that just like I had Kuma, I'll do whatever it takes to make sure that the baby knows that it is loved!

Chapter 56

The baby Finally came, and it was a beautiful baby boy named Michael Jr.. He had the most beautiful big blue eyes and longest eyelashes. Just as I feared, she was cold toward him. So cold in fact, that not only did she refuse to nurse him in the hospital, she refused to even touch him. The nurses were so shocked by her behavior that they began to visibly be rude to her, but Gia didn't care.

I played the role as a sort of surrogate mother to Mikey, so the nurses thought that I was Gia's sister. When I explained that I wasn't a relative and that I was just her friend, one of the nurses looked at me and said, "You know a heartless bitch like her doesn't deserve a friend like you?"

Unsettled by her frankness, I told her that Gia had been through a lot that they didn't know about, and that I was sure that very soon, she'd be back to being her old self again and everything would be just fine. I didn't really believe it myself, but I was hoping for Mikey's sake, that my words would come true. I knew all too well what that feeling was like, but in my case it was from both of my parents.

It was time to bring the baby home and since this was before car seats, they wanted Gia to hold the baby in the car. She still refused to touch him, and it turned into a little bit of a scene in the patient pick-up area of the hospital, but Gia held her ground. I was there too, so I said that I would ride with them and I would hold the baby in the backseat with me. I had to leave my car at the hospital and thought, well I'll get *someone* to drive me back to pick it up later, let's just get Mikey home.

As much as I hated Michael, I almost felt sorry for him, because I'm sure that he thought that his wife's contempt toward him would never be passed along to his son. He was Italian and was very proud that he finally had a son, and expected this to be a joyous time, but the little scene that just took place in front of the hospital staff and everyone within ear shot, made it crystal clear that this was *not* going to be good for anyone.

During the ride to their house, he began to demand that she had to start acting like a mother. She never even glanced toward him. She just kept saying, "You wanted him, not me, so you'd better be able to be father and mother to it."

"It?...He is your son, not an it!"

"It's an it to me…and you're even less."

Michael was furious and said, "Gia, if I wasn't driving this car, I'd beat the shit out of you right here!"

I couldn't believe what I was hearing and I tried to say something, but Gia responded with, "Well then, I guess you should have killed me when you had the chance, like the night you raped me and brought this *thing* into the world!"

He took his right hand off the steering wheel and swung at her, but thank God he missed.

I yelled, "What the Hell is wrong with the two of you? We'll all be killed. I don't care if you both kill each other when you get home, but I want to live, so stop it right now! Ok?!!"

Neither of them said a word for the rest of the ride, and I could only think, – What the Hell is it going to be like in their house once we get home? I found out pretty quickly, and it wasn't pleasant.

We got to the house and Michael still looked a little embarrassed, but Gia held strong. I went to the baby's room and set him in his crib. I asked Gia what she wanted to do; feed him, bathe him…what?

She looked right at me and said, "Gee Mar, I don't know. What do you want to do?"

I couldn't believe it…I thought,…oh my God, she really *isn't* going to do anything for the baby.

"Gia, he's your baby, what…?" that's as far as I got when she emphatically said, "Oh no, it's not my baby. That bastard wanted it, so he can take care of it. I'm going to bed. Good luck Mar.", and with that she left the room.

I thought, Dear God…Please let this all be a dream.

I heard Michael and Gia fighting in the kitchen and thought, I've got to stop this madness somehow. So I went into the kitchen and yelled, "Stop it! Listen you two, I have a family of my own to take care of, so I'm leaving, but before I go, I just want to make sure that *someone* in this house will take care of that baby!"

Gia said, "Well it's not going to be me." And again she walked out of the room. Michael went after her and I moved to block him. I said, "Michael, don't. She's obviously very upset and I think that it's probably best for now, that *you* take care of the baby. I can come over when you need a break, but *she* needs time…Ok?"

"Well I'll be damned. Who does she think she is?! That's *her* job…she's his mother."

"Michael, some women go through things like this when they have a baby, but they always snap out of it. So if she needs some time, give it to her. It's the *least* you can do under the circumstances…don't you think?" I hated to play the rape guilt card, but I had to for Gia and Mikey's sake.

You could see him instantly calm down and he said, "You're right Mar…but can you feed him and give him his bath before you leave? I'm too upset."

"Sure," I said, "where's the formula?"

"Formula?" Michael said.

I thought 'Oh My God, this is not your first baby for Christ sake!' I had to calm myself down, take a deep breath and said, "Ok, so you don't have any. Well that's fine. I'll make you a list and while you're at the store, I'll give Mikey his bath."

I wrote out a list of everything that I could think of, from diapers to food, and sent him on his way. I was really hoping that once he was out of the house, I could talk some sense into Gia.

As I started to bathe Mikey, Gia came by his room to say thank you.

I asked her, "Gia, are you really not going to do anything for Mikey?"

Coldly she said, "No. I know this makes me sound like the world's worst mother, but I didn't want to be its mother and I don't feel like a mother to it. When I had Kimmy, it was out of love, and that's what I feel when I think of her. But this…well you know the story,…I'm repulsed."

"But Gia, it's not the baby's fault *how* he got here. He's here, and that's what you should think about. You should try and give him the *best* life possible, especially with how his life started."

"I want him to have the best life Mar, and that's why I want to give him up for adoption. His life here with me will be shit!"

"But Gia, it doesn't have to be?"

"Yes it does Mar. Michael is going to walk around as the 'Big Proud Father', when he's got nothing to be proud about. He should be ashamed, but his 'Italian Male Ego' won't let him…I HATE HIM…and everything about him…especially *that* baby!" She started to cry and ran off to her bedroom and slammed the door.

I didn't know what to do. Then I looked at this beautiful baby trying to look up at me, and said to him, "Mikey, everything is going to be fine. I'll make sure of it."

Chapter 57

I went over daily to help with little Mikey. I would get up early and go over to get the baby his bottle. I'd feed him, rock him, sing to him and try to make everything as happy for him as I could. This went on for months. Thank God that Bill and the kids were fine with the whole thing.

Bill finally said, "Mar, why don't we just keep the baby here? It'd be a lot easier."

I asked Gia and she was fine with it, but she knew that her husband's ego wouldn't allow it… and she was right.

Michael said, "Little Michael is *my* son and he stays in *my* house. That's final."

It really didn't matter to me and I know that it sounds crazy, but this running back and forth day and night, didn't bother me one bit, because

I loved this baby and his sister like they were my very own.

Just as I was beginning to feel like I *had* given birth to him, there was a terrible storm and the wind had broken off a tree limb. It smashed a window in Mikey's room and landed on the floor, just as Gia was having a dream about someone kidnapping him.

She ran down the stairs and scooped him up in her arms, and cried and cried. She kept telling him that she was sorry for being a bad mother, that she'd make it up to him, and that she would *never* leave him again.

Instantly she became 'Super Mom'.

The next morning when I came over to feed Mikey, I walked into their den and there was Gia in the rocking chair feeding the baby. I thought...thank you God!

She looked at me and said, "Mar, last night during the storm, I had a revelation. A tree limb crashed through Mikey's window and I know that it was a sign from God, to take care of my baby or he'll take him away from me."

"Oh Gia, I knew that you'd come around. This is wonderful."

As I went to pat Mikey's head, she pulled him away from me and said, "Mar, please try and stay away. I have to bond with *my* baby."

I felt like my heart had been torn out of me, but I agreed to keep my distance, for Mikey's sake.

It took about a year for her 'revelation' to calm down enough, to where she was comfortable and would let me see the baby. Day by day things seemed to normalize even more.

As the years went by, we just kept having more and more fun as sort of a blended family. We had a pool, and one day, while I was teaching little Mikey to swim, who came by to surprise me but Kuma. She was in town for a few days to look at property; her husband had passed away a year prior, and her stepsons were all out of the house and busy with their lives and families. She missed all of her friends back in Chicago, and thought that she should move back. She was up to speed on the entire baby Mikey saga, and was so excited to finally meet him.

During the time that Gia was *bonding* with him and my heart was breaking, Kuma would always say that it wasn't going to be forever, and that Gia would come around in time,...again she was right.

She was shocked to see a baby so at home in water at such a young age. I said, "Kuma, this is nothing. He's been in our pool since he was born." It's true, he was born in June and by July he was in the pool.

Kuma looked at Mikey and said, "Mikey, you are *such* a lucky boy to have two mothers that love you very much."

I looked around to make sure that Gia hadn't come outside from getting some wine from my kitchen, and I said, "Oh please Kuma, don't ever say that in front of Gia. She feels bad about all of that, and I'd hate to upset her."

"Oh child, I understand and my lips are sealed." She smiled and turned to Mikey, and said, "You know what I'm talking about don't you?" And with that Mikey started to laugh, and Kuma said, "Just look at that baby laugh. I hope it's not because of my new hat?"

I loved how Kuma could cover everything up with a joke. Just then Gia came outside and said, "Oh, we have company! Hello Kuma, would you like something to drink?"

"Oh no Gia, I'm fine. I can't stay, I was just in the neighborhood so I thought that I'd pop by and see if anyone was home. I didn't know that I was going to see such a handsome young man over here, or I would have planned to stay longer." With that she reached into her purse and pulled out a hundred-dollar bill and said, "Here Gia, I didn't bring a gift, so take this and buy him something nice, from his Kuma."

Gia didn't want to take it, but Kuma insisted. I told Gia to just accept it because Kuma always gets her way.

Kuma responded, "Madia – you're such a smart girl. I've trained you well. She's correct Gia, I always win…except in love. There was one that got away," and then she winked at me. "Well I'm off!" she said.

I asked her, "Say Kuma, where are you going next? To visit my mother?"

"Oh child, is she still living in that castle, with all of those flying monkeys?!"

We both giggled as she gave me a big hug and a kiss, and then she was gone.

Gia looked a little confused and asked, "How much wine have I had? Did she just say flying monkeys?"

I explained, "The Wizard of Oz, Gia. Kuma is the 'movie queen'...*and* she hates Mama."

"Well to be honest Mar, your mother scares me too."

"I'll drink to that!" I said.

Gia started asking me all kinds of questions about Kuma and our past. So that afternoon, Gia got to hear all of the stories *and* how Kuma saved my life.

Gia just looked at me and said, "And Mar, you saved mine. Can I call you Kuma?"

Chapter 58

Gia and her children finally seemed to be very happy, and she was even able to tolerate her husband. Everything was going *so* well with her that I barely remembered all of the madness of the past.

That is until Gia came down with a really bad cold that had developed into mononucleosis, thanks to a very stupid doctor. When she went to the doctor, he gave her some pills and didn't do any kind of tests. She got worse and worse, so I finally told her that she had to get to the hospital.

She said, "But Mar, what if they want me to stay in the hospital? Who'll watch the kids?"

"Gia, I'm here, your sister isn't far. Don't worry, just get Michael to take you to the hospital."

Once there, they immediately admitted her. Her condition worsened to where she ended up with uremic poisoning. When I went to visit her she looked horrible. She was yellow from jaundice and very weak. She looked at me and said, "Mar, I know that I'm going to die."

I tried to stop her, but she went on. "No Mar, I know...and I need you to promise me that if anything happens to me you'll take care of Mikey for me. Will you please?"

"Gia, you don't even have to ask...you know I will. But you'll be fine...just rest."

"Mar, I've never really said thank you for everything that you did for me and my family, – especially Mikey. I just want to let you know that he and I would have both been dead, if it weren't for you. Thank you my dear, dear friend. I love you so very much."

I started to cry and silently I begged God to please let her live. Her children need her so much."

Gia said that she was tired and that she needed to rest. I realized that there was a nurse behind me. She put her hand on my shoulder and told me that I had to leave.

Gia's eyes were already closed, but I took her hand, gave it a kiss and whispered, "Don't worry Gia, everything will be ok – and I love you too." Then I turned and left.

As I drove home from the hospital I suddenly felt so alone and so sad, and started to cry uncontrollably.

Walking through the front door I could see that my teenaged son Billy, was hanging up the kitchen phone and was crying. He looked at me and said, "Gia's dead."

He came over and hugged me, but I couldn't stop shaking. I told him that I needed to go and check on Mikey and Kimmy. He asked if he should come with me and I nodded yes. Just then, Bill came up from the basement and saw us heading out the back door and asked what was going on. As we passed him, Billy told him that Gia had died. His response was classic Bill, he said, "Awe Shucks, that's too bad. I liked her." Then he went back downstairs.

As I walked I thought, – 'Awe Shucks? That's all you can say about a woman who spent the majority of the past almost ten years at our house…Awe Shucks?' But that was Bill.

As we entered their house, I heard Gia's husband Michael on the phone, explaining to someone about Gia's mononucleosis and how it resulted in her untimely death. The thing that struck me, was that he wasn't emotional about it one bit.

I knew that I would have to give him a hug and offer my condolences, but I could only think of how the very touch of this man, will creep me out.

So as he hung up the phone I said, "Michael" and put out my arms. He came toward me and hugged me, and I *was* repulsed.

As I tried to let go, he kept me in his grasp and said, "Gee Mar, here I thought that you didn't like me."

I couldn't believe it. I said, "I *don't*! I'm here for your children." I pushed him off me, then he noticed Billy coming in the door, and he quickly told me that they were playing upstairs and then he excused himself to make more phone calls.

I motioned for Billy to follow me and we went upstairs.

Once we were up there, I hoped that I could keep up a brave face for them.

Their little girl was ten years old, so she sort of understood what had happened to her mother, where Mikey was not quite four years old, and all he knew was that his mommy was very sick.

Almost daily after the funeral, Mikey would ask for his mommy and it broke my heart. His sister would just point upward, and say that she was in heaven.

He would ask, "When is she coming home?" Even though we would tell him that she wasn't coming back, he'd still keep asking.

I thought that maybe he was hoping that one day, we'd give him a different answer. Periodically, he would say how much he missed her, so I made sure to always talk about her and show him pictures of her so that he wouldn't forget her.

Their father tried to be father and mother to his children, but eventually it became too hard. We would do all that we could to help him, so would some of the other neighbors, but he still became overwhelmed.

One day when he appeared on our back porch deck, I didn't really think much of it. I noticed that he had a brown paper grocery bag in one hand and was holding Mikey's hand with the other.

I said, "Hi Mikey, Hi Michael, what's in the bag?"

Very calmly Michael said, "Mikey's clothes. Here you go Mar, since he's so close to you, – he's all yours." Then he turned and walked out.

I was shocked. I didn't know what to say. Mikey walked over to me and said, "Mar, can we have pizza?"

I knelt down and embraced him and said, "Of course Mikey…whatever you want."

I told Bill and the kids what had transpired and their reactions were all the same. They said that since he was here most of the time anyway, it made perfect sense that he should live here with us. They also said how much they loved him and that they really were thrilled, but they all wanted to know what was going to happen to his sister. I explained that I didn't know and that Michael didn't say anything about her. So I decided to call Michael and see what was really going on.

On the phone he said, "Mar, I can handle one kid…not two. Plus she's older and can take care of herself…Mikey can't. I don't have time for that."

"Time for *that*? That *that*, is your son!" I was furious.

He said, "Mar, I don't have time for this right now. I've got dinner plans."

"What about your daughter?"

"Oh she's going to spend the night next door at Toni's."

"Michael if I were you, I'd think that I'd want to spend as *much* time as I could with my two children."

"Well you're not me. I've gotta go, bye Mar." and he hung up.

I didn't think that I could detest him anymore than I already did, but it reached a new high, or in this case low. These kids needed their father more than ever and he's farming them out like they're puppies.

As I was going on and on about this, Bill told me to calm down, and that Michael just probably needed a break, that after a day or two, he'd be back to take Mikey home.

Oh, the ever optimistic Bill.

Well that couple of nights lasted more than twenty years, and he is as much a part of the family as if I'd given birth to him.

Chapter 59

Time went on, and early on a Saturday morning, there was a knock at the door. It was Kuma and she had a big bouquet of flowers.

"Kuma, what are you doing here and who are these for?" I asked.

"Oh Madia, for you of course."

"But why?"

"Oh child, don't be so modest! I read the article about you in the paper last night, and the other one last week. Don't you realize how much good you've done for kids, and for the neighborhood? The work you've done is amazing!"

"Oh Kuma."

"Don't, 'Oh Kuma' me. Not only did you see the need for pre-schools and summer play camps, but you started them *and* you've been doing it for so long, that you're now teaching those children's children! Don't you wish that you had someone like you to look out after *you,* when you were a child?"

I looked right into Kuma's eyes and said, "Oh but I did, and I had the *best*...I had *you*. So it's you that deserves these flowers, not me. Don't you see that if I didn't have *you* in my life, that I'd be dead or crazy? Kuma, you showed me *how* to love, and more importantly, how to *be* loved. My own mother made me feel worthless, but you told me that I was wonderful and that I was *deserving* of love, and that's why I'm able to show all of these children love. It's all because of you."

With that, Mikey walked in said hi, that he was going out with his friend John, he'd be back by dinner, and then ran out the door.

Kuma said, "See, there's more proof of the joy that you brought to this world. Why that boy was dropped off here like he was nothing, by a man who had money, a lovely home and a great life, but didn't want to be bothered by the task of raising his *only* son. A man who should've been in jail, and not only did you take him in, but you've made him a part of your family...and with no legal rights! That was a big risk and I don't know anyone but *you* that would have done something like that."

"But Kuma, you're the one that told me that it's every adult's obligation to be kind to children. God knows that my mother was raised by a crazy woman and that's why her view of parenting was so distorted, and if you hadn't shown me that there *was* a different path to go down, I would have repeated it as well. See Kuma, it's *you* that made the difference. You were a great teacher.

"And Madia, you were the best student." She gave me a big hug and a kiss on my cheek.

I looked at her and said, "Well I guess we just made a great team."

She looked into my eyes and said, "Madia, I am so very proud of you, but there's someone that I bet is even prouder, and that's your father. He loved you so very much, he just didn't ever have the time or the know how to tell you. He was a quiet man but he was full of love, and I know that you've made him very happy."

Then the phone rang and it was my mother. Kuma motioned to me to stay on the phone with her, she blew me a kiss and left.

"Mama, what's going on, I asked. I tried calling you yesterday twice but there was no answer?"

"Well Madia, I just wanted to let you know that I had hip replacement surgery yesterday and I'm going to need a ride home from the hospital in a few days. Can you do it or are you going to be too busy with *all* of your friends?"

"Surgery! Mama, why didn't you tell me? Do Babe and Loretta know?"

"No one knows and no one cares. If they'd let me leave in a taxi, I wouldn't have even called you. After all, according to the newspapers, you're too busy saving the world. You'd think that you were the first person to ever be nice to children. Well *I* was wonderful to all of the children in the neighborhood, and you don't see them writing articles about me, do you? Anyway, will you do it?"

"Of course Mama. What hospital are you in?"

"Why do you want to know right now? I'll call you with all of the information once I find out when they're letting me out of here."

"But Mama, I want to know, so that I can come up and visit you."

"Why, are you going to have them write an article about what a wonderful daughter you are too?"

"No Mama, I want to see you, that's all. I mean, I'm a little shocked to find out that you had surgery and didn't tell anyone."

"You don't care about me, but I'm sure that if it was your precious Kuma, you'd be fighting the nurse to wipe her ass! I'm hanging up!"

The phone went to a dial tone as I uttered, "Mama, be well. I love you."

I sat down and thought to myself about all the differences between her and Kuma. How could one love me so much, while the other one detests me? Here I am being praised for doing good things, and my mother is in a hospital alone. I started to cry and then I heard the door open, it was Billy. He asked what was wrong and I told him about Mama.

He replied, "Good, that's where the damn bitch belongs. Hopefully they'll do a lobotomy on her so that we can finally stand the bitch."

"Billy, that's your grandmother. You shouldn't talk about her that way. After all, she's all alone, and..."

He stopped me and said, "Listen, it's all by her choice. Hey, I know that somewhere in the back of your mind you think that she's going to come around and change and suddenly become this wonderful mother, well Mar, it's not going to happen. If it hasn't happened yet...it never will!"

He and Patty still kept calling me Mar – it's what the kids at the Parks called me and it stuck. It never went back to Mom.

"I know that she's difficult but she's still my mother, so I'm going to call every hospital in Chicago until I find her."

He said, "Have fun!", as he went to his room.

It took me a few hours, but I did it. She was at a hospital about twenty miles away and I informed Patty and Billy that tomorrow evening, we're all going to see Mama,...and that was an order. I knew they didn't want to go but too bad, she was their grandmother and that's all there was to it, plus I didn't want to go alone.

So after work we all got in my car and went to visit Mama. When we walked in she said, "What the Hell do all of you want? Or are you coming to see if I'm dead so you can collect an inheritance? Well I'm not leaving any of you shit! So you can all get the Hell out of here!"

Patty said, "Isn't there a plug we can pull or something?", as she walked out of the room.

Billy said, "It's good to see you too Gram. I'll be in the hall with Patty." Then he mumbled to me as he passed, "Good luck Mar."

"Mama, that's no way to talk to the kids. They came here because they love you and you're the only grandparent that they have left."

"Bullshit! Now go home until I call you."

I walked over to her, leaned in to give her a kiss and she pushed me away and said, "What the Hell are you doing? You just came from the outside and you may have germs on you and I've just had surgery! What are you trying to do… kill me?"

Then her tone changed as she said, "Oh my darling daughter, thank you so much for coming to see me."

I couldn't believe my ears. Then I heard a noise behind me, and it was a nurse.

She said, "Oh Mrs. Zovko, I don't want to bother you while you have company, but it's time for me to take your vitals."

Mama smiled and looked like a completely different woman as she said, "Oh this is my daughter. She and my grandchildren came to see me, isn't that sweet? My daughter is a very busy woman, but she found a few minutes to finally come and see me."

I could see that the nurse looked coldly at me as she said, "Well, I guess a few minutes is better than nothing, when your widowed mother has had major surgery and been alone for three days."

Before I could answer and defend myself she asked, "I know that it's none of my business, but did your mother really have to take two buses and a train alone to get here?"

I started to answer when Patty popped in and said, "Are you done with 'the visitation' yet? Can we go?"

The nurse looked horrified and Mama just lay there smiling.

Then the nurse said, "Yes please leave, so that *I* can tend to your mother."

I was so pissed that I couldn't even reply. Once again, Mama had worked her magic to make herself look like this poor, unloved victim of an uncaring daughter and some bitchy grandchildren.

As I marched down the hospital hallway, the kids asked me what was wrong, but I was so upset that all I could blurt out was that I'd tell them in the car. As I walked, I remembered what Billy said yesterday...that Mama will never change, and he was right.

In the car I explained what they'd missed.

Patty said, "Fuck her!"

Patty sort of inherited Mama's vocabulary, which explains why the two of them could never be left alone in a room without a fight breaking out. Patty would always say to me, "Why do you put up with her shit? I'd tell her to get fucked!"...which she did on many occasions.

Billy chimed in with, "Mar, why don't you take the same advice that you've always given us? 'Treat people the way that they treat you'. I'm with Patty on this."

"Kids, you don't understand. She's my mother and..."

"Big deal!" said Patty, "She's still a bitch!"

"Let's not talk about it anymore, while I'm driving, – ok?", and then I turned up the car radio.

When we returned home, I called up my sister-in-law Loretta, to tell her about the little scene that Mama put on in the hospital.

Lor said, "Mar, I don't know if I can make it up there to see her because I have to do the payroll for the business, plus if she's that mean to you, heck, I won't stand a chance."

"That's fine Lor, I just had to vent to somebody that would understand. Have a good night and tell Babe Mama's room number, just in case he wants to go up and see her."

"I will Mar, but I can tell you right now that he won't…you know your brother."

"I know, thanks for listening Lor. Good night."

"You too Mar, and try not to dwell on it…ok?"

"I'll try."

CHAPTER 60

Well it was time to bring Mama home and I elected Billy to come along with me. He was strong and she was heavy, so he was the likely and unlucky choice, plus he was able to deal with Mama better than Patty.

All the way up there he reminded me that he would be nice to her, *if* she was nice to me. He said, "Mar, I don't care if she's mean to me, because I don't really care what she says to me, but if she gets shitty with you,…then all bets are off."

I told him not to worry because there'd be a lot of staff around, and Mama's always on good behavior when there's an audience.

"But Mar, you don't know what kind of crap she's been telling them? They probably all hate us."

"That's fine. We don't have to see them after this, and *we* know the real truth…it'll be fine."

Just as I suspected, the staff was very cold toward us, and they were all fawning over Mama. The minute the car door was shut she started by saying that they were stupid, *and* they were all assholes.

Then she complained the Babe and Loretta never came up to see her. I explained that they were busy with their business.

Then she said, "Well if it wasn't for *my* money, they wouldn't even have a business."

Billy asked Mama what she was talking about, and she explained that she gave Babe the money to start his business.

Billy said, "Well Gram, since you gave your son thousands of dollars, what are you going to give your daughter?"

"Not a Goddamned thing. That's her husband's job…not mine."

I thought, that's fine with me, because I know her, and she would throw that in my face every second of my life. Poor Babe and Lor.

Once we got her home to the old apartment that I grew up in, we got her upstairs and settled. She told us that one of us would have to visit her daily so that someone could watch her walk back and forth, as part of her physical therapy. I told her not to worry and to just call us when she woke up. Then I went to give her a kiss on the cheek and she turned her head away from me, stating that she was tired and just wanted to go to bed.

We only lived three houses away from her, so going over wouldn't be a problem. The problem was, just having to be with her on a daily basis. It had been over twenty years since I had to be around that woman everyday and I wasn't looking forward to it, so I asked Billy if he wouldn't mind doing it. He said that he didn't have a problem doing it since he was out of school for the summer.

When he came back after the first day of therapy, Billy said, "Ya know ...there's something up with Gram."

"Really? Like what?" I asked.

"Well, she's being really nice. She even said that when she can walk again she wants to move to her land in Hawaii, and wants to dye her hair blonde."

"Billy, you've got to be kidding?"

"No Mar, it's like she's a new person *and* she gave me twenty dollars for helping her. It's very weird."

The next morning when Billy was going over to Mama's I said that I'd go with him, but then the phone rang and I told him to go on and I'd catch up.

It was Kuma. She wanted to know how Mama was doing and even said that she was thinking of dropping by Mama's to bring her some flowers.

I said, "You know Kuma, normally I'd say that it might me a bad idea, but Billy just told me that since her surgery, Mama is a new woman. She's actually being nice."

"Well I'm happy for her but I'm even happier for you."

"Me? Why?"

"Well Madia, maybe she'll be nicer to you – finally. Wouldn't that be a miracle? Anyway child, I'll let you go so you can witness the all new Madia for yourself."

"Bye Kuma, see you later."

As soon as I hung up the phone it rang again…it was Billy. He said that Mama had fallen down and that I should hurry over. And even though we only lived three houses away from each other, it seemed as though it took forever to get over there.

I went up those back stairs that I had been dragged up for so many years, and suddenly remembered every moment of my past, even things that I had hoped to never relive again.

Then my thoughts changed to Mama and I could only think, 'I hope that Mama didn't hurt her new hip.' But as I reached the top of the stairs, there was Mama. She was lying on the floor. Her glasses were off and lying next to her and there was a small pool of saliva emitting from her mouth. Billy said that she was gone, but I wouldn't let myself hear it.

All I kept thinking and saying was, "Please Mama, don't leave me, I love you. You can't leave me alone."

I looked up at Billy and said, "Call an ambulance!"

Calmly he answered that he already did, even though he knew it was too late.

"No, don't say that!" I screamed.

I felt as though I was flown back in time, and I was suddenly that scared little girl. I began pleading to her lifeless body, saying things like, "Mama please, please don't leave me. I need you. I'll be good, I promise." I then clutched her head and placed it in my lap, and with tears rolling off my cheeks and onto hers, I tried in vain to breathe life back into her.

I could see that it was too late, but I thought maybe if paramedics could get her to the hospital quickly, somehow, someway, they could save Mama.

I heard the sirens getting closer so I tried even harder to resuscitate her and when I looked up, I saw Billy just staring at me with no expression. By now Patty was there too, and crying. Billy had called her, even before me.

Billy said, "Patty, why are *you* crying?"

Patty was the only person who would ever fight tooth and nail with Mama. Swearing at each other and punching each other. It always amazed me how brave my children were, especially when it came to Mama. I told them when they were very little, that they were only to answer to me, and to tell me if Grandma ever treated them badly. There was no way I was letting that woman do to them, what she did to me.

Patty said, "I don't know why I'm crying. I just see Mar crying, and it makes me cry."

The paramedic's finally arrived and immediately took over. They worked on her, but they said that she was unresponsive.

"Well then get her to the hospital. Maybe they can do something there!" I yelled.

They looked at each other, and then at Billy, and I could tell that they all thought that I was crazy, but I didn't care…she's *my* mother!

The paramedics carried her down in a kitchen chair, because of a turn in the stairway, which wouldn't allow them to use a stretcher. I kept begging them to be careful because she had just had hip surgery and I didn't want them to hurt her. Again they looked at me as if I was crazy. They asked me if I wanted to ride in the ambulance, but the reality of the situation finally hit me, and I just shook my head no.

Billy said, "I'll go. It's a lot safer to be near her when she was dead, than when she was alive."

I didn't want to believe that she was dead, so to block that out of my mind, I asked Patty if she'd drive us to the hospital. I still had hope.

It seemed like in an instant we were at the hospital. I asked the nurses how Mama was doing and when I could see her. One of the nurses came around the desk and told me that she would take us to her. They had her in a separate room. When she opened the door, I saw Billy standing next to a bed, or table or something...it's all a blur. They had a sheet over her. I finally had to face the fact that she was gone. The nurse uncovered her face, which was now an unbelievable color, and I walked over to her. I looked at her face and I didn't feel sad any more. I bent down and gave her a kiss on her check and just softly said, "Good bye Mama...I forgive you."

Then the door swung open, and my sister-in-law, Loretta came in and asked why the doctors weren't doing something to help Mama.

Billy said "It's because she's already dead."

"Are you sure?" she asked.

Billy added, "She's turning blue Aunt Lor, so I'm sure she's dead."

Lor, still in denial, shook her head and mumbled under her breath, "Seems like they should *still* be doing something."

At her wake and funeral, everyone was waiting for me to fall apart, but I didn't. I guess Mama finally got her wish. I *was* strong.

I wanted Mama's love and approval all my life, and now she was gone. So I guess I'll never really know. All I *do* know is that I spent half of my life fearing her, but I also spent the other half loving her. I hope that she knows that too.

Now that time has past, I realize that through her distorted logic of wanting me to be strong, that this was the only way that *she* knew of teaching me…just as her mother taught her, on how to be strong. The only thing that saddened me is that she didn't have a chance to read this before she died. Maybe then she could see how a child's love for their parent, is so strong and pure, that it can transcend anything, even pain and torture to the point that in the end, a daughter would try to breath the life back into someone who gave them nothing but years of unhappiness.

Finally, my point to this whole story was not to make you sad, but happy. I survived and I was shown by another woman, that even though you can be mistreated by someone that you love…there is always hope as long as someone cares enough to help you see past the bad and experience the good...and that person was Kuma. Because for every negative thing that Mama imposed upon me, there was my Kuma to show me another way of life and love.

So later, when God granted me children of my own, I didn't perpetuate the abuse. I stopped it from entering their lives and broke the cycle. So to the millions of people who have been victims, please don't be a victim anymore. Most of all,...please don't create anymore.

Remember, abused children aren't born that way...we create them. Unfortunately, many times in our own image.

AUTHOR NOTES:

I must tell you why I was compelled to write this story. It's not because I was abused, you see, I was raised by "Little Madia." Yes, she was my mother, and I felt that her story *had* to be told. She felt that it was all in the past and that no one would care to hear about it. But I knew that it had to be told because of the extreme interest in the perpetuation of abuse.

People had to see that even a battered and abused child could be turned around *if* they are shown love.

Love that is unconditional and true.

"Little Madia" was not only turned around, but has also helped to turn around others - countless others. People whom under different circumstances, might have not ever felt that true form of love.

All I can say is that she made sure that we had one of the most wonderful childhood's that I've ever heard of.

I just hope that by unleashing these demons that have haunted her for so many years, that they will finally be banished once and for all.

It's true that the past is the past, but the past has a purpose - and that is to learn from it.

So thank you Little Madia, for not only giving your story to the world for knowledge and understanding, but most of all, I'm giving this story to you, for your freedom.

So thank you Mar, for letting me tell your story, and remember…I love you Mom!

Printed in the United States
By Bookmasters